The Ebbing Tide

The Ebbing Tide
by Elisabeth Ogilvie

DOWN EAST BOOKS / CAMDEN, MAINE

Copyright 1947, 1974 by Elisabeth Ogilvie
Reprinted by arrangement with the author
ISBN 0-89272-218-5
Cover design by Michael McCurdy
Composition by The Sant Bani Press, Tilton, N.H.
Printed in the United States of America

5

Down East Books / Camden, Maine

To my mother and father

Other novels by Elisabeth Ogilvie
reprinted by Down East books:

High Tide at Noon
Storm Tide

1

THE LITTLE BOY SQUATTED contentedly in the warm muddy spot in
front of the barn, eating a cracker and savoring its crisp saltiness.
He was eighteen months old, sturdy and round-bottomed in his dark
blue overalls and the blue sweater that fitted so beautifully over his
hard little stomach. A yellow bang escaped from his helmet and lay
on his forehead, almost touching his blond eyebrows; beneath them
his blue eyes bent a benign and judicial gaze on the large drake which
stood before him.

The drake, a mallard whose father had been wild, stared at the
cracker. "Qua-qua-quack," he said whisperingly. A small neat brown
duck joined him. Together they looked at the cracker and whispered
polite hints. The small boy, who was very perceptive, broke off a
piece and offered it. They were happy, the three of them, in the sunny,
sheltered barnyard. The sun struck an iridescent blue-green glimmer
from the ducks' feathers. The same sun brought out the kinglets and
crossbills and chickadees to chatter in the tops of the spruces and hang
upside down from the top branches. The golden horse on the weather-
vane above the barn gleamed and flashed in a sky that was soft with
blowing plumes of white on a blue as clean and shining as the boy's
eyes.

He was a peaceful little boy. For the moment his world was this;
the deliciously soft, sun-thawed mud around him, the courteous voices
of the ducks; the chickadees, the golden horse veering in the wind
that blew over the tops of the spruces, and the never-absent sound
of the sea. The sea was not in sight, for the boy was bounded by
the house, the barn, the woods, and a field with more forest beyond.
But the sound of the sea had been in his ears always, since he was

two weeks old; and perhaps it had reached him in the secure and ancient dark where he had lived before he was born.

His father and mother watched him from the back doorstep. Though the month was March, they had brought their afternoon coffee outdoors, for there was no wind here behind the house, and the sun fell warmly through the bare lilac bushes that edged the walk. The bushes were thick and rough with age, but their knotty, slender branches made a clear and delicate pattern on the wide planks that had come many years before from a shipwrecked schooner.

Safe from the cutting edge of the wind, the air here had a certain promise of freshness, not definite enough to be spring, but more of a reassurance that spring would sometime come. The fragrance of the coffee blended with it.

The boy's parents sat on the end of the doorstep, their long legs stretched out before them. His father, Nils Sorensen, had finished his coffee and was smoking his pipe. He was thirty-seven years old, a slim, sparely built man; he was not so tall, perhaps, as his brothers-in-law, but his body, in cleanly faded dungarees, flannel shirt, and rubber boots, had as much agile ease about it as it had ever had, and his eyes, watching his son, were as sharply, disturbingly blue as his wife had always known them to be. The years rested lightly on Nils Sorensen, and always would; it seemed as if he had never been without a certain, finely carved maturity in his face, and it had merely grown deeper and more sensitive with time.

He watched his son, and his wife looked fondly at the back of his neck, wondering why it should touch her heart so much that Nils' blond hair grew in the same sort of drake's tail that Jamie's did. . . . She had been Joanna Bennett once, and the Bennetts were all tall, with broad shoulders and narrow flanks, overpowering laughter or despair, and an odd charm in their black eyes that seemed alien to Maine; though it amounted practically to a coastal tradition that no Bennett could retain his health and happiness for long away from the red rocks and wind-tormented spruces of their island. Joanna was like the others, tall and supple with glossy black hair brushed back from her face, a warm dark skin under which the blood made rich color; her eyes were almost black under clear-etched brows like wings, and her spacious Bennett forehead was marked with a widow's peak.

There was a certain likeness between her and her husband; in their strong jaws and the firmness of their lips. Joanna laughed easily and often, her lower lip had a rich fullness, but in composure she showed the years of pride and self-reliance that had made her the woman she was now, at thirty-five.

As for Nils . . . he smiled now, suddenly, as the mallard left off being polite and took the cracker from Jamie's fingers. His smile was a Sorensen smile, not as quick and ready as a Bennett smile, for the Sorensens had never had as much to laugh at in childhood as the Bennetts. But it lit up his face with the warm steady glow of a lamp as compared to the lightning-flash grins of his brothers-in-law.

He got up slowly, and the sun struck off glints from his blond head. "Come on back to the shop with me, Jo. Bring Jamie."

She put up her arm, lazily, and he pulled her to her feet. "All right. You call him while I take the cups in." She went along the walk into the sun parlor, moving with erect ease in her comfortable saddle shoes, tweed skirt and cardigan. The Sorensens looked like two healthy, intelligent, and happy persons. *Which we are,* Joanna told herself stoutly, putting the coffee cups in the sink and adding another piece of birch to the stove. *As happy as anybody can be during a war.*

She took a jacket from behind the door — it would be cold walking down to the harbor — and remembered how many times in the last two years she had slipped on this jacket to walk down to the harbor with Nils, because the Coast Guard boat had come to take him back to duty. But this afternoon they were simply walking down to the fish house. He'd had a ten-day furlough; something out of the ordinary, because he'd never had anything more than a seventy-two hour pass since he'd enlisted. He told her the Lieutenant Commander at the Base thought he deserved it.

"Well, I should think so, too!" she said hotly. "After all, you're practically the only man they've got left who knows these waters — and will you tell me why only boys from the Middle West seem to get put on patrol duty here?"

Nils had smiled and said they had to be stationed somewhere, and his crew were darn' good kids, even if one had come from a sheep ranch in Utah and hadn't known how to row, and another one came from the mountains somewhere.

"Oh, I don't care!" Joanna had exclaimed happily. "Anyway, you've got a whole unexpected ten days, and so we're lucky — and we're darn' lucky that nobody else does know these waters the way you do! Maybe they won't send you away from Maine at all!"

She hadn't been selfish in hoping that. It was simply that she had two brothers in the Pacific, one on a destroyer and one on an LST, and knowing how she worried about them, she didn't see how she could endure the even more intense worry about Nils. Besides, his function here, skipper of a patrol boat whose run was anywhere that he might be sent in Penobscot Bay, was extremely important. There was much going on outside the rim of the bay and the Islanders realized it, although they had grown used to the shudder of the ground from depth charges, and the furious rattle of windows from not-too-distant firing of destroyers and cruisers.

When she went out Jamie was coming across the barnyard, lifting his small rubber boots with deliberation.

"On the double!" said his father, and Jamie hurried, his somber face suddenly transfigured with deliberation.

"See the boat?" he demanded.

"Not today, Tyke," Nils said cheerfully. "We're going to build some pots."

That was almost as good as seeing the Coast Guard boat. These departures were never hard on Jamie; almost his first words had been "Bye, Papa!" and he accepted everything as a matter of course, and had a fanatic adoration for the Coast Guard boat and its crew. But building pots was fun, and he could have a hammer to pound with. He reached up for his father's hand.

They went around the corner of the house that Nils' grandfather had built, neat, white, steep-gabled, and passed by more lilac bushes. These were white lilacs out here at the front door. Then they came out past the end of the spruce windbreak Nils' grandfather had planted after the house was finished, and the northwest wind blowing up from the harbor tried to take their breaths away.

The field was a tawny brown now, but in a few weeks the path would be showing green, and the grass would be growing tall around the well. The harbor was a bright, eye-hurting blue overlaid with shifting silver this afternoon, the boats rolled at their moorings, and a little edge of surf chuckled and tossed at the base of the red rocks that walled the harbor's curve.

Beyond the long island of Brigport, a mile to the north, the sky gleamed like a thin, polished shell of pale turquoise with a mysterious light behind it. It was one of the days when the Maine coast shone like a jewel.

The wind was a knife, but it was the wind that had brought this day. Joanna refused to lower her head to it as they walked down to Nils' fish house.

It was warm in the fish house, with the sun streaming in from the long low windows over the bench, and a fire of driftwood and lath ends dozing along in the oil-drum stove. The sound of the water muttering under the little wharf and surging up over the pebbled beach so nearby added to the snugness. The war seemed to exist only in another world, when Joanna could watch Nils working at the bench. He had spent most of his ten days building pots to add to her brother Owen's string. Owen fished his own gear, to which Nils' pots had been added, and the income from those traps belonged to Joanna.

It was always a pleasure to watch Nils work, even if he didn't talk. He moved with such smooth, unwasted energy, always at the same competent pace.

"I'm glad Owen hasn't got in from hauling yet," she murmured peacefully. "He'd be in here slatting around . . . and this is so nice. Nils, when it's like this I almost feel as if the war might be over tomorrow . . . it seems as if it can't go on much longer."

"I'm afraid it's going on for a lot longer than most people think." He was building bottoms this afternoon; he took three blows with his hammer to drive a nail in the end of a lath. Jamie, over in the corner, was having a deliriously wonderful time with a pile of red and white buoys and an old warp. "We'll invade the continent any time, and I don't think we'll breeze right in big as Billy-be-damned. . . . Then there's Japan to lick."

"You don't have to be so realistic when I'm having a nice little daydream, do you?" She went over to the bench and stood beside him.

His mouth twitched a little, but he didn't look at her. He set another nail in place, and lifted the hammer. Then he laid it down on the bench, and looked at Joanna.

"What is it?" she asked calmly enough, but her heart had begun a slow, hard pumping. It was the impact of his eyes, as tangible as if he'd put his hand on her shoulder and gripped it hard.

"Joanna, I've been putting this off too long," he said simply. "But the ten days are up, day after tomorrow, and it's only fair to you to tell you now."

"Nils, I wish you'd tell me quickly." Her voice was low as his. Jamie pawed happily among the buoys.

"When I go back this time, it's for keeps, Joanna. I go overseas."

She wondered in that first stunned moment why she hadn't guessed. It seemed as if she should have; how could she ever have been so confident and so happy? Now when she looked back, everything pointed to the truth. But she hadn't known, and so it had to hit her now, with this dreadful, shocking *suddenness*.

For an instant the fish house was unbearably hot, and the sound of the water and the wind outside grew into a roar that deafened her ears. Through that instant her eyes didn't shift away from Nils', and then everything moved by degrees back to normal again. Everything but herself, but that didn't matter as long as she didn't show it in her face. She took in a breath, carefully and experimentally, and let it out again.

"Well," she said. "I wasn't expecting that, I guess. But I don't know why not."

"I didn't expect it," he said soberly. "But then there's no reason why they should keep me here, if they've got more use for me in the Pacific."

"How long will it be, Nils?"

"I don't know. Nobody knows." He picked up the hammer again.

Her hand reached out and covered his, and then the world that was the Island — and would continue to be the Island, no matter what countries fell — broke loudly in upon them. A boat was roaring into the harbor, wide open; that would be Owen in the *White Lady,* back from hauling at last. Jamie dropped a buoy on his foot and burst into a howl of rage and pain.

2

THE NEXT MORNING was just like any morning when Nils was home. He got up quietly before sunrise to build the fire and make the coffee. Jamie still slept soundly in his crib in the corner of the room that had belonged to Nils' grandparents, but the dog, a benign blend of collie and shepherd, crawled out from under the bed when Nils got up, and went downstairs with him. Joanna lay in bed listening to the faint sounds below. Nils had thought she was asleep, and she hadn't moved when he kissed her cheek. Now that he was out of the room she could lie there in the grayness just before sunrise and stare at the ceiling as she had stared up through the dark for so much of the night.

She listened with an almost aching intensity, yet without consciously thinking that it would be a long time before she heard those early morning sounds again; the back door opening to let Dick out, and shutting again; the faint rattle of a stove lid; the distant, tinny clatter of the dipper against a pail as he took out water to wash in. Then the sky was paling over the black frieze of spruces outside her windows, and then the pallor was flushed with rose-gold. She slid out from under the quilts, her feet feeling for her slippers, her hand reaching for her dark-red flannel robe. Though it was cold in the room she stopped before the massive, old-fashioned dresser and brushed her dark hair quickly.

When she opened the door at the foot of the stairs she smelled coffee. She could look through the dining room into the kitchen, and see Nils making toast. He turned his head and smiled at her.

"Hi. Come and get it while it's hot."

"It smells like heaven," she said. She went past him to the sink and thought how much simpler and easier it would be if she could stop and put her arms around his neck and say, "Nils, hold me tight, because I'm scared."

But he'd look at her in amazement if she did. She'd never hugged him before breakfast, she couldn't start now. . . . She splashed icy water on her face and buried it in a towel. Then, together, she and Nils set the table in the dining room. In the Bennett homestead, where she'd grown up, the kitchen was the core of the house, and all meals were eaten there. But in this Sorensen house, the kitchen was barely big enough to work in. Nils' grandmother had been a little woman, no big-boned, long-legged creature like Joanna.

The first cup of coffee had become a ritual in their married life. He might have his bacon and eggs, or beans, or fish hash, with her brother when Owen came down—or *in,* if he'd been on one of his all-night poker games over at Brigport. And then she'd be busy with the children, and the day would be on its way. But this first cup of coffee, drunk in silent comradeship while the rest of the house slept, symbolized their life together.

Owen was stirring around upstairs. Their little interlude of quiet was at an end, and there was no telling when they would be alone again today. Tonight, yes; but she didn't want to wait for the dark. She wanted their eyes to meet with no veil between them, she wanted to reach out to him from her own need and have him reach out to her for a similar urgency. Not the hungers of their bodies would drive them, but their common dread of what lay before them, their fear of the unknown. . . .

He caught her gaze across the table. "What are you thinking?" he said, smiling faintly.

Thinking that I want you to need me, she answered, but it was a silent answer. Aloud, she said, "Owen's coming. He was out till two this morning, so I expect he'll be ugly. I wish he wouldn't drink so much."

"Owen will always drink, and more so now that there's a war on that he can't get into," said Nils. "Don't think that he's gotten over it— that his kid brothers were taken and he wasn't. Go easy on him, Jo."

"I'm always easy on him," she said bitterly. "Maybe if he thought I wouldn't cook for him, or wash his white shirts so he can impress his lady friends, he'd pull himself out of it. Some day he'll catch pneumonia and die *like that.*" She snapped her fingers.

Nils shook his head. "He won't die, Jo. People like Owen don't die." He began to fill his pipe, his blue eyes tranquil and remote. Something caught at her breath and turned it to a quick stab of pain. No, Owen wouldn't die. People like Owen didn't die because they were safe here at home, safe to rot alone. But men like Nils went out to the Pacific and died in the surf off tiny islands that suddenly became tremendous and bloody names. . . . She had been through all this with her two younger brothers, looking for their letters, trying not to think what it might mean when no letter came, listening to news dispatches, studying maps, and then re-reading the letters in an attempt to discover something tangible from their careful vagueness.

Now Nils would be added to the others. . . . Her desire to touch him, to cling to his squarish, strong hands, as they filled his pipe, grew so strong in her that she got up hastily from the table.

"I'll dress," she said, "and then get breakfast."

She dressed in the cold bedroom, with Jamie still sleeping in his crib. She looked out of the windows while she put on her clothes. After the crisp, boisterous wind of yesterday the day was calm, almost silkenly so. Over the harbor the sky was a pale, luminous blue, and the harbor lay below it, a placid shimmer of reflections. Already Sigurd Sorensen and Matthew Fennell had gone to haul. The *White Lady* remained at her mooring, and the *Donna*, Nils' boat. The *White Lady* would go out day after day, in kinship with the sea and the wind and the gulls, but the *Donna* would stay behind, on her mooring, until Nils came home again.

The *Donna* had been left once before, but her skipper had put her on the bank. He'd promised to come back, but he had died before he could fulfill the promise.

"You'll never go on the bank, I promise you that," Joanna said soundlessly to the lovely, high-bowed boat that had been her father's and was now her husband's.

There was a man rowing across the harbor now in a peapod, the oars stirring the still water into ripples of pale gold. The same pale gold gilded the oar-blades and the sides of the peapod, and invested the man himself with a touch of mysticism. He was edged with light. . . . Sometimes on mornings like this one, when each spruce across the harbor stood out separately and brightly green in the clear pale light, and the gulls floated high over the ledges to drop their crabs and sea-urchins, the emptiness of the harbor had an almost dreamlike quality for her, as if it couldn't be true that there were only four fishermen here now. Sometimes it seemed as if the others had gone to haul, and they'd all be back in the afternoon . . . but the absence of skiffs and peapods at the moorings gave the lie to that.

But when the war is over, she promised herself, *they'll be back.*

Owen was going down the front stairs, and Jamie was stirring with little animal noises in his crib. She went back to him and picked him up. He was a warm, sleep-heavy bundle in blue flannel, who gave her a shiny, drowsy smile and hooked one arm firmly around her neck.

By noon, when Joanna brought Jamie in for his dinner, the twittering and chirping in the alder swamp had reached almost hysterical heights of gratitude for the flooding, windless sunshine. The day had a soft, evanescent beauty, the boats coming into the harbor moved without effort between glistening crystal wings and left liquid silver in their wakes; there was more crystal and silver—or was it pure, living light?—captured where the water swirled casually among the rocks.

From the kitchen window Joanna saw the *White Lady* come in. Owen was home early today. Usually the others were in by noon or soon after, but Owen, whose string was set farther from the Island than any other man's, didn't come in till mid-afternoon. Sigurd Sorensen, Nils' brother, came in first, because he bought the other men's hauls for a company in Limerock, and so he had to be on the car when the other men came in. Francis Seavey was in early because he hated lobstering, and had never done it in his life until his wife had made up her mind to it; Matthew Fennell was never late because he went to haul in the morning as soon as it was light enough to see a potbuoy. But Owen, who considered himself the only proper fisherman of the lot, was in with the rest today. Probably his headache was too much for him, she thought skeptically. She hadn't found out yet whether the festivity of the night before was a poker-and-drinking party, or simply a drinking party.

She was opening a jar of greens at the dresser when Nils came in, moving quietly. He came up behind her without speaking, and put his arms around her, resting his lean cheek against her hair. She put down the jar and turned quickly in his embrace, as if she had been waiting for this moment all morning; she put her hands on his shoulders.

"Nils, I —" *I'm going to miss you,* she'd almost said. And it was such a silly thing to say. The way she would miss him, and he would miss her, was too great a part of them to be reduced into mere words. But as if he knew her thought, he tightened his arms, and drew her close and kissed her. His lips were cool against hers.

"Jamie asleep?" he asked.

"Yes, he was so tired he didn't fool around today."

"Owen's coming." Nils nodded at the window, and she knew Owen was on his way to the house. "Let's leave him to hold the fort while we put the *Donna* on her mooring."

"What have you been doing with her?" she asked curiously.

"Oh, I ran her around the harbor a couple of times, and then took her in to the wharf while I tidied her up." He released her and stood away. "Well, are you coming?"

She dumped the greens hurriedly into a saucepan and set them on the stove. "You bet I am!" she laughed, but she was thinking, *Tidying up the Donna!* As if she needed it! She was already spotless, but tomorrow he was leaving her.

Owen came in, kicking the door shut with a vicious swing of his rubber boot. The kitchen was smaller than ever when he came into it and stood scowling at them, his thumbs hooked into his belt, his black yachting cap on the back of his head. He was in one of his silent rages, when his black brows made a thick bar across his face and his full, squared lower lip was prominent. He was as dark as an Indian, and his repressed fury made him darker.

No need to ask him what the matter was; a hangover always affected him this way. "I'm going down with Nils to put the boat on her mooring," Joanna told him. "You can help yourself to dinner if you don't want to wait for us . . . Jamie's asleep."

Owen grunted and brushed by Nils to the sink. Nils, undisturbed, stepped out of his way. He was far more patient with Owen than Joanna could ever be. Men had a strange, tight kinship, she knew, that a woman couldn't understand. Nils and Owen were poles apart, but still they understood each other.

She went out and Nils came after her. It was high noon, the

air was at its height of warmth; the sunshine poured without stint or shadow over the Island and a sea as blue as in midsummer.

"You had a wonderful idea," Joanna said. "I couldn't sit down and eat with Owen right now. He's in one of his I-hate-everybody moods."

"He probably enjoys having us out from under his feet for a little while, too," said Nils.

The rest of the Island—three houses were occupied besides the old Sorensen house—was busy with dinner, so no one came out to break the warm harmony of their mood as they walked down to the shore. The *Donna* was tied up at the end of the Sorensen wharf. She hardly moved, the water was so calm. The tide was high, and they stepped onto the buff-painted deck and then down into the cockpit; Nils cast off the single line that held her gently against the spilings and started the engine.

Responsive as it had always been, after years of painstaking, loving care, the engine began its soft refrain, and the big boat moved away from the wharf; the water churned up by her wheel went chuckling and swashing around the green-mossed spilings and over the rocks shaggy with seaweed in the dark shade under the wharf. The boat headed so quietly out into the harbor that a gull standing on the almost-submerged peak of a ledge didn't fly upwards in fright, but remained like an ivory carving, breast to breast with its reflection.

Joanna stood beside Nils at the wheel. It would only take them a few moments to go to the mooring at the outer edge of the harbor; but she could drink in those moments as if they were some rare essence, and remember all the silent, sun-flooded noons of her life, especially when she and Nils had had the harbor to themselves. But that was in the first month of their marriage, when the Island had begun to take on new life again. The *Donna* moved across the harbor, cleaving gently the soft brimming blue, that glimmered into quicksilver in the boat's wake, and then broke in little glistening lines against the saffron and rose-red rocks. Above the rocks the spruces stood in sharp exquisite detail against a sky that ringed the horizon with light and became the soul of all blues at the zenith. A day like this came rarely to the Island, and it was a heart-shaking thing.

There had been a time when she and Nils had been actually alone on the Island; she had gone to haul with him in his peapod on mornings like this, and when they had come back the house was waiting for them alone. It had stood open in the sunshine, with the woods hovering close, and nothing to disturb the light or the still depths of shadows but the birds. Now there was noontime smoke from other chimneys — and until the war had come, and begun to rage through the Atlantic, there had been someone in almost every house. Their solitude had not lasted very long, but they hadn't cared too much, because it was for the Island's good to have people again. . . . Then most of the young men had gone into the service, the old-timers had left because married sons and daughters had found work in war plants, and the grandchildren needed someone to watch over them. They didn't mind leaving so much; there was no mail boat now, and often the telephone was out of order or shut off because of secret communications from the Rock. . . . One woman frankly admitted she was glad to be leaving the Island because the depth charges were too close and there were too many stories of submarines, and they didn't like the sight of fighting planes and bombers flying high in the thin mist of clouds.

Now Nils was going, and as she stood beside him watching the *Donna's* steady bow against the horizon, she had the feeling she had had so many times as a child, that the world consisted of a flat expanse of sea, with Bennett's Island and Brigport in the midst of it, a line of blue unreal mountains along the northern horizon with nothing beyond them, and an immense half-sphere of sky inverted over it all. When Nils left, he would drop into nothing beyond the edge, as her younger brothers had dropped. Their letters always seemed to arrive out of blank space, and so would Nils' letters. . . . She turned her face quickly from the horizon beyond Brigport, and waited for Nils to slow down the big marine engine and go forward to gaff the mooring buoy. But he met her eyes with a faint sparkle in his, and turned the *Donna* out past Eastern Harbor Point.

"Come and steer," he said. Words that had always sent her to the heights of ecstasy, from the time he used to say them to her when she was a gangling, eager twelve-year-old.

She took the wheel and Nils sat down on the washboard, watching the Island as it slid by. There was no need to talk; there was only motion, the steady vibration of the engine, the shining sea flowing past, the little sea pigeons flying up with a flash of their small red feet. She knew now why they were doing this, and if she had known any questions in the early morning, they were being answered now. Nils was saying goodbye to the Island. Perhaps he would never tell her in words what he felt about the Island, but he was taking her with him to share this final moment.

Long Cove was gliding by, a long stretch of beach whose rounded rocks gleamed white in the sun, white as a gull's breast against the blue line of sea. Above Long Cove flat fields stretched across the Island to Schoolhouse Cove, on the seaward side. In the marshy places she and Nils had picked cranberries, and where the fields bordered on the beach there were blackberries in August whose purple-black sweetness was richened by spray. There was high, densely wooded ground after Long Cove, and the empty buildings that shone palely against the dark high wall of trees, overlooking the fields and the two coves, were Bennett property. In the big barn that dwarfed the other buildings Joanna and Nils, her brothers and his cousins, had played hide-and-go-seek. . . . She glanced sidewise at Nils and saw that he was not too remote from her, so she spoke.

"Remember swinging out of the hayloft on a rope?"

"If I ever knew of Jamie doing that, I'd want to wring his neck," said Nils. "And I thought your uncle was an old fussbudget for objecting." He shook his head and laughed.

"Nils, d'you think we could ever get hold of that place—if Aunt Mary was willing to sell?" she asked eagerly.

"Maybe she'll be ready to talk business when I get back," he said. *When I get back*. . . . It was like a little cold wind skimming across the water and turning the surface to a darker, colder blue.

After the woods ended, the Eastern End began, a narrow neck of land whose shoreline on both sides, lee and windward, was guarded by a brutal jumble of rocks. But the tide covered them today, and the empty buildings looked serene and not too lonely in the sunshine. The Eastern End land looked barren, if one didn't know what strawberries grew in the deep grass in July, what birds nested in the low bushes, and how incredibly lush the field could look when there were people living at the Eastern End, and stock to keep the land shaven and green from one shore to the other.

The fish house built up against the steep bank above the cove wore sunshine on its weathered shingles, and wavy ripples of light from the water that lapped around its spilings. A line of gulls sat on the ridgepole and were not alarmed by the *Donna's* calm purring progress; but on the high rocky ledge that rose outside the cove like a seabound castle the gulls started up in a cloud of harsh cries and beating wings when the boat went by. The young gulls circled with the old ones, gray-brown wings only slightly less graceful, but already as strong.

"Remember the day we went ashore there?" said Nils. "Rowed down from the harbor in a skiff—"

"Nobody would have known if Owen hadn't been down to the Eastern End playing with the Trudeau kids, and went home and *told*," said Joanna.

They were silent again. She turned the wheel and the *Donna* began to round the Head, which rose up from the fields as a rocky hillside and ended in a bold, massive face of tawny-red rock below which the *Donna* looked tiny but indomitable. There was always a surge here, even in this fine weather. Glittering sheets of water swelled in long slopes, and the boat rode gently with them. Nils was looking up at the Head against the sky. The softness that had been around his mouth and eyes when he remembered the forbidden trip in the skiff was gone. Joanna felt a gradual tightening in her chest; it was reflected in the way her strong brown fingers tightened on the spokes of the wheel.

Remembering was no good, because the present was upon them, and there was no escape. Tomorrow he would be going. It would be bad enough for her, but at least she could remain with the Island. Nils would be leaving everything, and the Island was as much in his blood and bones as in hers. Their grandfathers had come here together.

In all the years she had known Nils, since her earliest memories began, she had had to make up for herself what he was thinking. Now, because she knew him as well as anyone could ever know Nils, she was almost certain of his thoughts. She longed to cry out to him that she knew what he was thinking; but Nils never wanted to burden anyone, even herself who was waiting, with the things that lay heaviest upon him.

If she knew Nils, and she *did* know him, she knew that nothing could ever take him by surprise. Not even death. He had taken death into account from the moment he had received his orders. All these ten days at home, when he had let her think it was an ordinary furlough, he had been taking death into account, and because of that, everything he had done and said had been for the last time. When he was talking with Owen, there must have been the quiet certainty that he might never again set or haul a trap, or take his own boat out of the harbor.

When he was rocking Jamie at night. . . . Her throat began to ache; she kept her eyes straight ahead over the cabin roof, though they were filled with a burning mist of blue, and glittering light, and wavering rocks. She wanted to hold Nils against her breast as he had held Jamie. It seemed at once a hideous monstrous thing that she could not comfort Nils as simply as she could shelter Jamie and stop his crying. She held herself rigid there by the wheel, without looking at his face. He mustn't know what she knew. He would want her to think he was like her brothers, who went out into the blue hell of the Pacific with their self-assurance around them like armor. Other men were killed, other men came back maimed. But not they. Wait and see! That was the Bennett of them.

But Nils came of a different strain. The knowledge of death, and sin, and punishment, and hell, had been his since he was little older than Jamie. Night after night his grandfather Gunnar had read the Bible to his wife and his grandchildren—the Old Testament with its grandeur and terror; and he had added his own warnings of the doom that awaited all human flesh. It was true that Nils had taken it stolidly, and Sigurd had all but laughed in the old man's face, and it was their sister who cried and had nightmares; but it was now, when Nils was a man of thirty-seven, that Joanna recognized what part of Gunnar's teaching had borne fruit.

In the room where Nils had slept as a boy there was a framed verse on the wall at the foot of his bed; it had been there always, he had told her, and he knew it by heart. Morning and night for almost all his life he had read it. It must have become deeply, irrevocably ingrained in his being.

> As for man, his days are as grass;
> As a flower of the field, so he flourisheth.
> For the wind passeth over it, and it is gone;
> And the place thereof shall know it no more.

She could endure it no longer, and turned toward him quickly.

"Nils!" she cried, surprising even herself. He got up from the washboard, smiling a little, and put his hands lightly on her shoulders.

"What's the matter?"

"A cramp in my leg—I've been standing still too long." She reached down and rubbed the back of her knee, not looking at him.

"Then sit down for a while." He took the wheel, and she sat down on the engine box, wanting to look at the clean, lifted line of his face as he steered, but not trusting herself to look too long. They were passing Schoolhouse Cove now, and a seal was turning over and over lazily in the surge around the rocks; the same rocks threw back the sound of the engine, magnifying it to a roar. Then they rounded a long, out-thrust point whose crest was a thick cap of tangled grass and raspberry and rose bushes. Joanna looked up, watching. Nils was watching too. They passed between the tip of the point on one side, and a rounding ledge on the other, where gulls and shags flew up in a tangle of black wings and white ones, and then the *Donna* slipped quietly into Goose Cove.

It was a long, narrow oval of a cove, walled by the point on one side and the woods on the other, the same woods that marched thickly to the very end of the Island. In the shadow of the trees the water was a glassy surface of jade and emerald; where the shade ended, the blue began, and lay hardly moving against the shelving, warm yellow rocks that slanted down from the ridge of the point like rudely cut massive steps.

And at the end of the cove, above the little pale curve of beach, the Bennett homestead stood. It was the house where Joanna had grown up, and the house to which she and Nils had returned day after day when they had once lived alone on the Island. There it stood, four-square and solitary on its headland. It was across the Island from the harbor, and its nearest neighbors were the spruce woods, the gulls that perched familiarly on the ridgepole, the crows that flew over from the Western End woods to the Eastern End woods; the swallows that made their nests under the eaves. The house was alone now, but it did not look lonely.

Nils shut off the engine, and in the sudden hush the silence was as tangible as the soundless flight of a gull's wings. Without speaking, Nils stepped upon the washboard and went lightly up to the bow. The killick made a silvery splash as he dropped it overboard. When he came back and jumped down into the cockpit with hardly a sound in spite of his rubber boots, Joanna stood up. He came toward her, and his smile was gone. There was a subtle change in his face; no longer the mask of a man who is calmly certain of death, or with the faint, warm smile of a man for his comrade. The tension showed through now, the tension that rose of his soul's need and his body's passion. The way he loved Joanna, and had always loved her, was the most powerful force of his being. Perhaps it was easy for him to view all other things with quiet acceptance.

She knew it, and her eyes didn't move from his. His hands came out to touch her shoulders; not to rest lightly but to grip hard. His mouth seemed hard, but it was not; neither were his eyes furious as they darkened. Only intent. The grip on her shoulders, biting through her jacket, drew her closer to him.

"Jo—" He started to say her name, and the word was smothered as his arms went around her in an embrace like steel, and his mouth was against her throat. She stood motionless in his arms, seeing the dark empty woods towering over them, feeling the sun warm on her lifted face. She was still, but there was a slow trembling inside of her, as if deep within the tears were beginning to well. She brought up one hand and laid it on the back of his neck; her cheek was against his fair hair, it smelled cleanly of wind and sunshine.

"Nils, my darling," she said quietly. It was not often the word was used between them. *"My darling . . ."*

After a moment he lifted his head and his eyes blazed into hers. "It's—leaving *you*—" The words came harshly, with difficulty. But they were enough for her to understand, and she felt a fierce joy. He wanted her to be sure that nothing else mattered but her; not even the Island could have any part of him at this time.

"But not for the last time," she told him passionately. "Nils, it isn't the last time! I know what you think, but I know what I *know!*"

"Don't talk," he said. "Don't talk, Joanna." He cut off her protest with his mouth on hers.

The cabin was open and waiting; the *Donna* swung gently at anchor in a globe of shining silence.

3

IN THE MORNING THE RAIN blew in from the east in gray sheets. The warmth and stillness and color of the day before seemed like a dream. The wind was strong enough to sway the birches and the alders, and edge the seaward side of the Island with surf; but there was only a faint quiver to the tips of the spruce boughs. By Island standards, it really wasn't a wind at all. Certainly, not enough wind to keep Nils from going. Owen would take him to Brigport to meet the mail boat, which had stopped coming to Bennett's when the mail did, years before.

Joanna didn't plan to go over to Brigport with him. They had had their good-byes, it would mean nothing to them, the waiting around the harbor of the other island, watching the freight being taken off, and the gulls perched on the wet ledges in the rain, feeling the chill that was not alone from the March rain but from the occasion itself.

She left Jamie with Nils' cousin, Thea, who lived on the other side of the windbreak, and walked down to the wharf with Nils. Owen had gone out already and brought the *White Lady* in. She waited at the old wharf, over by the long pebbly beach where the boats were hauled up for repairs and the skiffs and dories kept. Nils was in his uniform today as a Chief Boatswain's Mate in the Coast Guard. Until this morning he had been the familiar Nils, the lobsterman. Now, in navy blue, with the dark trim raincoat and the neat bag, she recognized once more the futility of believing that he was hers alone. He was going because he must, he would go where he was sent, and nothing she might do or say could alter his course. For the duration, neither she nor Jamie could come first with Nils.

It was nothing to cry about, nothing to brood about. She was simply one of millions of women, and the wonder was that she had come to accept it so calmly, she thought, as they walked along together in the rain, through a village that was almost deserted. She'd always had such a strong sense of her own individuality as a person that it had got in her way at times. Well, there was nothing like a war to snap you out of it.

They turned by the fish houses and walked along the shore, past the Arey house where Nils' brother Sigurd lived. Sigurd's housekeeper knocked on the window and waved frantically at Nils, who smiled and touched his cap.

"I'll try to get down to Pruitt's Harbor this afternoon and see Ellen," Nils said as they walked on.

"She'll love that," said Joanna enthusiastically. "Especially if you go to the school. She considers you an honest-to-goodness hero, and all hers."

"She's a good girl. More of a lady than you were at twelve, too."

"She takes after Mother," Joanna said. She slipped her arm through his and tightened her fingers on his sleeve. He *would* go down to Pruitt's Harbor, too. It was typical of Nils, and the deep comradeship between him and his stepdaughter. She knew he wasn't her father, and Joanna didn't know if Ellen considered Nils in the light of a father, at all; in some things Ellen was rather a mystery to her, but she was certain that Ellen considered Nils an indispensable part of her universe. *And so do I,* thought Joanna, and tightened her fingers even more.

Nils glanced at her sidewise. "O.K., Jo?"

"O.K.," she reassured him. "I'm just overcome with the idea that I'm walking along Bennett's Island main street with a C.P.O. It's making me conceited as anything."

"And everybody looking at you, too," said Nils, pointing to the long baithouse on their right and the boatshop on their left. He nodded at the row of gulls on the boatshop's ridgepole. "The reviewing stand. Politicians, every damn' one of 'em."

"I wonder if they have parades in the Pacific," said Joanna. "Politicians in the Solomons ought to be a change from the Limerock brand, anyway."

We're doing wonderfully, she thought, and then they had reached the old wharf, by the boatshop, and the *White Lady* was waiting, her engine idling. Out beyond the shelter of the baithouse, the east wind swept in from Schoolhouse Cove, raced across the marsh, and tried to wrap them in rain. But nobody noticed it, it was Island weather. Owen grinned up from the cockpit. "You want to be piped aboard, Admiral?"

Sigurd came out of the cabin, waving a bottle of beer and whistling "Semper Paratus." He was a big, yellow-maned Viking of a man, who gave the impression, even when he was in a roaring rage, of an utterly friendly and humorous person. "You pipe down," he advised Owen. "You want to pipe, you can pipe down. Hi, Nils. God, I wish I was goin' with you!"

He took Nils' bag and clapped his younger brother on the shoulder with a heavy hand. Nils, however, bore up under it. "Well, you're going as far as Brigport, aren't you?" He took his bag back, and went into the cabin to stow it. Sigurd hovered hugely in the companionway.

"Sure, but my God. You know what I mean. I could kill a lot of those yellow beggars—"

"He's been goin' on like that for an hour," said Owen. "I'm intendin' to drown him as soon as we get out by Tenpound. Put him out of his misery."

Nils forced a smile. "Well, I guess we'd better get started—"

Joanna stood on the edge of the wharf, shivering. It seemed as if the east wind had never cut so deeply; yet her tweed coat was warm, and so was her wool kerchief. *I'm not really cold,* she thought. *It's just the excitement. After all, I'm not falling on his neck and crying, and making it hard for him. It's all right if I feel a little funny. . . .* She saw someone coming by the baithouse, and called quickly, nervously.

"Wait a minute, here come Francis and Matthew!" She met Nils' eyes and grinned, and took her hands out of her pockets and blew on them so he'd think the jerky note in her voice came from the cold. He looked back at her steadily, standing in the roomy cockpit while the others baited each other noisily behind him. She wondered what he was thinking in that instant; if he would carry this picture of her, standing there in the rain with the dark clouds scudding beyond her head, and seagulls walking on a wetly shining roof, and the wind making color in her face; or if the picture would be of yesterday, while the *Donna* moved gently at anchor in Goose Cove.

Francis Seavey and Matthew Fennell came up, their rubber boots clomping on the loose planks, nodded at her, and jumped down into the cockpit to shake hands with Nils. She stood watching the scene; now she wondered what all of them were thinking; the one who must go, the others who must wait. Francis Seavey was Thea's husband, not a lobsterman by training but a carpenter, and when the draft board turned him down, Thea had brought him out to the island where she'd grown up, moved into her father's house, and informed Francis that they had just as much right as anybody to make money out of lobstering. Consequently Francis looked unhappy most of the time. He was a slight, mouse-colored, youngish man, whose rubber boots were always tripping him up, and who was terrified every time he went out to haul. Yet there was probably nothing Francis desired more than to be going to fight Japs with Nils.

Matthew was a sturdy man in his forties, sound and good as a Baldwin apple. He loved lobstering, he loved the Island to which he had come a few years ago, he loved his young wife and his grandmother, who was very old now and who was apparently intending to live forever. He made good money, put a great deal of it religiously into War Bonds, and was completely oblivious of the fact that his wife had been having Gram around for a long time now, and that the situation in his house was as potentially explosive as a mine field.

"Good luck, Nils," he said simply. Francis didn't say anything, but he swallowed when Nils took him by the shoulder and shook him gently. "You take care of yourself, Franny," Nils said. "I want to see you here when I get back. When it's too bad for this big ape—" he nodded at Sigurd—"to go out, it's too bad for you. Understand?"

Francis nodded earnestly. Nils had given him a weapon. Next time Thea cast aspersions on his manhood when he was reluctant to go haul, he could quote Nils at her.

The good-byes were over. Francis and Matthew climbed out of the cockpit, Joanna cast off the bowline, and Owen maneuvered the *White Lady* delicately away from the wharf. She backed out with the engine lifting into a high, powerful roar, the wheel churning the pewter-gray water into a foaming chaos; then her bow swung around and she headed out across the harbor, her wake fanning out behind her. Joanna waited a moment, the rain beating at her back, to watch the boat and the men standing around the wheel. Nils lifted his arm in farewell, and she waved back. Then as the *White Lady* cut by the *Donna*'s bow at the mouth of the harbor, and left her rolling in the wake, Joanna turned sharply and walked up to the road.

The two men who were left had gone across to the baithouse. She heard them talking in there—not about Nils, but about the respective merits of bream and corned herring for bait. No one who was left on the Island would talk much about Nils today.

She walked home alone. Out of the wind, the rain fell with a soft, shushing sound on the rocks and the dead grass. The roofs shone. Across the Island there was surf and wind, but here in the shelter of the almost empty village the roar was muted until you could almost forget it. Here you heard the giant whisper of the rain, the mewing of a gull who stood aimlessly on a ledge in the middle of the harbor and said the same thing over and over. The slight wash of the water against the rocks, made by the wake, had died quickly away, as quickly as the *White Lady* had gone around Eastern Harbor Point.

Joanna found herself obsessed with the emptiness of everything; the village, and her thoughts. It was reaction, probably. Her life wasn't empty. It couldn't be, simply because Nils had gone, like so many men, to war. Even after Alec, her first husband, had died, and she was so wildly young, she had never had the sense that her life was empty. There had been Ellen. Now she had Ellen and Jamie.

She found herself wishing that Ellen were with her, not staying with her grandmother so she could go to school in Pruitt's Harbor. Well, she could wish a lot of things, but nothing would be changed. And she had enough to do to fill every moment. Gardening, sewing, berrying, canning, writing letters, reading. . . .

Feeling like the very soul of no-nonsense, she stopped in at Thea's to collect Jamie. The dog came out from under the doorstep, waving his plumy tail and looking at her from benign bronze eyes; Thea wouldn't let him in, she was too fussy a housekeeper. "Wait for me, Dick," Joanna told him as she went in, and he crawled back under the doorstep again.

Jamie sat on the floor playing with a pack of cards, and Thea was peeling potatoes at the sink. She had golden hair that was too bright to be natural, always done up in bobbing curls, and she was never without high heels and brilliant rayon print dresses, even when she was faintly blue around the lips with cold.

"Nils gone?" she asked brightly. "Well, come in and have a cup of coffee, why don't you?" She bustled around, her curls dancing, her lean hips swinging under the bright print. "Gawd Almighty, you could probably do with more than coffee, couldn't you? If you was a drinkin' woman, that is . . . I know how I'd feel, sendin' my man off—if I had a man like Nils or Sigurd." The cups clattered on the table. "No chance of Franny ever goin', with his flat feet." She giggled. "And that ain't all that's flat. Ask me, I know!"

Joanna stood by the stove, holding her hands out over the covers. "I don't feel like coffee, really, Thea. Don't go to all that trouble."

"I suppose you won't have much appetite now." Thea sighed. "I don't blame you. The awful things that happen. . . . Did you see that picture of what the Japs did to a Marine?" She flicked her sharp tongue over her thin bright lips. "It was awful. They—"

Joanna, smiling steadily, buttoned Jamie into his jacket and helmet. "You've been good to look out for him," she said.

"Any time, any time!" said Thea airily. "He's real good, too. Not much like his uncles!" She laughed. "They were all sure-enough hellions when they was kids—the Bennett uncles, I mean. I remember how Owen was when we was all goin' to dances together." She moistened her lips the way she did when she was talking about the Marine killed by the Japanese. Joanna felt her anger beginning in her, slowly but hotly. She urged Jamie toward the door.

"Well, thanks, Thea. Any time I can help you out in return—"

Thea followed her to the door, chattering continuously. "I like kids, but I don't guess Franny knows how to make any!" More laughter at her own wit. "Too bad Sig's my first cousin—and him livin' all alone with a housekeeper—"

"I guess she keeps him happy," said Joanna over her shoulder, keeping her smile fixed. Once she was out, and the door was shut between her and Thea, she lifted her head and took a great cleansing breath of the damp, cool air. It smelled of wet bare trees, of the east wind, of March; it smelled wonderful.

With Dick and Jamie tagging along, she went back up through the spruce windbreak and came into her own house. In the kitchen she stood still and listened to the small familiar noises that made up the silence of the house. An ember falling in the stove; the glug of the oil stove in the sitting room. The loud, asthmatic ticking of the old-fashioned clock on the shelf in the dining room. She gathered the sounds around her as protection against the loneliness which she knew would assail her when she least expected it. Nils would take comfort in visualizing her here, and the thought gave her a sort of comfort now.

She put Thea from her mind, and took off her damp things, divested Jamie of his. He went immediately to playing, advancing upon his toybox with deep concentration. Now there was dinner to start; oh, even on a rainy day there was always something to do *right now*. She brought out salt pork from the cellerway — from their own last-year's pigs — and tore strips of meat from a dried salt fish. She realized, as she worked at the dresser, that finally she felt as if this was her own house; it was as if Nils' departure had sealed the knowledge. For so long she had felt strange here in this small house almost enclosed by the woods, except for the field beyond the dining-room windows. She had grown up in the Bennett homestead, which was all light and space and air, with the sea almost below the windows, and the sun shining in from the time it rose until it dropped into the sea. And then she had hated the man who had lived in this house; Gunnar, Nils' grandfather. He had built the house on a rocky ledge in the midst of marshy ground, and it was a tribute to his industrious Swedish blood that the house stood so firm today, the big barn so tight, and that such lushly abundant gardens could grow in the field that had once been a swamp.

But Joanna had hated him. Most of the other Islanders had disliked him intensely, but there was a special antagonism between the rosy-cheeked, indomitable old man and the equally indomitable girl. He had been dead a long time when she married his grandson, but when Nils wanted to move into the empty house, because it was his, she'd had to fight the feeling that Gunnar was still in the house. Nils had never known about that; Nils, who had hated his grandfather with a cold, impersonal hatred while Gunnar was alive, had ceased to hate him when he died. So she didn't tell him of the hours she lay awake while he slept; lay awake because the big bed with its ornate headboard had been Gunnar's. And she wouldn't sit in his chair. . . .

But little by little they had changed the furniture, and then when he'd suggested a more modern bed, or a simple maple style, the war was beginning and her natural economy had got in the way of her aversion to Gunnar's possessions. And the aversion left with the advent of Jamie.

After that she concentrated on keeping the dining room bay filled with plants, as Nils' grandmother had done; she kept Anna's beloved dishes, tureens, chocolate set, and the decanter that never held anything stronger than elderberry wine, displayed in the cupboards, and still made chowder in the old black iron kettle. She had fond memories of that kettle herself, and she'd loved Anna, who was the only mother Nils had ever known. Anna had done the best she could for her widowed son's children; she'd bathed the boys' sore backs with tears of Balm-of-Gilead lotion after Gunnar had beaten them, and she had stood between them and her husband as much as she had dared.

And yet Gunnar had thought he was right. After all, it was the way he had lived from the time he was a cabin boy on a square-rigger at the age of eleven. Joanna knew that now, and she could understand why Nils had been so quick to forgive, once his younger sister and brother were out from under the old man's thumb.

It was good not to hate anyone. It was good to be getting a dinner made from pigs you'd raised yourself, and dried codfish you'd caught on a handline in the lazy blue trough of the sea on a warm, tranquil September day, you and Nils. It was good to be holding the fort for Nils, knowing he was proud because you'd proved yourself to him, and he had a right to be proud.

It was good to be in the house that was yours and his. . . . Joanna lifted her chin unconsciously as she thought it, in the old gesture of pride and self-assurance. Nothing could ever violate the security that she and Nils had built for themselves and each other in the years of their marriage.

4

OWEN TOOK HIS OWN GOOD TIME about coming home from Brigport. Dinner was on the back of the stove, and Jamie was asleep when he came in. "Get me some water before you take your oilskins off," Joanna called to him.

"What do you do—pour it right down the sink?" he demanded, but it was a good-natured growl. He prowled through the kitchen, big in his glittering yellow oilskins and sou-wester, and grabbed up the pails with a great deal of loud clashing.

"Give me the mail first," she said as he started out again.

"Oh, hold your pucker," he answered and kept on going. She watched him stride down to the well. He was the brother next oldest to herself, and the most troublesome of all; once he had disappeared for seven years, and had returned without a word of explanation for anyone but Nils. And Nils had never told. There was nothing at all to be certain about, in those lost seven years, and everything to conjecture. Joanna still wondered sometimes, but not so much as at first. Now she was faintly amused that she and Owen had been thrown together, to be the last of the Bennetts on Bennett's Island. The two older boys lived prosperously at Pruitt's Harbor, the two younger boys were in the service. Owen had tried to get into the Navy, but he had been rejected; his heart beat too fast. No one had ever dreamed it would be his heart that would keep him out; it had always seemed to be a strong and perfect mechanism operating in a body of steel.

It was impossible not to love Owen, but sometimes even sisterly affection couldn't condone his behavior. She found it safer not to wonder what he did when he stayed a night at Brigport, or a week on the mainland twenty-five miles away. . . . Nils had told her to be patient with Owen. For Nils, she would be patient when her own store of tolerance was exhausted.

He came back, whistling, and set the brimming pails on the dresser. Then he peeled off his dripping oilclothes and pulled off his rubber boots. She stopped moving between the kitchen and the table to watch his black head with a narrow gaze as he leaned over to put on his moccasins.

"Did you ever take Thea out?" she asked.

"The Dutch heifer? No, thanks," he drawled. "I never wanted anything that'd been pawed over by the population of two islands. . . . Why?"

"I just wondered. She was hinting around this morning. If I thought you'd ever been out with her, even twenty years ago, I'd stop speaking to you."

He looked up, his eyes squinted reminiscently. "Nope, Thea never looked very enticin' to me. . . . I can tell you everybody that ever rolled her under a spruce tree, though," he offered.

"No, thanks," she said dryly. "Where's the mail?"

He took it out of his hip pocket, a newspaper and two or three letters. "Here . . . Well, I set Nils on his way. Probably he'll just about get out there and they'll send him back." She knew he was offering her reassurance and so she nodded.

"I don't expect it to be for long," she lied casually, looking over the envelopes. "Do we want an encyclopedia? Here's an ad. . . . Letter from Ellen . . . and Aunt Mary!"

She gazed at her brother in astonishment. "What do you suppose she wants?"

"Most likely she wants me to shingle the barn roof or something. . . . Tell her I got more women with wants than I can handle already." He took the cover off the kettle of squash and breathed deeply. "Lord, there's a lot of yearnin' females in the world these days, you know it? If they don't want their roof shingled, they want somethin' else—"

Joanna laid the envelope down without opening it. "I want my dinner first. I need to be fortified."

"The old witch," said Owen amiably. He sat down at the table, and opened the newspaper. Joanna set the food on, put coffee and water in the percolator and put it over the flames. Her mind worked as rapidly as her hands. It was true, she didn't trust Aunt Mary, who was not her aunt but had married her Uncle Nate. The comfortable set of buildings over against the Eastern End woods, a good part of the woods themselves, all the fields between Long Cove and Schoolhouse Cove down to the schoolhouse, and the two coves, all this belonged to Uncle Nate's Place, and in Joanna's childhood it had been a well-ordered and prosperous farm that supplied the rest of the Island with vegetables, eggs, and milk. Then, because of his wife's mysteriously bad health — which was pure legend as far as the other Bennetts were concerned — Nate Bennett had left and gone to the mainland to live. His sons hadn't cared about the farm, and for a good many years now the Place had stood empty, the golden cow on the barn as empty a symbol of the past as a forgotten flag flying over a deserted fortress.

Uncle Nate was dead now, and Aunt Mary was blooming; and for whatever reason she had written, Joanna was suspicious. Of all her relatives by marriage, Aunt Mary had liked Joanna the least. The boys would blarney around her with their bold charm, but Joanna would never stoop to charm anyone whom she despised.

She read Ellen's letter while she ate, and saved Aunt Mary's letter to go with her coffee. "Put down your paper," she ordered Owen. "If you're still behind it. I'm about to read out Auntie's letter."

"If it isn't the roof, it'll be a paint job. Tell her I've got a defense job. I'm defendin' myself from graspin' women —"

"Can you get your mind off that one track it's been on for thirty-seven years, and *listen?*"

He flashed her a glowing grin, white against ruddy brown. "Darlin' mine, read on."

" 'Dear Joanna,' " she began, and scanned the pages quickly. " 'I am writing in haste, but know you will forgive me . . . when you hear . . .' " Her voice trailed off unbelievingly. " 'I have been lucky enough —' " She felt a chill going through her that was quickly replaced by burning heat. " 'I have sold the place.' " She read, her voice clear-edged and expressionless. She laid down the letter and looked at Owen, who was not grinning now.

"The old witch," he said softly, but not amiably. "Ornery old witch." His long arm shot across the table and he picked up the letter. "Who's she sold it to? Rich New Yorkers? They want to turn it into a summer resort?"

—

He scowled at the letter, his brows drawn ferociously. "Can't read her scratchy writin'. . . . Let me see . . . Sold it to a man, she says." He snorted. "That tells us a great lot. Hey, you didn't read the rest of it. She wants you to feed and sleep him for a week when he comes out to look it over."

The impact of her outraged astonishment pulled her out of her chair. "I won't do it," she said softly, knowing that if she lifted her voice she would storm. "I won't do it. I won't even answer the letter."

"She'll send him anyway. You know the old buzzard." He crumpled the letter savagely in one big brown hand.

"She can't do it." Joanna came to a stop by the window, and stared out past the geraniums at the tawny field fenced in by a fringe of spruces. But she saw nothing. "She *can't!* I know she always hated us—and all the Bennetts—but even at that she'd give us a chance to buy, wouldn't she?"

"You still surprised at what people do?" Owen cocked an eyebrow at her. "People that hate us? Listen, kid, she's been waitin' for years for a chance to say, 'To hell with you beggars.' Now she's said it. She's sold out Bennett land to outsiders, and this one time you can't do anything about it, so relax."

"And asking us to look out for the—" She put her hands against her burning cheeks, trying to cool them. "I can't imagine what he'd be like except that she'd be sure to find somebody that would be horrible—he'll shut off the road—he'll—Oh, I wish I had her by the throat! Darn her smug soul!"

"Say 'damn,' " Owen advised her. "Damn her soul. It tastes better. Damn Jeff and Hugo too, for my money. Even if they don't want to live here, they could at least hang on to the land."

She stood by the windows, gazing out at Uncle Nate's Place, that had been Bennett property since Grandpa Bennett had bought the Island from the State of Maine. Was it for this those earliest Bennetts had toiled, living in a log cabin through their first winter on an uninhabited island twenty-five miles from the rest of the world; building the homestead with the sheer strength of their hands and shoulders; was it for this that her grandfather, and then her father, and then herself, Joanna, had fought to hold the Island community together? So that a Bennett's wife could betray him as soon as he was in his grave by selling his and his children's birthright?

If Jeff and Hugo hadn't wanted it, Jamie might have had it some day. But it was a stranger who had the deed. He owned the barn where she'd played, and the close-cropped meadow land above Long Cove where the cows had come home at night, with all the western sky and sea ablaze with sunset behind them. He even owned the wild roses that grew against the seawall above Schoolhouse Cove. He owned the fields that were spangled in June with blue flag, red and white clover, daisies, buttercups in a shimmering sheet of gold, the sudden hot flame of devil's paintbrush; he wouldn't care about the strawberries that came in July, sweet and small, in clusters of rubies among the tall grasses; the Queen Anne's lace that made the field look frosty in the late August moonlight, the blackberries, and in October the glossy purple-red crop of cranberries. A stranger would claim the great pink pond-lilies that Uncle Nate had planted one year in the ice-pond, among which the seagulls came down to drink, settling themselves like white blossoms among the pink ones.

Her throat constricted. She wanted to cry, to swear, to go out and walk for long furious hours in the rain until she could wear out this passion of rage. She wanted Nils terribly, but even as she wanted him, she knew he couldn't help her.

She swung around accusingly on Owen. He sat at the table, his arms folded before him, his dark face set in harsh lines.

"I won't have him in my house!"

Owen shrugged. "I don't want him either. But we've got the little end of the stick and about all we can do is find out about the gink. We won't know much if he stays with Sig—or Thea."

That decided her. Whoever he was, and whatever he was, it was certain that he'd heard a good deal of nonsense about the Bennetts from Aunt Mary, and he'd hear even more—of an unmistakably low caliber—from Thea. Out of self-defense, she would have to take him.

"I'll write to her," she said.

"He might not be so bad—how do we know?"

She gave him a look and didn't answer; neither of them spoke of the letter again that day. When she wrote to Nils, she didn't tell him about it. Nothing was certain. Perhaps he hadn't bought it yet, anyway. Who ever heard of anyone with money to spend paying it out on something sight unseen? No, he was coming out to look it over, and then decide, and for a Mainlander the Island in March would be a bitter, barren place; the buildings needed repairs and it was next to impossible to get materials. For a little while, just before she went to bed, she felt a faint stir of relief, a lightening of heart. And then, when the lamp was out, and the finality of Nils' absence was a flat, irrevocable fact, the heaviness came back and stayed with her, pressing on her like the windy dark, until she fell asleep.

5

AUNT MARY'S FINAL WORD, ornamented lushly with many thanks, said that "the man" would arrive on a date set in the first week in April. He was simply "the man" to Joanna and Owen, since they couldn't read the writing when she told them his name. Variously, Owen called him "that gink," "that son of a gun," and "that beggar," until Joanna felt constrained to tell him it wasn't really the stranger's fault. In all fairness, he wasn't to be blamed. But she knew even while she was speaking that she resented him as furiously as Owen did and perhaps more, for Owen's rages burned up in him like a fire in dry driftwood, and went out in a cloud of steam like the very same fire when smothered with wet rockweed. Her own anger burned long and steadily . . . and she had always had a more ardent, deep-rooted kinship for the Island anyway.

No one else knew what was about to happen. Joanna forebore from writing the news to her older brothers and her mother at Pruitt's Harbor. She prepared Ellen's room for the boarder, and because there were certain rules of hospitality that had to be followed, her most beautiful quilts came out of the chest to blow for a day in the sunshine and wind.

Nora Fennell, Matthew's wife, came down on one of her rare

visits that day, and her eyes widened at the sight of the prismatic colors glowing against the dull background of the barn. *"They're beautiful!* Are you cleaning house so soon, Jo?"

"Just airing quilts," Joanna said briskly.

"Gram's made some nice ones." Nora stood by the line fingering the corner of the Log-Cabin quilt. In her slacks, and with her thick glossy chestnut mop tied back by a ribbon, she looked barely twenty instead of almost thirty. Her gray eyes and wide, laughing mouth had made her irresistibly attractive when she had first come to the Island. Now there were two little dents at either corner of her mouth, from holding it so firmly, and her laughter came slowly. "Gram made some really lovely ones, but I won't use them."

"Why?" Joanna shooed Jamie off the rug she wanted to sweep, and he stepped doggedly to one side.

"Because she made them, of course. Anything to annoy the old—" She stopped, and took out her cigarettes. "She hates this too. I'm a scarlet woman. Married, smokes, and won't have children."

"Because she wants you to have children," Joanna added, and Nora nodded. Joanna went on sweeping, aware of the aura of helpless resentment that hung around Nora. There was a hardness, too, about the girl that she didn't like. At first Nora'd been hurt or embarrassed by Gram's frankness. This was much worse. And Matthew was apparently unaware.

"I've heard about having children since before I married Matthew. She started talking about it then. Well, I wasn't going to have one at the end of the first nine months! If she'd kept quiet . . . honestly, Joanna, I think the devil's in her! She's eighty-eight, and she can make me mad enough to want to strangle her!" Joanna looked up, because the hardness had been replaced by something like panic. "She about drives me crazy! I don't know what it's like to live alone with Matthew! It's not my house, it's Gram's. When I go home she'll start in, telling me I wouldn't have time to run around if I was doing my wifely duties." Her eyes filled suddenly. "She hated Bosun, and after he died I knew I hated her, because he'd never done anything in life that was bad, poor little feller. . . . But I couldn't even cry for him, because she'd made it sound as if I was . . . *crazy* . . . somehow, loving a dog that much. I'd have had a baby, once. I wanted one. But not now."

Her voice hardened again. She wiped her eyes on her sleeve, ground her cigarette into the dirt. "Excuse me, Jo . . . huh?"

Jamie put his arms around her knees, and looked up. "Hurt finner?"

"He thinks you've hurt your finger," Joanna said, and understood when Nora put the child away from her without answering him or looking directly into his anxious face.

"I'll go back and put the potatoes on, I guess. Gosh, I envy you, Joanna. Even if Nils has to be away, you know what you've got is yours, and nobody's telling you or criticizing—"

Joanna wanted to say something reassuring to Nora, but there was nothing to say, so she let her go.

The small room looked pleasant enough when she was done with it. She washed the wide, blue-painted floorboards, and made up the old spool bed with the quilts, set a blue-and-white pitcher and basin on the white washstand, hung fresh curtains. She put several books on the stand beside the bed, and an ash tray. *He'll see that we know how to read, anyway,* she thought grimly, knowing that Aunt Mary was prone to describe her Bennett relations as something akin to a gypsy encampment or a settlement of half-breeds.

On the morning of the day he was to come, she awoke before dawn and wondered about the weather. A trip across the bay in the *Aurora B.,* and then the final three miles from Brigport Harbor to Bennett's, had been enough to discourage some visitors from ever trying it again. So if it were a very bad day today, it would help. On the other hand, Owen had to go to meet him, and she still had stomach-wringing moments of apprehension when a boat set out for Brigport in really bad weather.

But there was no wind; the silence before dawn was a heavy and absolute thing. Perhaps it was going to be a day like the one before Nils left, so beautiful that it hurt. She would have to wait a while to see. She watched for the sky to pale above the saw-toothed wall of spruces, and she must have dozed, because almost before she knew it the sky had turned a flaming and treacherous red. The bar of color ended abruptly against the rim of the cloud ceiling, which reflected faintly rosy waves. Then, as she watched, it faded and she knew this would be a gray, still day with a raw-edged cold that seeped into the bones and permeated every corner of the house, even with two fires. At this time of year, without the saving grace of snow on the spruces, or the evident beginnings of spring, this sort of day could be the most dismal and discouraging of all.

Faintly ashamed of her elation, she slid out from under the warm covers, put on her robe and slippers, and went down to build the kitchen fire. The dog padded down the stairs behind her.

Owen went out to haul before he went to Brigport, and when it was almost time for him to come home, she took Jamie and went out. She had her dinner started, a substantial lobster chowder and a thick squash pie. There would be hot biscuits, too, apple jelly, and coffee. She hoped he'd enjoy it, because she wouldn't. She wouldn't relish any meal eaten while he was in the house.

She walked down to the shore, pacing her step to Jamie's. Now he was ahead of her, now behind her, and the dog Dick was all around them. In the sullen quiet Jamie's voice was loud, and the harsh cries of the crows flying over the woods were thrown down to earth by the low, dense ceiling of cloud. The woods looked black, the fields below were dun-colored; the empty houses looked desolate, like people who are waiting in bleak loneliness, with their shoulders hunched up and their hands driven into their pockets, their faces passive and blank. She felt a chill of homesickness for the old days, when the established things were safe. Now nothing was safe; neither the Island nor the world.

She turned to the left by the fish houses and walked around the shore toward Grant's Point, twin to Eastern Harbor Point; the two high, spruce-crested arms of rock made the harbor. The Grant house, long empty, stood drearily against a dreary sky. Below it, half on the wharf and half on the solid ground, the building that had been the store and post-office for so many years huddled against the shelter of the point. The shingles were curled at the edges, and there were scarred places where the shingles were gone altogether. The wharf itself was in worse repair. No one ever used it now, preferring the Old Wharf across the harbor.

Jamie pulled hard on her hand. "Come on, Mama . . . come on." He wanted to go out on the wharf, and she shook her head.

"It's not safe, Jamie. We'll fall into the water." Jamie pulled his brows together, looking comically like Owen, and stared down through the long shed at the forbidden territory. Until Pete Grant had closed

up shop and gone to the mainland, the mail boat had landed pas-
sengers and freight on this wharf for over forty years, and the lobster
car, where Pete had bought thousands of pounds of lobsters from
Island fishermen, had lain in the shelter of the wharf. Before the war,
Nils and the other men left on the Island had put the wharf in fairly
good shape, but two years of storms had undone their work.

She thought with a blend of humiliation and pleasure that the
principal wharf of Bennett's Island wouldn't present a very favorable
impression to a stranger.

A chill struck through her coat and seemed to permeate her very
thoughts. She turned restlessly, still holding Jamie's hand, and walked
back along the shore. "A boat!" Jamie shrilled, and she listened, her
heart quickening unpleasantly. But it was Sigurd's boat, coming in
around Grant's Point. Against the sleek, gunmetal sea the long line
of the wake gleamed with unnatural whiteness. The big boat cut swiftly
across the harbor toward the Old Wharf, and Jamie listened raptly
to the engine. He waved, and was not discouraged because Sigurd
hadn't seen him. He was waving to the boat and not to the man.

Francis Seavey came in right behind Sigurd, in his smaller, din-
gier boat, whose engine sounded spotty and harsh after the expensive
purring roar of Sigurd's marine engine. Joanna began to wish that
Owen would come soon. Of course, if the stranger had to stand around
over at Brigport in this penetrating chill, after the cold ride on the
mail boat, he might be discouraged altogether from wanting to buy
on an inaccessible island. But it was nerve-wracking to wait.

She gave up, finally, and went home. And they came when she
wasn't looking for them; she had barely gotten Jamie's things off, established him in his high chair with a cookie and milk, when Dick
barked on the doorstep. There was something uncanny about the way
they had come. She hadn't heard the boat, or glimpsed it crossing
the harbor, she hadn't even seen the men when they came up from
the shore. But suddenly there they were in the house, with Dick circling them in excitement, and Owen laughing.

Owen laughing! He had been swearing when he went out this
morning. She went slowly into the doorway and stood there, until
they noticed her. The man who was scratching Dick's ears was as
tall as Owen, but very lean. She couldn't see his face, but she saw
his sandy, close-clipped hair and the back of his narrow head; she

saw the hand scratching Dick's ears. It was a long flexible hand with squarish-tipped fingers.

She saw all this in the instant before Owen, who was hanging up the man's heavy trench coat and hat, saw her.

"Jo, this is Dennis Garland," he said, and she knew by his voice that he was no longer resentful. Feeling betrayed, she put out her hand to the man who came toward her. She saw deep-set gray eyes with a faint, questioning smile in them; it spread over his angular lean face and took away the austerity it might have had in repose.

"How do you do?" he said, and at the sound of his voice Dick pressed against his knees. It was an unhurried voice, an easy voice. Tired, too, Joanna realized. His hand closed firmly over hers.

"How do you do?" she murmured, and knew why Owen wasn't sullen. It would be hard to be set against a man who was so obviously tired, whose pallor had so gray a tinge, and whose manner was so friendly. He was young, perhaps forty; and he had the easy erectness of a man who has lived actively.

"I can't tell you how kind you are," he said. "This is a great imposition, I know . . . in more ways than one."

"Not at all," she said. "You'll want something hot right away, won't you? After the trip on the mail boat—"

"He didn't suffer much," Owen grinned. "Rode all the way in the pilot house with Link."

Joanna raised her eyebrows. "You did well. Link's usually pretty stuffy about that."

"I guess it was a case of fools rushing in where angels fear to tread." He followed her into the kitchen and spread his hands out gratefully over the stove. "I didn't know till your brother told me that the pilot house is the sanctum sanctorum. . . ."

"Link counts on his cigars to drive people out," said Owen. He opened the cupboard door and took out a bottle and two glasses. "Have something to warm your bones?"

Garland shook his head, smiling a little. "No, thanks . . . I've smelled worse cigars. I stuck it out, and he told me quite a bit about the Island."

Joanna said crisply, "Owen, why don't you take Mr. Garland's bag upstairs, and show him his room? I'll be getting dinner on."

"Huh! I can't fly on one wing!" Owen took another, quick drink, and then picked up the bag. Garland, turning to follow him, saw Jamie standing in the doorway. Jamie, hands behind his back, looked up, his blue eyes calm and contemplative under the yellow bang; the tall man looked down, and his thin face lightened. "Hello, son," he said softly.

"Hi," said Jamie. "What's that?" His hand lifted; unswervingly his finger and his gaze went to the one thing Joanna had missed, the small gold discharge button in the lapel of the old tweed jacket.

She stood quietly in the kitchen for a moment, listening to the men's footsteps on the stairs, and the voices from above, Owen's vibrant and clear as it always was, Garland's no more than an easy murmur. She couldn't describe her feeling at the moment. It was not that she felt cheated. It was more of a let-down sensation. Owen had apparently gone over to the enemy; even Link, who never allowed anyone in the pilot house, had sold out. What's more, he had *talked* to the man. He'd told him about the Island. She had all this to stir around in her brain, and then there'd been the discharge button. Here was a man older than Nils, who had gone, and had been discharged while the war was still going on; it made her faintly uncomfortable, as if it was unfair to hold resentment to a man who had perhaps been wounded or made ill in the service.

Well, there was nothing to do about it but get dinner on, and wish this week to be over quickly. But in the very instant that she wished it, she knew how endlessly it would reach across the hours.

6

DINNER WAS A PLEASANT MEAL, on the surface at least. Owen and Dennis Garland kept up the conversation, and Joanna listened, marveling. The two men were so different, and yet Owen was as free from self-consciousness as if he had known the other man all his life. Not that Owen was inclined to be self-conscious anyway, but she had expected some inner reserve in Owen, some withholding of himself, as she was keeping herself remote.

She was courteous, she spoke often enough not to seem sulky, but she excused herself as soon as possible to take Jamie up for his nap. She took her time about it; there was the small pink pot, the shoes to take off, the overalls, the presentation of the one-armed teddy bear which had belonged to Ellen, the snuggling down, the drawing of shades. When she went downstairs Owen was sitting by the radio, which he had turned very low; he sat leaning forward, his elbows on his knees, his hands clasped loosely between them. The scent of his pipe was strong and sweet in the room. Dennis Garland wasn't there.

She began to clear the table. Presently Oven turned off the radio and came out into the kitchen, carrying stacked cups and saucers.

"Has he gone to look at the Place?" Joanna asked without looking up.

"No, he's up in his room." Owen lounged against the dresser, watching the boiling stream from the teakettle explode the soap flakes into foam. "Not a bad guy, Jo."

"I could tell that you thought so." She slid the silver into the pan, ladled in cold water from the pail.

"Could have been much worse!" said Owen. He shoved the dishes back from the edge of the dresser with a nerve-wracking clatter, strode across the kitchen and got his jacket and cap.

After he had gone she waited in the kitchen, watching him go down past Thea's and Sigurd's to the fish house. She listened. There was no sound in the house at all; no human sound.

It was late in the afternoon when Dennis Garland came downstairs. She had lit the Aladdin lamp against the encroaching gray dusk and sat reading by the table in the dining room, while Jamie played around the floor with his trucks and airplanes. She heard the footsteps on the front stairs, and coming through the sitting room, but she didn't look up until she knew he was standing in the doorway.

She had a faint shock when she raised her eyes; it was one of those disturbing impressions that seem so familiar, but that pass so swiftly one cannot be sure. He stood in the doorway, touched by the outer edge of the lamplight, a tall, lean figure in tweeds; the light touched his strong nose and caught the glint of his faint smile in his eyes. He glanced from her to Jamie, and his gaze lingered for a moment on the baby's yellow head; then his glance moved back to her. All the while he was filling his pipe.

"I slept too long," he said. "I expected to walk over to the property this afternoon. What sort of silence do you have on this Island? I couldn't fight against it."

He came forward into the light. The familiar sensation was gone. "I don't know," she answered. "But it's not often this quiet. There's the rote and wind—" She put her book aside politely, thinking, *Now I'll have to make conversation until Owen comes back again.*

"Don't stop reading," he said quickly. "I shan't disturb you. I'm going out and walk on your Island, so I'll know it's real."

She understood, and was for this reason uncomfortable. She had felt the same way about the stillness herself. She picked up her book again, but instead of reading she watched him as he walked out through the kitchen. He moved quickly and easily, as quickly and easily as his hands had moved to fill his pipe. There was a freshness about him that had come since he'd slept, and she remembered that while he had been speaking about the silence the lines in his face had seemed less deep, the pallor less gray. He brought in his trench coat and hat from the sun parlor, and stood by the stove as he put them on. Before he went out, he scratched a match on the stove and lit his pipe. In the dimness of the kitchen the quick puffs of light illumined his face, the strong lean features and deepset eyes, and again she had that baffling moment of recognition. Then it was gone, as quickly as it had come.

Now he will go out, she thought, and was ready to breathe deeply again, as if his presence in the house were stifling. He turned toward the outer door; then suddenly, he came back into the dining room and the yellow circle of light. He dropped his hat on a chair and stood before her, hands in the pockets of his trench coat.

"Mrs. Sorensen," he said quietly, almost without expression, "there's something I'd like to say. Perhaps it will make it easier for us if I say it now. I realize how much of an intolerable imposition this is—and believe me, I shan't subject you to it for long."

She felt confused and embarrassed, and angry because Joanna

Bennett should be feeling none of these things. Conscious of her rising color, she said stiffly, "It's no imposition. I wouldn't have told my aunt I'd board you, if I'd thought it would be too much work for me."

"You know I don't mean that," he corrected her gently. "You see, I know something of the situation. And my family has lived in Maine — for — well, almost as long as the Bennetts." He smiled a little. "Don't you think I know how you feel about family land? Your aunt — and by the way, she's only an aunt by marriage, isn't she? — was quite frank. So I know just what sort of unfortunate position we have put you in. But if I hadn't bought the property, there was a strong chance of a New York man's buying it, with intentions of making it into a resort."

"I see," said Joanna. It was all she could manage, and she was quite sure that she hated him for knowing so much, for seeing so much.

"Well" — He put his pipe in his mouth and picked up his hat. Dick emerged from under the table and looked up at him, tail wagging, bronze eyes turning black with pleading. The man touched the broad silky head briefly. "May he go?"

Joanna nodded. Then Bennett pride reasserted itself; he should not think she was rude or ignorant. She stood up, strongly slender and erect. "Thank you for explaining. It makes it easier . . . when we know what you've saved us from."

"Does it?" He gave her a searching, candid look from gray eyes. Then, unexpectedly, he smiled, and it was not faint, but a warm and sudden thing. "I'm afraid it doesn't make me any less of a foreigner, though. . . . Coming, Dick?"

As quickly as that, he was gone. He had gone out to find the silence, and when the door shut behind him the silence swallowed him up. Yet something of himself had been left behind, so that even if he never came back there would be the echo of his voice, the wraith of his tobacco smoke, the sheen of lamplight across his hair, and that swift and final smile. And there would always be the memory of her stubborn antagonism. He was right. His explanation hadn't made it any easier; for whoever bought the Place would be an outsider, whether he was from Maine or from New York or from South America.

The next day was gilded by faint sunshine, and the day was mild and warm, with a spring-like dampness in the earth and on the wind. The alders were beginning to show an amethyst tinge, their branches cloudlike against the wall of spruce, and along the edges of the brook there were spears of clear bright green. Behind the blowing, shredded, wisps of cloud the sky showed blue; the tender blue that came only in early spring and in the warm days of fall.

Owen went out to haul, and Dennis Garland went out to explore his new property. He asked Joanna to make him some sandwiches, and said he wouldn't be back to dinner. Tormented because he was going to lay actual claim to the Place by walking on it, relieved because he would be gone most of the day, she made a lunch for him, of lobster sandwiches, coffee in Nils' thermos bottle, and an apple turnover.

No sooner had he gone than Thea was scampering across the yard, her curls bobbing—they were always "set" at night—her skimpy skirts blowing about her knees in the boisterous spring breeze. Her pale blue eyes were wide and shiny with excitement.

"Jo, who's that?" she demanded.

Joanna was getting beans ready to bake. "Who's who?" she said flatly, measuring mustard into the pot.

"*You know!* The fella Owen brought home yesterday! He just went down by . . . Who is he, anyway?"

"He's a man who wanted a place to board for a few days," said Joanna.

"He must be nuts," Thea observed. "Anybody'd come out here when he didn't have to . . . Kerosene lamps and outdoor toilets, my gosh!"

"That's what you were raised on," Joanna reminded her. "Along with fish and potatoes, like the rest of us." She forbore to remind her that no one had forced her to come back to the Island to live, and that anytime she wanted to leave, it would be perfectly all right with the Island.

Thea arranged a curl, standing on tiptoe to examine her reflection in the mirror over the sink. "Oh, sure, I know all about it. But even if you was raised on it, you don't have to like it. In most cases, anyway." She giggled and Joanna was thankful that Owen wasn't there; Thea's remark would have been the signal for a ribald exchange, punctuated by insults from Owen and more giggles from Thea, who never knew when she was being insulted.

"Well, anyway," Thea went on cheerfully, "what's he like? Is he nice? Gee, he looks like a professor or somethin'. He isn't a *preacher*, is he?" she added with alarm.

"I don't know what he is," said Joanna. "He's very quiet, that's all I know." She went down on her knees before the stove to slide the beanpot into the oven.

Thea hovered around for a few minutes more, and then went out. Most likely she would now go down to Sigurd's to check notes with Leonie, Sigurd's housekeeper. In a few days now they would know; the fact was inescapable. But until then, Joanna reasoned, let them stew.

It was so warm and sunny at noontime that she let Jamie's nap go by and took him out for a walk after dinner. Dick, who had escorted Dennis Garland across the Island in the morning, met them by the fish houses and decided to go with them. What was Garland doing over there? Joanna wondered, and looked into Dick's kind, shining eyes as if she could see mirrored there what he had seen this morning. He would have followed the stranger's feet around through the house and the barn, he would have sat down beside Garland on one of the great, flat, shelving rocks that looked out to sea; perhaps he'd even shared a sandwich with him, and Garland had talked to him, as lonely people will address their thoughts to dogs and very small children.

Lonely! Why had she thought of that word? Perhaps because the man walked in an aura of solitude. Nils had always been like that, but it was a self-sufficient aloneness. Not a loneliness. And this man looked as if he had always been alone.

She walked slowly along the path toward the Old Wharf and the long beach, with a half-intention of going up the road past the marsh toward the Bennett homestead. That, at least, remained irrevocably Bennett; the sloping meadow before it, the long point between Schoolhouse and Goose coves; Goose Cove, and then the woods. And Sou-west Point belonged to the Bennetts too. When you thought of all land in the Island's three hundred and sixty-five acres, you knew Uncle Nate's Place wasn't so big after all.

The sun lay warmly on her head, and there was a mild, dreamlike atmosphere around her. The wind had gone down. The harbor moved against the shores in pale blue peace, the gulls stood in a white row on the boatshop roof. Dick, his coat gleaming with bronze lights, followed Jamie toward the beach. When Jamie grew up, he would walk like Nils, she thought, and the idea brought Nils before her almost as vividly as if he'd been hauling his skiff up over the beach rocks. She hadn't heard from him since he'd left, but he had warned her about that. Ellen had written that he'd come to Pruitt's Harbor to see her and the rest of the family. Beyond that, she knew nothing of his movements. But she wasn't disturbed by the blankness. When she could see him as clearly as this, in the soft bright clarity of the silent noon, she could not worry. It would be only when she could no longer summon him up, or recollect exactly the tones of his voice, that she would be afraid.

"Joanna!" The hail rang out in the stillness, shattering her mood of peace. It was Sigurd, standing on the wharf above the lobster car. His blond head gleamed, so did his grin. "Come over and see what I found today!"

Jamie, his hands full of stones, was almost down to the water's edge. He gave her a pleading look, and she nodded. "You can throw them, Jamie." She walked out on the wharf, and Sigurd, looking immensely proud of himself, pointed out at the harbor.

"See? Found it driftin' out by the Hogshead, and I towed it in."

"What?" She couldn't tell where his big scarred forefinger was pointing, and he jabbed it in annoyance.

"There! On Stevie's moorin'!"

She stared, frowning and perplexed, at the big black cylinder, bobbing gently in the tide. Light reflected brightly from its wet rounding surface. Sigurd went on eagerly, his big voice reverberating against her eardrums.

"I tied it up out there, and then I called up the Coast Guard. They're sendin' a boat out to see if it's any good—"

"Well, what *is* it?" she demanded.

"A mine," said Sigurd. "Can you figger that?" His voice cracked in ludicrous amazement. "There it was, floatin' around . . . must of got loose from somewhere. *"Almagstige Gud,'* I said to myself, "Sig, you're a lucky kid. Lucky you didn't run into it.'" He laughed uproariously, and Joanna smiled, but her impression was that of pure horror.

"Do you think . . . it's a good one?" she asked quietly, resisting an impulse to run down to the beach and pick up Jamie.

Sigurd shrugged violently. "How do I know? That's why I called the Coast Guard."

"You'd better watch out none of the others run into it coming in to the car."

"Sure. Be just like Franny to smash to hell into it. Be the biggest noise he ever made, huh?" He threw back his head and laughed again.

"Well, I'll get on with my walk. You did fine, Sigurd. I'll expect to see you towing in the *Deutschland* some day." She left him standing in the self-satisfied contemplation of his find, and went down to the beach.

"Come on, Jamie," she said with a sharpness she didn't mean for him. "You can throw more stones later." Jamie threw all his stones at once, with a fine tragic air, and climbed the sloping beach laboriously. He would walk with her, but his disapproval was plain.

They went up toward the homestead, and the sky was as blue, the colors in the marsh as lovely, but the dreamlike feeling was gone, and she felt her nerves tightening. She fought against the increasing tension; she took deep breaths of the soft air, she concentrated on watching Jamie stamp ahead of her, and on Dick ranging through the marsh whose bronze grasses reflected the glints in his coat and in his eyes. She watched the flight of crows from the trees behind the schoolhouse, jet black against the little white belfry, which in turn shone against the sky. But again and again she saw the big black tube, made fast to the mooring, rising and falling gently on the calm water. There was something deadly in the very contrast; like a battle in a field of ripe wheat ready for the harvest, under autumn sunshine. The mine, anchored in the sheltered little harbor, had suddenly brought the complete ugliness of the war to Bennett's Island.

She'd planned to sit on the sunny granite doorstep of the homestead for a little while, but as soon as she had reached the weathered and silvery gateposts, she knew she must go back to the harbor. Perhaps it would not look so bad this time. She would not know until she had looked again.

7

THE COAST GUARD BOAT came out from Limerock in the late afternoon, and by that time everyone who could make it was on the shore. Even Nora Fennell came down, bright-eyed with excitement. "Gram's taking a nap . . . Gosh, seems as if something's happening around here, doesn't it?"

She stood beside Joanna on the wharf and watched the dinghy from the Coast Guard boat circle around the mooring. "Why don't they go close to it?" Her excitement began to fade. "Golly, you don't think it's dangerous after all, do you?"

"I don't know," said Joanna. She had only come down because Jamie had seen the boat from the kitchen window and had gone into a delirium of ecstasy about it. The men stood in a little knot at one side, watching it without speaking. Even Sigurd's first exhilaration over his find had died out. Thea stood between him and Franny, hanging onto their arms. Her voice was more high-pitched than usual, perhaps because no one was answering her questions.

Leonie came along the wharf and joined Joanna and Nora. "Housekeeper" was a courtesy title only, and in the old days Leonie wouldn't have presumed to speak so freely to two decently married women, nor would they have greeted her so calmly. But it was somehow impossible to regard Leonie as a light woman. She was slight and trim and mousey, she walked on sensible shoes and looked at her world through horn-rimmed glasses that were always shining.

"That one," she said acidly, looking at Thea's back. "She turns my stomach . . . So does Sigurd, today."

"Why?" Nora asked obligingly.

"Towin' that thing in . . . I suppose if he found Tenpound adrift he'd come bringin' it home. Some people can't leave anything lay. We're like to be blasted out of our beds to Kingdom Come."

Nobody answered. The truth of her statement was too evident, and Joanna tightened her grip on Jamie's fist when it wriggled protestingly. "No, you can't go to Owen," she told him.

"Well, I'm not intendin' to stand here and watch my doom comin' at me," said Leonie, and started out for home, putting her feet down with no nonsense on the planks.

"I keep forgetting she's living in sin," said Nora in mild astonishment. "Thea acts more like a scarlet woman than Leonie. They say Leonie plays poker with the men, and she can drink too." She giggled softly. "I wonder what she's like when she's drunk."

"She teams Sigurd around like mad," said Joanna. "I'm not keen on watching my doom approach, either. Come on, Jamie."

"I guess I'll wait for Matthew. Gram's good for another hour, and I'm going to have some fun while I can . . . if you can call it fun." She gave Joanna a wry grin, and went toward the men.

Joanna left the wharf. The sun was going down and she felt chilled; yet it was still warm. The chill was not from the weather, she knew, but it had something to do with the thing tied up at Stevie's mooring, around which the Coast Guard dinghy moved so gingerly.

Jamie slowed, Dick bounded away from her, over toward the marsh. She saw Dennis Garland standing there by the old anchor sunk into the ground where the beach joined the marsh. His clothes blended with his background, and she would have missed him if Jamie and the dog hadn't seen him. He stood there, motionless, his hat brim slanted so that his face was shadowed. He was, somehow, an anonymous figure. He could have been anyone. But because she knew who he was, and why he was on the Island, she thought of him as she walked home; of him, and the mine, together.

In the evening the men talked about the mine. The captain and crew of the Coast Guard boat had been afraid to touch it. When they left they cautioned the fishermen about touching it again, and added that they would send for a mine expert from Boston to come down and look at it. Meanwhile, it remained in the harbor, a quiet, black, ominous thing.

During the evening Joanna added a little more to her scant hoard of knowledge about Dennis Garland. He had been in the Navy. Owen told him about Stevie and Mark, and he was interested. He had been in the Pacific himself, he said, and then turned the subject abruptly, asking a question about the Island. The change was so sudden that Joanna looked up at him, but his face told her nothing. He lay back in Nils' chair, watching the smoke from his pipe drift toward the ceiling, and his sharply rugged profile was remote and seemingly at peace.

Owen lounged in his own chair, his moccasined feet outthrust, a drink at his elbow. Dick lay between the two men, showing a fine impartiality. Joanna, sitting at the table, trying to write letters, glanced at them often. It was a pleasant, companionable scene. So had Nils and Owen sat during many an evening, sometimes with a cribbage board between them, and so had she glanced first at the fair head and then at the black one, and marveled at the easiness that was in Owen when he was with someone who could gentle him. Now he had that same easiness, and it gave her a pang, as if somehow he were being disloyal to Nils.

She gave up trying to write her letters and went out into the kitchen and turned up the lamp. She put more water in the tea-kettle, and laid out the things for getting breakfast. The woodbox was full of seasoned birch and spruce, and fine stuff for kindling. Owen had been outdoing himself at keeping the woodbox full, she thought dryly. She washed her face and brushed her teeth, took her lamp from the shelf and went up to bed.

It was one of those nights when she felt an onrush of loneliness for Nils. The bed looked big and cold, the towering headboard was too imposing for a woman sleeping alone. She turned back the covers so that they would look more hospitable, and began to undress. After the itching nervousness she'd felt downstairs, her skin received the cool air gratefully. She stood naked for a moment, rejoicing in her freedom from clothes as simply as an animal enjoys freedom from its harness. She could see her reflection, all dim shadows and brief golden highlights, in the mirror; she was supple, as narrow-flanked and high-breasted, as if she had never had two children and nursed them both. One thing she had always enjoyed was her superb physical and mental health.

Jamie turned over, murmuring, in his crib, and she reached for her pajamas. In bed she sat cross-legged, brushing her hair and reading. The men were talking so softly downstairs that she couldn't hear even a murmur. How much longer would Dennis Garland stay? she wondered. But he had bought Uncle Nate's Place. There was no hopeful doubt about it, and tomorrow she would have to write to Nils concerning it, and the boys. Tomorrow . . . She blew out the light and slid down between the chilly sheets.

That night she dreamed. It was the first time she had ever dreamed like that since she had been grown-up, waking up to the sound of her own incoherent moans, reaching out into an emptiness that suffocated, feeling clammy and chilled with sweat. She lay in the darkness for a long time, huddled into a tight ball, rehearsing over and over the horror of the dream. She had been watching the mine rising and falling gently on a sea as friendly and blue as Jamie's eyes. She could only see one bit of the mine, since most of it was under water; but what she saw had not been terrifying. It flashed in the sunlight as it moved. Then, though she didn't see the boat, she knew it was there, she heard it coming nearer and nearer, and knew Nils was on it; she'd felt a great surge of happiness.

I hadn't expected to see him as soon as this, she thought. *They must have come back for something. This is a little unexpected gift.*

But he mustn't bump into the mine. She said it quickly, and then she tried to call to him, because as the sound of the engine grew louder, the mine looked suddenly malignant, as if it had a life of its own, and there was something horrifying even about the shining, tranquil water around the mine. But when she tried to call, her throat closed up. It ached with her effort to be heard, but nothing happened. . . . Nothing but the flash. There was no sound, just a flash that frightened her more than a sound could have done.

When it cleared there was the shining water again. It stretched to the horizon on either side, reflecting the sun like one vast uneasy mirror. The mine was gone, there was no sound of a boat, no friendly mew of a seabird, nothing. . . . Nothing but Nils' head, and a wave breaking over it with lazy finality.

His head had been covered with blood. The one ghastly glimpse hadn't shown his face. *Maybe he hasn't any face,* someone kept whispering, and she awoke and knew it was herself, whispering.

In the morning she felt sick and slow, as if she were coming down with some sickness. Even in the light of day she couldn't escape the dream. It carried its own atmosphere, and she was surrounded by it. When she was getting breakfast she thought miserably, *It'll torment me till I tell someone about it.* And she decided to tell Owen when he came down. He would jeer at her, and that was what she knew she needed.

She heard feet on the stairs and her heart lightened wonderfully, and began to shape the way she would tell her dream. And then Dennis Garland came into the kitchen.

"Good morning," he said pleasantly.

"Good morning." She turned away, busy with measuring coffee, and neither of them spoke again until Owen came down. Then there was no chance to tell him about the dream. But her annoyance with Dennis Garland had tempered the horror somewhat.

"Well, we didn't blow up last night, by God!" Owen announced and plunged his face into a basin of cold water. Coming up, he groped for the towel, found it, and emerged from it pleasantly, his brown skin glowing. "Nope! But there's still plenty of time. Wait till the expert gets here."

There was more talk of the mine at breakfast. She thought she would go crazy. It was Owen who did most of the talking; Garland asked more questions about the Island, but she answered them briefly. It was like having a toothache, when even to move the jaw hurts unbearably. She thought they would never get through the meal, and down to the shore. But when she was alone with Jamie, she was also alone with the dream again.

She was upstairs making the beds when the doors banged downstairs and Thea called. "Yoo-hoo! Anybody home?"

Joanna thought first of not answering, but Thea was quite capable of exploring the house if she thought it was empty. "I'm home," she called from the head of the stairs. "What's the matter?"

"Nothin', except that the boat's here with the mine expert from Boston! Franny says they're gonna tow the thing ashore and take it apart on the beach!"

"Oh . . . Well, thanks for telling me, Thea."

"Ain't you goin' down to *watch?*" Thea asked in shrill incredulity.

"I don't think so —"

"He's the cutest thing I ever see in a uniform, that expert. Well, so long!" There was a sound of Thea's high heels trotting through the house, the doors banged again. Joanna went into Dennis Garland's room because it was the nearest, and sat down on the bed. She felt suddenly weak; the back of her neck was wet with sweat under her hair.

She wasn't afraid because they were going to take the mine apart, but it was the dream. She got up again, feeling light-headed, and smoothed out the spread. From there she went into Owen's room. There was enough work here for a half-hour. But the windows looked down to the harbor, and she was drawn to them as irrevocably as a nail to a magnet.

The day was full of April's uncertain sunshine and when she opened the windows the cool air smelled even more strongly of spring. She leaned out, looking over the tops of the white lilac bushes and the spruce windbreak, over and beyond the fish houses, and saw the Coast Guard cutter riding at anchor at the harbor mouth, its gray paint washed in sunlight. The mine was gone from Stevie's mooring, and that meant they had taken it to the beach.

The village was deserted. There was nothing in sight that moved except the gulls, and the blowing grass, and the water that surged and withdrew endlessly on the shore. Everyone was at the beach.

She went downstairs, slipped on her coat, and collected Jamie from his mudpies on the back doorstep.

"Goin' to see a boat?" he asked eagerly, trotting along beside her.

"Yes, a boat," she said. She walked fast, as if she couldn't wait to get there, now that she had made up her mind to go see what was going on. The men had towed the mine in to the foot of the beach, and everyone stood around on the wet, smooth stones that shone faintly in the morning sun. Lying in the wash of the retreating tide, the mine was about five feet long, and there was some sort of mechanism built on one side. A very young seaman and a youthful lieutenant, both in rubber boots, stood ankle-deep in the water and stared at the mechanism.

The officer looked up, grinned at the nearest knot of men, and pushed back his cap. "That's a new one on me," he said candidly. "And I'm supposed to know 'em all."

"You think it's German?" Owen asked.

The lieutenant shrugged. "I can't tell. We'll go to work on it, anyway." The sailor waded ashore to a tool kit lying on the stones and opened it up.

"Where's the best place to be," Leonie demanded, "if that thing's liable to go off? Should I turn off my oil burner?"

"Lady," said the lieutenant, "if that thing went off, it wouldn't matter where you were. And I wouldn't worry about the oil burner, if I were you."

Joanna stood at one side, away from the others, watching the mine with fascination. She could see it as it had appeared in her dream and in a way, this was as horrible. It lay half in the water like some great, vicious sea monster that has been beached but is still deadly. Jamie, to whom beach stones and water presented one fixed idea, pulled to get free, and automatically she picked him up.

This is what faces Nils, she thought. *Torpedoes, mines, bombs and then the Japs themselves.* His bloody head on the water, his bloody head without a face, and she couldn't put out a hand to save him.

Inside her, as she watched, the sickness grew swiftly and quietly, until she felt like a cold, bloodless shell enclosing not a woman, but a mass of terrors. Fantastically it seemed as if she stood completely alone, that no one else existed because no one else could understand. That group, standing around watching, asking questions, making macabre jokes—in this instant they had no relationship with her whatever. Her arms tightened around Jamie.

A beach stone moved, close to her; it moved under someone's foot. She became conscious that someone was standing quite near her. It was Dennis Garland. She hadn't seen him when she came to the beach, she had no idea how long he had been standing beside her, and for a moment she had the frightening thought that he had seen what had happened to her. Then she realized that no one could have seen, and she smoothed her face out carefully, loosening the lips that had drawn tight, dropping the veil of a smile over her eyes.

"Hello," she said. "Exciting, isn't it? Nothing like this ever happened to the Island before."

"I'm sure of that," he said. "May I take Jamie? He must be heavy."

She handed him over, and Jamie put his arm confidently around the man's neck. "What's that?" he pointed at the mine.

"An ashcan," said Garland. "Do you want to look at an old ashcan? It's not much fun, is it?"

Jamie shook his head uncertainly, and pointed at the cutter. "Papa's boat."

"I've got to go home and start dinner," Joanna said abruptly. "I'd better take him . . . he thinks a visit to the beach isn't legal if he can't throw stones overboard."

"He's probably right," Garland said with his pleasant smile, and set Jamie down. He didn't offer to walk home too, and Joanna went quickly, before he could decide to go with her.

8

BY EVENING THE MINE EPISODE was closed, as far as the Navy was concerned. The cutter had gone off into the windy April sunset, taking everything but the outer shell. Someone dragged the empty cylinder over to one side of the beach, out of the way of the skiffs and dories. The mine had been harmless, after all; but discovery of the mine could be added to the other things which the Islanders took with some nonchalance and a certain pride, in this the third year of the war. At first the radio towers and the gun crew at Matinicus Rock had brought the war a little too close; the stringent regulations about boat numbers—big, bold black figures along the side and an extra set atop the cabins—the identification each man must carry, the shudder of depth charges, the patrol planes before dawn—all these things had tightened the nerves at first, and some of the people had gone ashore to stay. But those who had remained on the Island were casual now.

Joanna felt anything but casual about the mine, and knew some of the others had been as uneasy. But they wouldn't show it, any more than she would. Owen talked about it at supper time until it was all she could do not to flare out at him, in front of Garland, and order him to be quiet. But of course he was interested, he couldn't know how it was forever before her mind's eye, the black thing bobbing peacefully in the bright water . . . and then Nils' head going down.

And there was no diverting Owen, anyway. He had had a few drinks with Sigurd before he came home to supper, and if he wanted to talk, he would talk. She knew what his answer would be if she tried to change the subject.

So she tried to eat, and said nothing, but kept busy with Jamie. Garland had little to say. He looked tired; the grayish tinge had come back into his flat cheeks, and the lines had deepened from his nostrils and the corners of his mouth. Already, in the few days he had been there, she had noticed that his eyes darkened toward night. In the daytime they were the clearest gray she had ever seen, but tonight they were almost slate-colored when he looked at her directly, and seemed more deep-set than usual. When he spoke to Jamie his smile started in his eyes and took away the fatigue for a moment; but the smile didn't come to full life across his spare, strong features.

Owen went out as soon as supper was over. Joanna stood in the doorway of the sun parlor, for a breath of fresh dusky air after the heat of the stove and the Aladdin; there were stars beyond the points of the spruces, they showed distant sparks of brightness and then were obscured by the blowing clouds, and then appeared again. The air was cold, but it kept its April smell, that spoke of green grass in the paths and sap stirring in the birches. On the far side of the Island the surf was piling up with a long roar. But it was not a wintry sound tonight.

Owen's voice roared out in a song, shattering the quiet of the dusk.

Every ship has a mainmast, an upstanding stick;
Every lass loves a lad—

She shut the door abruptly and went back into the kitchen. Jamie was sitting on the floor by the stove, struggling with his shoes, and Dennis Garland was on one knee beside him, not touching him, just watching the chubby fingers battle with the stubborn shoe laces. Jamie's face was red, his lower lip prominent. He puffed angrily; and just as he was about to explode into a howl of protest, Garland reached down and untied the knot. Jamie looked up at him with an instant, sunny smile. At the same time Dennis saw Joanna in the doorway. He stood up quickly.

"A little complication," he explained gravely.

"I see." She felt displeased and antagonistic, as if the man were a usurper. As if he had come in unbidden and taken Nils' place. She wished he would not stand there so quietly, looking at her. He behaved as if he were on the verge of asking something, and she had a half-desperate fear that he might ask it now if she didn't do something quickly. . . . Jamie saved the moment. He lifted his other foot up toward Garland.

"Come along, Jamie," she said swiftly, and bent to pick him up. Taking his sleeping suit from the oven door, she sat him on the dresser and began to undress him. She didn't look around at Garland again; and after a moment she felt that he had gone. She heard his quiet footsteps on the stairs, and then his door closed.

She felt guilty for a moment, as if she had been rude to a guest. But only for a moment. After all, she hadn't agreed to furnish conversation along with bed and board. . . . Still he was an odd man, she couldn't help wondering about him and his background.

The day had been a wearing one. Unexpectedly, she was ready for bed, so tired that she ached as she finished the dishes. She blew out the Aladdin and turned down the kitchen lamp, and went upstairs. There was no sound from Garland's room. Later, she lay in bed, ostensibly reading, but her mind wandered. More often she was staring at meaningless text while she thought of the tiny scrap of knowledge she had acquired about Dennis Garland. His name, the fact that he was born in Maine, that he had been in the service; he was neat, the few clothes he'd brought were well-worn but good, the sort of tweeds and pullovers she'd always liked. His toilet articles were plain but good, too. He liked to read. He smoked a pipe. . . . She went on enumerating even the little inconsequential things. Black coffee, not a very heavy eater, though he ate more now. And that was all she could list.

I might like him, she thought, *if he hadn't bought the Place.* It was the last thing she thought before she fell asleep.

She woke up violently, to a harsh, rasping sound. Her heart was pounding, her mouth so dry that her tongue felt thick and swollen. The sound went on, sharp, rough, rhythmic. . . . She realized with a sickening sense of relief that it was Dick barking. He'd gone out with Owen and had come home again. She felt for her robe and slippers in the dark, and made her way across the room, sure-footed and noiseless, her one aim to let the dog in before Jamie woke up.

The rooms downstairs always looked strange when she came down in the middle of the night to find the lamp still burning. The furniture had an expectant look; things that were friendly and familiar in the day stared in a hostile fashion at night. The folds of the tablecloth, now. . . . She didn't look at them, but went swiftly out through the sun parlor and opened the door.

Dick was whining between barks. "Come in, you idiot," she said sharply. "Standing out there yammering like a gorm." The dim light from the kitchen lamp shone out through and cast a faint glimmer on the doorstep. The wind was rising, it made a sound like surf in the windbreak, and there was a sibilant, muted roar in the air all around. Dick came into the whisper of light, eyes shining, tail apologetlc and anxious, and stopped.

"Come on, Dick," Joanna insisted. The tail went faster and he made a little whimpering sound in his throat, and turned away, leaving the light for the darkness. She was conscious that she was afraid. That wasn't like Dick, and it caused an instinctive stir of alarm in her senses, too sharp to be ignored. She went out on the doorstep and stood listening for some informative sound through the Island's familiar night voice, wind and surf. Her ankles were cold; involuntarily she tightened the sash of her robe. The stars had moved a long way since just after supper.

Now it was Dick who was saying, "Come on." He said it with little noises; she heard him near her, making a great stir in the thick shadow beyond the lamplight. And it would be only by getting away from the lamplight that she could see. . . . She left the doorstep and walked slowly along the path between the white lilacs, toward the windbreak. The damp ground wet the soles of her slippers and a chill went through her. It turned to abrupt and sickening cold when her toe touched something that shouldn't have been there.

Owen lay huddled in the tall dead grass under the first spruce in the windbreak. It was his foot she had touched. She knew it was Owen; that was her first thought and she confirmed it when she knelt, her hands quick and sure on his head and face. That was his hair, thick and crisp, and his face. His skin was warm, and when she leaned closer she smelled gin on his breath.

She went back to the house, furious to the verge of tears, and disgusted. "You get in this house," she ordered Dick. "Leave him there. If he doesn't know any better . . ."

"Mrs. Sorensen, is something wrong?"

She started. Dennis Garland was there, he had come into the kitchen and turned up the lamp. He was still dressed, she observed dispassionately, while she was hating him for being there, hating Owen for being drunk out in the path.

She lifted her chin. Her eyes glowed somberly in the lamplight. *No, nothing is wrong.* Her mind framed the words; but she heard herself saying aloud, in a clear, proud voice, "I'm afraid there is. My brother is outside. He's very drunk."

He made a movement toward the door, and she shrugged. "Leave him there. If he doesn't know any better than to drink cheap gin, it'll teach him a lesson to lie out in the field all night."

"Pneumonia would be too much of a lesson, wouldn't it? And you'd be the loser—you'd have to take care of him."

"If you weren't here, I'd have to leave him. I can't manage him alone."

"Well, I'm here, and I can help with him," he said seriously. "Let's get him in, before the neighbors discover him and want to help."

Neighbors. Thea. A fine thing for Thea to behold when she got up in the morning. She'd love that; she'd relish it for months, and serve it up whenever she got a chance, with innovations. And Owen wouldn't care. It would be Joanna's pride that would burn, and the rest of the family who would be shamed, when the news reached Pruitt's Harbor.

She followed Dennis Garland outdoors, and together they got Owen into the house. He was an inert weight, and they were both out of breath by the time they put him on the sitting-room couch. Garland brought in the lamp from the kitchen; they stood and looked down at Owen, and Joanna was shamed as her brother had shamed her so many times before. Tonight she had reached the end of her rope, but Garland had been there, and so once more she had "done something." But not because she wanted to. . . .

"Attractive, isn't he?" she said. Owen slept heavily, his face putty-white except for a bloody scratch on his temple. "It'll be worse before morning, because gin makes him sick." She glanced at Garland defiantly. There was nothing but defiance left. But she dreaded his sympathy.

He wasn't sympathetic. She couldn't read his face, except that it was intent and impersonal. "I'll clean that cut up," he said. "And he ought to get out of those clothes, they're damp. If you'll get me some dry pajamas for him, I'll attend to it."

She started toward the stairs and he called after her. "Have you any bandage and tape?"

"All my first-aid stuff's in the first cupboard, second shelf." She went on up the stairs and into Owen's room. Coming back with the heavy flannel pajamas, and a blanket, she was faintly amazed at herself. It was almost funny . . . as quickly as that her tension broke. She couldn't help it, but she was glad Dennis Garland had been here tonight, because she couldn't have left Owen out, after all; she might have gone to bed, determined, but she'd have been up again in fifteen minutes, and the vision of the struggle with a dead-drunk weight wasn't a pretty one.

When she came downstairs, there was a pungent, biting whiff of alcohol in the room, and he was just placing the last strip of tape over a small bandage on Owen's temple.

"That was a nasty little dig," he said. He began to pull Owen's boots off. Joanna unzipped the jacket and unbuttoned his shirt.

"Don't you mind this?" she asked. "Undressing a—a drunk?"

He shook his head, and for the first time his slow smile touched his eyes. "But you do. Look, why don't you make some coffee, and I'll finish this job? It's nothing to me, but I know how you feel."

"You know a lot," she said without rancor, and went out into the kitchen. By the time the coffee was made, Owen was in his pajamas, and tucked efficiently under blankets. Garland and Joanna sat down to coffee; the clock said ten minutes before two.

The coffee was strong, and boiling hot, and Garland looked at his with pleasure. "You make wonderful coffee, Mrs. Sorensen." He was as serene as if nothing untoward had happened, and it was breakfast time. Joanna looked down at her cup. Her throat felt closed and tight, because she knew what she must say, and it was never easy for a Bennett to apologize. Yet she would do it before she touched her coffee; else the coffee would not go down.

She lifted her head, folded her arms composedly on the edge of the table, and said, "Mr. Garland—"

He glanced up, but his hand still moved, stirring his coffee. For the first time she could put words into his expression. Kind and sensitive at once. It made it somehow easier for her to speak, that kindness that tempered his weariness and kept it from being harsh.

"You were right when you said I resented your buying the Place," she said. "I did, at first. But I don't now. . . . If I've been rude, and not too hospitable, I'm sorry." Her jaw tightened, and her eyes stayed on his without faltering. "I really mean it. And I don't know how to thank you for helping me out tonight. I don't know what I'd have done if you hadn't been here."

"You don't have to say all that, you know." His expression was quizzical.

"Yes, I do." A faint warm glow of red came into her cheeks. "And I want to apologize because this happened tonight."

"Why should you apologize, Mrs. Sorensen?"

"It's a sure thing Owen won't! He drinks too much, but he's proud of it."

"I doubt that. It's probably just self-defense. It's more likely that he's ashamed of himself, but he thinks he can't do anything about it."

Joanna could drink her coffee now. It tasted better than her coffee had tasted for a week. She found herself eager to speak; now that the barriers were down, and Garland had seen Owen at his worst, there was no sense in skirting the subject and she wanted badly to talk to someone. With Nils gone, she had to keep so much to herself.

"Owen always drank, but not the way he's drinking now. It's bad for him, and he knows it. Sometimes I think he's doing it deliberately." She paused, listening again for that harsh breathing from the sitting room. "He had pneumonia once, when he was away from home. What you said about pneumonia tonight—well, I've thought about it more than once."

"A big man like Owen can go down like a felled ox," Dennis Garland said. He looked at her seriously across the table. "What's on his mind, anyway?"

"I think it's the war," said Joanna. "They wouldn't take him. He was drunk for days after they turned him down."

The man took out his pipe and tobacco. "Heart," he murmured. "I listened to it while I was putting him to bed. He looked so bad I thought we had something worse than a drunk on our hands. His pulse was very slow—and uneven."

Joanna felt a certain dread grip her like nausea. She watched Dennis fill his pipe with strong, square-tipped fingers, his head bent, almost fair in the lamplight. The moment was dream-like, but it was a bad dream. First Nils had gone, and then this stranger had come, and it seemed as if she had taken one blow after another since then. Common sense told her that he had nothing to do with the floating mine, the nightmare, Owen. But he had been here through all of them, and in her mind he would be irrevocably a part of them.

She moistened her lips. "Is he all right?" she asked him steadily, but it was as if her steadiness didn't deceive him. His head came up quickly, and across the table his eyes considered her, tired but perceptive. She felt herself clinging to that gaze as if it were a tangible support. "Is he all right?" she asked again.

"He's all right for now. But he isn't all right as far as his life's concerned. It's not pleasant to be getting on for forty with only a sense of your own failure to live with. Maybe he *is* drinking deliberately. That's his escape. Everybody has an escape—"

"Even you?"

He smiled faintly. "Even I. Even you."

"Escape from what?" She straightened her shoulders even more.

"Don't be offended. It's no disgrace . . . it's the only sensible way, sometimes. It's wrong only when you try to run away from the ordinary realities of life, instead of facing them, or finding a way around them." He leaned back in his chair, and the scent of his tobacco smoke was aromatic, like the kind Nils used. "And then it's a disgrace to choose the wrong escape."

"Liquor is wrong—" she began quickly. "I know that. I know Owen's unhappy. But if he'd stop drinking long enough to put himself into good condition, he'd have a new slant on life, and he could figure out what to do."

" 'If he'd stop,' " he quoted gently. "Do you realize what that entails? He's got to *want* to stop, so violently that the desire will carry him through that horrible period of cure and readjustment. He won't—

and can't—stop just on the chance that he might discover some reason for living."

"You say that as if right now he had a reason for dying."

"He has. He's wretchedly unhappy, with nothing to live for."

She looked at him with pain, knowing that he was right, wondering why she hadn't seen it in all its merciless clarity before. It was what Nils had tried to tell her, but she wouldn't believe it until this stranger came and told her. Who was he, anyway? It became suddenly imperative that she should know.

"Who are you?" she said. She leaned forward, her dark eyes luminous with their questioning, her strong round chin in her hands. "*What* are you?"

He didn't answer her at once, but watched her quietly. Then he took his pipe out of his mouth, and looked down at it. "Right now I'm a wanderer. I've no roots, unless buying your uncle's place is an attempt to put down roots in Bennett's Island soil. Until last winter I was a Navy doctor. A surgeon."

"I saw the button in your lapel. But you're still a surgeon, aren't you? I mean—a man doesn't simply stop being—"

"You're wrong there." He was smiling, but she couldn't read the smile. "It's the simplest thing in the world to stop being anything, or just to—stop being. I said I was an escapist, didn't I?"

Suddenly she felt embarrassed, as if she had gone too far. It was as if she had touched a scar, and realized that the scar was a surface thing, that underneath the wound was still festering. She stood up.

"More coffee? . . . Yes, and you said I was an escapist. I've been waiting for you to explain that." She went out into the kitchen, and came back with the coffee pot. He pushed his cup across the table.

"When your husband left you to go overseas, you made up your mind that you wouldn't brood—didn't you?"

"If I did, I'd go mad. My imagination is too vivid." Her hand tightened on the handle of the coffee pot, and she loosened it with a conscious effort, but already he had glanced down and seen the whitened knuckles.

"You've got all sorts of things to do to make the time go fast and to keep your thoughts moving constructively. . . . That's a form of escape, but a sensible form. A creative form . . . Do you understand?"

"I think so." She poured coffee for herself and took the pot back to the stove. When she came back, frowning a little with a dozen unformed but urgent questions, he said in his unhurried voice, "You've always been a strong person, and you intend to keep on being strong. Whatever you've set out to do, you've done. You've prepared for your husband's leaving, so you could take it in your stride. And when he comes back—" He looked down at his pipe again. "And when he comes back—" he repeated, and she felt a hurrying of her heartbeat, a quickening awareness along her skin of some unsaid meaning behind his words; as if the simple phrase had some connotation for him that she would never know. The pause lengthened; into it came the asthmatic ticking of the clock, and Owen's breathing.

"And when he comes back," Garland said at last, "you'll be as steady and strong as you've always been. That must be a wonderful thing for him to know. It should give him peace of mind in spite of everything. So many hundreds of women have cracked up and gone under since the war began. They're soft as putty. They just can't take it."

"How do you know about me?" she protested. "How do *I* know? He's only just gone."

"Do you know what I thought when I came here, and in the first few days?" Their eyes held gravely.

"I thought you were the most at-peace woman I'd ever met. As complete and self-contained as a tree. Or as the Island itself."

I should be embarrassed, she thought, *but I'm not. It's the way he speaks.* . . . Aloud she said, "It's not true. Oh, I don't mean I intend to crack up. But I'm not really at peace . . . things bother me sometimes." It was incredible that she should be admitting this. She was being astonished at every turn of the talk.

"Storms shake the trees, don't they? But when their roots are deep, they're safe. And the Island goes fathoms deep down into the sea, it's based on rock rising out of the very core of the earth. Surf can't hurt it." He looked very tired now, his voice was slow. "The mine bothered you, didn't it? But you're all right now."

"I had a terrible dream about Nils and that mine," she admitted. "It was . . . awful. But as soon as it fades, I'll be all right. You see, I really worry about Nils, or why would I dream like that?"

"Of course you worry about him. You love him. He's part of

you. But you love him so much that you don't intend to crumble in a disgusting welter of self-pity while he's gone. . . . You're helping him in every way you can." He stood up, and knocked his pipe gently on the edge of the ash tray. "You'll dream, but you know how to handle that. It's when you don't know how to handle dreams that you go to pieces." His face shouldn't have been gray when the lamplight was so yellow. . . . "I know about dreams. Nightmares. When you begin to have them in the daytime, you give out. If you're lucky, it won't be *both* your mind and your body that goes. I don't know which is worse."

"You were discharged," she said quietly. "You gave out—"

"They convinced me that it wasn't an insult to my manhood to give out," he said with a wry twist to his mouth. "Three years in the thick of things, operating through battles. . . . I suppose it was when I began to get tired—they didn't seem to be able to spare any time for leaves, and I could have done with thirty days—that things crowded in on me. But it wasn't till after I got—well, a letter—that I began to have a hard time distinguishing where reality left off and the nightmare began."

He stopped abruptly and stood as if he were listening. After a moment he said, "You know, I've been back in the States since January but I still can't get used to this quiet. . . . Will you forgive me for talking about myself? I didn't intend to—"

"Forgive me for probing," Joanna said.

He put out his hand and smiled. She had been avoiding his smile since he came; but now she would not avoid it, nor his hand. She put hers out, and felt the warm, dry grip of his fingers.

"You had an explanation coming. And I didn't mind telling you. That surprises me, since you're the first person to whom I've spoken about it since I left the hospital. . . . Will all that coffee keep you awake?"

"I don't think so. But I ought to listen for Owen—"

"I'm not a heavy sleeper. I'll leave my door open and I'll hear him if he moves."

"You shouldn't be bothered with this," Joanna protested, but he shook his head.

"We're friends, aren't we? No protests then." He stood out of her way. "Sleep well, and good night."

When she reached her room she knew she was aching with tiredness, but her mind was alert and racing. She lay down, feeling her muscles quivering against the sheets; after a few minutes she heard Garland come upstairs and go to his room. In the cool dark, she remembered their conversation and was grateful for it, but stirred in spite of herself. It had helped to tell him that she'd dreamed, but her chief and most vivid sensation was not of relief, but of compassion. The letter he had mentioned so briefly was from a woman, she was sure of it; a woman who had in some way gone under, who hadn't been able to wait for him with strength and serenity.

Nils, she said soundlessly in the dark; *Nils, I wouldn't do it. . . . I'd die before I'd let you down. You're sure of me and you can always be sure.* It was at once a pledge and a prayer.

9

THEY DIDN'T MENTION THAT NIGHT AGAIN, but the next few days passed with a feeling of ease, almost of relaxation. Owen mentioned it when he was alone with Joanna, having breakfast at dawn before he went out to haul.

"My Lord, you've sure stopped waggin' around here like a broody hen. I thought you didn't like the guy!"

"We've been through a battle together," Joanna said flippantly. "Dragging you in before the dew fell on you. The dew *and* Thea. It makes us comrades."

"Jeest, that was rotten gin." Owen contemplated his evening in retrospect. "I don't remember anything after Leonie shoved me out the door. Just remember she was some mad."

"What for?"

Owen glanced at her with a fiendish twinkle in his black eyes. "Seems to me I sullied her honor by puttin' my arm around her."

"It's a wonder Sigurd didn't knock your head in," Joanna remarked dispassionately.

"He was pegged out in the corner. Leonie and I were holdin' the fort and I wanted to hold Leonie. But she stayed pure. I don't remember anything else till the next mornin', and my stomach burnin' like I'd drunk iodine."

"Spare me the details. I was around, remember?"

"You and Dennis! Jesus, I was some sick. I haven't got over it yet." He was pulling on his rubber boots and when he straightened up he was breathing hard, his high cheekbones were stained with dark color. "Don't know what that poison does to anybody's wind, but a man's a fool to drink it."

"I know," Joanna said. Usually she could think of some withering remark to supplement Owen's after-a-bout observations; but since she and Dennis had talked, she didn't want to be sarcastic. She saw Owen as a sick man, and it was easy enough, when he looked as he did now.

He went out without whistling; she wondered with an unpleasant start of alarm if that took too much of his breath. Jamie wasn't awake yet, neither was Garland, and she took an empty water pail and walked down to the well. It was a clear, warm morning, more like August than the middle of April. The sun had not yet risen from the sea in the east, and the pale, windless light was without sound or brilliance. She could not even hear the rote on the back shore, and knew that all around the Island the water lay as still as it lay in the harbor, like faintly rippled, silver-gray silk.

A song sparrow trilled out suddenly from the alder swamp, and then she became aware of all the sleepy chipping and chirping, as chickadees and sparrows and nuthatches — and all the other small birds that brought April to the Island — began their day.

But they added to the stillness, rather than took away from it, and she heard a clatter and rattle from the beach as Owen pushed his punt down; the thud of rubber boots on the firm ground as Matthew Fennell came along the path on his way to the shore, Sigurd's front door closing ith a small explosive sound in the hush. The Island was awake and stirring, and she had stood dreaming long enough at the well.

She drew her pail of water and set it on the curb in time to say hello to Matthew; when she walked back toward her house she met Francis Seavey coming out of his, oilclothes over his arm, swinging his dinner box. He gave her his bashful nervous grin, and ducked his head.

" 'Mornin', Jo!" He hurried on down to the shore, as if Thea were coming after him with her grandfather's horse whip.

Joanna, smiling, went into her own house. *I'll write about this morning*, she thought. *I'll put it all in a letter to Nils, how quiet it was before the gulls were up, how still and yet how busy. . . .*

Dennis Garland was to leave the next day. He intended to wander around through the New England spring, he said, and then come back in the summer to see what the Island was like then. Joanna was nsure whether she would miss him or not, but she *was* sure that she as glad he had come. She had written about him to Nils, telling him at last that the Place was sold. She wasn't afraid that Nils wouldn't ccept the news well. He always accepted everything with equanimity, because he said that everything had its reason. And if she said that Garland was a decent, quiet man, that would be enough for Nils.

The morning of that day she woke up to see the spruces swaying gainst the great fluffs of wind-clouds that blew boisterously across the un. She'd slept late, she thought with astonishment; she'd been sleeping long and soundly ever since the night when she'd sat with Dennis Garland over coffee. It was as if in some way she'd lost a weight from her soul.

Jamie was standing up in his crib, looking at her over the side, his mouth tucked in disapprovingly. *"Mama,"* he said sternly.

"Oh I know it!" She laughed as she lifted him out. "Scold me. . . . By the sound of the wind I don't guess our Mr. Garland is leaving us today after all."

Owen and Garland were eating breakfast when she came down. "Fool, crazy westerly," Owen muttered blackly. "Wanted a breakwater for years. Anybody'd think we didn't even belong to the States out here."

"Maybe it's the administration," Garland suggested. "Maine's too hard-rock Republican to expect anything from the Democrats—or want anything. To hear my brother hold forth, anyway—"

"Lord, it's always the wrong administration." Owen dropped sugar into his coffee with a fine disregard for rationing. "They've been promisin' a breakwater now since before I was born—"

"Can you remember that far back?" Joanna said, and received a look. She laughed, and went about fixing Jamie's breakfast.

"First the Republicans promise it, and then the Democrats. I guess maybe I'll start bein' a Socialist."

"That won't get you anywhere." Garland's lean face was serious but his eyes, unclouded gray this morning, held a twinkle. "You don't think they'll do anything for you millionaire lobster fishermen, do you? My boy, you Islanders are plutocrats these days. Or didn't you know it?"

"Sure, I know." Owen pushed back his chair and walked into the kitchen, to stare down at the harbor. "But one crazy westerly can turn us into paupers. Where can you get new trap stuff now? Nails and riggin'? What do you do if your boat goes ashore and smashes up?"

Garland joined him at the window. "Your harbor's wide open, isn't it?"

"Yeah. Look at those old seas comin' in past Grant's Point. Look at those boats jumpin' around."

Joanna, listening, didn't have to look to know what the harbor was like this morning. She knew too well how the combers drove into the little harbor, breaking in a surge of swirling white foam against blue-green sea. She knew how the surf was piling up on Eastern Harbor Point, in literal explosions of water that sent spray as high as the tree-tops in smoky plumes. Alternately the day dazzled and darkened under the blowing clouds. Sometimes the harbor and the Island lay under moving shadows that turned the water to dark emerald and peacock shades, and blackened the woods, and deepened the yellow fields to bronze; then the roof of clouds would part, and through the widening rift one glimpsed the high, shining, blue arch of the world. The gulls circled in soaring arcs, borne on the wind and exultant in their surrender to it. When Joanna was young she had wanted to be a gull, and she still felt an excited beating in her throat when she watched the wide, sweeping patterning of their wings.

The men went down to the shore; it was not a day to stay indoors. Though the house was set back from the harbor, and sheltered by the windbreak, the wind made itself felt in quick shudderings of the window panes. The tawny grass in the field rippled like a yellow sea, and the smoke from Sigurd's and Thea's chimneys blew away in shreds. And Jamie was excited by the wind, like all young animals.

He drummed his heels and his fists until Joanna took him out of his highchair, and then he raced around the house shouting at nothing, his eyes shining.

Washing the dishes, she looked down at the harbor, and between the fish houses she caught glimpses of the boats, plunging and bucking at their moorings, their bows to the wind. The moorings were laid as stoutly as could be made possible, heavy ground lines and heavy anchors, thick hawsers for the pennants. But even at that it was enough to make a tight uneasiness in Joanna's chest; the boats pulled so hard and seemed so helpless in the merciless march of combers from the sea.

There was enough to do in the house, but she was drawn back to the windows over and over again. She went upstairs to do the bedrooms, after she'd put Jamie out in the sunny lee of the house to play, and found herself at the window in Dennis' room. Brigport was ringed with surf, and the mile-wide stretch between the islands was feather-white. She half-shivered with excitement, loving the wind and yet fearing it with some deep primordial instinct.

Up here the gables shuddered with the impact of each gust. And every time the window panes rattled she was drawn inexorably across the room to look. . . . She was watching the boil of surf on the outer ledges as she swept, when a nearer movement caught her eye and she looked down to see Francis Seavey come into view between the fishhouses and Sigurd's house. He was running. His jacket flapped out behind him and he ran clumsily. She smiled at the picture he made. Francis always had such a time with his boots, as if he wore flatirons in them as well as his feet.

Sigurd came along behind him, his big body moving swiftly and easily, his bare yellow head bright against the silver shingles of the fish houses. He outdistanced Francis and turned down by Nils' fish house; for an instant, as the wind struck him, he halted and then went on, toward the front of the fish house where the broken, shifting, green and white water boiled on the edge of the shore. Francis followed him; and then she saw Matthew and Owen and Dennis coming. There was such urgency in them that it hit her like a blow. Her hands tightened on the broom handle. *What were they running for?*

She knew in a moment when they came back into sight, the five men, dragging Nils' dory. It had been hauled up in front of the fish house. Two men on each side, and one ahead straining with all his weight on the painter, they set out around the shore toward Grant's wharf and went out of sight beyond the old house called the Binnacle.

"It's a boat," Joanna said aloud. "That's all it could be. A boat's dragged her mooring."

She ran downstairs and pulled on her coat, tied a kerchief over her hair and under her chin. Her heart was pounding with dread but it didn't slow her down. She went out the back way and swooped up Jamie from his sand-box. He protested, and braced his sturdy small body against her.

"We're going to the wharf, Jamie," she told him crisply. "Behave yourself."

"*Walk,*" said Jamie firmly, and wriggled.

"Not this time." She went past the lilac bushes with him held against her shoulder, his arm around her neck. Dick was affected by the wind too. He barked and dashed ahead, the wind sleeking back his coat and flattening his ears.

She thought she'd never reach the wharf; but she didn't have to go to the wharf to see what was wrong. When she came out by the fish houses, with the wind tearing at her so that she must lean forward into it, she saw the boats that were out of place. The *Donna* and the *White Lady* shared the same mooring, whose ground-line reached from a heavy anchor just inside Eastern Harbor Point to the massive ledge which showed at low tide between Nils' wharf and Grant's. And they weren't where they should have been, where they always had been. They were out of place with the same sickening *wrongness* as a broken bone showing where no bone should be.

She needed only a moment to know what had happened and what would happen. Somehow the groundline had chafed, near the ledge; the anchored end, near the harbor mouth, still held fast, but the wind had driven the two boats back to the rocky and deadly wall of Eastern Harbor Point. Unloosed at one end, the ground-line was pulled across the harbor floor. It was high tide and the boats were almost in the edge of the frothing surf. If they were not rescued within an hour of the tide's turn they would lie in the foaming welter and could be smashed, helplessly, against the rim of rock, thrown at it with heavy breaking sea, until they were matchwood.

On the inner mooring Matthew's and Sigurd's boats were safe though restless, and on the innermost mooring Francis Seavey's boat was secure. But the *Donna* and the *White Lady,* laying huddled together as if for comfort, were on the way to destruction. Something like a sob tightened Joanna's throat, but she forced it back. Island women had no time to blather and bleat. She went on steadily toward the wharf and found all the men there.

Here in the shelter of the wharf was the only real lee spot in the harbor, and the nearest approach to the endangered boats. The planks of the wharf were bad, and the spilings trembled with every sea that broke against the exposed end, but the men, moving lightly and quickly in their heavy boots, were lowering the dory by means of the old derrick and tackle that had once hoisted Pete Grant's freight.

Joanna stood in the shed, where there was some shelter, and watched. The little knot of five men, and one of them an outsider, looked pitifully small against the wilderness of white and green water beyond them. Yet there was no hesitation. Down went the dory, to bob restlessly on the surge and swell of the lee; and, down over the side of the wharf Sigurd and Owen went like cats. When they had put the thole-pins in and had the oars ready—Sigurd forward and Owen aft—Matthew went down over the side and took his place in the stern.

The two at the oars began to row. It was an old story to Joanna, she had seen it at intervals all her life; but she would never be able to watch with the calm certainty that they'd reach the boats safely and be safe themselves. She watched with a dry throat and an ache in her legs and shoulders as if she were at the oars with them, driving the dory across the wildly heaving expanse of harbor waters. When they went out past the end of the wharf the gale hit them. To go directly across its path would be dangerous; they went in a quarterly direction toward the boats, of necessity letting the seas take them to leeward for a few yards and then straining against the wind and water pulling to windward, but always creeping on toward the *Donna* and the *White Lady.* It was a task that demanded every ounce of their strength, and Joanna could almost feel the strain upon her own muscles as she watched the dory rise and fall and lurch over the enormous hills of shining green, hills that shattered into a boiling confusion of jade green streaked with swirls of white. She saw how Matthew waited in the stern, every muscle tightened, his body pulled together in taut anticipation of the moment when he must jump aboard the first boat they reached.

Even Jamie was quiet in her arms, and she was watching so intensely that she was startled when Dennis Garland spoke to her.

"This is new to me," he said. "Frankly, I'm nervous. This harbor is a horrible sight right now."

"It's not new to me," she answered. "And I'm nervous." Her lips felt stiff. "I always wonder—I mean, there's always a chance—"

He nodded. "I know . . . Tell me something. Your brother said it could be worse, but I don't see how it could be. Do you?"

Francis joined them in the sparse shelter of the shed. He looked bleak and rabbity, and he was sweating. Joanna felt an impersonal pity for him; this was all new to Francis too, and he wasn't merely a bystander, he had to make his living here.

"Of course it could be worse," she said, sounding cheerful. "It's high tide now, and the boats are comparatively safe there until the tide begins to go—then they'll be getting surf coming and going. If they'd drifted down on the point at half-tide, they'd be a mess by now. They'd be on the rocks for sure. The flood is what's saving them."

They watched the dory go; it was almost half-way now, and it was gaining. The gain seemed agonizingly slow, but at least the dory wasn't being driven off its course by the wind, and the oars held.

"Be sumpin now if that anchor let go," Francis muttered. "That's all that's holdin' those boats—"

"The anchor won't let go," said Joanna with more assurance than she felt. She was gazing so hard that her eyes felt hot and strained, and her arms had tightened on Jamie until he began to squirm.

"Come here, Jamie," Garland said, and took the baby away from her. She had to talk. She couldn't watch in silence any more. She began to explain to Garland, trying not to gauge the aching slowness of the dory's progress.

"They'll have to go up into the wind and ride down on a sea. When they're right off the bow—they'll probably go to the *Lady* first—they'll slip their oars at the same moment, and when the dory rides past the boat Matthew will jump aboard. Then he'll grab the dory painter and make it fast around the winch head—" Garland was listening, his thin face absorbed as he followed each move in his mind. Francis was smoking a cigarette in violent puffs. He kept moving out onto the wharf to stare and then came back, shaking his head.

"You've probably seen worse things in the Pacific," she said to Garland.

"I've seen worse, but here the enemies are the sea and the wind. There's something monumental about the struggle, when you think how many hundreds of years it's been going on. . . . But you're not interested in my maunderings right now." His mouth twitched.

"Yes, I am. I've thought about it often, only I've never said it to anyone. No use saying it to the ones who're living through it. They *are* the struggle. . . . I know what I mean but I'm getting mixed up."

"Never mind, I know what you mean." And she knew that he did.

"*Jeest!*" said Francis wildly. He swallowed a mouthful of smoke and began to cough. "They're almost there, by gosh," he got out, his eyes streaming, "but what ails Owen?"

Joanna had seen it before he told her, that split second when only Sigurd was pulling on the oars and Owen wasn't moving. She ran out on the wharf, Garland with her, Jamie blinking in the wind. They saw Matthew move forward as Owen slumped, his hands on the oars before Owen's hands left them; then Matthew was rowing, standing up and pushing forward on the oars, facing Sigurd, who was pulling. Owen had gone down into the bottom of the dory; even at this distance there was something final and frightening about the completeness of his collapse.

"What is it?" Joanna turned desperately to Garland, her eyes strained wide. "What's happened to him?"

"He's played out," Garland said. He spoke quietly, without alarm. "He's not over his bout yet, you know."

"No matter how much he's drunk, he's never given out like that before," she cried furiously. "He *can't* be—"

"Can't he?" Dennis Garland looked at her with compassion in his gray eyes, and yet with such certainty that she stopped protesting.

She realized she had put her hand on his arm, her fingers were gripping through the rough tweed. She took them away, swiftly, and turned back to stare at the harbor. Sigurd and Matthew were rowing as if Owen hadn't been with them at all. She tried not to think of him lying in the bottom of the dory, his head close to Matthew's boots and the water sloshing against his face.

Dennis Garland was still close to her. He said against her ear, "He's probably fainted. Don't worry about him."

"Jeest," said Francis again. "If that ain't the damnedest thing!"

Fighting against the wind, the dory moved up a length or more beyond the boats, and then the men let her ride down on a sea. It carried her at an incredible speed toward the port side of the rearing *Lady*. For a moment Joanna forgot Owen. With one man gone, this job of boarding was doubly hard. To ship the oars an instant too soon or too late meant they must maneuver into place all over again, and they would be very tired by now. She saw the dory coast down, with a sea breaking under her, toward the rearing bow of the *White Lady*, and with a swift gesture Matthew shipped his oars; there was a moment when Sigurd fought to hold the dory in place, and Matthew was crouched and waiting. She felt the breath go out of her in a long weakening sigh as Matthew scrambled aboard the *White Lady*, and Sigurd shipped the other oars. The big power boat plunged down into the trough, and Sigurd, with the strength born of sheer desperation, plucked Owen from the bottom of the dory and rolled him quickly over the washboard of the other boat. Matthew had made the dory painter fast to the winch head, and Sigurd, waiting while the *Lady* reared again and the dory tossed helplessly, climbed aboard as soon as the copper-painted bottom slammed down against the water.

"Made it, b'gosh," muttered Francis. Joanna and Garland stood side by side, without moving or speaking, only watching. From the other end of the shed Thea and Leonie were coming, Thea's voice shrill above the roar of wind and water. Joanna didn't look around.

Once aboard the boat the job wasn't done. The *Donna* and the *Lady* had to be brought to the safety of the beach. Matthew took the dory painter from the winch head and slacked her off astern, while Sigurd inched forward on his belly over the deck to the paul-post, and began to loosen the mooring line. It was a precarious business, with the big boat rising high at every sea, slamming down with a sickening impact as the sea rolled on to explode on the rocks so wickedly close astern. Sigurd lay pressed flat on the wet deck, holding to the paul-post to keep from being thrown overboard as he slackened the line. Every now and then a breaking wave sent a deluge of spray over him as he lay there. He couldn't let the mooring chain go until he felt the vibration of the engine through the planks and knew Matthew had started it up. Even then he would wait until Matthew put the *White Lady* forward a few feet; when the mooring chain slackened he could quickly cast it from the bow, and the *Lady* would be free and under her own power.

On the wharf the watchers only knew the engine had started up when they saw Sigurd cast off the mooring. One boat was safe; Owen's boat. And Owen lay on her platform. The others had no time for him now, the boats were their chief concern.

Matthew edged the *White Lady* close to the *Donna*, close enough for Sigurd to jump over into the cockpit. But now there was no extra man to cast off the mooring for Sigurd. He took a line with him from the *Lady* and crawled forward over the deck as he'd done before. The *White Lady* must tow the *Donna*, because if Sigurd cast off her mooring, she could be borne to destruction in the brief interval that it took to start the engine. With the tow line made fast, the mooring off, and the *White Lady* started on her careening trip for the beach in the shelter of the Old Wharf, Sigurd crawled aft. Now he could start up the engine and the *Donna* could come in under her own power as she'd always done, when she was Stephen Bennett's boat. Now she was Nils' boat, and his brother was manning her; but she was still the *Donna*.

"Give Jamie to Thea," Joanna said tersely to Dennis Garland. "Thea, watch him for me, will you?" She took him herself from Garland and put him into Thea's arms.

Thea said, "Well, for heaven's sake! Sure, I'll take him, but where's Owen gone to? I thought he started out—"

Joanna didn't hear her. She ran up through the shed and Dennis came behind her. She had no compunction about leaving Jamie with Thea and Leonie, they weren't able to run around the beach in their high heels anyway. And Francis would tell them about Owen.

Going along the narrow path toward the fish houses she saw the *Donna* come up abreast of the *White Lady*, and glimpsed Matthew coiling up what he could of the slackly trailing tow line before he cut it. The boats were rushing in, wind and sea driving them. Then they were hidden by the fish houses, and she thought she would never get to the Old Wharf. Francis caught up with her and Dennis, and with a masterful effort got by them.

They arrived, all three, at the Old Wharf just as the *White Lady* came roistering in on a breaking sea, leaving Francis' boat rolling frantically, and headed straight for the beach. "You take this one," Francis told Dennis, breathing hard. "Get aboard and make the bow line fast."

He headed down the wharf as the *Donna* came in, riding the *White Lady's* wake. A comber lifted her stern, pushing her nose down. But in another moment she was around the corner of the wharf, sliding in close with a gracefulness that was a tribute to Sigurd's handling. Francis was aboard at once, making the bow line fast while Sigurd tended the stern line. Matthew had put the *White Lady* up ahead, her bow nosing the smooth beach rocks, and he and Dennis had made the lines secure.

The boats were safe, and it seemed years ago in another life that Joanna had looked down to see men running for a dory. . . . Now she looked down again, into the cockpit of the *White Lady*, and saw Owen lying on his back on the platform, his face to the sky. He lay flat and unresistant, in his drenched clothes, his wet forelock soot-black against his gray pallor and his eyebrows an incredibly dark line across it. There was no expression at all in his face. He looked as if he were dead.

Then someone hid him from her; it was Dennis. He jumped lightly down into the cockpit and went down on one knee, she was looking at his tweed shoulders and the back of his narrow, intelligent head instead of Owen.

Matthew had lighted a cigarette and was taking long, hard breaths of it. He stood by Owen's feet. "What's the matter with him?" he said. The others came and stood by Joanna, without speaking; even Sigurd and Thea were quiet this time. Jamie held out his arms to his mother and said pleadingly, *"Mama!"* She took him, without looking away from Dennis. When he stood up, he looked at her as he spoke.

"We'll all have to lend a hand," he said. "Where can we get a door to use for a stretcher?"

10

Quietly, Dennis Garland took over. As quietly, his authority was accepted. There was no waiting to discuss the morning's work; the exhilaration and danger of those minutes were of the past, and besides, they had been tempered by the shock of Owen's collapse. It was incredible and it was frightening. One might have expected it of anyone but Owen. Sigurd's face was drawn, the big hand holding a cigarette was shaking. He had been terrified out there in the dory, not of the sea or of the wind, but of the power that seemed to strike Owen down before his eyes. Owen was strapping and strong and apparently inexhaustible, and now he lay limp as kelp on the boat-shop door.

The four of them carried Owen home, trying to walk gently over the beach rocks. Joanna went on ahead to open the door and stir up the fire. By this time Jamie was in a fury of frustration; he had been snatched up from his play, and to add insult to injury he hadn't been allowed to set his feet on the ground, but had been carried first by one person and then another as if he were eight months instead of eighteen months. The roaring surf and the howl of the wind had excited him, and he was frightened, without knowing why, by Owen. By the time Joanna reached the house with him he was howling without reservations, his eyes streaming, his face red. He was her first responsibility; she talked to him calmly, washing his face with cold water. She gave him a cookie for each hand and took him back to his sandpile.

Now that her first dread was past, she could move swiftly. She went back into the house and saw the men coming up by Thea's. The fire was still alive; she revived it further with some small birch pieces to make a quick hot blaze, and then made ready the sitting-room couch.

The men put Owen on the couch and flocked out nervously, to stand around in the kitchen and sun parlor. Joanna and Dennis were alone in the sitting room. She watched Dennis pulling off Owen's boots as he had done the other night.

"What's the matter with him?" she asked at last. "You haven't said. . . . What do you want me to do?"

He looked up at her with a brief smile. "His system has put up a big protest, that's all. As long as he's down, you don't have to worry, because he'll have to rest. Time enough to fuss when he's up again. . . . I'll want hot water bottles, heavy pajamas—same as the other night." She went obediently toward the door, but she had to look back. He was so quietly sure of himself, the way Nils was, and she had a blessed sense of not being alone. If he hadn't been here this would have happened just the same, and she could imagine her rising panic, her ignorance of what to do, her terror that Owen might be dying under her eyes.

She brought down pajamas and blankets, and when she went out into the kitchen with the hot water bottles, the other men were still waiting, and Thea and Leonie hovered by the sun parlor door. Sigurd, chewing his lip, looked like a cowed Viking. It was Matthew who spoke to her, his pleasant face soberly concerned.

"How is he, Jo? What's the matter with him?"

"Too much cheap liquor," she said frankly. "Too much hell-raising." It was easy to say it, even in front of Thea, now that she knew she wasn't alone. "You know as well as I do how he's been going. Maybe this will shake some sense into him."

"He looked awful when he keeled over." Matthew shook his head. "I was watchin' the boats. I dunno what made me look around, and his face was like wet ashes. Like to scared me silly for a minute, but he was even more scared. Couldn't get his breath, seemed like. I had to grab those oars some quick."

She filled the hot water bottles with a steady hand, even when Thea moved suddenly close to her elbows. "Who is that feller, Jo? He acts like a doctor. *You* know, don't ye?" Her round blue eyes were sly, her whole peaked face avid.

"Yes, he's a doctor," Joanna said briefly, without looking at Thea. On an impulse she threw something else into the conversation to keep them busy for the next few days. "He's bought Uncle Nate's Place."

Thea's gasp was satisfactory; it proved that something had gotten by her. She didn't linger, but took Franny's arm. "Come on, Franny," she commanded him brightly. "No sense hangin' around bein' a nuisance at a time like this. You can come over later and inquire." At the door she collected Leonie, and Sigurd followed his housekeeper with less spirit than Dick showed, accompanying Joanna to the well. Thea would drag them all into her kitchen and make coffee, and talk over the latest bombshell, making up the angles she didn't know. Well, at least it would keep her tongue off Owen for a while. Joanna had heard in a round-about way Thea's insinuations to the effect that the only reason she wouldn't "go out" with Owen was that he had contracted something more than pneumonia in his seven-years'-absence.

Matthew waited until the others had gone. "If there's anything I can do, Joanna—"

"Thanks a lot, Matthew. But there probably won't be anything. I don't know."

"At least I can get you a pail of water." He took the empty pail and went off down to the shore. Matthew was a good man, she thought. One of the kind she had known during her childhood, industrious, sober, thoughtful. She took the hot water bottles to Dennis.

He had Owen undressed and wrapped in blankets, and he tucked the bottles around Owen's feet. "There, he'll do for a while," he murmured, and straightened up. His hands were as sure as ever, and they had been gentle, yet strong with Owen, but Joanna, seeing his face, was dismayed.

"You're tired!" she said involuntarily. "You've done too much. I forgot—"

"I'm glad you did. I'd have been annoyed if you'd begun telling me to take it easy." His smile softened the lines in his face. She had begun to appreciate that slow smile. It came rarely, but it was comforting as the warm steady fire from seasoned wood. To have him here now was almost as good as having Nils.

"I'll make some coffee," she said. "I guess we can stand it. How about some eggs, too?"

"Eggs it is. How many years since breakfast?" When they came into the kitchen Matthew was setting the water pail on the dresser.

" 'Y gorry, damn' lucky you were here, doc," he said earnestly. "You sure there's nothin' I can do?"

"I'd like to get a prescription filled at some drugstore in Lime-rock. How would I go about it?"

"Well, you could call up, but I figger the storm's prob'ly put the cable out again between here and Brigport. But I can get over to Brigport as soon as the wind goes down." His good-natured face puckered in concern. "But I dunno how I could read all that stuff over the 'phone—"

Dennis laughed, and reached for his pipe. "I'll go with you. If they send it out next boat-day that'll be soon enough." After Matthew had gone, he said, "Good chap. They're all the best sort. I'm proud to know them."

"Finest kind, my brother Stevie would say." *He'd say you were the finest kind,* she added silently. She'd had something to write to all of them; whatever resentment her brothers might feel at the idea of the Place going out of Bennett hands, it would be lessened considerably by this incident. The house would seem empty when he had gone.

"You missed your boat," she reminded him. "You wouldn't have been able to get over there anyway—but it's come and gone, and we've never given it a thought."

He drank coffee and smoked, looking at peace in spite of his obvious fatigue. "I'm not going for a while, if it's all right with you. Owen will have to be kept quiet, and I want to talk to him."

"Yes, of course it's all right with me," she said calmly. But she felt her hands go nerveless with relief, so that she had to set down her cup.

She got Owen up to his own room the next day. It was an agonizing trip, as much torture to Joanna as to Owen. She knew now what Matthew had meant when he said Owen's color was that of wet ashes. It was hard not to let her fear show in her voice when she and Dennis came downstairs again.

"I've never seen Owen sick," she protested. "And he looks so terrible. Will that prescription really help him?" It was a senseless question, but she wanted assurance badly.

"Part of that comes from his nerves. The prescription will help, yes. It's a sedative. He'll have to leave liquor absolutely alone, and it's going to be hell for him. The sedative will take the edge off it."

"What makes it worse is that he's afraid, himself." She had seen the silent panic of the trapped animal in Owen's eyes.

"Yes, he's afraid, but he needs fear." Dennis' easy voice, the impersonal, almost academic tone, was like a reassuring hand laid on her shoulder. "This may be a big help to him in the long run. He's been through a terrifying experience, you see. His own boat was almost on the rocks, and he couldn't save her—he didn't have the strength. That realization took the last shred of his resistance, and he gave up."

"My father's boat, too," she said. "The *Donna*—it's my husband's boat now, but my father had it built when we were small. Owen still thinks of it as father's boat, and if anything happened to her, it would go as hard with Owen as if he lost the *White Lady*."

Dennis nodded. "He'll never tell you these things, because to a man like Owen, such a confession is an open show of weakness. To know the disease is half the cure, somebody said once. This experience may force Owen to look at the facts."

"I'm glad you're here," Joanna said. "I can't tell you how glad—" She had a desperate fear that her voice would quiver, so she said nothing else. But she lifted her chin, and looked at him directly. If she couldn't say anything more elaborate, her honesty must be enough.

A unique atmosphere of peace pervaded the house while Owen lay in bed. Dennis sat with him for an hour or more at times, and Joanna could hear the murmur of voices, but Dennis never told her what they talked about. She only knew that little by little the trapped look was fading out of Owen's eyes. One day when she brought him breakfast he gave her the old, mocking grin.

"What a life! Layin' abed while those other poor sons o' bitches have to go haul!"

"I know you love it. Resting on your laurels—"

"Rustin' on 'em is more like it," he drawled. "You know how long I've been sober, my girl?"

"So long I can't believe it," she said tartly. But her eyes held a twinkle that answered his. It was good to be swapping remarks with him again; better to know he had his feet braced.

After the rush of the day, when both Jamie and Owen were asleep, the evenings were long and slow and pleasant. Sometimes she was astonished at how contented she felt, whether she and Dennis were talking, or whether he sat on the other side of the lamp reading. Sometimes at the minute sound of a page turning, she would look across at his long-jawed face with its finely cut, yet strong mouth, and wish passionately that Nils could know him. Oh, Nils would know him when he came home, since Dennis had bought the Place, but she wanted him to know Dennis now, and she wanted Dennis to know Nils.

He knew how Nils looked from the photograph on the radio, and sometimes she tried to tell him about the real Nils; the inner serenity and fortitude of the man, and the goodness. But she had rarely talked about Nils to anyone like this, and she was grateful when he said simply, "Owen's told me about him."

"He's always been more patient with Owen than I've been. He tried to tell me almost what you've told me, but I thought it was a case of men sticking together."

He smiled, and walked across the room to look at the photograph. "He wouldn't have had that taken, if I hadn't told him it was for Jamie," she said. "He's so darned self-effacing—"

"Not self-effacing. Self-assured."

Thus they could talk almost freely about Nils. And he asked question after question about the Island. She told him all she knew about it, from the time her grandfather had bought it from the State of Maine. He was delighted with everything she could tell him, and she found herself remembering old anecdotes she thought she'd forgotten, and bringing down albums of old photographs from the attic. She wanted him to see the harbor when it was full of graceful sloops, and schooners that brought out the mail and groceries, much as the lobster smack brought the groceries now.

"Then Pete Grant opened a store and spoiled us for forty years," she told him. The mention of Pete Grant began a whole new period of recollection; how Pete lived as a young man in one of the camps and baked beans every Saturday night for himself and his bachelor chums, and eventually was selling them to everybody on the Island who didn't have a woman to bake beans for him. The life of the Island about the time of Pete Grant's advent and for the next twenty-five years or more had been a golden time. In Joanna's mind, filled with the stories she had heard, that period stood for snug winters given over to quilting and social evenings, knitting bees when a man's trap-heads for a whole season's need would be done in a single evening; indeed, the winters seemed to be long, unhurried seasons of content and abundance. Her grandfather had been in his prime, and his sons Stephen and Nathan were young men, ambitious and industrious, but willing to limit their ardent young energies to the boundaries of the Island. It had been like a little principality, lying far at sea, its existence known to so few that even in Limerock there were people who said wistfully, "Seems to me I've heard of Bennett's Island . . . where is it, anyway?"

Joanna showed Dennis pictures of Uncle Nate's Place as it had been once. He was intensely interested, and his interest led her on to talk more. It was only at the end of these evenings that she realized she knew nothing more about him than he had told her that one night. He spoke as if he had no family and no past, and she wondered increasingly if he had been married, if it had been his wife who had let him down, what the woman looked like, what their life had been together. It was a matter for endless conjecture. She lay in bed, falling asleep, and thinking. There was one thing that she did know. Whoever and whatever the woman had been, Joanna despised her.

She's as much of a fool, she thought coldly, *as I'd be if I let myself lose Nils.*

11

APRIL WAS PROGRESSING toward May now, and the annual miracle was taking place when color seeped slowly and unmistakably into the fields and trees. The dead bronze of the marsh had an emerald sheen where the new grass sprang from the damp black earth, the buds took form on the sleek lilac branches and on the knotty boughs of the apple trees in the orchard. The old maple tree in the cemetery, sheltered by the big spruces that walled in the little plot, showed red buds against the wind-broken sky, and Joanna, looking up through them, her hand on the smooth strong trunk, knew she was not dreading the spring as she had expected. It had seemed as if she could not enjoy it with any fullness of heart when Nils was gone, and the little canker of worry lay always deep in her mind; but when she saw the red buds against the delicate blue and white, she knew there were some things that would always fire her spirit. Red buds, and the first roseate flush along the apple boughs, the first bluebirds to light on the raspberry canes in the field—she always forgot how blue they were; the early morning crying of the gulls circling and calling over the harbor after their winter silence; the new traps outside the fish houses, and the repainted buoys hung in the sun like beads to be strung by a giant, red and yellow, blue and white, black and orange.

Owen was walking down to the shore every day now. He'd be going out to haul soon, and there would be no further reason for Dennis to stay. The thought held some slight sadness for her. She had grown used to him. . . . Owen seemed to be on sure footing now, he had been living without liquor for two weeks and there was a fresh, clear-eyed vigor about him that was convincing. It was Dennis who had done it, in those long hours when he and Owen had talked. He'd helped Owen over the edge, and for this Owen—and the rest of the family too—would be eternally grateful to him.

She came home one afternoon from a long walk up through the Bennett meadow to the orchard and cemetery, and thence down through the Fennell's field; walking slowly in the soft late light, with Jamie and the dog forging ahead, she was in a gentle, half-melancholy mood. Dennis had bought Uncle Nate's place, but somehow it seemed to form no ties. She had the feeling that once he had left he would disappear into the emptiness from which he had come. Nils would never know him, and they would all have lost a friend.

She went down the narrow lane that passed the clubhouse, a long low building nestled flatly under the spruces, and then came to the closed-up Gray house, set back from the lane among its trees. The sun had gone down behind the high part of the Island, and the lane where she walked lay in cool shadow. But as she turned into the path that led close by the windbreak, the long shadows of the spruces stretched across the tangle of tawny grass, and the gables of her own house were gilded with ruddy sunshine, the windows ablaze.

"Hello!" Jamie crowed out, and she saw Dennis coming from the house to meet them, smoking his pipe and wearing his old tweed jacket. It was odd how much a familiar part of the scene he had become in a few weeks.

He admired with gratifying interest Jamie's handful of somewhat crumpled alder tassels, and waited until Joanna reached him.

"I've made a decision," he said. She stopped in the path.

"What?"

He laughed. "Don't look so horrified. Not until after I've told you, anyway. . . . I'm going to stay on the Island."

"I'm anything but horrified!" said Joanna. Her dark eyes began to shine. "I was just thinking how we'd miss you—"

"Don't think I'm going to impose on you further, though. You have enough to do. I've been talking to Sigurd, and I'm going there."

"You haven't imposed." They walked along together toward the house, and she thought, *Better Leonie than Thea*. She didn't protest because he was leaving the house; they both knew the impossibility of his becoming a permanent boarder. Aloud she said, humorously, "Sigurd's place is considered the local sink of iniquity, because he and Leonie are living in sin. But you'll get good food and a clean room."

"I like that couple. I shan't mind the iniquitous part of it. Do you know why I decided to stay?"

"Why?" They loitered along the path. Between the trunks of the windbreak the late sun streamed with a summery warmth, and the harbor burned brightly blue in the ruddy light. It was too pleasant to hurry.

Dennis took his pipe out of his mouth and cradled it in his hand, staring at it. "For years I've been preaching against escape; and now that I've decided to run away from the unpleasant aspects of life, I've discovered that escape is a very restful and delightful thing."

"What are you escaping from?" she asked him candidly.

"I've already told you. The unpleasant aspects of life—"

"It's not always pleasant here. It can be hellish."

He stopped again, and gestured with his pipe. "Look. To put it simply, I like it here. I feel happy and at ease. By all the rules of convention, I should go back to a place and a manner of living that has become very repugnant to me. By all my personal philosophy I should go back. But I'm not going."

They had reached the end of the windbreak and he stood looking down at the harbor, his eyes narrowed against the brilliance of the setting sun. The harsh radiance illumined his face, and she saw how much younger it seemed than when he had come; as if he had cast off all the anxieties and silent fears and weaknesses that had come with him, and had forgotten himself entirely here on the Island. He had eaten plain food and slept long hours in the silence he'd found unbelievable; he'd become involved in the life of the place. And now he was going to stay.

She wanted him to stay. It was not for her to say anything now. But she had a moment's misgivings when she glanced at his hands, the surgeon's hands. She remembered her blunt question. *But you're still a surgeon, aren't you? I mean—a man doesn't simply stop being—*

He'd spoken of escape then, she remembered, and she'd felt that she'd unwittingly touched a raw wound.

"What are you thinking about?" he asked suddenly, and she realized he had been watching her.

"Supper," she answered promptly.

"If I knew you better I'd call you a liar," he said, smiling, as he walked with her to the house.

He moved down to Sigurd's the day that Owen went out to haul for the first time. The house echoed with its stillness when they had both gone. Joanna turned on the radio and was beating up a ginger-bread to the accompaniment of a cowboy singer when Thea came in.

"I see you lost your boarder!" she shouted above the music.

Joanna nodded and went on beating. Thea flattened her bony hips against the dresser, licked her fingers and rearranged a curl.

"How'd he happen to go, I wonder?"

The cowboy yodeled piercingly. Thea glanced around the corner at the radio with an ostentatious shrug of her shoulders, which Joanna chose to ignore.

"I said," Thea repeated loudly, "How'd he happen to move?"

"Oh!" Joanna gave her a bright look. "He wanted to."

Thea's eyes narrowed. But her thin, reddened mouth still smiled. "S'pose he couldn't very well hang around with Nils bein' away and all. . . . You seen Nora Fennell lately?"

"What?" said Joanna. From the next room a voice made a plain-tive query. *Why do you treat me as if I were only a friend . . . ?*

Thea's smile was an effort now. "I said . . . Nora hasn't been down to the harbor for a long time. Maybe she's in the family way."

She giggled. "That'd be somethin' wouldn't it? I've been thinkin' Matthew must be a lot like Franny — couldn't make —"

If you don't love me I wish you would leave me alone, wailed the bereft cowboy.

"I wonder if there's anything else on," said Joanna, and went in to the radio. When she came back to the kitchen, Thea was gone. Joanna smiled.

12

SOMETIMES IT SEEMED TO JOANNA as if there were four Joannas, each a distinct personality, whose pattern of thought was as different from the other Joannas as the east wind from the west. There had been the girl who'd existed from birth until the time she married Alec Douglass; no, until the time she'd *met* him, for surely she had begun, without knowing it, a new design in life on the day he had come up the ladder of Pete Grant's wharf and taken off his hat to her with as much courteous charm as if it had been a top hat, and himself in white tie and tails. He'd been gaunt and hollow-cheeked, and his clothes were worn thin; the wind had blown through them that raw March day. His boat was the same — his name for it was *The Basket.* It showed up pitifully among the sleek prosperous boats in the harbor, and Alec Douglass himself had looked too thin, too white, too impermanent among the five Bennett boys and Nils — who in those days had been like another brother to Joanna. Yes, Alec Douglass had blown from nowhere, with his battered old hat under one arm and his fiddle under the other, and he had seemed as evanescent as the dreamlike hush before a storm. But he had stayed, and married the Bennett girl. Nils Sorensen wanted to marry her, but it was Alec who got her.

The life Joanna lived then bore no relationship to her wild-bird teens, or to the life she had lived since. She had been happy as she had not believed it was possible to be happy. That was at the first of it. In three years she knew an all-consuming ecstasy, then a slow but damning awakening to reality; aching pride, and a humiliation during which her chin never lowered. Alec was a gambler. He carried cards in his pocket as he carried her in his mind, and one fever equaled the other. It was a tribute to Alec's heart-breaking charm that Joanna never grew bitter, and it was a tribute to that proud chin of hers, and the level black eyes, that Alec chose betwen her and his other love, and she won out. The June evening when Alec was drowned in the harbor, he was the man she had believed he would be.

The interval between his death and the birth of Ellen was barely an existence. She kept herself carefully numb; she never wept for Alec. Not even when she was alone did she loosen the iron barriers she'd set on grief. *Once I give in, I'll go mad,* she had thought. There was the baby to think of. She owed the child some sort of life, even if she herself never felt anything again but this cold blankness.

But when she looked at the hour-old baby, she knew she was ready to go on. . . . The next period was a strange one. Something happened to the Island. One by one her brothers left; even Nils went away, after the day when he had faced her across Ellen's basket, with Ellen's minute fingers gripping one of his, and she'd told him she would never marry him or anyone. The other fishermen went, and then her father had to go. He couldn't hang on alone. The Bennett homestead was empty for the first time since the earlier Bennetts had built their log cabin on the slope above Goose Cove. . . . Except for the tangible evidence of Ellen, who had her father's long slim body and his quicksilver smile, the three years with Alec had been a dream; only it was as if she had fallen asleep at home, with the sea murmuring in her ears, and had awakened in Pruitt's Harbor. She had worked in the sardine factory to take care of herself and Ellen, she had friends, she participated in the life of the town. Not for her to live in a shell of solitude, knowing only her family. But there had been no roots. Her roots belonged somewhere else.

So she had come back to the Island, and the fourth life began. It was with Nils, and it was so complete that she looked back on the other periods as fragments, as parts of a whole; the entirety was *now*. In her childhood Nils and the Island had always been there. The Island had at once surrounded her and pervaded her; Nils had been so close that sometimes she felt more tied to him than to her brothers. Now it was the same, only in a deeper sense. She no longer accepted Nils blindly, she knew his value, and the senseless thing that life was without him.

The knowledge of the entirety was with her now, even with Nils overseas. So if Dennis Garland told her she was serene, she had reason to be. *As long as I don't dream again,* she thought. The dream about Nils and the mine had so shaken her she still remembered it at odd moments during the day.

It came to her one day while she was waiting for Owen to come in from hauling. It was well past noon, but he was shifting traps today, from deep water to more shallow places around the Island, where the lobsters crawled as the year warmed. Jamie was asleep, and the silence grew more and more oppressive, and in it the memory of the dream blossomed viciously. The house seemed to suffocate her all at once. When sweat sprang into the palms of her hands, she put down the book she had been trying to read, and went out.

The lilac buds looked ready to break, and the seven-sisters bush over the front door was showing signs of life. A robin who'd been wandering over the wet lawn—it had been raining gently all morning—flew away when she came out, and lighted in the field beyond the lawn. She examined the swelling buds carefully, and inspected the tulip bed on the western side of the house. There were small green blades piercing the damp dark earth. She must remember to tell Nils that, she thought, scrupulously ignoring the dream; but it lay treacherously beneath her forced calm, like the ledge called Tumbledown Dick at high water.

It was a gray, gentle day, the air was cool and moist to breathe, and there was hardly a sound. She couldn't bring herself to go back into the house again. Jamie was good for another hour's sleep, so she walked down to the harbor. It lay at high tide, silvery except where the trees made reflections of translucent green, and even they were overlaid with a silver stipple. The timothy was hung with cobwebs; they were truly gossamer, she thought. She walked around to the old wharf. Sigurd would be tending the car, and she'd have a few words with him, and then come home again.

There was no one in sight when she walked out on the wharf, but she could hear Sigurd's voice, reverberating through the silver hush.

"Nothin' to it, by God! Only thing is, I like to grab a nap when I finish my dinner, and I can't, long as I have to tend the goddam car!"

He was down on the car, with the doors open; he and Dennis Garland stood looking down at the lobsters moving like shadows through the water. Sigurd leaned on the scales and gestured largely. "The most work's gettin' the critters bailed into crates when the smack's comin'. That'd be a hell of a chore for you —" he squinted at Dennis' hands —"till you got hardened up some. But Christ, everybody'd turn to and help. We'd get 'em crated up faster'n you could spit through a knothole. . . . Hi, Jo."

"Hi." Hands in her pockets, she grinned down at the two men. "What are you doing, trying to foist off your job on somebody else?"

"I'm trying to talk him into it," said Dennis.

"It sounds as if he's convinced."

"Well, I am," said Sigurd bluntly. "Damned if I ever wanted to tend car in the beginnin'. But Richards, he was set on havin' somebody take over after Jud Gray went ashore to live. If I wasn't doin' it, I could set out more pots —"

"And take a nap after dinner," Joanna added.

Sigurd laughed mightily. "Well, if Dennis here wants somethin' to do, he don't have to start twistin' my arm to get it. He can have it!"

"Congratulations," Joanna said to Dennis. "I hear you're the new lobster buyer."

"When you say it like that, it sounds pretty important. And I don't mind admitting that I *feel* pretty important." His grin was un-affectedly happy; she marveled at the simplicity of a man who had lived as Dennis had lived, who knew as much as Dennis knew, and who would come here to this small and unknown spot and be happy because he'd been accepted.

She couldn't stay to talk much longer, but she felt rather pleased with life as she walked home. She had forgotten the dream, and she was composing a letter to Nils, which she would write as soon as things had quieted down after supper. *My darling, the tulips are coming up. . . . Jamie said "Keep still your noise" to Dick today, his first real sentence, and of course it was for his pal and nobody else. . . . Owen is shifting pots, he looks five years younger. He has played poker twice down at Sigurd's and didn't drink either time. . . . Dennis Garland is going to tend the car for Sigurd. He loves it here.*

13

SUDDENLY DENNIS WAS NO LONGER a man from the mainland, a "foreigner." The Islanders treated him almost as a native. If they pondered and discussed among themselves — and they did — Dennis knew nothing of it, for they accepted his presence on the car with equanimity. They might have wondered with burning curiosity why he was here, where he had lived, why he wasn't practising; but if he'd chosen to stay on Bennett's Island, that was his affair. Men had come to Bennett's Island for a variety of strange reasons in the past, and had gone without the Island's knowing any more about them than it did about Dennis Garland. And they liked Dennis. He was neither a talker nor a show-off, he didn't act as if he knew more than anybody else, and when he came down on the car in overalls and shirt-sleeves, with his old felt hat pushed back on his head and his pencil tucked over his ear, he was pleasant to meet.

After he had been on the job for a week, he came up one evening to have supper with Joanna and Owen. The smack had come that day, and although the men had helped to bail and crate five thousand pounds of lobsters, he had done a good share of it himself, and he showed his blistered palms with a certain humorous pride.

"Hey, good enough!" said Owen. "Marks of honest toil, huh? You're doin' all right, son. You were doin' all right with that bail net this afternoon, too."

"I thought it was going to throw me, at first. But there's one thing I'm really proud of." He looked at his fingers and wiggled them. "No lobster's pinched me *yet*."

"They will, chummy," Owen assured him. "They will." He tilted back his chair on its rear legs, scratched a match with his thumbnail, and lit his cigarette.

Dennis glanced across the table at Joanna. She was looking at his hands, her face locked in thought. "What's the matter?" he rallied her mildly. "*Should* I have been bitten by a lobster, for purposes of initiation?"

She smiled. "I was wondering if you men were ready for your dessert. Indian pudding."

The front legs of Owen's chair came down with a crash. "Bang," said Jamie with enthusiasm, and tried to rock his high chair.

"Why didn't you tell me there was dessert?" demanded Owen. "Lord, I wouldn't have been such a hog with the baked lobster!"

"I haven't had Indian pudding since I was a youngster," said Dennis reminiscently.

Out in the kitchen Joanna spooned the golden brown aromatic pudding out of a baking dish, and thought of Dennis Garland's hands. She understood his pride, and she was proud for him, as if he had been one of her brothers. But at the same time she had remembered the skill that belonged to those hands, the training they had received, the work they had done. Somehow the waste seemed terribly wrong; and yet he was happy, he looked calm and well-satisfied with his day's work. Involuntarily she shook her head, and carried in the dessert and the coffee.

Owen intended to play poker with Sigurd that evening. A couple of men were coming over from Brigport to join the game, and it was going to be a good one, Owen said. With the spring crawl everybody had been making money hand over fist, and the Brigport men were known as lucky fishermen.

"We'll see if Bennett's can't take their money away from them," said Owen complacently. Joanna looked at Dennis and shrugged. She hated gambling, but she never worried about it where Owen was concerned, especially when he wasn't drinking now.

"Dennis, why don't you ever sit in?" Owen asked suddenly. "Ever play poker?"

"Sure, but I can't hope to keep up with you fishermen. Poker's too expensive for me."

"You ought to have enough in your pockets. Tonight, anyway, when the smack's just been and gone."

Dennis lifted an eyebrow. "What's that to me?" he asked pleasantly. "I'm not in the business—I just look out for things for Sigurd."

Owen folded his arms on the table and leaned forward. "You mean to tell me that son of a gun took the—" His voice rose mightily. "Listen, you're supposed to get three cents a pound—the man on the car gets it. *For himself.* You ain't workin' for Sig now, you're buyin' lobsters for Richards. Sig's out of it." He pushed back his chair and stood up, towering over the table. Jamie looked up at him with fascinated blue eyes, Dennis with mildly startled amusement.

"The dirty crook! I'm goin' down there now and tell him what he is." Knocking his chair out of the way, Owen went for his jacket.

"Listen, Owen, *I* don't want the three cents," Dennis protested. "It's enough for me just to have something to do—"

"Oh, my God!" Owen said savagely. "It's yours. Why should Sig have it? Of all the two-bit racketeering square-heads—what are *you* laughing at?" He glared at Joanna. "You think it's funny? Your own brother-in-law pullin' a fast one like that?"

"No, it's not that." But she couldn't help laughing. "It's just— well, because it's Sigurd, I guess. He was always crazy. . . . Like bringing the mine in, when he didn't know whether it would explode or not. He was so *proud.*" She plucked Jamie out of his high chair, and he put his hands on her cheeks, looking for the dimple. "And now he probably thinks he's been very clever, he's probably been patting himself on the back and telling Leonie what a remarkable fellow he is."

Dennis was smiling too. "But if you told him he was dishonest, he wouldn't understand why you were so wrought-up about it. And he wouldn't be at all resentful about being caught."

"You two," muttered Owen. But his first fire of righteous wrath was dying out. He knew Sigurd of old. He took out his cigarettes, "But I'll tell the low-life beggar. The three cents is yours. And that Leonie!" He gave them a sidewise look, his black eyes glinting in the lamplight. "She ain't your type, Dennis, most likely, but she's got an awful snug waist for a man to get his arm around. And if she thinks Sig is so remarkable, she ought to be put wise."

"I didn't think she was *your* type, Owen," said Joanna.

"Well, she ain't *rightly* my type," he conceded in the deliberate drawl that meant he was in fine fettle. "But beggars can't be choosers, and there ain't much choice around here."

"Considering that she's Sigurd's housekeeper, she behaves like a pillar of virtue," said Dennis. "Don't tell me you ever got close enough to learn how snug her waist was!"

"The last time I was down there," said Owen, "I not only had my arm around her waist, I—" He broke off to grin at them. " 'Course, she'd been havin' a little toddy—and Sig was snorin' on the couch. But she's a good woman, you can believe that. She'd only let me go just so far. The first time I tried it, she booted me out. The second time—oh, what's the sense of givin' away the secret of my technique?"

He reached over to rumple Jamie's silky yellow hair with a big brown hand, pinched Joanna's cheek ungently, and went out.

"Exit the hero, whistling," murmured Dennis.

"He's pretty impossible when he gets on the subject of women," said Joanna. "but I can stand anything as long as he's not drinking. Well, I have to get this boy to bed." She ran her hand lightly over Jamie's head, smoothing down the devastation Owen had left. "It's funny, but for a long time it felt like a baby's head. Now it's a boy's head, and he's only a baby when he's sleepy." She glanced almost shyly at Dennis, who sat back in his chair, smoking his pipe. "I love watching him grow, and yet sometimes—"

"You think he's growing too fast."

"Yes. I want him to love the Island, and to live here if *he* wants to. But it's not an easy place for children to grow up in."

"I shouldn't worry about him," Dennis said peacefully. "He has his father's eyes and his mother's chin."

She began to unlace Jamie's shoes. "Thank you for having so much faith in the eyes and chin. I wish you could meet Ellen. She's twelve, and tall for her age, slim and almost blonde. She goes into silences so much like Nils' silences that she could be his own daughter. She'll be here when school's out." Suddenly she knew she didn't dread the summer as she had thought. Even without Nils it would be bearable, as this spring had been bearable.

He stayed until she had Jamie in bed and the dishes washed. When he left, she walked with him to the end of the windbreak. The April night was still and cold; the Island lay in unreal clarity under the moon. The rooftops looked as if they were covered with snow, the trees stood in painted silence against the steel blue sky. Over Brigport a row of tiny white clouds lay motionless. Occasionally there was a flash of moving silver as the water curled lazily over the harbor ledges; but the movement was the exception rather than the rule.

"A bomber's moon," Dennis said.

"Yes, we can't even enjoy moonlight any more, because it helps the enemy." But tonight the enemy seemed far away and not actual, because the Island in the moonlight was such a familiar thing. She stood there in the cool stillness, trying to make it seem possible that it was daylight where Nils was, that he had actually gone from the Island. A little shudder touched her flesh.

"You're cold," Dennis said. "I'll be getting along. . . . And speaking of that, I wonder how Owen's getting along. It'll be a great hardship to go right up to my room and not peer into the kitchen on the way." They laughed, softly, because in the silence their voices were so clear. He knocked his pipe against a tree and put it in his pocket.

"Good night."

"Good night," she answered. She waited in the black pattern of shadow thrown by the spruces while he walked down the path toward the harbor, and Sigurd's house. The moonlight was so clear and bright that he was recognizable all the way. Dick materialized from behind her, coming back from his evening prowl. When she spoke to him his eyes were liquid light.

There were the last minute things to do in the kitchen before she went to bed. The house was close with the heat of the stove and from the Aladdin lamp; she left the sun parlor door open to allow the cool fresh air to come in, while she moved around on her late tasks. Owen had done his chores at supper time, filled the water pails, brought in wood and split kindling. There was not much for her to do, but since Nils had gone she found herself roving around the house at night, not wanting to go to bed.

When the warm weather comes, and I can start my garden, she thought, *I'll be so tired at night I won't feel like this.* To climb the stairs, to get into bed and never think, but to slide instantly into deep sleep. . . . It was right now a heavenly idea, when she was so wide awake and there was nothing to do. Or rather, nothing that she wanted to do except lie beside Nils holding hands in the dark, her head against his shoulder.

Dick had been waiting for her patiently as she moved from one thing to another. Now he went out into the sun parlor, his toenails clicking on the linoleum. Deep in his throat there was a mutter, more of a vibration than an actual sound.

"Come on, Dick," she said to him. "You know there's nothing out there." She walked through the sun parlor to shut the door on the rectangle of pale field, dark harbor, and moon-washed sky. Dick reached the door before her and ran out on the doorstep, his growl unmistakable now. At the same time she heard the voice. It sounded hardly human; she felt her scalp prickle as if her hair was standing on end like Dick's hackles. It splintered the dreamlike silence with merciless clarity, there was no escaping it.

The voice came again. It was Leonie's, lifted in shrill fury. Joanna's scalp pricked again and she went out behind Dick, catching at his collar before he could charge off down the path. They moved through the lacy pattern made on the turf by the bare white lilacs, and reached the safer, blacker splash of shadow that came from the windbreak, and stood still.

There were two people in the field, and in the bright pale light there was no missing them. Owen and Sigurd; Owen stood very still with his feet planted apart, his hands on his hips. He said very distinctly, "Shut up, Leonie. Don't be such a gorm, Sig."

Sigurd went steadily toward him, his great shoulders crouched. The moonlight was so intense it was possible to tell his hair was yellow. There was something animal in his slow advance.

"Oh for God's sake," said Owen, sounding annoyed rather than angry. Then there was Leonie again. She came out past the corner of the porch, her light dress glimmering; her glasses caught the moon in their lenses and Joanna saw them flash and gleam.

"Don't you call him a gorm, Owen Bennett!" she shrieked. "You know what you are? You're a cheap lowlife!"

Leonie is drunk, thought Joanna with interest. *So this is how she acts.* Sigurd would be drunk too, but Owen wasn't. She could tell by the level tone of his voice, which was scarcely raised above normal. "You've already called me that, Leonie," he said patiently. "And you told me to get out. Well, I *am* out."

"Why don't you go home where you belong, then?" she railed at him. Impossible that this was the trig Leonie of the polished shoes and horn-rimmed glasses. Screaming in the moonlight like a fish-wife, while all the time Sigurd moved steadily toward Owen, slowly but irrevocably.

"Why don't you git, then?" she repeated. "We don't want any of the likes of you around here!"

"If you think I'm intendin' to turn my back on that Neanderthal man of yours, you're crazier than he is," Owen returned. "Get him in the house, will ye?"

Sigurd said nothing at all. "Yellow-belly," jeered Leonie. "I knew you was a connivin' son of a gun, trying to steal a man's woman when he was drunk. Now I know you're yellow, too."

"Sure, I'm yellow as a goddam buttercup," Owen agreed. "I'd as lief turn my back to a fifteen-foot sea as to him."

"I hope he murders you," said Leonie with loud relish.

A movement at Thea's front door attracted Joanna's attention; Thea and Franny were there in the doorway. The moonlight spared no detail of Thea's avid attention and Franny's befogged wonder. Joanna was invisible in the heavy shadow, and Dick wouldn't growl as long as she held his collar. It was not possible, she thought sardonically, that this affair could take place without Thea's presence; and then she remembered Dennis. It was incredible that he should be sleeping through this. But that was not half so annoying—that he might be watching—as the thought of Thea, who took every such incident to add substance to her insidious campaign against the Bennetts.

Sigurd was only a few paces away now. Owen didn't step back. "I don't like knockin' out a drunk," he said. "But by God, if you don't call him off—"

"Even if he's drunk, he can knock your head off!" She pranced around them light-footedly, as if she had never set her feet down flatly and firmly on the wharf. "Take him on, if you ain't soft as—"

"You like shoutin' those words out for the whole Island to hear?" Owen inquired with ominous politeness, and his right fist came up. It was smooth and swift. There was no sound or outcry. Sigurd's head snapped back; for a moment he was motionless, appearing to look up at the moon, and then he crumpled. Owen caught him.

"Get hold of his feet," he told the transfixed Leonie, "and we'll take him into the house."

For answer Leonie leaped at him like an embattled wildcat. Owen was holding Sigurd by the armpits when Leonie struck at his face, and Joanna suppressed a gasp, while Dick whimpered, and pulled against his collar.

"My Gawd," Thea hissed. "You see that, Franny? He won't have an eye left in his head!"

Owen dropped Sigurd and for the next instant there was a chaotic struggle over Sigurd's body. She was an avenging fury in horn-rimmed spectacles, she was kicking as well as scratching, and Joanna prayed silently that Owen wouldn't lose his temper and strike her down as he had struck Sigurd. But he'd never get free of her without hurting her, and Joanna's fingers were already loosening their grip on Dick's collar; the dog wouldn't hurt Leonie, but he would startle her into sanity.

There was no need to let him go. Dennis came out past the corner of the porch, moving with speed and purpose. He walked up behind Leonie and took her by the arms, pinned her back against his chest.

She raged incoherently, but she couldn't move.

"*Jesus!*" said Owen. "Thanks." He wiped his face. "Good God, talk about thunderbolts. What am I goin' to do with this?" He touched Sigurd lightly with the toe of his boot.

Dennis' answer wasn't audible, but after a moment Owen turned and came up toward the house. Thea seized Franny, who was now craning his neck with unabashed fervor, and pulled him back. The door shut with an obvious click. Thea was never one to be surreptitious about her eavesdropping.

When Owen came abreast of Joanna she spoke to him, and as he turned his head, she saw the dark trickles of blood streaking his face. "You here? I wonder who else is sittin' in on this?" he said dryly.

"The Seaveys have been watching. And I shouldn't wonder if the Fennells *heard* it." They walked together toward the house. With remarkable self-control Joanna said nothing more. In the kitchen she turned up the lamp, and Owen ladled cold water into the basin and splashed it over his face. Joanna moved quietly behind him, getting out cotton and alcohol. She handed him a clean towel, worn thin and soft by years of wear, and he dried his face tenderly. The scratches showed up viciously now, as they began to swell; they raked his brown skin from cheekbones to chin.

"She went for my eyes," Owen said. He was angry now; his fury, repressed while he tried to deal with Sigurd and Leonie, smoldered in his voice and glinted blackly behind his lashes. "She went for my eyes, the damn' cat. I should have got her around the neck and strangled her."

He took the alcohol bottle savagely from Joanna's hand and shook it with the same violence over a wad of cotton. "Probably I'll get rabies . . . or worse!" In front of the mirror over the sink, he swabbed at the scratches, wincing and cursing. Joanna leaned against the dresser with her arms folded.

"What happened, anyway?" she asked calmly.

"Oh, Sig was on the bottle—practically out—and I got a little close to her, and that was hunky-dory till Sig came to." He leaned over the sink to examine closer a deep dig near the corner of his eye. "So he told me to get out. Bein' too much of a gentleman to point out that the lady was willin', I got out. But she didn't have to come waggin' out on his coattails actin' like she was so damn' chaste and I'd raped her, or somethin'."

He swung around and added with quiet rage, "There was a time when I thought she was a very interestin' woman. Now I know what she is. She's what every woman is, except you and our mother."

"And what's that?" said Joanna with interest.

"A perverse little witch." He prowled past her, his eyes slitted, his lower lip eloquent, and went upstairs to his room.

Dennis Garland had come quietly through the sun parlor and was standing in the kitchen doorway. He and Joanna looked at each other. His thin face was concerned, but there was something like a twinkle in his eyes.

"Disgraceful, isn't it?" said Joanna. "But when you've lived on the Island as long as I have, you'll take it without batting an eyelash."

"I'm not batting one now. Leonie's asleep, I gave her a bromide that's guaranteed not to cause internal combustion when it meets up with all that cheap vodka they've been drinking down there."

"How's Sigurd?"

"Oh, he came in under his own power while I was looking out for Leonie. Do you suppose she'll be the perfect lady tomorrow?"

"She'll be so lady-like that Thea will be snorting about it for the next week." Joanna couldn't help chuckling. "In a way I admire Leonie. When she's a lady, she's a lady; and when she's the other way, she's a—"

"Trollop," he supplied. "No dithering around for Leonie. No shilly-shallying. She's either one thing or the other."

Joanna sighed. "Well, Owen's off the liquor, now he's off women. I wonder where he'll break out next. . . . How about some coffee?"

14

IT WAS MAY AT LAST, and all at once everything seemed to hurry. The green spread like a pool of tender color over the fields. It would be June before the lilacs and apple blossoms and violets were out, but by the end of the first week in May there were strawberry blossoms like white stars in the sheltered, sunny places. The crocus ringed the heavy, twisted trunks of the old lilac bushes with purple and gold, and Joanna's few hyacinths released an exotic sweetness into the wind-cleansed air.

The birds were coming; in the early morning Joanna awoke to the valiant trilling of the song sparrow, full-throated and blithe even through a raw, beating rainstorm. In the spruces that towered beyond the alder swamp the nuthatches called back and forth all day, and in the alders there was a continual flash of movement as the early warblers arrived. There was a wood peewee who would answer as long as someone whistled to him. And there were the days when the field was dotted with robins, chipping and pecking like so many chickens; the rainy afternoon when five Baltimore orioles, in a glory of black and gold and orange, stayed around the windbreak for hours. And one early morning, when the sun cast long shadows across the dew-silvered grass, Joanna watched from the kitchen window the courting dance of the flickers.

The gulls were busy. From the first moment of dawn they were noisily active, their clamor was music to Island ears. They worked all day, dropping to rest on the harbor ledges, meeting the boats that came in from hauling, settling on the water in a vast whipping and rushing of big gray wings as the baitbags were shaken over the side. In the evening they flew in silent groups to the outer ledges where they lived, until the last of them had patterned the violet air over the harbor and then were gone.

There was so much to see and hear and smell, and the half-pagan urge that had always been a part of Joanna stirred in her now. It had been subjugated through the years by the responsibilitles of maturity; but it was there, a nostalgic something too ephemeral to be called happiness, too restless to be called peace, and it was made poignant by the ache that never quite left her; the ache for Nils, that she must be seeing the spring come in without him, and that he must be so far from home when May came to the Island. She wrote it all to him in detail, trying to see it as if it were all new so that every impression was fresh and vivid; and to do that, she tried to see it through Dennis Garland's eyes.

His quiet happiness in his new life tempered the ache for Nils. Each day he saw something new, and mentioned it to her and she was secretly pleased because there was someone else in this small, strait universe who saw the Island without taking it for granted.

The wild pear buds opened into white blossoms with a tenuous fragrance, the cranberry and strawberry blossoms spangled the slopes above the sea like faint, glistening drifts of snow. May was a white month.

There was a wild pear tree at the edge of the alder swamp behind the barn. It stood on a little knoll above the brook, the brook that was a real brook only in the spring, when it mirrored flying clouds and a sky the color of forget-me-nots or slate-blue with storm, and the violet branches of awakening alders, the dark green tips of the spruces; and now the wild pear tree.

Ten spotted brown ducklings paddled in the brook one morning; splintering the blue and green and white into silvery fragments. The handsome drake and his small spouse had produced a family, and Joanna contemplated them as raptly as Jamie did. They were so downy, so baby-like, and yet so complete. Dick watched them, with remote interest, Jamie with his blond eyebrows pulled together and his lower lip out, his hands behind his back.

Nils had wanted to know in his last letter if the eggs had hatched yet. Down there among those green alien islands, where the blue water covered so many skeletons of ships, and broken bodies washed up on the white beaches, Nils had written about the duck eggs. She stared at the ducklings, seeing Nils instead, Nils' mouth so quiet and steady, Nils' hand moving so evenly as he wrote, Nils' head bent. She could see it so strongly that her hand made a little unconscious gesture, as if she would run it lightly over the back of his head and rest it for an instant on his neck.

Dick stood up, his tail waving, and she came back to the moment with a start. Dennis Garland walked toward her around the corner of the barn, in overalls and shirt sleeves. He walked lightly, almost with suppressed resilience.

"Come over to the brook and see what's here," she said softly. "Don't make a quick move."

He reached the knoll beside her without a sound and looked down at the brook. She glanced sidewise at him; he was as absorbed as Jamie. He had a deep tan now, with no tinge of grayish pallor under it, and the lines had smoothed out almost completely. A vision of the lonely man who had come to the Island, who had stood alone by the anchor that afternoon, seemed unreal in this instant; this was the real man, who turned to her now and said, "I imagine Joe's pretty conceited about this."

"I don't know. He's been acting as if it's all a darned nuisance." She laughed softly. "Judy sails along ahead of them and Joe keeps fooling around behind the procession, muttering."

"Saying, no doubt, that all the wife thinks about are those darn kids," said Dennis.

"Do you know how we got them? My brother Charles was coming out this way to go seining, and he called up to see if we wanted a duck. We hadn't had any fresh meat for so long, so of course we said *yes.*" She contemplated the drake's smooth iridescent head. "We thought he'd bring it out all dressed, but he brought him alive. And the poor thing was so terrified, his eyes so bright, and he was so pretty—" she shrugged. "We put him in the barn until Nils could get around to kill him. But Nils kept putting it off, and Owen kept asking when we were going to have a duck dinner. . . . Well, Nils and I didn't say anything to each other at first, but after about a week somebody had to give, and believe it or not, it was Nils. Every time he went out to the barn for anything, the drake talked to him, so he couldn't kill him."

"You could have given the job to Owen," Dennis suggested.

"The way Owen took on when we broke the news to him, you'd have thought we were a couple of cowardly idiots. He stormed out and went to haul — and when he came back he'd been over to Brigport and gotten Cap'n Merrill's wife to sell him a duck to keep the drake company." In the midst of their laughter she waved at the family in the brook. "Their names are Joe and Judy. I'll let Ellen think up names for the offspring."

"Oh, is *this* where you are?" Thea came around the corner of the barn, and Joanna walked to meet her; Thea's arrival on the knoll would throw the ducks into panic. Dennis came along behind her, with Jamie, and Thea's eyes widened in careful astonishment.

"My heavens, I didn't know you was here too, or I wouldn't of barged in!" Eyes and teeth gleamed at him. "Ain't it a perfectly gorgeous day?"

You're acting, Joanna thought. *You knew he was here all the time. You came along on his coattails so fast it's a wonder you weren't walking up his back.*

"A beautiful day," Dennis agreed courteously.

"You must like it here, the way you're stayin'," Thea said, keeping her face turned up to his. The path was too narrow for two people to walk abreast, but Thea was managing it somehow. "Looks like somebody's loss is our gain!" She giggled, and lurched grotesquely as her ankle turned. Dennis caught her arms and steadied her.

"Oh," she moaned softly, shutting her eyes, and leaning against him. "I think I've sprained it."

"Try standing on it," Dennis suggested, but Thea gripped him with shrill squeals. Over her bobbing head Dennis looked at Joanna, his face completely grave, except for his eyes, and Joanna looked back. By the way Thea was brandishing her foot around, her pain couldn't have been too intense.

"Come on, Jamie, let's get out of the way," Joanna said, and took her son's hand. "Come on, Dick." They went on ahead, Jamie looking over his shoulder at Thea with grim fascination. On the back doorstep Joanna stopped to examine the opening green leaves on the lilacs. She was amused by Thea, and by the glance she and Dennis had exchanged over Thea's head. Smiling faintly to herself, she waited, and presently Thea came out by the barn, limping slightly. Dennis came behind her, fishing out his pipe and tobacco pouch from his overalls pockets.

"Whaddya know?" Thea exclaimed brightly. "It's hardly sprained at all!"

"That's good," said Joanna. "A sprained ankle is an awful nuisance."

"Not when there's a doctor around to look after it." Thea's glance at Dennis was all but languishing. "But I guess it's not a sprain. . . . I'll be gettin' home. Remember you're comin' to supper next Saturday night, Dennis!"

"I'll remember," he said.

"So long, then. So long, Jo!" She beamed at Joanna, and went around the house with no trace of a limp at all.

"How did you do it?" asked Joanna. "Convince her, I mean?"

"Stood her on her own two feet before she realized. Odd little character, isn't she?"

"Very odd," said Joanna with restraint.

"No one can say there's a certain type of Island woman, because both you and Thea are Island-bred, but you're poles apart." He stood contemplating her in the May sunshine, her dark head against the white clapboards, her brown hand still holding the green-leaved twig, the dog pressed close against her legs, and the child playing in the sand pile at her feet. "Do you mind if I say that I never expected to find anyone like you here?"

She was pleased, but she didn't show it. "Is that a compliment, or not?"

"A compliment," he said candidly. "I love the Island, but it makes it all the better to know someone like you lives on it. If your husband were here, I imagine I'd feel the same way about him, from all I've heard. In the meanwhile, I intend to take full advantage of our friendship."

"It looks as if I were the one who had taken full advantage of our friendship," Joanna said. "You've done so much already — you're always on hand when something happens —"

"Do you know what you've done for me?" He shook his head. "No, you probably don't. But I assure you —" He broke off and looked down at Jamie, who was staring at him with solemn, unwinking blue eyes. "All right, Old Hundred, I'm leaving . . . Jamie thinks I talk too much." He grinned at Joanna, a sudden, warm grin, and left her.

She sat down on the doorstep to let the sun soak in, and remembered what he had said. Here on the Island, she was his friend. Her pleasure was as comforting, as exhilarating, as the May sunshine. None of the men on the Island really spoke his language, much as they liked him and he liked them; as for the other women, there could be no sympathy between him and Leonie, or Thea, or Nora, who was clean and good, but young. She knew how she, herself, valued the understanding that had sprung up between her and Dennis; the shared humor of a situation, the shared delight in the sky-colors at sunset, or the ducklings; the unselfconscious discussions over coffee, the lending of books and the talking-over, afterwards. It was good, and besides, it tempered the edge of her heart's loneliness for Nils.

15

HER CONSCIENCE BOTHERED HER about Nora Fennell. She awoke one morning from a dream that Nora was the fresh, wholesome young thing she'd been when she arrived on Bennett's Island, and the contrast between the dream and the reality stung her.

As soon as her morning's work was done, she went out into the yard to call Jamie. He was wandering toward the alder swamp, apparently in an aimless manner, and she wondered what he was thinking as he canted his head toward the trees. Dick walked along behind him, his tail moving slowly, benignly. Joanna hesitated for a moment, to smile at the sturdy little figure in blue overalls and sweater, the round and intent yellow head, the big dog following him, and then called.

They both turned around, Dick with a quickening tail, Jamie with a scowl fantastically like Owen's, for all his blondness.

"We're going to see Nora," she told him. "What are you looking for in the alder swamp? Birds? Chickadees?"

He made a vague, ambiguous sound which could have meant almost anything, and approached his mother at a dreamlike gait. As soon as he had placed his small firm hand in hers, with the air of royalty bestowing a favor, they walked across the Sorensen field to the lane that led to the Fennells'. They went out through a break in the raspberry thicket, opposite the clubhouse. It was a long low building settled among the trees, and the men of Bennett's Island had built it, back in the days when her father was a young man. In all Joanna's growing-up the clubhouse had been the scene of school concerts, Christmas parties, Valentine masquerades, Fourth of July suppers; dances when accordian and guitar had rung out the tunes for Boston Fancy and Lady of the Lake. Now it was locked up and looked oddly unhappy there among its spruces. But not unkempt; a year or so ago the men had assembled to tar the roof and sand it, and as proof there was still a pile of sand behind it, below the kitchen window.

Perhaps they should try to have some dances this summer; certainly there'd be a crowd over from Brigport. The dance floor was a joy to behold, and it was more of a joy when you danced on it. . . . She found herself humming softly—"Put Your Little Foot Right Out—" as she swung open the iron gate to the Fennells' field.

The Fennells owned the house now. It had been hers before that, left to her by Alec. It had been a little hard to rent the house to strangers, but later, when they wanted to buy it, she had been contented with Nils and so it wasn't hard to let the house go. She'd only hoped that they would be very happy under the roof which had sheltered the first rapture of life with Alec. But now the Fennells had been there four—or was it five—years, and as she walked up toward the old-fashioned white house, set against the spruce-banked hillside, she thought again what she had realized so many times; the Fennells weren't happy.

Nora loved Matthew with her whole being, it leaped from her eyes when she looked at him. And Matthew loved her, with the slightly bewildered love of a man who has married a tree sprite or a mermaid.

But Nora was moping because her dog had died, and Gram was

gloating. Sometimes Joanna had been moved to say that it would be a blessing for the young Fennells if the old lady would quietly die. "Oh, she'll up and die one of these days," Owen snorted, "but she won't be quiet about it. Not that one!"

Gram had brought Matthew up, and she had been old in his babyhood. Now she seemed incredibly ancient.

Matthew came to the door when Joanna knocked. His broad, patient face crinkled into a smile. "Hello, Joanna. Come in! I guess you caught me all right — I haven't gone out to haul yet."

"Don't apologize, Matthew. A man's entitled to sleep late a couple of times in his life, isn't he?" She went past him into the long kitchen where she'd fixed so many meals while Alec played his fiddle at the end of the stove. But the kitchen was so different now, with Nora's color scheme and furniture, and a white stove instead of a black one, that there were no memories . . . except of Bosun, who until recently had always met her at the door, all frantic tail and laughing tongue and whiskery black face.

Nora was standing at the dresser, breaking eggs into a bowl. She leaned against the woodwork as if she were very tired. Her smile was subdued, her eyes heavy.

"Hi, Joanna . . . Sit down." She'd been like a glossy young colt when she came, five years ago, always throwing back her head with an impatient vigor, her eyes forever changing like the sky on a windy bright autumn day. "Jamie with you?"

"He and Dick are outside. You don't want those two tykes in the house. . . . How've you been, Nora?"

"I've been having a cold," Nora said vaguely. "It hangs on. It bothers my stomach, mostly."

"Well, I have spells of being pretty dull," Joanna said. "Why don't you come down, and we'll be dull together?"

Matthew, bringing his rubber boots in from the entry, said, "I try to get her to go out more. But she doesn't. I know it's lonesome without —"

He stopped, and leaned over to fuss with his boots. Joanna knew what he had almost said. *Lonesome without the dog.*

"Who's lonesome?" demanded Gram from the sitting-room doorway. Tiny and erect, without even a cane to help her, she marched into the kitchen in her starched black and white print. She looked at all three of them in turn from her sunken but still fiery gray eyes. "Nora, stand up straight. Matthew, them your ashes on the floor? Must be. Man hadn't ought to smoke a pipe if he don't know how to manage it. . . . Hello, Joanna."

"Hello, Mrs. Fennell." Joanna smiled at the small tyrant, feeling like a hypocrite.

"I want to know who's lonesome," announced Gram. She sat down in a straight chair, her back as stiff as the chairback. Nora's hand slowed on the egg beater. Matthew, sweeping his ashes onto the dustpan, didn't look up, and Joanna hurried into the imperceptible pause. It didn't do to mention the dog.

"I get lonesome, Mrs. Fennell," she said. "With Nils gone."

"But you've got the boy." Gram's beaked nose quivered at the tip and her mouth set hard. "You got the boy and the girl too. You know a woman's duty on this earth. Take Nora, now." Joanna looked remorsefully at Nora, whose head was bent lower than ever, one wing of hair sliding past her cheek and hiding her face. "Say Matthew got drowned today—what'd Nora have left? What's Matthew got, so's he can be satisfied he's leavin' kin behind? Nothin' but the back of her hand!"

"Gram," said Matthew with his customary patience.

"Ask her why she don't have a baby, a big healthy girl like her! Moanin' around about a *dog*. . . . It ain't natural."

Joanna stood up. "I guess it's time for me to be starting dinner."

"I'll walk down to the gate with you." Nora turned quickly from her work and went to the door, waiting there with defiance in her pose.

"Good-bye, Mrs. Fennell," Joanna said.

"Good-bye," Gram said acidly, and looked with open appraisal at Joanna's figure in the fitted percale print and cardigan sweater. With the door shut safely behind them, Joanna turned to Nora, laughter welling up in her dark eyes.

"Nora, does she think I'm going to have another one?"

"She's got a complex," said Nora. She looked around at the field and at the newly leaved birches against the rim of the woods with her eyes narrowed and her forehead creased as if her head ached. "Where's Jamie?"

"He probably was bored, and started for home." Joanna nodded down toward her own house; often she and Jamie had come up diagonally across the open ground instead of coming up by the lane. "He'll be soaked to the knees, it's so wet in there. But it won't hurt him."

The field had a shimmer of green among the clumps of dead, brownish-yellow grasses, the strawberry plants showed along the path, tiny white petals against green leaves. There was sunshine, and a fresh soft breeze blowing from the west, where the mainland was a violet line between blue sea and sky. Impossible not to walk lightly; but not impossible for Nora, who walked with her head bent, and her lower lip bitten in.

"Nora, how long since you've been to the mainland?" Joanna said suddenly. "I think it would do you good. You need movies, and something new to wear, and some meals you haven't cooked yourself—"

"I need more than that," Nora muttered. "I need—" She stopped short. Her eyes, when she faced Joanna, were wide now, and filled with a sort of liquid desperation, like a trapped animal's. "Joanna, why do you think Matthew didn't get out early this morning?"

"I don't know," said Joanna. Her heart was beating fast, with the urgency of the other girl's terror.

"Because I was sick, and I didn't want Gram to know. I was miserably sick, Joanna! Matthew was running up and down stairs, waiting on me, and I made him promise he'd tell her I had a sore throat or a bad headache, or something—"

"Sick?" said Joanna slowly. Nora nodded. She looked sick enough now.

"I'm going to have a baby, I think. And I don't know what I'm going to do." She put her hand out and gripped the top of the gate, her knuckles were marble-white through the taut flesh.

"Why—you'll have it, I should think," Joanna said. "Nora, it isn't so terrible. You've probably heard lots of stories, and been scared silly by them—but most of them weren't true."

"It's not the pain I'm scared of," Nora spoke with difficulty. "I could stand any amount of pain. It's—" Her cheeks flooded with angry color, the desperation in her eyes turned to fire. "I *won't* have it! I promised myself I'd never have a baby when Gram was alive, and I won't! It wouldn't be my baby; it'd be hers, because she's thrown nothing else at me since the day I married Matthew!"

Joanna watched her and listened in compassionate silence. A few years ago she would have tried to talk Nora down, she would have argued with fierce ardor, trying by sheer overwhelming will-power to *make* her think straight. But she was humbler now, and more pitying; and she knew that all the determination in the world couldn't change Nora. The years of the old lady's domination had set up such an unreasoning obsession in the girl that nothing could break it down, except Nora herself.

"Nora, think of Matthew and not of Gram," she said finally, because she must say something.

"I'm going to think of *me!*" said Nora fiercely. "Gram's always come first. It was always what *Gram* wanted. Well, this is one thing that Gram wants that she isn't going to *get!*"

There was nothing to say, even while she was fighting back her dismay. "Be careful." That was all.

"Oh, yes, I'll be careful!" Nora was smiling now and it wasn't a nice smile. "But I guess I'll be taking that trip to the mainland, the way you said. Maybe I'll go, in a day or two."

"Come and see me before you go," said Joanna, in one last effort.

Nora's smile was crafty. It chilled Joanna. "Maybe I won't have time. So long, Jo!" Almost blithely, she started back to the house. Joanna shut the gate quietly behind her. For a moment, as she walked along the lane, she was almost blinded and deafened by her dismay. If ever there was disaster in the air, it hung around Nora Fennell in an unmistakable aura. At the thought of the girl's probable aim when she went ashore, Joanna winced. No reputable doctor would do as she asked; but from Nils Joanna knew there were plenty — not doctors — who were making a profitable business out of the war, since Limerock was swarming with hundreds of new people, servicemen and the women who followed, inevitably, in their wake. And when Nora discovered how wrong she was, and how completely a fool, it would probably be too late.

If only Nils were coming home to dinner, in from a day's hauling. There was nothing he could do, but she needed his sanity and his composed outlook. Thinking of Nils took her mind off Nora, and the day came back to her again, the essence of the Island spring that was composed of sun-warm spruce, ripening bay, the damp spongy soil and growing grass under her feet, the ineffable, tenuous sweetness of the wild pear tree by the clubhouse, and the west wind. She breathed deeply of its cleanliness, and everywhere she looked there was more cleanliness, the stark, geometric beauty of firs piercing the sky, sunlight on her own steeply gabled roof, the vibrant whiteness of a gull sweeping close over her head, and the neat black hood of a chickadee in an alder.

Without complacency, but with a heart-shaking intensity, she realized her own good fortune, and she walked home with thanksgiving in her mind; thanksgiving blended with a yearning compassion for Nora.

16

WHEN SHE CAME INTO THE YARD she was so sure that Dick would come bounding across to meet her that the certainty almost evoked him before her, wide mouth, smiling eyes, ears lifting as he ran. So the emptiness was the more complete for his absence, and Jamie's.

"Jamie," she said. She didn't raise her voice, yet it seemed to echo in the sunlit silence. At the same instant the mother-animal-instinct told her that the yard was empty. When she said his name again, there was an undercurrent of fear in it, and she set her lips tightly together. He could not be far away, and Dick was with him. She went toward the barn, saying to herself, *Don't hurry, he'll be at the brook with the ducks. Don't hurry.* But her feet wouldn't obey the cool logical message from her brain, they were responding to the quick terror that had sprung up in her from that feeling of emptiness. It was as if Jamie had never been. One moment he was sitting on the bottom step up at Fennell's, in the next moment he was gone.

He wasn't at the brook behind the barn, and neither was the dog. She wanted to whistle for Dick, but her mouth was too dry. She stared at the alder swamp, where the thicket of smooth gray-barked branches was taking on a warm violet sheen, and the green-

gold tassels were beginning to form. There was no sound. Even the
birds seemed to have gone. A little breeze sprang up from nowhere
and ruffled the blossoms of the wild pear that leaned over the brook,
rippling their reflection into nothingness. The ducks weren't there.

Suddenly a crow called out from the dark belt of spruces beyond
the alders, and other crows took up the warning until the air was
suddenly shattered by their voices. There was no more stillness. She
felt a jolt of excitement in her chest. Crows always shrieked like that
when an alien element came into their territory; it meant Jamie and
Dick could be wandering out toward the Bennett meadow.

She crossed the brook and ran along the path among the alders.
There was nothing to fear if he had gone along here. *If* he had gone
along here. . . . She reached the spruces, and there was no sign of
dog or child in the clear, cold brown shadow. The crows had quieted
again, the silence settled down around Joanna like a heavy and tangible thing. She reached the Bennett meadow. It stretched before her,
a sea of golden grass that rippled faintly and noiselessly in a little
wind from the sea. It was an immensity of sunlit space; it would be
like walking around the world for Jamie's not-quite-two-year-old legs.
The dark wall of woods ringed it until it came out at Goose Cove.
Again there was the jolt in her chest, sickening this time. But he
couldn't have reached the shore in such a little while. Unless — her
mind circled frantically. Unless he'd gone up into the woods behind
the Fennell house, those dark, ancient, deep woods that walled the
meadow.

But he hadn't wanted to leave the yard this morning; and he
was so stubborn that she couldn't rid herself of the idea that he'd started
home under his own power. She ran back along the path through
the alder swamp and came to the barnyard again. From the yard
he might have gone to the shore — she'd taken him sometimes to meet
Owen when he came in from hauling. She tried to think casually;
He'll be playing around in somebody's skiff, that's what he loves.

Thea came out as she went by the house. "Where you goin' in
such a pucker?" she demanded.

Joanna didn't look at her. "Jamie's gone," she said, and kept on.
She heard Thea's heels clattering down the steps.

It was a year before she reached the harbor beach, below the
old wharf. She knew she should have been prepared for its emptiness,

the high tide brimming blue-green with only a narrow border of white and lavender and gray beach rocks between the water's edge and the path, a few skiffs jostling against a dory like puppies against an old dog. Nothing else. She stood staring, not knowing which way to turn next.

But the wharf was behind her. *Please not the wharf,* she said steadily inside herself. That was one thing Nils had mentioned often, because when he was Jamie's age he was always running away to the wharf. Once he'd fallen overboard, but there was a boat at the car, and he'd been fished out and sent home with a sound slap across his bottom. But there were no boats at the wharf this morning, there was no sign of life anywhere. The Island might have been deserted; it lay still, unstirring, in the full flood of May sunshine.

"Mrs. Sorensen," said Dennis Garland's voice. "What is it?"

She turned then, and saw him standing on the wharf just above her, and remembered him with a great surge of relief. If he had been around the wharf all morning, he would have seen Jamie.

"I've lost Jamie," she said to him quite simply, looking up. "Have you seen him?"

He was tall against the sky. "No, I haven't, but I'll look for him."

"I don't think he's gone too far." She managed a creditable smile, but she knew his trained gray eyes could see beyond the smile and sense her growing panic. She framed her words carefully.

"We were up at the Fennells'. He and Dick stayed outside—they always do. When I came out they were gone, and I thought he'd got mad and started home. He didn't want to go up there with me in the first place. But when I got home he wasn't there." Her mouth wanted to tremble. She tightened her jaw. "I think he might have gone up *behind* the Fennells', there's an old path up through the woods—"

"We'll find him," Dennis said. He jumped down onto the beach. "Do you want me to start up there, behind the Fennells'?"

Thea and Leonie came hurrying toward them. Joanna said, "Maybe they'd look up there, if you'd go through the Fennells' field into Barque Cove. I've taken him that way along the West Side."

His eyes said, *Don't give in.* "Good. I'll go now. Matthew hasn't gone out yet—I'll put him to work too."

"I'll go back through the swamp," she said. "I only ran through there before. But this morning he was going toward the swamp when I called him." Why hadn't she remembered that before? She could feel her face grow cold as it whitened. "There are holes—deep ones—"

"Don't forget, Dick's with him," Dennis reminded her. "Well, let's start." His quiet composure braced her, and she felt strength come back into her legs. They turned toward Thea and Leonie. Thea was puffing, Leonie stern with anxiety.

"Why don't you go along?" Dennis said to Joanna. "I'll tell them where to look." For an instant his fingers went around her arm, gripping it hard through her sweater sleeve, and then she found herself walking along through the May morning.

She was grateful for Dennis Garland's impersonal attitude. It kept at bay the bone-dissolving terror that was trying to sweep over her like the persistent wash of surf over Eastern Harbor Point. But of course Jamie wasn't his child, of course he couldn't think of the hundred things she knew and feared about the Island; he didn't know the rocks by heart, and the granite-walled ravines in the woods, and the deep, dark places in the swamps where a child might wander and become suddenly beyond the reach of the voices that called him.

Her throat constricted. *If only Jamie won't be afraid,* she thought. *Don't let him be afraid. Dick, stay with him.*

Joanna had lived through many long hours in her life, but this one was beyond any doubt the longest. She went from panic to a sort of frantic reasoning with herself, and then to a sickening leap of hope when a gull's cry sounded like a child's voice. In the alder swamp she scratched her face and tore her dress, making her way through the dense interweaving of branches. Jamie could get through all right, and she must go wherever it was possible for him and the dog to go. She called, making her voice sound warm and unafraid, but her voice came back in a thin ghostly echo or not at all. She didn't know which was worse, the echo or the silence that swallowed all things up.

Soaked to the ankles, her back aching, her face bleeding from a deep scratch on her cheekbone, she emerged from the alder swamp into the Bennett meadow. She listened. Nothing anywhere. No *halloo* to call in the searchers and say that Jamie was found.

She walked across the meadow to Goose Cove. He might have found his way here; she'd brought him over here to play on warm afternoons. When he was not there she kept walking, following the old wood road along the edge of the woods above the shore.

When her weariness became too great, and she had to sit down, she was in a little cove that was too tiny to have ever been named. She used to play here once, among the rocks; it had always seemed a snug, secure place, its infinitesimal beach sheltered by a steep, densely wooded hillside rising above it, and by great black ledges on either side. Now, as she sat on the bank, she looked up at the monstrous tangle of ancient spruce boughs above her, hung with moss, confused with dead and fallen trees, stricken with an immense and brooding silence. When she looked away, it was to see the lazy, treacherous curl of surf on the ledges. Either way, it was no longer snug or secure. Far above her, so far they were mere shining specks as their white breasts caught the sunlight, the gulls continued their impersonal circling. She could not hear their cries. The sea stretched away into a luminous haze, and the noon sun was hot and unkind in this windless place. There was nothing here. It seemed that she had been moving in a vacuum ever since she had first called Jamie's name into the emptiness of the yard.

She wanted to get away from this place, but her legs wouldn't let her. "Nils," she whispered, holding his name in her mind like a talisman in her cupped hands. But her whisper faded into the hot, glistening silence, and Nils was as far away as ever. Perhaps there was a battle going on now. Perhaps—her hands went up to cover her aching eyes, to press hard against the lids. No, she wouldn't have it that way! Nils was all right. There would be a letter . . . maybe tomorrow. . . .

But what would she be writing to him tonight? She got up, knowing she must leave this place even if she had to crawl. Perhaps already they had found Jamie and taken him home, maybe giving him a glass of milk and he was asking where Mamma was. But she was too tired to hurry, or to feel the shock of hope sending new energy along her veins.

When she finally reached the back door of her own house, the silence remained undisturbed, and it pressed on her like stone. She stood for a moment by the lilac bush, staring at the tender young leaves without seeing them. If only someone would speak or call out from somewhere.

Her mouth was parched. She would have a drink of water and then go out again.

When she stepped on the doorstep, Dick growled. She stood rigid in the doorway, looking at him, not believing that it was really Dick. He came to her as she had expected him to come in that last instant before she realized Jamie was gone. She shut the door carefully behind her, and put her hand on Dick's head, feeling the broad hard skull under the silky coat. Automatically her fingers sought the tender spot behind Dick's ear, and when he pressed the ear into her hand, leaning blissfully against her fingers, the moment of unreality was past.

"*Joanna—*" It was Nora, hushed but radiant, coming out of the kitchen. "I've been making you some coffee—Jamie's asleep." Nora had tears wobbling on her lashes. "He's in there."

Joanna went into the dining room, putting back a strand of hair from her forehead with a heavy hand. Dennis was sitting in the biggest rocking chair, and Jamie was asleep in his lap, pouting, his lower lip looking furious and his cheeks red and streaked with dirt and tears.

"He was playing in the sandpile behind the clubhouse," Dennis said. "Dick was guarding him. Jamie was mad because I interrupted him, and he called me a son-of-a-bitch. When we were almost home he decided he was outnumbered, and fell asleep."

Joanna contemplated them both, the man with the gray eyes, the child. Her eyes came back to the gray ones. "Why is it always you?" she said. "Give him to me, I'll put him in his crib. Nothing will wake him for hours now."

She took the warm burden into her arms, and when the sleep-heavy blond head rolled against her shoulder she put her lips against the moist forehead for a moment; then she turned toward the stairs.

"I'll go along home, Joanna," Nora said from the kitchen.

"Thanks for everything, Nora." Joanna smiled at her over her shoulder, the warm Bennett smile, vivid in spite of her untidy hair and blood-stained cheek. Then she went up the stairs, and laid Jamie in his crib. She took off his shoes and socks, and covered him up. For a moment she stood looking down at him, her face locked against the impact of her relief. And he hadn't been terrified, after all. Just furious at being found.

Son of a gun. She felt a sudden irrepressible desire to laugh.

When she went downstairs, Dennis was standing in the middle

of the dining room. "Well, everything's under control," he said easily. "But I'm wondering if you ought to have a bromide—you need rest as much as Jamie."

"Don't go yet. I haven't thanked you."

"You thanked me. The way you looked at him was thanks enough for me." His eyes were smiling a little, and his voice was as blessedly serene as sleep without dreams.

"I want to thank you properly, but I don't know how," she said haltingly. "I'm really happy. But I—" Her voice was unsteady. She tightened her lips, and turned her back to him instinctively. She had always hated display, she had always fought wildly against showing her emotions. Standing at the window she looked out at the field and spoke again.

"I'm so grateful. You've already done so much I feel ashamed. Whenever anything happens, you're there. And everything seems to be h-h-happening—"

The relief was too great. She began to cry, so suddenly and so easily she hardly knew it until she felt the tears sliding down her cheeks. When she tried to speak it was worse. She put her hands over her face, but she would not lower her chin. Shamed, and yet proud, she stood Indian-straight, Bennett-straight, and wept.

"Don't try to stop it," he said quietly, moving close beside her. "You need to cry."

She couldn't have stopped then, but it was agony to be like this, with no defenses against his eyes. It seemed as he were always seeing what she intended no one to see.

"Its just that—it's just—" She tried to explain, but she didn't know what she wanted to explain.

"Don't talk," he said, and put his arms around her, drawing her into their comforting circle with a light, firm pressure. It was his touch that had done it, and now she was helpless. With a sudden blind gesture she pressed her face hard against his shoulder and shut her eyes. His arms tightened.

After a few minutes they moved apart. She should have been embarrassed, she thought, or confused, but she wasn't. She took her handkerchief from her pocket, and Dennis looked out the window, his face as dispassionately kind as always.

"Thank you," she said. "I guess I can say it now. Thank you for everything."

"You're welcome." He looked at her then, and with concern, touched her cheek gently with his fingers. "You've a nasty scratch there. Have you anything to put on it?"

She nodded, and at that instant the front door opened, and Thea trotted through the sun parlor and into the kitchen. For a moment she hesitated in the doorway, looking from one to the other, her eyes narrowing in almost imperceptible speculation. Then she smiled — broadly.

"Jest thought I'd see how you felt, and if there was anything I could do," she explained. "But you look like you're in good hands."

"Yes, I'm fine," Joanna said. "Thanks for helping out, Thea. It was wonderful of everybody to go running around over the Island this morning."

"Well, gosh, a lost kid," Thea mumbled. She bent nervously to pat Dick. For Joanna, her moment of pliant uncertainty and weakness was gone. Thea had checked on the time Nora had left, waited to see if Dennis had gone too, and then she'd had to come over. Joanna knew it as thoroughly as though she could look into Thea's brain under the yellow curls. And Thea had been rewarded; she'd seen Dennis' hand touch Joanna's cheek.

When Thea straightened up Joanna's dark eyes looked into hers with a challenge the other woman couldn't miss. "I've been telling Dennis I don't know how we ever got along without him."

Thea threw back her head, smiling, her glance flashing between the other two. Her hand went to her hip; she laughed over her raised shoulder at Dennis. "Yes, he cer'nly come in handy for you, Jo! Well, you prob'ly want to take it easy, so I won't hang around."

She hurried through the sun parlor, her heels clattering. She let the door slam behind her.

"It looks as if life might be getting back to normal again," Dennis said mildly. "Are you going to let me fix that cut?"

She shook her head and smiled. "I can do it. You've already done enough, and the men'll be coming to the car now."

"Oh — reminding me of my duties, are you?"

She managed to laugh as she walked with him to the door. When he was gone she went into the kitchen and poured out a cup of the coffee Nora had made; but another scent was in her nostrils, that of sweet tobacco clinging to an old tweed jacket; and her forehead still felt the imprint of that tweed, and the hard bone under it, against which her face had so blindly pressed.

It seemed, all at once, as if it had been long years instead of weeks since Nils' arms had held her tightly; and each year was a burden. In this moment, almost too heavy a burden to carry alone.

17

By the end of May, the gardens on the Island were planted. Everybody had one. Joanna's was out in the field beside the house, where Gunnar Sorensen had grown prodigious gardens fertilized with seaweed and rotten herring, as the Indians had done. There was no horse on the Island to pull a plow, as there was at Brigport, but Owen turned the soil in his spare time, and Joanna herself was handy with the fork. Then she did the planting; turnips, potatoes, carrots, beets, Swiss chard, bush and pole beans, squash. In the sunny dining-room windows she had started tomato plants and cabbages.

Though the planting season was sometimes late, everything grew with an almost tropical speed once it had a start, and by early June she was setting out tomatoes and tiny, pale green cabbage plants. The field behind the windbreak was sheltered, and sometimes she worked out there all day, the sun beating warm on her head, the earth moist and friable under her flngers. At night she reported everything in her letter to Nils.

D-Day had come and gone; gone, but life had changed suddenly. The Island alternated between furious optimism and abysmal depression. Some said it would be all over in a month, that the Germans were ready to crumble, they knew it was the end. Others swore there'd be a year or more of dirty fighting. And there was Japan, wasn't there? The Japanese would surrender as soon as the Germans did; no, the Japs would fight to the last man, they had nothing to lose. Look at the way they were always committing suicide. It wouldn't bother them to keep on fighting.

The papers and the radio commentators were even more confusing. Owen read everything and listened to everything. Joanna, feeling her nerves beginning to tighten unbearably, and bad dreams threatening, took sensible steps. She read only one newspaper, and listened to only two commentators. And even then she found herself wondering if she would have been able to listen if Nils were off the coast of Normandy instead of in the Pacific.

I should be praying, she thought as she knelt in her garden. *But what would I ask for?* She could see Jamie's little red wheelbarrow, tacit evidence of his being. *All I can ask,* she thought, *is for God to save something for Jamie and all the other children in the world.* She remembered the monstrous sufferings inflicted on those other children, and her stomach knotted with cold rage and sickness. *Maybe God's given us up as a bad job and turned away for keeps.*

Much of the news made D-Day sound terribly easy, as if the Americans and British were simply walking ashore, after crossing a stretch of water like the twenty-five miles between the Island and the mainland; they were to be met by the French patriots, wearing tricolor sashes and carrying bouquets, and the Germans would simply be eliminated with no effort on anybody's part. She'd listened with her tongue in her cheek, and Owen had been darkly cynical.

"It ain't that much of a strawberry festival over there," he said. "It's pure hell, most likely. We'll hear about it after awhile." He moved uneasily about the house, as if it were too small for him, and she wondered if he would go looking for a drink; if anything could tempt him to backslide, this would be it. This helpless immobility, this waiting here, tormented by the belief he was letting his brothers down, that his manhood was at fault, that in this monumental struggle he was nothing.

But he hadn't got drunk after all, though there was enough reason for it. The news from the Normandy beaches grew progressively worse in the next few days. And the fog came. A warm fog which seeped insidiously into the house and turned all the woodwork whitely damp, and kept the clothes clammy. It was too mild to keep fires going, too damp without them. The wind stayed stubbornly to the eastward, and all day and all night it bore the moody bawl of the foghorn from Matinicus Rock.

Too much fog could ruin the wild strawberries, and this year more than in the past few years it looked as if there would be an exceptionally good crop. There was no chance to go to haul, the fog hung so smotheringly thick it was hardly possible to see the bow of a boat from her wheel. The price of lobsters was climbing all the time, the traps were probably full—and the prospect was certainly a tantalizing one.

Tempers were short. Viciously short. Because of the shortage of trap stuff, some of the men didn't have any extra laths laid by, so they couldn't put in their spare time building new gear. There was nothing to do but stick by the radio, listening, cursing, and finally falling into morose silences. There was a noticeable lack of complaint about the shortage of cigarettes, the O.P.A., and Roosevelt during that week when the whole world, and Bennett's Island were thinking about the coast of France.

Joanna was grateful for her garden and for the letters from Nils. They were so calm, so matter-of-fact, that they took away some of the horror that she knew could grow upon her like an obscene fungus if she read all the stories about the Pacific and brooded upon them. She worked in the garden, fog or not, and at last she was rewarded. The wind shifted to the west, the last fog blew over like a silvery veil across the sun, and she knelt in clear warm light, seeing the diamond sparkle on the grass all around her, and over against the house the lilac plumes nodded among their leaves. Rich, oriental, purple fragrance against New England's white clapboards.

Jamie would sleep for two hours and she had a sense of freedom as she thinned the delicate, pale-green cabbage plants. Owen would be in soon, but his dinner was ready on the back of the stove. She wondered what Dennis thought about D-Day. She'd hardly seen him to speak to, alone; whenever he'd come to the house in the past week Owen had been there and they'd sat and talked. When he'd first come to Bennett's, he hadn't wanted to talk about the war.

She was so closely aligned with the Island that she felt a personal sense of achievement whenever she looked at Dennis and saw the tangible evidence of change. Without smugness she knew she had a right to be proud. He had singled her out, he had told her more of himself than anyone else knew, there was a companionship between them that she considered rare and satisfying, and that she knew he valued. He had told her so. She was not naive enough to give their friendship the complete credit for his new health and serenity, but she knew that it had helped greatly. There were some things the Island couldn't do alone.

Footsteps fell on the grass. She looked up quickly, half-expecting it to be Dennis, and in the next second expecting Owen; but it was Thea. Joanna sighed, and leaned over the cabbages with renewed and quite fervent interest.

"Hello, hello!" Thea's angular shadow fell across her, Thea's voice bounced merrily against her eardrums. "Workin' hard improvin' your figure, I see!"

"Working hard improving the food situation," Joanna said dryly, and sat back on her heels. "How are you?"

"Finest kind!" She jigged up and down, hands on her hips, her brief skirt waving around her knees, which were unpleasantly thin and unpleasantly bare. Joanna remembered Owen's comments on them, and her mouth quirked.

"I must say you look gay enough," she murmured. "Make-up and everything. What's going on?"

"Oh, nothing! You know I always dress so's I'd be presentable anywhere." She slid a supercilious glance at Joanna's open-necked blouse and smudged slacks. "Not that there's anywhere to go on Bennett's, but it's sort of good for the morale, *I* think."

"Oh, yes," said Joanna sagely.

"Well, I only run over to say hello. I have to be gettin' Franny's dinner on." She giggled. "It's short lobsters—only I hadn't ought to say so in front of you—the Bennett's bein' so fussy about keepin' to the law."

A small tinge of premonition shot through Joanna's mind. She felt herself growing wary. *Thea is a scheming bitch,* she thought calmly, *and she's like her Grampa Gunnar. She's on the prod today.*

"Don't worry, I won't tell," she said pleasantly. "Besides, it wouldn't be the first time, would it? Anybody knows what lobster shells smell like, burning."

Thea's eyes narrowed, their shiny blue darkened. "If everybody burned stuff, they'd never get caught, would they? That's what I said to my cousin this mornin' when we were talkin' on the phone—I went down to the store and called her up to see if she's heard anything from her boy in England." She nodded confidentially at Joanna. "You know Signe, that lives in Pruitt's Harbor. She knows Charles, and all of them."

Joanna's shoulders were tight and square under her blouse. But her fingers heaped earth about a tiny plant, patted it into a bulwark of strength for the fragile stem. "How is everybody in Pruitt's Harbor?"

"Seems like they're in an awful stew right now," Thea went on. She was trying to be airy, but an inner excitement made her words jerky. "*Your* family, that is. I imagine your mother's just about sick over it, but of course Young Charles ain't really one of her boys, just a grandson—" Joanna sat back on her heels and looked up steadily at Thea's face, waiting. Thea's eyes were glistening. She seemed a little uncertain under the dark contemplative gaze. She moistened her lips.

"I thought you ought to know, and me bein' one of the family, by marriage—of course I wouldn't start claimin' I *wasn't* connected, the way some people might do, seein' as there's never been anything like this in the Sorensen family—"

Joanna stood up, with no impression of hurry. She was taller than Thea, she was erect and lean in slacks and shirt. Now she put her hands carefully into her pockets, before she could get at Thea's shoulders with them, and said mildly, "Whatever are you getting at, Thea? Can't you seem to say it, right out?"

That did it. A furious and ugly blush spread like wildfire over Thea's neck and face. Her voice lashed out shrilly, like a curling whip, or a snake's tongue. "If you want to know, Young Charles and some of his pals broke into the hardware store D-Day night and stole a whole lot of shotgun shells, and God knows what else, and the sheriff found the boxes right in Charles' wood-house!" She went on and on, a vicious noise in the quiet day. "They've been stealin' stuff right along, breakin' and enterin', and the sheriff's been layin' to catch 'em. Well, now he's caught the little bastards, and he's likely to get 'em all sent to Thomaston for a good long while!"

Joanna stood quietly, simply staring at Thea. The echoes of Thea's voice seemed to jangle hideously in her ears.

"Go on home, Thea," she said at last. "You've been around to everyone with the story, and now you've told me, so your job is done. Go home."

Thea's bravado was gone. She flounced around, switching her shoulders and her thin hips under the tight rayon skirt, but the flourish was weak. "Well, anyway," she said loudly and vindictively, "your mother won't be goin' around lookin' like she thought she was so much of a lady, with her grandson in Thomaston State Prison!"

The last word was a gasp. Joanna, looking beyond her, saw Owen standing at the corner of the house, a silent but ominous figure against the white lilacs.

"Get home, Thea." His voice was quiet, for Owen. His feet were set wide apart in rubber boots, his hands were in his pockets. His thick black eyebrows made a bar across his face. "Get home, before I wring your goddam neck."

Thea took a step forward. "Scram," said Owen. "Shove off. And don't ever set foot on this side of the windbreak again."

"Nils is my own cousin—" she protested feebly, but when Owen took his hands out of his pockets she moved swiftly sidewise, and all but ran across the lawn and out of sight beyond the windbreak. They heard the back door slam. Joanna shrugged, and went toward the house. Owen came in behind her. He went directly to the sink and splashed water into the basin, clattering the dipper as if he wanted to hurl it through the window.

Joanna set the food on the table for his dinner. When she came back into the kitchen he was standing in the middle of the floor, his face black with thought. They looked silently at each other, and he exploded at last.

"Somebody's a damned liar!"

"We'll know the truth of it pretty soon," Joanna said, over and above her own inner sickness. "Of course, everybody's got it to talk about now. Sit down and eat."

He sat down mechanically. "Still . . . the kid was always wild. Hates school, just like I did."

"I won't believe it's so bad," Joanna said stubbornly. But she felt tainted and shaking inside, as if Thea's malice had sprayed filth over her. The house threatened to suffocate her; she couldn't stand Owen's storming.

On an impulse she said, "Watch out for things, will you? I'll be back in a little while. Jamie's asleep."

Owen nodded, blackly, and she escaped into clean space. She began to walk with no aim, her feet carried her swiftly through the leafy alder swamp and out toward the Bennett meadow, but she was hardly conscious of her direction.

She felt the same scalding, impotent wrath she'd always felt whenever a Bennett fell publicly from grace; a harmless misadventure of hers, at fifteen; Owen's behavior; Charles' marriage to Mateel, when he'd "got her into trouble". . . Whatever one of them had done exposed not only that one, but all the others, to gloating eyes like Thea's, or to the indignant pity of those who defended them. And now Young Charles had been arrested for burglary, and no one had ever been arrested in the Bennett family. As Thea had said, jibing, the Bennetts had always kept to the law.

If they'd all stayed on the Island where they'd belonged, this wouldn't have happened. It was almost a relief to feel angry because Charles had moved his family away to make more money. She was angry with Mateel, too, for having so many children that she didn't have time to spend on Young Charles; angry because her older brothers hadn't taken Young Charles on the seiner, the *Four Brothers,* last year when he'd wanted to go with them.

But not even anger could drive away the reality. Suppose he *had* been breaking and entering for a long time; suppose they *did* send him to Thomaston prison for several years. Did they really put sixteen-year-old boys in the State Prison?

There was no way to escape this, and she walked across the Bennett meadow, up toward the woods, and the cemetery, without any knowledge of the usual comfort the Island could give her. The war was here, suddenly, in this sea of sunlit grass, under this blue Maine sky, where the gulls had always scissored the air with their wings. The war was responsible for what Young Charles had done; it had caused death, destruction, disease, madness, every crime under the sun; and it had taken Nils away from her. She wanted Nils so terribly that when she reached the edge of the woods, and stood in its shadow, she gave herself up for a moment to the intensity of her longing.

And then, with tears making a shimmer of light in her eyes, she walked up through the blooming orchard to the cemetery.

18

A FAINT, DAMP COOLNESS that smelled of grass and wild roses touched her moist forehead. The birds were singing. By the time she had entered the shadow of the big spruces that fringed the woods, the clear sun-washed air around the treetops was cut into a lace-like pattern of sounds. Joanna's senses quickened, in spite of her preoccupation, her ears and nostrils were as sensitive as an animal's so that she heard and smelled these things without thinking consciously of them.

In the orchard there was the heavy drone of the bees around the apple blossoms, and sunlight topping the little trees with silver; her head brushed the lower branches and petals began falling, floating into the deep cool grass around the gnarled trunks. When she looked up she saw the sky, shining with a burnished intensity after the week of fog, blue between the masses of pink and white. A white-throat sparrow sang out suddenly; the first this year, and the three steady, sweet, fluting notes half-stabbed Joanna.

The cemetery lay at the end of the orchard, so that the farthest apple trees leaned over the fence and scattered their petals on the grassy graves. The flowers set out on Decoration Day were still bright. She had bordered Alec's grave with the pansies Ellen had sent out — bought with Ellen's own money for the father who had never seen her. Their brilliant, velvety little heads trembled in the faint breeze. But the apple blossoms were over them all, a canopy of fragrance.

She walked around the corner of the little cemetery and up onto a little rise, where an old fence roamed out of the woods and joined the cemetery wall. There was a stile over the fence and she sat down on it. Here was silence, sunshine, sweetness, and one tall birch, that she had known for a good many years. She always thought of it as being golden with autumn against the spruces, but today it looked springlike in its young green.

She closed her eyes and sat without moving. There was no sound but the rustling of leaves, the far-away crying of gulls out on Goose Cove Ledge, the sibilant rush of a cuckoo's wings. She closed her eyes and waited for peace to come to her.

She felt, rather than knew, that someone else was there. When she opened her eyes she saw without surprise that Dennis Garland was standing at the edge of the woods where they marched up from Goose Cove. She thought, *He always comes,* and then felt her first astonishment. He did always come, didn't he?

"I'm sorry," he said. "I've disturbed you."

"No, you haven't." She smiled faintly at him. "I've just been listening to the birds. This is a wonderful place for them."

"So I've discovered." He came toward her, running a hand through his fairish hair. The slanting light struck through the branches, highlighting his strong-bridged nose and gaunt cheekbones. He looked austere, but she was used to that now, knowing how he changed when he smiled.

He smiled now, as he sat on the other side of the stile and took out his pipe. "Every day I discover something more enchanting about the Island. I don't know if you like that word, but I do. The Island *does* enchant."

"I know. Look what it's done to me all these years!"

"You looked enchanted when I came along. The sun on your face, and your eyes closed, your head lifted as if you were invoking some secret god."

She loved the way he talked. It took her out of herself, it was balm on the sore Young Charles had made. Already the tension was easing in her chest. She found herself watching his face, the shifting sparkles of light in his eyes, the way his thinly cut mouth said words in that easy voice, and she was suddenly embarrassed because she was staring. She looked down at his hands as he filled the pipe. His hands were always clean, for all that he worked on the car, and the nails were cut short, they weren't bruised or broken. A surgeon would have to keep his hands immaculately clean. His hands were his whole work, his whole life.

He went on talking, describing a bird he'd seen, while she

watched his hands. There were tiny, short gold hairs on the backs of them, and he wore a wristwatch. She'd always wanted to give Nils a watch, but he could tell time by the sun; and now that he was in the service, he'd bought himself a watch. The thoughts slipped idly through her head, without pain, and it came to her suddenly that she was not miserable any more. It was as if watching those square-tipped, strong fingers, the long, capable thumb, had steadied her as much as those strong fingers had steadied her when they gripped her arm the day Jamie was lost; and later on that day, when they had held her against his shoulder for silent comfort.

With an effort she pulled her gaze, and her mind, away from his hands. She looked out across the cemetery, and her eyes seemed heavy-lidded, as if relaxation had come too soon.

"That must have been a Maryland yellow-throat you saw," she said. "A little black mask—yes, that's a yellow-throat."

"He was a brazen little chap," said Dennis. "He looked me over as thoroughly as I took stock of him." He looked off across the cemetery. "You know, I have never known a cemetery that was so full of friendly peace as this one is. I don't wonder you come here often."

"I've always loved it," she answered. "Ever since I was a kid. It was a favorite hideaway."

The smoke from his pipe rose upward in a thin turquoise column. "Sigurd tells me there are some unmarked graves here—shipwrecked sailors—"

"Over there, at the far side, where the apple blossoms have fallen on the grass." She pointed, and turned to him, eager to tell him the story that had always seemed so romantic and sad. "The ship went ashore off Brig Ledge—it was a brig, so that's why it's Brig Ledge now—and my grandfather, and Nils' grandfather, and some of the other old-timers, saw it, but they couldn't do anything, they couldn't even launch a dory. It was horrible. Later these five bodies were washed ashore, and three of them were very young, hardly more than boys."

He was listening, but a remoteness seemed to have passed over his face; she remembered then that he had seen hundreds of boys' bodies lying in the surf. The tragedy of these five wouldn't impress him. Her voice flattened.

"Well, anyway, they buried them. And that apple tree always has the best apples. When we were kids we thought it was some sort of gift from those boys to us."

"It was a nice thought," he said gently.

"Yes. We called them the Sailors' Apples."

At once the words echoed in her head. She heard her own voice, shadowed with some unknown emotion, saying those words into the sunlit silence, *We call them the Sailors' Apples.* The words were repeated over and over again, with the persistence of lights flashing and dancing on the sea. A tremor ran through her and her skin felt chilled, and then warm.

With an effort she threw off the spell the words had cast and looked up. Dennis was watching her. The remoteness had gone, in its place was an absorption, as if he were studying every plane and contour of her face and throat. Red showed richly under the brown of her cheeks, and she must have made some movement, for suddenly awareness flashed into his eyes, as if his thoughts had come all at once into focus.

She stood up quickly. "I ran away from home. Jamie'll be waking up and roaring." She spoke with an ease that hid the unreasonable quickening of her heartbeat. Now everything was going back to normal. That funny, frightening moment there on the stile was over, and Dennis was unfolding his long legs and standing up.

"I'm afraid I ran away too. Leonie'll be keeping dinner hot for me."

They walked down through the alley of blossom that was the orchard, stopped to see where a cuckoo had gone, and turned down the damp cool path that led into the Bennett meadow. Conversation was desultory but pleasant. It was no different from all the other times they had met, and yet, in a distant, secret part of Joanna's mind she was remembering Dennis' face when she had looked up. *He was looking at my face the way I was looking at his hands,* she thought. And she had watched his hands because they fascinated her. The inevitable conclusion set her heart to beating again with a thick jolt, half-sickening.

His hands fascinate me because he's a surgeon, because they can do wonderful things, she reasoned with herself. *But it's impossible for him to be—* her mind rebelled at using the word *fascinated* again, but it rebelled even more at saying that he might be in love with her. It was ridiculous.

They went through the alder swamp, Joanna walking ahead. He had sought her out in every way, he had made no secret of preferring her company, yet he was always the same, courteous, half-remote, never intruding. *It's because he knows what I am,* she thought, *what sort of woman I am . . . what sort of wife. . . .*

She looked almost with astonishment at her own back door, smelled the familiar strong sweetness of the lilacs, and remembered slowly Young Charles. She felt as if she had been in another country.

19

"Doc! DENNIS!" The voice assailed them violently, ripping harshly through the mantle of silence in which they had walked. They both turned and saw Matthew Fennell running down from his house, plunging awkwardly in his rubber boots over the uneven ground. He ran like a man driven by demons.

"It must be Gram," Joanna said her lips drying. "It's sure to be Gram."

Dennis nodded his head curtly toward the running, stumbling man, "Come on," he said, and started up to meet Matthew. From the back door Owen hailed her.

"What goes on?"

"Something's wrong up to Fennells'," she called back. "I'm going to see!"

"O.K.!" He stood on the doorstep for a moment longer, his hands on his hips, scowling in the brillance of the sunshine, and then she was running after Dennis, lightly, over the ground she had known all her life.

Still Dennis reached Matthew before she did. Matthew's tan had turned muddy, his forehead dripped sweat, and he breathed in long sobbing gasps. The sight of his urgency was shocking to Joanna. Dennis gripped him by both shoulders.

"Take it easy, man. Speak slowly. Now, what's happened?"

"Nora," Matthew said hoarsely. "She's bleedin' to death, I think. Hurry, will ye?" He twisted away from Dennis, who still held one arm as they walked along.

"What happened?"

"She fell downstairs, and she—she—" He mopped sweat out of his eyes with a blind and hopeless gesture. "She was goin' to have a baby."

Dennis glanced over his shoulder at Joanna. "You any good at this? I'll need help."

"I can obey orders, if that's what you want," she said crisply.

"Good." He broke into an easy run, still keeping his grip on Matthew's arm, and Joanna ran with them. But something twisted inside of her. Nora hadn't gone to the mainland, after all. She'd taken things into her own hands. To Joanna, the big white house seemed hung with tragedy, as if death had already come into it. It had looked like that, the night Alec was drowned.

"How long since it happened?" Dennis asked Matthew.

"It was around dinner time she did it, but she said it was all right, it hadn't hurt her or nothin'. And I believed her." His face contorted. "Mebbe if I'd come for you then—"

"You can't be blamed!"

"I was sort of worried, but she kept on smilin'. . . . It wasn't till she collapsed that I see how bad it was. I come out on the porch and I saw you. Like it was meant to be."

"Probably it *was* meant to be," said Dennis. "Now get hold of yourself, man. You can't help Nora by collapsing yourself. She's young and she's healthy, she's got plenty of chances."

They had reached the steps. Dennis had to help Matthew, the man seemed to be nerveless with terror. Gram awaited in the kitchen, looking smaller than ever, her eye-caverns immense.

"She's in there," she said sternly, her forefinger stabbing at the doorway into the living room. "In my bed. A fine mess she's made, for all her foolishness."

Joanna had a moment of pity to spare for the old lady, who had known in one brief instant both the realization of her hope for Matthew, and the cruel destruction of those hopes.

After that there was no time for pity. There was Nora, her eyes circled in blackness, her face so white it seemed already transparent, her chestnut hair dark and stringy with sweat around her forehead. She didn't speak, and her lips were pressed tightly together; lips so pale that it seemed as if they had been drained of blood. If Matthew was terrified, and Gram was gazing bleakly at ruin, Nora was something else. Whatever she had done to bring this on, she was paying for it now; her face was rigid, as if she were willing herself to show nothing.

Dennis did what he could with the materials at hand. For Joanna, it seemed as if the next few minutes were incredibly long; when she looked at the clock, and saw that only fifteen minutes had passed, she was amazed. The brilliant day outside, the ethereal light across the apple blossoms, the cuckoo's wings—they had all been relegated suddenly to the distant past. The present was made up of silent hurry and a man's voiceless fear; and it was the color of blood.

Gram stayed strictly out of the way. Perhaps, at last, her old legs were tottery. Matthew wandered around the rooms, his face twisting when he looked at Nora, and then lined with anxious hope when he looked at Dennis. Dennis gave him a quick smile sometimes, but he worked silently. Joanna found herself watching his hands again; they drew her as inexorably as a fine pianist's hands draw the listener who is lifted beyond himself by the music.

At last it was over, they could take a long breath, and some of the fear died out of Matthew's face. But Nora, lying in a clean bed whose sheets seemed no whiter than her skin, looked the same. She started at the ceiling, her eyes unmoving, her lips a taut line. Joanna and Dennis, who had gone out into the kitchen to wash up, and to set some coffee going, came back into the room and saw Matthew standing beside the bed. He glanced at them miserably.

"You sure she's all right? She won't speak to me."

"Of course she's all right." Dennis touched Matthew's shoulder briefly. "She doesn't feel any too good, that's all."

He moved a chair beside the bed, and sat down. He had been deft and impersonal as he worked over Nora, his face drawn and almost mask-like in its absorption. Now he was smiling faintly, his eyes tired and very kind. He put his hand on Nora's forehead.

"Are you feeling better now, Nora?" he asked her gently, and she began to cry. Abundantly and without effort the tears welled out and ran from the outer corners of her eyes to the pillow. Her mouth was shaking and she stared up at Dennis with mute pleading. Matthew made a small agonized sound and started forward, but Joanna stopped him. Her lips shaped the word, *No*. In a moment now Nora would talk, and Matthew wasn't going to like what he heard. But it was his household, and it was time he set it in order.

"I want to know," whispered Nora, "if I can still have a baby."

"No reason why you can't have a dozen, if it's all right with Matthew. But you'd better stay away from the stairs."

Matthew gave Joanna a watery smile, and she smiled back, but inwardly she was not sure what to think. Perhaps Nora was going to cover up as best she could; Joanna couldn't blame her for that. "I thought —" Nora swallowed hard. "I thought it was a judgment on me for not wanting the baby. I didn't, at first."

"A great many girls feel that way at first. That wasn't any crime, Nora."

"But you don't *know* why I didn't want it!" Her voice rose in faint, frantic protest. "I thought it would be Gram's baby, not mine! And I was going to do something, and not have it."

She turned her face away and put her hands up to cover it. "I'm so ashamed," she whispered.

"Nora, honey," Matthew said hoarsely, but Joanna put her hand on his arm and wouldn't let him go. Nora would talk to Dennis as she would talk to no one else.

Dennis said quietly, "But after a while you wanted the baby, didn't you? What changed your mind?"

"It was the day Jamie was lost. I kept thinking how it would be for Joanna and Nils if anything happened to the baby, and then I thought about Nils, and about Matthew . . . how much Jamie meant to Nils, and how much *our* baby would mean to Matthew." She took her hands away from her face and looked up at Dennis with a desperate honesty. "Then all of a sudden, I knew that if I — had anything done — it would be killing Matthew's baby. And then I knew I couldn't do it, even if Gram *was* still around."

Dennis nodded. "What happened today, Nora?"

"I was feeling so darned *good* — " her smile was shaky, but real — "because I was beginning to be happy about the baby, and I hadn't been sick for a couple of days, so I had to be smart and run up the stairs. But when I started to run down, I — I caught my heel, or something."

She was ready to cry again. "And I've made an awful mess for everybody, and I've lost my baby, just when I wanted him."

"Don't forget that dozen or more you're going to have." He held her wrist in his fingers for a moment, and looked at his watch. "Well, can you sleep now?"

"Yes." It was the slightest whisper of sound. Joanna began to pull down the shades, Dennis moved the chair away from the bed.

"Doc," Matthew whispered harshly. "Can I speak to her for just a minute?"

"Five minutes if you want to. We'll go out."

"I don't care if you hear. I guess I been pretty dumb." He looked at both Dennis and Joanna in sheepish apology. "I never knew just how it was with Nora — about Gram, I mean. The poor kid, I — "

"You're all right, Matthew. Don't start worrying now, when everything's going to clear up." Dennis nodded toward the bed. "You'd better talk to her before she falls asleep."

"Sure." He cleared his throat and went cautiously across the darkened room. Just outside the door Joanna stopped.

"I'm going to listen," she said shamelessly. "I've been worried about Nora for a long time."

"We'll both listen." They waited by the unlatched door, standing close together in a silence made eloquent by the shared battle of the last half-hour.

"Nora, honey," Matthew murmured. "Look, darlin', when you have that baby, Gram can go away. She's got that cousin over in Liberty. Or she can go away *now,* if you want."

Nora's voice was faint, tenuous as a dream. "Not now, Matthew. She'd just die if she thought you didn't need her any more. Maybe after we have the baby she'll want to go, she'll know that we're all right."

Joanna turned her head and smiled at Dennis. "Nora's grown up overnight."

"She's a game kid. You won't have to worry about her any more."

They moved away from the door, toward the kitchen where the coffee was bubbling with a self-important, cheerful sound. "Is there anybody on the Island that you *don't* worry about?"

"My brothers call it minding everybody else's business," she explained candidly. "But I guess I take after my father. He fussed about all the Islanders as if they were kin to him."

"Well, all you Islanders *are* kin to each other," he said seriously. "Because of the Island."

She met his eyes without glancing away; her lids were heavy with fatigue, she looked at him through her thick Bennett lashes. "Then you and I are kin, because you're an Islander now—aren't you?"

There was a sort of inner gleam that came sometimes instead of a smile. "How about some coffee? We'll drink a toast to each other and the occasion."

So swiftly she couldn't have drawn away, he put his arm through hers.

20

THERE WAS NO SIGN OF OWEN or of the dog in the house; the doors stood open to May. Joanna ran upstairs and found that Jamie wasn't in his crib, and his scuffed play shoes and overalls were gone too. Owen had taken him up and dressed him then, she thought with the little warm amusement she always felt whenever Owen attended to his small nephew. Probably Jamie was down in the fish house brandishing a hammer, and he'd have a new swear word in his vocabulary; but she was too tired to worry right now. She felt as if she'd like to sleep for hours. When her mind wound backward over the trail it had taken since she'd begun to work in the garden just after dinner, the cabbage plants seemed a hundred miles away.

When she went downstairs again, Owen was coming up by the well. Jamie roved ahead of him. Dick sniffed expectantly at the well-curb and Owen shouted at him to come away.

He was grinning when he came in, and she remembered, as if it were a fragment of a dream, the black rage that had been consuming him when she had gone out.

"I've been down callin' up," he said. "Mother's fine. She says Mateel's upset and Charles is all hawsed up, but things are calmin' down." He dropped into a chair, fishing for his cigarettes. Joanna looked at him blankly. It came to her with a shock that she'd forgotten about Young Charles. Guiltily she glanced at herself in the mirror over the sink. Her cheeks were flushed with tiredness, the same tiredness that made her eyes look veiled, half-mysterious, but fortunately she didn't appear as blank as she'd felt for a moment.

Owen was lighting a cigarette and Jamie waited, his rosy mouth pursed, his intent blue eyes holding twin reflections of the tiny flame. Owen lowered the match and Jamie blew it out, then trotted off through the sun parlor and out the back door.

"Well?" said Joanna. "How bad is it? How long has Young Charles been up to this business?"

"He never did anything but snitch the shells, to celebrate D-Day with. The other kids been raisin' hell around there for a year, but Young Charles never got in on it till just now." Owen took a long breath of smoke and expelled it slowly. "The Judge talked to him, and took a shine to him, I guess. Anyway, he's given him a chance. Put him in Charles' custody."

"Maybe Charles'll have sense enough to take him on the *Four Brothers* this summer. Philip would be willing, I know."

"Philip could get along with the devil himself, but those other two are too damn' much alike. Nope!" Owen shook his head. "They gowel hell out of each other, those two. Charles has got other plans for the kid."

"What are they?" Joanna stacked dishes in the dish pan.

"Perk up," said Owen, grinning. "He's bringin' him out to you. The White Man's Burden. You're supposed to have the iron hand in the velvet glove, or somethin'."

Joanna looked at him in dismay, dropping a handful of silver on the plates. "What are we going to do with a sixteen-year-old boy?"

"Oh, Charles is bringin' out a peapod for him, and he wants me to stake him to some traps. We keep him busy, and set a shinin' example."

Joanna gave him a glance of twinkling malice. "You're a fine one for that, I must say." She leaned against the sink, mentally rearranging beds. "When is he coming?"

"In a week or so. As soon as school's out, so he can bring Ellen at the same time. . . . You particularly happy about this? You feel able to wrastle with Young Charles, do ye?"

Joanna straightened her shoulders and returned his grin with composure. "Of course I do. It's a job, but I can do it. It's not going to be very handy for either us or the boy, but if his father wants him out here, out of the way —" She shrugged, and took the teakettle off the stove.

"What happened up at Fennells', anyway?" Owen said idly, after a moment.

"Oh, Nora fell downstairs and knocked herself out. Scared Matthew silly. But she's all right now."

The *Four Brothers* came as soon as Ellen's school was out. It was a crisp day, with a little north-west wind riffling the water and turning it as bright in the sun-glare as crumpled tinfoil. There was a cold edge to the air, but a fragrance, too, and over by Schoolhouse Cove the wild roses were opening, and the blue flag was appearing in the marsh, in stiff ranks of pale green, blade-like leaves and purple-blue flowers.

Joanna's emotions were a compound of dread and delight. Dread because Young Charles was coming, and yet she couldn't refuse to have him. But what were they going to do with him? There were no other boys his age, there were no amusements, and he was a high-spirited handful. . . . Delight because Ellen was coming, Ellen who would have grown a lot since last Christmas and whose blue-gray eyes were as undisturbed, as candid, and as quick to sparkle as her grandmother's eyes. Joanna was glad the Island looked at its best. The fields were full of flowers, daisies and buttercups growing intermingled so that they were shifting gold and silver when the wind blew.

She went down to the well, Jamie tagging along behind her, and just as she brought up the dripping pail from the cold, mossy darkness, the *Four Brothers* came in sight off the southern end of Brigport.

She rested the pail on the wellcurb and watched. Her two older brothers, Charles and Philip, had bought the seiner, and later the two younger brothers, Mark and Stephen, had joined the crew, and it was then they had named her the *Four Brothers*. Everybody along the coast knew her and the Bennett boys. If Owen had joined them, she would have been called *Five Brothers,* but Owen had been out discovering life on his own when the other four became a team. Now Mark and Stevie were in the Pacific, and two other men, not family, had taken their places; but the *Four Brothers* was a family boat, to Joanna, and there was the familiar tightening in her chest as she watched the boat come toward the harbor, cutting glassy, curving wings and leaving a wake that glittered.

Jamie was watching too. He pointed a plump, rigid forefinger. "A boat!" he cried.

She set the pail down and took Jamie's hand. "Come on," she said, suddenly as excited as he was. "We'll go meet them!"

Charles, over forty now, had gray at his temples and a glisten like frost over his black hair. But like his father before him, he had kept his strong, agile spareness. His face had settled into a lean and determined cast. As the boat slid alongside the old wharf, he looked up at Joanna and grinned, and for a moment he showed the vivid Bennett charm that had combined with his natural talent and ambition to get him most of the things he'd wanted out of life. But when he was not smiling, he seemed grim, with a cut to his mouth and a narrowness to his eyes that his father never had. This business about Young Charles would have gone hard with him, Joanna thought.

Philip came between Charles and Owen in age. He was one of the quiet Bennetts. When they came up on the wharf, it was to Philip that Joanna went first, realizing as she put her arms around him how *nice* he was. He smiled at her from blue-gray eyes like his mother's and Ellen's, and hugged her.

"You're almost handsome, Phil," said Joanna. "Why doesn't some woman grab you up?"

"Because every time a female looks at him he hides behind a damn' spruce tree," said Charles. "Hey, can't you kids get your gear out of there?"

Ellen emerged from the fo'castle and waved at Joanna. "Hi, Mother. I was combing my hair, so I'd look neat when you saw me!"

She climbed nimbly up on the washboards and then on to the wharf, and hugged Joanna with all her wiry young strength. Ellen was twelve, and tall like both her parents, but her movements had the half-awkward, half-graceful, lankiness of her father. Her hair had darkened to a pale soft brown, and lay on her shoulders, smooth and shining and straight. Her profile, as she turned away from Joanna to gaze happily around her, was delicate and strong at once, a hint of maturity in the firm cut of her mouth; yet her forehead had the wide innocence of childhood.

"Looks as if the bait house'd blow down in a good gale," remarked Charles.

"I think it looks beautiful just the way it is," said Ellen passionately. "I think everything looks beautiful."

"Even the smell, huh?" That was Young Charles, who had thrown his bags out into the cockpit and now appeared behind them.

"You'll get used to the smell of bait after you've been baitin' up all summer, son," said Charles dryly. "Throw that gear up here, and speak to your aunt."

"Hello, Charles." Joanna spoke casually to the boy, smiling, and he grinned back. He was a handsome boy, not as tall as his father and Philip, but strongly, compactly built, light on his feet, with thick bronze curls and a foreign, velvety texture to his glance, an almost liquid quality. But when he laughed, he was pure Bennett. It was easy to see why he was a worry to his parents, but it was also easy to forget the shame he had caused and to like him very much. He had possessed the same endearing make-up since babyhood.

Jamie stood by, looking at his uncles with somber blue eyes, and his lower lip was definitely anti-social. He stood with his hands behind his back, watching Young Charles toss the bags up to Philip, and his stomach was out as defiantly as his lip.

"Come on, Jamie!" Ellen went down on her knees to hug him and he accepted her homage imperturbably. With the children going on before, and Philip and Young Charles coming behind with the bags, Joanna and Charles walked up through the village to the house. It was dinner time, and no one was in sight. Sigurd didn't come out to hail Charles, Thea didn't call from her back door.

"Lord, it's empty around here," said Charles. "But it's still home."

"Why don't you move out here again?" Joanna asked him lightly.

"I might, at that." His face was somber. "What we've just been through—with that kid—" He shook his head. "I've got other boys growing up. And girls too. Young Donna's wearing lipstick now whenever she gets a chance and she's only fourteen. I'll be damned if I like what they learn on the mainland."

"I never could understand why Young Charles couldn't go with you, on the *Four Brothers.*" She watched Ellen and Jamie walking on ahead, Ellen straight and slender in her dark slacks and sweater, Jamie sturdy and square, but just as straight, in his corduroy overalls and jersey. *Nice children,* she thought. *But I work hard to make them nice and keep them that way. . . .*

"I'm not like Father," Charles was saying impatiently. "We strike sparks from each other. He gowels me and I know I gowel the hell out of him. Well, we've got the peapod on the stern, and he'll pick up the hang of things pretty soon. You can send him in on the mail boat when he gets too much for you, and you need a few days to breathe in."

It seemed definitely settled. She didn't mind that Charles had taken it for granted; he thought that she had the best place for Young Charles, and so he had brought the boy to her. With a gesture that had become an integral part of her, through the years, she hardened her shoulders under her blouse, tilted her chin a little higher, and accepted the responsibility.

She gave them all a mug-up when they reached the house, delaying dinner until Owen came in from hauling. Now she had four Bennett men at the table, and she was happy—as happy as she could be without Nils. When she stood at the stove taking out the vegetables, her back to the dining room, and listened to the deep Bennett voices, she made herself think, deliberately, that Nils was there, sitting in his own place, listening, smiling a little, his blue eyes moving from face to face. In a moment now there'd be a small spell of quiet and in it Nils would speak, his voice so easy, almost light, after her brothers' voices. But they would listen to him as they always did; for some reason they had never shouted Nils down, even when they didn't like what he was saying.

The break came, but Nils' voice didn't. Its absence was almost a shock. Then she said cheerfully to Ellen, "Take the mashed potatoes in, Ellen. I'll bring the lobster."

No, nothing could bring Nils back, not even her love when she lay alone in the dark and tried to evoke him. She could remember how he spoke, and remember his hand stroking her hair in the absent-minded way he had while he talked; but when she was sliding under the waves of sleep, lulled with the sense of his nearness, she might turn over and put out her arm, as if to put it over him, and the touch of the cool sheets, and the damning fact that he wasn't there, would plummet her into awareness. Then she must think with fierce concentration of the garden, of the canning she intended to do, the sewing to be done for the children, Owen's mending and the problems of rationing. . . .

But today she was lucky to have the boys here, at least, and she would make the most of it. Tonight she would write every bit of it to Nils, remembering their jokes and the way they chaffed each other, and she'd tell him that she wasn't really worried about handling Young Charles. If she told him that, he wouldn't worry either; he knew she was capable.

She sat down at the table. Owen and Charles were holding forth, in time-honored fashion.

"Good Lord, man, you can make more lobsterin' these days than you can at anything!" Owen scowled at Charles as if his older brother were slightly moronic. "Don't ask me if I want to go seinin'! I'd be pretty dumb to leave what I've got here."

"I don't know as I want ye, now that I got time to think about it," said Charles. "So stow it. Just answer me this—" He looked at Owen without a flicker of a smile on his dark face.

"What?" said Owen belligerently.

"Do you still get as drunk as a fiddler's bitch every Saturday night?"

"Drunker." Owen grinned, and winked at Joanna.

"Attractive conversation," she said. "Full of nice words for the small fry to pick up. And Ellen and I are ladies—or didn't you know?"

"I have to apologize for Charles, Jo," said Philip. "He's lived off aboard the boat so long he's forgotten how to behave. It's a wonder he isn't eatin' mashed potatoes with his knife."

"I never make excuses." Owen stated grandly.

In the late afternoon Charles and Philip left. Ellen and Young Charles had taken Jamie and had gone for a walk over toward Goose

Cove, Young Charles with Owen's .22 under his arm. Joanna and Owen went down to the shore with their brothers. The little wind had died down, and the day was bright and still, the stillness seemed not born of emptiness but of peace. The harbor gleamed a translucent, polished blue against the red rocks, and the boats lay at their moorings like white birds resting. On the fish house roofs, on the ledges, the gulls stood sleepily in the sun; only a few circled over the Island in wide arcs, their great wings balancing with lazy power. And everywhere there was the scent of lilacs.

Thea and Leonie sat on Sigurd's front piazza, sewing decorously, when the Bennetts walked by. Thea squealed, not so decorously; there were greetings, rather self-contained on the part of Charles and Philip, and Joanna introduced them to Leonie. Thea found it necessary to inquire for each member of Charles' family. Joanna, remembering the premeditated malice with which Thea had informed her of Young Charles' scrape, waited politely, her contempt for Thea leavened by her amusement at the way Thea avoided her eyes. She stood erectly by the corner of the porch, letting the mixture of voices go past her ears, and looked about her at the Island. . . . She saw, then, Dennis Garland; he was coming up the road from the Old Wharf.

She was totally unprepared for the sight of him, and for the odd quickening of her senses. She had not consciously thought of him all day, but now it was as if she saw him twice. He was coming toward her, walking briskly, the sun shining on his tanned face; but at the same time she saw him, very near herself, on the stile by the cemetery. There was that odd little jump in her breast again.

The voices around her, Thea's high-pitched gushing enthusiasm, her brothers' deep tones, seemed very far away. She watched Dennis Garland coming toward her. *I wonder how I look to him,* she thought without vanity. If he were in love with her, she did not feel vain about it, but had instead a rather hurting blend of compassion, curiosity, and tenderness. She remembered that once long ago Simon Bird had desired her, and only a few years ago a boy named Randy Fowler had been infatuated with her. She had loathed Simon, and Randy had annoyed her. She couldn't remember ever feeling about anyone as she felt now.

It's because Dennis is so fine, she thought. *I feel almost honored.* It was a daring idea, but true. And of course, because Dennis *was* fine, their friendship would never be endangered, it would always be firm and unspoiled.

He was almost up to them now, he caught her eye and the smile began in his. She knew a surge of pride, of excitement. He should meet her brothers; and they should meet *him*.

21

IT WAS A WONDERFUL strawberry year. They grew everywhere. Jamie could take a cup and wade through the tall grass beyond the garden, to put green berries in the cup and eat the ripe ones until his mouth and his jersies were stained bright red. On Sou-west Point the berries had always grown abundantly, and this year they spread in a fantastic, fragrant carpet over the treeless slopes. They ripened in the wind and fog and sunshine, and grew to a glistening crimson in the sheltering grass, hanging in rich clusters almost too beautiful to eat.

The annual pilgrimage to the Point began, but no matter how many people picked, or how long, there were always plenty of strawberries. This year there were more than plenty, with only four women to pick them and very little sugar for canning. Joanna had managed to save some sugar, and the men on the lobster smack, who brought out everybody's grocery orders, had been clever enough to find some syrup. She wanted, almost passionately, to make some jam, even if it were no more than two or three jars. Then, when Nils came home, he could have some of this year's strawberries.

She and Ellen and Jamie went several times to Sou-west Point; Owen took them when he went out to haul, and rowed them ashore in the furthermost cove. Joanna and Ellen picked, and talked, while Jamie and Dick roved around in the grass, and they ate their lunch at noon. Then, when Owen was on the way home, he came and picked them up.

But Joanna always liked to go alone at least once during the season; from childhood she had loved to go berrying alone, and that was when the Point seemed to belong solely to her, and she could enjoy, unencumbered, her familiar sense of oneness with the Island. Those who moved around her drew from her; and as generous as she was, there were those moments when she wanted to keep herself for herself. It was a gathering-together of her strength and resources, a refreshing of the ever-welling spring of her personality.

She awoke one morning early, before dawn, and as she lay there listening to the first tentative chirpings and twitterings from the woods, she knew that she wanted to go alone to the Point on this day. And the strawberries she picked today would make the jam for Nils.

As soon as she had decided, she could stay in bed no longer. She dressed quickly in the dim room, and only Dick knew she was up. He went downstairs with her, and she fed him. Then, while her coffee bubbled, she wrote a note to Ellen and put it at the girl's place. Ellen would look after Jamie and start dinner. Owen and Young Charles had already gone to haul. They started early these summer days.

The air was cool and pale, and her feet stirred elusive scents from the wet grass. The trailing blackberry vines were in blossom, white, dew-spangled stars of heavy, exotic sweetness, almost alien against the rocky slopes of Maine. She picked a blossom and put it in her hair, behind her ear, as she had done when she was a girl. Blackberry blossoms at sunrise were something wonderful. In the moonlight they were ghost flowers, and their perfume stabbed like a knife.

She followed the twisting path along the West Side, above the rocks. The sea made a little hushing sound; it brightened slowly as the sun lifted, and the gulls began to stir. The birds in the woods were fully awake now; the old spruces, lifting in saw-toothed silhouette against the clear, luminous pallor of the sky, echoed with the minor, persistent flutes of white-throats and phoebes, the forthrightness of the chickadees and nut-hatches, the impudent chatter of the warblers and the candid, bubbling tune of the song sparrows. A robin kept saying, "Giddy-ap, giddy-ap," at Joanna, until a crow, sighting her, drowned out all the other birds with his hoarse alarms.

Where the path descended into a cove, she stopped to watch two seals playing lazily among the ledges, and was pleased because they did not dive out of sight when she appeared. It was as if they knew her. With her feet wet with the dew, and the scent of ripe strawberries around her, and the gulls setting out on their morning business, and hardly a boat in sight, she could almost imagine that no one else lived on the Island at all. Not that she could do without Jamie and Ellen; but still, this richness of solitude —

Sou-west Point began to rise before her, the woods thinned out except for a few wind-twisted spruces, and she came across a patch of strawberries growing on a slope that plunged forthrightly toward the sea. She dropped to her knees and her hands separated the wet leaves, sought for and found the first cluster of plump bursting-ripe berries. They made a round, pleasant sound, dropping into the pan. At once she was very happy.

She cleaned out the patch, working upwards, and eventually reached the highest part of the Point; she stood on a long ridge, and could look out across the glistening sea to the east and south, or turn and look at the cloud-blue mountains and mainland in the north and west. A light salty wind blew against her body, cooling it under the light cotton dress. She lifted her hair from the back of her damp neck, loosened if from her scalp with her fingers. The ridge was the same, the sea was the same; Matinicus Rock rose out of the water as it had always done, and even the fact that there was a gun crew out there, and newly built radio towers, couldn't change the everlastingness of the Rock itself. It was the same with the Island. It had existed before Joanna had, it would exist long afterwards. In the life of the Island her life was only a sigh.

The thought lifted and exalted her. So many times she had stood here alone, on the austere heights of Sou-west Point, and felt her insignificance. Once it had hurt her, and she had fought against it, but now she accepted it and was glad. Was this a sign of maturity? She wondered.

She hoped she would be able to write a little of this to Nils. He loved the Point too, and he loved solitude. There were ways in which Nils was suffering, even if he hadn't yet been physically hurt; he had mentioned in one of his letters that there was always someone talking aboard ship, there was never absolute silence, never the sense of being alone. . . . Nils wouldn't let himself become obsessed with a need for silence, but how he must dream of the silences he had known, the long hours alone in his boat on familiar waters, the nights when Joanna's breathing, and the far-off sighing of the sea, only deepened the hush.

When she was tired and hungry, she sat contentedly on the dry, aromatic turf under twin spruces that grew in lonely silhouette on the seaward side of the ridge. She ate her sandwiches slowly, savoring them along with the smell and sight of the day; her eyes dreamed on the horizon, she tried to make it seem possible that three thousand miles beyond the Rock there was carnage and brutal clamor and destruction. It was hard to keep the truth in her mind, when her back was comfortable against a tree trunk, her lard pails were rounding over with berries, and there was an agreeable mixture of warmth and coolness playing over her as the sun fell through the branches of the spruces, and the little wind that always blew over the Ridge moved the boughs in a continual, gentle quivering.

The crows had long since stopped their hoarse worrying about her presence and had accepted her. The gulls went about their daily business, there was an industrious chirping from the thickets where the ground sparrows nested and raised their families. A few feet beyond Joanna the grassground ended abruptly in a bluff, and the land dropped steeply to the beach below. She could lie against her spruce tree and watch through her lashes the glimmer and sparkle and shifting diamond sheen of the water that crept quietly up the beach and slipped back, only to return and retreat again. The beach, small, deep, sloping, was a dazzling and unexpected break in the volcanic black rocks of the seaward shore line; the white pebbles fairly danced with light in the sunshine. Yet, if you were on the beach, the pebbles would not be white, but every pale, sea-polished color you might name.

Joanna's fingers closed peacefully around a bleached sea-urchin shell she had found near her in the grass. Sou-west Point was littered with them, where the gulls had had their daily feasts. This shell was almost perfect, it might have been fashioned of fine, thin white porcelain.

She came awake again as a peapod slipped into sight from among the big ledges off the very tip of Sou-west Point. It was Young Charles, of course. No one else fished from a peapod. He handled it well, sending it forward across the bright water with long, swift strokes. She watched him with pleasure. The paint of the peapod was still clean and white, his oilpants still maintained their brilliant yellow newness. The long visor of his duck-billed cap shadowed his face; but she could tell the shape of his shoulders under the blue shirt, and she could see his arms' ruddy brown, and almost for an instant or two—she could imagine it was Owen at sixteen, or Mark. All of her brothers had hauled their pots in these coves from a peapod at one time or another, and their father before them. It was good to have a boy on the Island again, a boy and a peapod.

She'd had misgivings about Young Charles; but in the two weeks since he'd come, most of the misgivings had gone. Under Owen's supervision, he'd taken to lobstering the way a Bennett should, he had a natural instinct for the right places to set his pots, and he was lucky besides. Owen said he was a good worker in the fish house, he didn't chafe at the necessary drudgery of patching pots and knitting heads, and he wasn't squeamish about plunging his hands into bait. And it was easy for Joanna to have him in the house. He was quick to fill the water pails or the woodbox, and he had a noisy, infectious good humor that didn't plunge suddenly into gloom, as the Bennett temper was prone to do.

The peapod shot swiftly forward across the cove, and she realized that he was coming ashore. For a moment she thought that he had seen her, and then remembered that it was next to impossible to see anyone sitting where she was, from down in the cove. *He's going to explore,* she thought in quick understanding. He'd finished his hauling, and he was going to wander around for a bit before he went home. She wondered what was in his mind as he shipped his oars and beached the peapod, and climbed over the side to haul the boat on, his boots splashing in the little line of surf. She and her brothers had always been imaginative; to them, the heights of Sou-west Point rising barrenly against the sky had been every citadel, every pirate-haunted or cannibal-inhabited island they had ever read about.

He was making the painter fast around an old spar that had been there for years. She put down the sea-urchin shell and moved forward cautiously to watch him. She wouldn't interrupt him—not she, who loved her own solitude so much, and she would be going home soon anyway, now that she'd eaten and rested. But she wanted to see how he stood and looked at the timbers that reached out of the shifting beach rocks like giant whitened ribs—and ribs they were, the ribs of some ship that had once been "an able handsome lady," like the *Lucy Foster* in the song. What dreams might a sixteen-year-old boy dream, when he was a blend of Bennett and Trudeau, and stood like this on a deserted beach, on an island where his father's and mother's people had lived before him?

She reached the edge of the bluff and looked down. He was half-running; and he went by the stark gleaming ruin of the ship, the stones rolling and clattering under his feet.

Thea was there to meet him. *Thea*. While Joanna had dreamed on the hillside above her, Thea had come along the wooded south side of the Island and out onto the beach. Joanna realized all this in the one incredulous moment before she saw her nephew take Thea into his arms. She went rigid and cold, and then her senses swung so close to the edge of actual nausea that sweat broke out icily in the palms of her hands, and she had to shut her eyes until the monstrous sickness passed by. When it had gone, she was furious. Her first impulse was to go down there, to descend upon them like a totally unexpected williwaw, to take Young Charles by the ear and send him back to his peapod with a well-aimed kick; and then she would get Thea by those *curls*, and she would shake her with her steely fingers and wrists until there was no starch left in Thea and she would drop on the beach as foolishly and flaccidly as the Raggedy Ann doll Ellen used to have.

But of course she wouldn't do it. There was the minute or so before she could get away, when she saw Thea take off the boy's cap and run her fingers through his curls; and the nausea came again, so close that the water ran in her mouth. She moved away from the edge, then, picking up her lard pails with a careful, automatic gesture, and went down over the other side of the ridge.

She saw nothing as she walked home, and her rage carried her along much faster than she had made the trip before. The day that had started in such shining peace was shattered. The sun was high, the sky without a shred of mist across the blue, and the drone of engines mingled with the wash of water around the rocks; the birds were in full swing. But if she heard them, she didn't know that she heard them.

She passed Barque Cove and cut through the woods behind the

clubhouse, thence across the lane and her own field. She didn't meet anyone, no one hailed her, and she was grateful. She saw with thanksgiving her waiting house, with delphinium a cool deep blue against the white, and the seven-sisters bush spilling out its fragile sweetness to meet her.

22

IT WAS DARK before she had a chance to speak to Young Charles and then she had to make the chance. He was in and out a dozen times, and always there was someone else there, or he was gone before she could get his attention. He was noisily exultant, teasing Ellen, carrying Jamie on his shoulder, wrestling with Dick; but then, he was always like that, especially when he'd had a good haul.

You had a good haul today, my lad, she thought grimly. She wasn't quite sure what she was going to say to him. Several times she was on the verge of telling Owen about it, but at the end of the day she hadn't said anything at all. Owen would rant and swear, he'd take the boy by the scruff of the neck, and he'd barge in on Thea and give her enough to talk about for the rest of her life. She'd be all outraged innocence, and Young Charles would be an abnormal child who'd made advances to her.

Joanna could imagine it all, seething, and by the time Owen had gone off through the mild evening down to Sigurd's, and Ellen had gone to bed, she had no longer any doubts as to how she would approach Young Charles. This was no time for doubt. The job must be done, it must be done tonight, and she must do it alone.

He had been out all evening, and by some peculiar coincidence there were no edges of light showing around Thea's shades. Thea hated to go to bed early; she sat up listening to the radio and drinking tea when Francis had been long in bed. But who knew if Francis was home tonight? He might have gone up to the Fennells' to play cribbage with Matthew, he might be down with Sigurd and Owen. And Young Charles was out, either wandering around in the mild, murmuring night, or—

He came in suddenly, so suddenly that she was startled, even though she had been waiting for him ever since Ellen had gone to bed. She looked up from her book and saw him standing in the kitchen doorway, beyond the rim of the Aladdin's sharp yellow light. His grin showed white, and he reached up and shoved back his cap. The gesture was so much Owen's that for an instant she felt confused, as if Time had played a trick on her.

"Hello," she said briefly, and he came forward into the light. There was a sheen of perspiration making bronze highlights across his brown forehead, and on the fine dark down on his upper lip. His cheekbones were red, as if he'd been in the wind.

"Hi, Aunt Jo." He gave her the grin again, and fidgeted around the room, his hands first in his pockets and then out of them. She watched him while she pretended to read. It wouldn't be hard at all to tell him she knew about Thea. The way was opening before her.

"Sit down, Charles," she invited him. He didn't answer, but went into the dark kitchen and glanced out toward the harbor. He stood there, motionless, for a long moment; she had the impression that he was watching for something in the darkness outside, something of his taut expectancy communicated itself to her. He was like a glossy young animal, waiting in a thicket.

"What ails you?" she said casually. He came back then, loosening the already-open neck of his shirt as if it were too tight.

"Aunt Jo—" He dropped down into a chair opposite her. "Aunt Jo, if anybody comes in here, say I've been here all evenin', will ye?"

"Why?" She smiled at him, but there was an instinctive tightening of her muscles. It was all so familiar, but she would never get hardened to it. He smiled back at her. It was a smile that could have charmed the birds out of the trees, but it didn't charm Joanna, who was used to rich and blazing smiles instead of straight answers.

"You know how boys are, Aunt Jo," he said winningly. "Lots of things there's no harm in, but—" He shrugged, and spread his hands deprecatingly. They were square brown hands that were never still.

There was a blaze and a sparkle in his eyes, fiery color along his cheek-bones as he talked on, vaguely but brightly, about the foolish little things the older people raised hell over. He was tremendously exhilarated; he might have been in the glorious, crest-of-the-wave stage of drunkenness in which she'd seen Owen so many times. Or he might have been in another sort of intoxication that she could also recognize. There was no liquor on his breath as he leaned toward her with a final, and very sure plea.

"You won't be sorry if you tell a little fib for me, Aunt Jo—"

"It's quite a big one, it seems to me. Who's going to raise hell about this, anyway? Are you afraid it'll get back to your father? But if it's so harmless—" She shrugged her shoulders, and laughed. "I can't understand what you're fussing about, Charles! Who is it that's supposed to think you've been here all evening?"

His eyes narrowed, as if he were trying to harden his face. He got up. "Forget it, Aunt Jo."

"Did Francis come in too soon?"

She was prepared either for sincere amazement—if he hadn't been in Thea's house—or for sudden, intense Bennett fury. Instead, he sat down again, and reached for a cigarette. She had the impression that his hand was trembling.

"How'd you know, Aunt Jo?"

"I was picking berries down on Sou-west Point this morning," she answered honestly. "I saw you when you came ashore."

"Does anybody else know?"

She shook her head, and a faint grin touched the boy's stiffened lips. "But Jesus, Aunt Jo, if my father ever finds out, he'll skin me alive. You ain't intendin' to tell him, are ye?"

"No, I won't tell him." She met the boy's eyes in all candor. "But Charles, it's only a matter of time before he finds it out for himself. Thea has a cousin in Pruitt's Harbor, you know. And nobody has any private life on Bennett's Island. Everybody'll be talking in a week."

He wiped his forehead with his arm. "God, it's a mess, ain't it? Francis did almost walk in on us tonight," he added frankly. "If I hadn't seen him comin' up from Sig's, I guess I'd have been a dead pigeon." His jaw tightened and a little bit of swagger came back. "Not that I'm scared of Franny. I could prob'ly knock him stiffer'n a maggot."

He got up again. "Well, I might as well hit the hay. Got a hard day tomorrow." He tried to say it with bravado, but standing there in the lamplight, he looked very young and subdued. He was not so much a man as he'd been thinking he was, and she felt a wave of indignant tenderness toward him; at the same time she had a strong desire to strangle Thea by her scrawny neck.

There was nothing more to say to Young Charles except a brief, "Good night." He was scared, badly scared; perhaps his escapade didn't seem so brave a thing now that it was out in the light, and there was the chance of his father's discovering it. He'd have a new idea to sleep on tonight, and perhaps that would do the trick. She could only wait and see.

The next few days went on as July days always went; she made jam from the berries she'd picked that morning, she weeded the garden, she walked over to Schoolhouse Cove with Nora Fennell and talked about babies while Jamie dug in the coarse white sand and threw stones into the water. Yet all the time, behind her eyes, there was the thought of Young Charles; and when he was near her, she watched him without him appearing to watch, trying to find some sign. But he looked at her without equivocation, and he seemed carefree enough. She didn't want to ask him, she didn't want to refer to the whole sickening business, and she began to wonder if she wouldn't be safe in assuming that he had broken off with Thea, that the thing had ended almost as soon as it had begun.

She relaxed then, feeling incredibly fortunate, and fonder than ever of the boy, because he had been so easy to handle. Much easier than her brothers had been; Owen in particular had been as stubborn as a yearling bull.

She went out into the barn one afternoon to look over the old furniture Nils' grandmother had stored before she went to the mainland. The barn was dusty-cool, slashed through with thin blades of sunlight in which the motes swirled goldenly. Joanna, in old slacks, moved around the stacked pieces, whistling faintly. She was contented, and had no reason to be. Gunnar had been right when he said work was the poor man's blessing. When there was always something to do, something you liked to do and knew at the same time that it was necessary and useful, you could be contented — after a fashion — even when your husband was in the Pacific. Nils' last letter had been one of the best, and besides, there was a growing possibility that the Japs might surprise the world by surrendering as soon as the Germans did. D-Day had happened over a month ago, and so the Nazis ought to be tiring pretty soon.

She whistled "Coming in on a Wing and a Prayer" and began to dig her way toward a little low chair that would do for Jamie. Scrub it and sandpaper it, and paint it blue—

"Aunt Jo, you out here?" Young Charles' voice had a hollow sound in the echoing spaces of the barn.

"Right here! Come and help me move this stuff, will you?"

He came, but not very quickly. She watched him move across the wide, cleared floor of the barn, a slim silhouette against the gold and green light beyond the open doors. His rubber boots seemed to be dragging at him, his shoulders drooped.

"Jamie said you were here. . . . What do you want me to do?"

She was shocked, but managed not to show it. His face was gray where there had been rich color, and when he reached out to move a table, his fingers clamped on the edge as if he were holding onto life itself.

"What is it?" She had to speak then. "Are you sick, Charles?"

"No, I'm not sick." His eyes clung to hers desperately. "Aunt Jo, did you ever do anything and think it was pretty good, and then afterwards you just about turned inside out with thinking what a goddam fool you made of yourself? You feel like pukin', and you almost wish you could die—so you could get rid of thinkin'."

"I know all about that," she agreed. "It's probably the worst feeling in the world. I guess everybody has it, at one time or another."

"It's bad enough when it's just yourself you've got to think about," said Young Charles. "But when somebody else won't leave you be— Aunt Jo, I hate like hell to bother you with this. But I don't know what to do!" His voice cracked, but it was tragic rather than ludicrous. "I knew right off, the other night, that I had to haul myself clip 'n clean right out of this. I'd been thinkin' proud of myself till you told me I wasn't such a hell of a guy. But—" He stopped to swallow hard, and to reach with nervous, jerking fingers for his cigarettes. "I thought if I just didn't go near her again it would be all right. But she come after me. Just now, when I was haulin' my peapod on!"

"Then what?" Joanna asked calmly.

"She asked me when I was comin' up again. She said Franny

was going to the Main in the lobster smack when it come. I guess I didn't put it very good, but anyhow, I got around it—I said I couldn't come up again."

"And she was mad," said Joanna, outwardly tranquil, inwardly knowing how Thea's face could turn into a vixen's mask, slit-eyed, the lips drawn back from the teeth.

"Sure she was mad." He wiped his face. "Like to turned my stomach, the way she looked. And then she said she—she liked me." He was dark red with embarrassment, looking away from Joanna. "I can't tell you how she said it. But anyway, she said that after Franny I was—well, anyway, she said I had to come up again." He was talking too rapidly now, trying to spill it all out while he had the courage. "She said she knew I was scared of my father, and if I didn't come, she'd fix it up so he'd find out. Only he'd think I'd been chasin' her around and botherin' her." His eyes came back to Joanna's, wide and liquidly dark, all black pupil like a frightened animal's. "She even said she'd tell him I come after her while she was pickin' strawberries, and—well, you know."

"I know," said Joanna softly. It was all she could trust herself to say. She took hold of the other side of the heavy table; together they moved it aside, and she brought out the little chair.

"I'll paint this up for Jamie," she said as pleasantly as if there had been nothing else said. "I think it used to be Nils'."

"I'll take it in for you." He lifted the chair and they walked across the barn into the sunshine and the warm breeze and the color of the afternoon. The air was brilliant, flecked first with coolness and then with warmth, the sky beyond the spruces held the blue of turquoise, dappled with tiny puffs of white clouds. The scent of grass and of flowers was everywhere, but the sea dominated it all, even here where there was no glimpse of the sea. The sound of the combers rolling up on the back side of the Island, the smell of rockweed and of salt— there was no escaping them, there would never be any escape from them.

Jamie ran across to meet them. "Is that for me?" he shouted, pointing at the chair.

"That's for you," said his cousin, managing a smile. They went into the house, Jamie leading the way. Ellen wasn't home, and Owen was down to the shore. Joanna dusted off the chair, since Jamie was determined to sit in it. While she started supper, Young Charles sat behind her on the woodbox; his unnatural silence conveyed his forlorn depression. She worked for a few minutes without speaking, wanting to reassure him and yet not quite sure how to proceed. "Your father's known Thea for a good many years, Charles," she said at last. "I don't think she'd be able to put much over on him, or on any of us."

"But I'd have to tell him what I been up to!" the boy protested. "And you don't know how he is. It wouldn't do any good if I told him I knew I'd been a proper damn' fool, he'd still give me hell."

"I think the best thing for you to do is to keep on working. Thea's a lot of noise and brag, but that's all she amounts to. She'd never dare to go to your father."

Young Charles argued with her miserably, and Joanna herself didn't believe what she was saying. Thea was capable of almost anything. She'd had her hands on Young Charles once, and if she lost him she'd be beside herself with fury and disappointment. The result might well prove to be one of the biggest hell-brews ever stirred up on Bennett's Island.

But still, she talked down the boy's doubts with a fine, brisk air of self-confidence, wishing all the while that Nils was here. Nils would know what to do. "It'll be all right, Charles. Now how about going out and splitting up a lot of nice fine kindling, enough for tonight and tomorrow morning? And I need plenty of chips if we're going to have biscuits for supper."

He gave her a feeble grin and went out the back way. Jamie deserted his new chair and tagged along behind him.

Alone, Joanna began to mix up her biscuits. She looked down toward the harbor, a glory of burnished silver now that the sun was sliding toward the west.

23

THE HOUSE WAS QUIET. She sifted flour, measured out sour milk, her strong hands moving swiftly and automatically. How brave a rooster Young Charles had been a few days ago, she thought with a blend of regret and humor. Now his comb was crumpled, his fine tail-feathers bedraggled, he wanted the safe enclosure of the yard and the familiar hands throwing corn, and shutting him in at night. Oh, once this was over he'd be strutting as finely as ever, and crowing the way young roosters crow when they discover their voices. But at the moment . . . At the moment she wasn't too angry with Thea; Thea was an incident, a milestone in the boy's growing-up, and if you considered her impersonally, you weren't as icily furious as you'd been a few days ago. If the thing were nipped in the bud now, it couldn't harm Young Charles, any more than Leah Foster had harmed Owen.

Leah Foster's name came suddenly into Joanna's mind, and she saw it with an actual sense of shock. Why, she'd *forgotten* Leah; she'd forgotten her for years and years, and once she'd thought she could never forget that pale, bland face, topped by the silken-smooth hair; the small, secretive smile, the meticulously shod feet, the smell of starched cleanliness and lavender. Because of her tidiness, Leah had been all the more horrible — for Joanna, at least. She had been more monstrous than the whores who'd walked openly on any street in any land.

Joanna hadn't been much older than Young Charles when she found out what Leah Foster really was. From the harbor window she could look down now and see the Binnacle, the house where the Fosters had lived; Leah and her husband, who looked as if he had been carved from a piece of gray driftwood. Not a man at whom you'd glance twice, Ned Foster. He came and went on the Island's horizons as silently as a shadow, as soundlessly as the cuckoo flying through the shade beyond the orchard. But not so Leah. Leah was quiet too, but not like a shadow. The boys knew her; the Trudeau boys, and Hugo Bennett and Owen. . . . They'd all carried water home from the well for her. When Joanna was certain of Owen, she had been sickened, she had seen Leah as a fat spider in a silken web. Now she knew her picture had been a trite one, and she could even feel a certain pity for the middle-aged woman who had tried to draw some sort of vitality from the boys' rich youth.

But she had stopped whatever there was between Owen and Leah Foster. She had been afraid of it, and so, with a calm courage born of her nineteen-year-old desperation, she had stopped it, in such a way that no one but Leah ever knew. It had ended almost as soon as it began, before it had a chance to start a fester in Owen that would have tainted his whole life. She had never regretted what she had done. She was as sure today that she had done right, as she was sure then. She had gone to Leah—

Gone to Leah. Funny, the similarity in names . . . Leah, Thea. She had gone to Leah, and had ended it. . . . Young Charles came in, he kindled the fire without speaking; when the flames were snapping, he went out again. Her hands still worked, but inside of her everything had come to a stop, on the threshold of a new idea. The house was quiet, there was a moment of quietness all around her, as if for an instant the world was holding its breath.

She found herself cutting biscuits, placing them delicately in the pan. She adjusted the dampers in the stove. The oven wasn't hot enough yet, the biscuits would have to wait for a moment. Just long enough for her to cross the yard.

Thea was getting supper. Her kitchen blazed with late sunlight, it winked from the rounded surfaces of the teakettle, kindled little fires in the lamp-chimneys on the shelf. Everything sparkled; good housekeeping was as much a part of Thea's heredity as the dangerous streak of Old Gunnar she had showed the boy. Of course it wasn't all Old Gunnar, there was something there that was pure essence of Thea, as she had always been and always would be.

Since Franny had gone to the mainland on the lobster smack, supper consisted apparently of tea and a sandwich. "Hi, Jo," Thea said listlessly. Her face was blotched, and her eyelids swollen so thickly that it changed her whole appearance. "God, I'm a mess. I got an awful cold. Or hay fever, maybe." She sniffed hard, as if to convince Joanna of the truth. "Sit down." She waved at a chair, her hand seeming scrawnier and more claw-like than ever, but Joanna shook her head.

"I've only got a minute. Go on with your tea. You look as if you need it." She made herself sound briskly sympathetic. Thea must have been crying all day — ever since she'd approached Young Charles on the beach. She looked old and ugly, there was no resilience to her.

She took a swallow of strong tea, and then looked at Joanna with a sharpening glance. "Did you come in for somethin' special, Jo?"

"Well, yes, it is something special," Joanna said slowly. "Maybe you know what it is. You couldn't expect it to stay in the dark forever. . . . It's about my nephew, Young Charles."

The cup clattered into the saucer as if Thea's wrist had suddenly given out. Tea slopped brownly onto the table cloth. Thea stared at Joanna, her eyes hard and shiny. "What do you mean? What's he done?"

"You know what he's done, don't you?" Joanna asked her with a curious remote gentleness. "And what you've done? We don't have to say anything more than this about it, Thea. Just don't speak to him again, and it'll all clear up."

The vixen's mask was there now, all the uglier because of the thickened eyelids, and blotchy cheeks. Thea got up and moved around behind her chair, gripping it until the knuckles shone white.

"I'd like to know what in God's name you're drivin' at. It sounds pretty nasty to me."

"It is nasty," Joanna agreed. "And I think you ought to know that Young Charles didn't tell me until I asked him. I have eyes in my head, you know. And what I can see, others will be seeing after awhile. So, don't you think it would be wise not to speak to him again?"

Thinned lips, pulled back, didn't scare her, or slitted eyes. She thought impersonally, *The woman's half-insane. Of course she hates me for this. . . . And she's not much the way Leah Foster was. . . .* She'd been terrified at Leah's manner when she'd told her to leave Owen alone. The woman's poise had been inhuman, to the nineteen-year-old girl who'd been as raw and as fiery as a colt. But she wasn't terrified now. It was like getting the witch grass out of the garden, a tiresome job that had to be done.

"Thea, I thought you'd be glad to pull out of it, before the talk started. You should know Charles well enough not to take any chances on having him drag the truth out of Young Charles. He wouldn't hesitate to go to court, and *you* know how much chance you'd stand there!" She added as a quiet reminder, "Young Charles is a minor, you know."

"You got no call to be stickin' your nose in my business, Joanna Bennett!" Thea said viciously. "You're as deep in the mud as I'm in the mire, any day!"

Joanna said distantly, "If you're wise, Thea—" She moved toward the door. Thea's voice flung after her, as crudely shocking as a slap across the face.

"You want to get out before I turn the tables on ye, don't ye? I notice you ain't so good at standin' around lookin' stuck on yourself when it's your turn to listen!"

"Explain that, will you?" Joanna said, without lifting her voice.

"I don't have to do any explainin'! You know better'n I do what you been up to—only I know enough to stir up the biggest stink *you* ever smelled!" She straightened herself, her cheeks flushed purple under the blotches, and her smile was a sort of crooked leer that sickened Joanna.

"There's a lot of folks wouldn't take it too kindly," Thea went on, "with my cousin out fightin' and maybe dyin', and you carryin' on the way you are. I wonder how Nils would like it, if anybody was to drop him a line—"

"Like what?" Joanna felt sick—sick at the sight of Thea, but she wasn't afraid. The woman was raving, that was all. Face her down, and she'd crumble. "Like what, Thea?"

"Like Garland sittin' in his chair, and maybe layin' in his bed!"

She wasn't expecting it, and so it was like a blow in the stomach.

And yet, curiously enough, she wasn't too amazed. It was just the sort of thing Thea would throw at her, like a hoodlum throwing manure. It was just the sort of thing Thea would *think*, because her mind couldn't function in any other terms.

This filth can't hurt Dennis or me, she told herself, and the fact spread coolingly over her rage and disgust. She looked back at Thea as if from a great distance. "You're babbling, Thea. You'll make yourself sick."

"Babble! I'll show you how I can babble!" Thea was choking on her own violence. "I *thought* somethin' was goin' on, you and Garland bein' such close pals. But you bein' so much of a *lady*, and always bein' too good for the rest of us bastards, and him supposed to be so much of a *gentleman*—but I found out what I wanted to know, the day Jamie was lost. You're nuts about him and his fine ways, and no man'll turn down what's offered him so free and clear!"

Joanna slid quietly through the door and shut it behind her. She waited for a moment in the shed, holding the knob, and heard a savage crash of china that meant Thea had thrown her cup against the wall. Then she went home.

When she reached her own doorstep she was trembling. She felt as if she would never be able to shut out the sound of that voice and the words it had hurled at her. And she knew too that she hadn't straightened things out so well, after all. For Young Charles, yes. She doubted that Thea would ever trouble him again. But if she had ever wanted to strike back at Joanna, she had done a complete and devastating job, without actually knowing it.

There was a ghastly humor in the situation. But laughter was an unknown element in Joanna's world at the moment.

24

IT WAS RIDICULOUS. It was the most ridiculous thing she had ever heard of. She should have been able to discount it for what it was worth; yet—what was it worth? She thought she had crossed it off, eradicated it as Thea's perverted mouthings, by the time she went to bed that night. But when she had propped herself up in bed, writing tablet on her knees, the yellow lamp flame flickering gently in the night breeze that stirred the curtains, Jamie's breathing soft and even from his crib, Dick sighing in his sleep—when she was all ready to write to Nils, she found herself unable to write. She leaned back and stared at the velvety dark square of the window with eyes that were as dark, trying to form words in her mind. The strawberries, the jam she'd made and put away for him, Jamie's new words, the lobstering, the news from Pruitt's Harbor—there were all these things but they were nothing, they could be encompassed in a few lines. She realized then how much of Dennis there had been in her letters. He was news, he made news, Nils always asked about him and was interested in his progress as lobster-buyer, and besides, her consciousness had never been clouded as far as Dennis was concerned; she had known no reason why she shouldn't write about him as freely and frankly as she wrote about anyone else.

Then why this reluctance tonight? She looked at her competent fingers holding the pen, and drew her peaked black brows together as if the fingers were responsible, as if they were holding back the phrases. *There is absolutely no reason for this,* she told herself in clear, cold, silent words. *If he is in love with me, we've both decided to ignore it, in the interest of our friendship.* It was rather a fine sentence, and she was proud of it. She contemplated it with some satisfaction. Why, already she'd half-forgotten that instant in the orchard, she rarely remembered that he considered her as anything but a friend; and to say that *she* was in love with *him*—all her hard-won serenity suddenly deserted her, she was aware of a wash of heat rising over her body, so that the room was stifling.

The day Jamie was lost. She heard Thea's voice, the indescribable venom of it; and at the same time saw Thea standing in the doorway of the sun parlor. She smelled the clean-laundered scent of Dennis' shirt and remembered its coolness against her hot cheeks, and the hardness of his shoulder against her, blessedly hard for her to press her forehead against; she remembered the relief of her crying. And then Thea had been standing in the doorway. *She must have seen more than I realized,* Joanna thought dully. But if Owen had been there, she would have been grateful for his shoulder as well, if she couldn't have Nils. But Thea would never think of that. Thea went by what Thea did.

I'm not in love with Dennis, said Joanna, and the wave of heat came again, burning and infuriating. *How could I be? Women like me don't fall in love with other men when their husbands are gone!*

One thing was certain, Thea had begun to make life difficult for her. She had nothing to feel self-conscious about, but it wasn't pleasant to think Thea was watching her every move. If she, Joanna, weren't a strong-minded person, the memory of Thea's remarks would cast a shadow over her association with Dennis. But she didn't intend to let anything or anyone taint something that had become so valuable to her. Not if she could help it.

She wrote the letter to Nils eventually, but Dennis wasn't in it; she was beginning to wonder if she weren't going into too much detail about him. She filled up the pages with descriptions of the Island, July, and local gossip, and went to sleep secure in the knowledge that to ignore Thea was the right course.

In the morning, she was setting the kitchen to rights after breakfast when she saw Dennis coming up the path from the shore. She felt a sudden and hitherto unknown confusion, and a swift onrush of fury against Thea who had caused this to happen, and then she went upstairs quickly. She was making beds when Ellen called to her innocently.

"Mother, Dennis is coming! Do you want me to make some more coffee?"

Joanna pounded a pillow into new fluffiness before she answered. Then she called back calmly, "No, never mind. He probably won't stay but a minute!" She wanted to wait quietly, and hear him come in, but instead she snapped sheets with great vigor, pulled out the blankets and made new mitered corners, and was deeply absorbed when Ellen hailed her again.

"Mother, have you got any mail? Dennis is going to Brigport with Sigurd—"

Joanna went to the head of the stairs then. "Hello, Dennis!" she called down to him cheerfully. "Thanks for asking. There's a letter for Nils—it's on the sideboard, Ellen."

He answered from the dining room, and for an instant she felt as if she had never heard his voice before, its deepness and ease, its own particular timbre. "Good morning, Joanna! Do you want to go over with us? It's a superb morning for a sail—"

"I wish I could," she said with convincing regret, talking to the picture of the Infant Samuel that hung where the stairs turned. "But I'm as busy as a three-legged cat with fleas!"

"A pretty way to describe yourself, I must say. . . . Well, what about this child of yours?"

"She can go if she wants to. Ellen, take a dollar from my pocket-book and see if they have any candy in the store."

"O.K.!" said Ellen rapturously.

There were sounds downstairs, of Ellen's quick feet; and the ghostly fragrance of Dennis' pipe floated up the stairs to Joanna. *This is silly,* she said to herself. But she could not go down there, any more than she could write about him to Nils last night.

"You won't reconsider?" Dennis' voice came after a moment, and she felt her heart jump. But of course he wasn't reading her mind. She answered him almost gaily.

"Don't tempt me, please. I'm a busy woman."

"Far be it from me to lead you from the path of virtue, then. Ready, Ellen?"

"Ready!" Ellen was in seventh heaven, Joanna could visualize the shine in the blue-gray eyes, and the unselfconscious happiness that is possible at twelve. She felt a pang of sadness as she went back to her work. She would have liked to have gone. It had been a long time since she'd been out in one of the boats. But because of Thea there was this new barrier. It was true, she didn't intend to let Thea spoil anything. But today was too soon, the ugly words were too fresh in her mind.

The dance was Young Charles' and Ellen's idea. They had disappeared on a walk one afternoon, with Owen's .22, and had come back at supper time to admit, unabashed, that they'd climbed through a window into the clubhouse and had banged on the old piano, and played the old records. Everything was just standing there going to waste, Young Charles pleaded eloquently. Here it was July, and in a week or so there'd be a full moon — perfect night-sailing weather for a crowd to come over from Brigport. Ellen chimed in with unexpected fervor; her cousin had been teaching her how to waltz, *why couldn't they have a dance?*

Owen shrugged and looked at Joanna. Sigurd, Thea, and themselves were the only club-members left on the Island. "If people that are so damn keen on dancin' feel like washin' lamp chimneys and cleanin' the dance floor, I s'pose we can do somethin' about it," he said gruffly but with humor in his eyes.

It turned out to be a gala affair after all. Sigurd volunteered to play his accordion for some square dances, and when the notice was posted at Brigport, one of the Pierces said he'd bring his fiddle, since they didn't have a fiddler on Bennett's any more. Young Charles ordered some new records to come out on the lobster smack. The preparations went on and caused a pleasant stir in Island life. Joanna had a moment when she was stung with homesickness for the days gone by, when her brothers were all home, and a dance was something more than a dance; it could stand for almost anything, especially on a moonlit night in July.

And the fiddler of Bennett's Island had been Alec Douglass. But that was a long time ago, and life was as worth living now as it had been then. She would not willingly give up the present to have the past again.

Just before supper on the great night, Young Charles and Ellen begged her and Owen to come up and see how they had cleaned the clubhouse. It had been a perfect day, it promised to be a perfect evening. In fact, the perfection was almost too much; in a few days there would be rain and wind. There was always a price to pay for such effortless warmth, for such a richness of color and purity of outlines, for the exquisite clarity of air that seemed to edge every spruce spill with gold-tinged light, and strike through every bird-song with an added, more poignant sweetness.

They walked up through the lane, cool and shaded now that the sun was behind the trees, and the scent of late wild roses was around them, and the robins were making their liquid-throated evening songs from the big spruces that stood over the clubhouse. Jamie and Dick went on ahead, Ellen walked beside Joanna; she stood as high as her mother's shoulder now. Young Charles and Owen came behind, talking shop.

"Mother," Ellen murmured, with a quick glance backward at her cousin. "Guess! Dennis asked me for the first waltz! I wish it could be Nils, but if it can't be, I'm glad it's Dennis." She didn't require any comment. "I don't want Young Charles to know, he'll plague me. He says I've got a crush on Dennis. Mother—" She tilted her head, her young brow creased anxiously.

"Mother, can't you just *like* somebody without having a crush on them?"

Joanna looked steadily into the worried eyes. "Of course you can. Only cousins and brothers who want to tease say things like that . . . or trouble-makers."

Ellen's frown smoothed out and she hugged her mother's arm happily. At the same time something smoothed out in Joanna. Her own words, made simple and short for a child, had placed the facts concisely for herself. Almost at once she felt a lightness come over her, she was looking forward to the dance for the first time.

In the clubhouse she admired the lamp chimneys that Ellen had washed and polished, listened to Charles' new records, and praised him for the way he'd cleaned the expanse of hardwood dance floor. Owen looked at everything with a hypercritical eye, while his niece and nephew waited in badly controlled impatience for his words.

"Looks all right," he said at last, one eyebrow lifted fiercely. "The talkin' machine's got enough dust on it to plant a garden in, and you swept all the dirt into the corners, but a man gallopin' by pukin' wouldn't notice it."

"Oh, *Owen!*" Ellen burst out, turning red.

Young Charles gave him a Bennett scowl. "You know what you're full of, don't ye?" he said belligerently.

Owen grinned suddenly. "It's all right. Looks fine. Now come home and get your supper. It'll take you an hour to scrape that top-soil off yourself."

It was a good dance. The crowd that came over from Brigport, except for the summer people, were old-timers and they gave a sense of familiarity to the proceedings. And it was like the old days to have Sigurd playing for square dances again. Inspired by whiskey and his own talent, Sigurd played tirelessly in a long and dazzling stream of jigs and reels that he had kept somehow in his merry yellow head. The square dances, Lady of the Lake, March and Circle, Portland Fancy, were almost the romps they'd been in the old days. If the older people's enjoyment was set in a minor key by memory, and their perpetual consciousness of the war, the youngsters had an unqualified good time.

Everybody came. Gram Fennell, in her best black silk, sat in a queenly manner to watch, tapping her foot during the square dances, nodding her head during the waltzes, though she told Joanna she didn't think much of the way people danced so close together these days. Joanna had brought Jamie, who looked on for a while, too enchanted to move from the bench; his eyes blazed deeply blue, his cheeks scarlet. All at once he was sleepy, and settled down with his head on Ellen's sweater, and Joanna's coat tucked around him. For the rest of the evening he slept in some hinterland far from the music, the sound of dancing feet and of laughter.

Thea and Franny were there, of course. Joanna nodded to Thea whenever they met during a square dance; sensing the reluctance with which Thea's hand came to meet hers, during Ladies' Chain, she made her own grip warm and firm, and smiled deliberately into Thea's eyes. Thea was nothing. Nothing at all.

Owen was happy enough. He spent the evening dancing with one of the summer people from Brigport, a slim little woman with a pert way of tilting her head to look up at him. Her smile was vivid; Owen's was brilliant, and it was doing its usual devastating work. Joanna, dancing with Dennis for a few minutes during a Liberty Waltz, nodded her head toward her brother.

"Do you see what I see?"

"Who's working on whom? That's what I want to know," said Dennis gravely.

"I've seen this before. She thinks she's taking him over, but she isn't. Owen's never impressed by that type, but he can't help impressing her, any more than he can help breathing."

It was easier than she'd thought it would be, to dance with Dennis. Of course the atmosphere helped, the music, and general good temper all around. Thea was watching, but Thea was nothing. As long as she could keep telling herself that, Thea would continue to be nothing.

Dennis waltzed with unspectacular ease, holding her neither too closely nor too distantly. Their bodies moved well together, and it was not necessary to talk, he seemed content to dance without speaking. Once he said to her, "That clear yellow is very becoming to you. And I like the black-eyed susans. I think all women should wear flowers in their hair."

"Black-eyed susans are plain little things. I only put them in for fun."

"Better than gardenias," he said. "Or camellias." His voice was very low, and she glanced sidewise at his face, but it was impassive in the momentary radiance of a hanging lamp. Then they turned, and shadow fell across his face, and she didn't look back at it.

"You look a lot different from the lobster-buyer," she said lightly. "Gray flannels—and I like those jackets in the dull plaids. I want Nils to have one." She concentrated on Nils in gray flannels and a muted plaid coat, and the image was dear and safe.

Bit by bit the dancers' energies ebbed away, the men began to remember that they'd have to haul tomorrow, the youngsters were growing heavy-eyed—Ellen was smothering huge yawns and trying not to look half-asleep whenever her mother glanced at her. The Brigport crowd began to collect up for the trip home in the moonlight. Franny Seavey, who'd been trying for half the evening to escape, won out at last and departed with Thea. The Fennells took Gram home. Sigurd reached the end of his repertoire and his pint simultaneously, and Leonie took the accordion under one arm, held on to Sigurd with the other, and escorted him out.

"If I don't," she explained succinctly to all within hearing, "he'll flop where he is and I'll never get him up."

Joanna, preparing to take her children home, looked around for Owen to carry Jamie. "He went out when the Brigport gang did," said Ellen. "He was walking with that school teacher from Pennsylvania."

"Oh, naturally," said Joanna. "I forgot about her. Well, I guess we can manage Jamie—"

Young Charles, still carrying his importance like a shining blade, called to her from the other end of the hall. "If you can wait till I get the lamps blowed out, Aunt Jo, and the place shut up, I'll carry him!"

"Never mind," said Dennis pleasantly. He came in from the porch, putting his pipe away. "I'll take him." He walked down the hall toward Joanna and she found herself standing there dumbly, watching him, while Ellen dropped on the bench and Jamie slept on. Dennis came nearer, his face gravely pleasant; and behind him Young Charles moved about his duties like a slim phantom figure at the back of some dimly lit stage. After the noise of the evening, the shadowy silence held some expectant quality, the stillness beat at Joanna's eardrums . . . or was it her own pulses that beat so hard, because she was tired and oddly nervous.

Then Dennis was lifting Jamie, and Joanna and Ellen went out behind him. They came into a world all sharp black shadows and blue-white radiance and a strange effortless warmth that was so rare on the Island that you wanted to take it into your hands; or to walk in it for hours and wonder if the moon were not casting its own silvery warmth.

When Joanna came downstairs, after putting Jamie into his crib and blowing out Ellen's lamp for her, Dennis was still waiting in the dining room. She hadn't bothered to light the Aladdin, and the moonlight fell in knife-sharp, lop-sided angles on the floor; Dennis was a silhouette by the bright windows.

"Come out for a walk," he said simply. He turned his head as he spoke, and she saw his profile against the moonlight. His voice reached across the room to where she stood in the dark, at the foot of the stairs. It was low, it didn't hurry, it wasn't urgent. There was no harm in this, she thought.

"All right," she answered as simply.

They went out the back way. The moment that Joanna had said *All right,* Thea had slipped maliciously into her mind. And then she knew Thea was more than nothing, after all. She hated her, because even the innocent gesture of walking with a friend must be tinged with slyness, and so seem less innocent.

But once they were out and walking across the field, and the rare and wonderful warmth enveloped them gently, she stopped thinking of Thea. The Island was always another world by night, and by moonlight it became a world that she could imagine sometimes in dreams, or when she listened to certain music. She didn't want to speak, to bring any ordinary note into this atmosphere, and Dennis was quiet too, as if he also moved in a hushed and precious unreality.

They went through the Fennells' gate—the white house stood sleeping against the high black ramparts of the woods—and down into Barque Cove. There lay the sea, immense, untroubled as the windless air, steel-blue and silver. In the deeply walled cove the water made a rhythmic whispering and shushing as it drew in and drew out. Joanna didn't stop here; she went up the grassy slope at one side, following the narrow, twisted path that led to Sou-west Point, and when she reached the top of the slope she stopped. From the woods behind them some small bird moved in its nest and called sleepily, and then was still. Not even a breath stirred the grass, only Joanna's and Dennis' feet released some aromatic scent from it that held a faint essence of sunshine and spray and wind.

"Let's sit down here for a few minutes," Dennis said. "I want to take this all in."

"We don't get a night like this once in ten years." Joanna sat down cross-legged, and the ground was still warm with its remembered sunlight. Dennis, beside her, reached for his pipe and then he stopped and smiled.

"No, I won't smoke. I want to smell the night. I wish I had a nose like Dick's, so I could pick out every little scent that's on the air right now."

Joanna felt relaxed and calm. She was glad she had come out with him, after all. "Well, there's the grass," she said. "There are several kinds. And there's spruce. And clover. Rockweed from the cove down there, and the salt water itself."

"I smell something else." He looked around him. "It's quite strong, and very sweet." He got up and walked toward the woods a few paces. "It's stronger this way—don't you smell it?"

Joanna got up and followed him, and the instant she moved she smelled it too. The exotic sweetness of blackberry blossoms, lying heavily on the stillness.

"I've found it!" he called back to her. "Come here!" She stood motionless where she was. She could see him very clearly in the pale white light. She could even see his puzzled smile. "Coming? Oh, I suppose it's an old story to you, you've known this all your life."

His voice was easy but as distinct as the shadow of the scrub spruce near which she stood. She answered him quietly.

"No, it never gets to be an old story. It always surprises me." She walked toward him then, and the blackberry vines trailed through the grass, their blossoms small and glimmering and white. She dropped down beside them; Dennis went down on one knee and broke off a little spray.

"Blackberries," he said. "Wild ones. Running over this hillside, and spilling out such perfume. . . . It's a perfume that doesn't belong to New England, does it?"

"Oh, I don't know." She kept looking down at the vines, not at Dennis who knelt so close to her. "Look at lilacs."

"But they're tamed, they live safely in dooryards. This is something wild and unexpected." When he twisted the spray in his fingers, its scent moved out from it, and with every breath Joanna felt a wave rise higher and higher in her; it was like a tidal wave, it threatened to sweep over her and drown her in a flood and foam of old memories, old emotions. She would not recognize them for what they were, she fought them back. Dennis, still kneeling, looked out over the sea that rippled gently and endlessly in a dull-silver pattern; the moon shone on his face and took away all color, but darkened to clear-etched black lines the manner of its carving; the eye-hollows, the brow, the curve of the nostrils and the lips and the indented lines at the corners of his mouth. *But that isn't the way he's supposed to look,* she thought with a quick, inward shock of surprise. *He should be laughing, and reach forward to put the flowers in my hair—*

For a moment her world rocked back and forth, she was actually confused. Panic rose; she had never known anything like this before, she felt as if she were swinging between two lives, one so long ago that it was like a dream instead of a reality. . . . *Reality.* Reality was a good safe word, she reached out to it and hung on to it, and it was a mooring.

That was fifteen years ago, she said distinctly to herself. *And it was just such a night, warm and with a flood tide, and no wind, and all the rest of the Island was asleep . . . and we found the blackberry blossoms like this.*

It was Alec who had put the blackberry blooms in her hair, and kissed her afterward, his hands cupping her face, and her mouth going soft and ardent under his. Alec had been dead for thirteen years now, and she was behaving like an idiot.

The wave engulfed her, but it was a wave of heat and shame. She stood up swiftly, and her voice came with a coldness she didn't intend.

"I'll have to be getting back. You needn't come with me if you're not ready."

But he was already on his feet, the white spray still between his fingers. "Of course I'll go back with you. I keep forgetting that you aren't a free agent—I've had no right to keep you out like this."

He wasn't smiling, and she said quickly, "But I wanted to be out. A night like this is too rare to waste. It's just that—"

"It's just that—it's now time to go home," he answered. But neither of them started down the narrow path. They stood looking at each other, and now his face was in the shadow, and hers in the moonlight, looking up. She knew that her heart was beating in slow heavy rhythm, she had a sense that something should be said—or shouldn't be said. Then she turned sharply and went down the steep trail to Barque Cove. He came behind her.

They spoke infrequently, but casually, on the way home, and when he left her at the back door he said "Good night," in his usual pleasant way.

"Good night," she answered, her voice brightly friendly. But when she came into the silent, unlit house, she stood for a long moment in the sun parlor, without moving. Dick padded downstairs and came out to meet her. She scratched his ears automatically, while she listened to the thudding in her veins.

Then, slowly, she went about the motions of gettlng ready for bed. Owen hadn't come in yet, Young Charles was sound asleep, looking very young and astoundingly innocent. For him, the Thea business had rolled past, he had probably half-forgotten it already. Ellen seemed to be dreaming happily, Jamie slept in his own profound fashion. Dick went in under the crib, and Joanna lay down in the big bed.

This was one of those nights when the bed seemed very big, and very empty indeed. Her mind was a chaotic jumble of square-dance tunes, of the sound of dancing feet and laughter, of the sudden, vibrant silence on the hillside, the water under the moon, the way the blackberry vines had looked in the grass, the way Dennis had knelt to break off a blossom.

Her whole body ached and throbbed, burned and cooled and then burned again. She tried to laugh. *It was all that dancing,* she thought. *Hypering around as if I wasn't any older than Ellen. . . . Nils will laugh when I tell him how I capered at the dance.*

All at once the ache increased. It was not from dancing, after all, it was for Nils, for a chance to lay her long body beside his, to feel his arm under her head, and his other arm across her so that she was encircled by him. Together thus, they made a sure, magic little universe of their own. But without each other the universe was in bits. She wondered if he had time to feel this sense of incompleteness, if it haunted all his days and then came to torment him in all its intensity when he was off his guard.

She moved her long legs restlessly between the sheets, she folded her arms behind her head and stared through the darkness. Then as her futile yearning groped inevitably toward its peak, her eyes filled with unexpected and incomprehensible tears. She could not fight them. Lying there in the soft night, she wept silently until she fell asleep.

25

IN AUGUST, CHARLES BENNETT came back to Bennett's Island to live in the Bennett homestead. He brought his wife, the other five children who came after Young Charles, and a schoolteacher.

Whether he had made up his mind suddenly to abandon seining and go back to lobstering, or whether he had been planning it for a long time, Joanna didn't know; Charles wasn't one to tell his ideas, he simply confronted the family with the facts. That was how he had left the Island, back when Young Charles was a baby.

The little community was practically revolutionized by the thought of his return. For one thing, it meant a school, and everyone looked forward to that, even if all the pupils would be Bennetts. And the teacher was one that Charles himself had hired. To have the State send a teacher meant a great deal of red tape. But if the families of the pupils wanted to share expenses, to pay a girl and supply her board, the State was agreeable.

Joanna spent a happy week getting the homestead ready. Ellen and Young Charles helped, but she liked to go up there alone, or with Jamie and Dick, and open all the windows to the ripe, full richness of August. She liked washing all the small square panes, remembering what a miserable chore she'd always thought it in the old days. She'd slatted and sulked on window-washing days, and now she was taking positive delight in it. Each pane framed a different picture, a brilliant little scene of water and sky, of glistening rocks and white beach, or grassy point, or spruce woods; sometimes a bird flew through the scene, crow or gull or barn swallow—the old barn was full of them.

Jamie would wander around behind her, making dusting motions with a piece of rag, or else he'd play on the big granite doorsteps, or he'd go down into the meadow and rove among the raspberry bushes in his bright jersey and overalls, eating what fruit he could find. Dick moved patiently behind him, lying down whenever he could in the aromatic shade under the bay bushes.

In the house Joanna washed white paint, and swept, and aired, brought down quilts from the chests where they had been carefully stored and laid them on the dry grass to be sunned; and she spent moments of inaction kneeling by the upstairs windows, looking out at the sea beyond Matinicus Rock, or in toward the mainland and the blue Camden hills, at Vinalhaven and Isle au Haut, which had always seemed to her to be an enchanted cloud-blue mountain rising out of the sea.

While she looked, she dreamed, hearing boys' voices in the low-ceilinged rooms behind her, noisy young feet on the stairs, the big kitchen ringing with its mealtime clamor. It was all going to happen again.

She remembered how she had hated it when Charles married Mateel Trudeau, whom he had "gotten in trouble," and whom he loved. The whole family had hated it, until they realized why Charles loved her and they began to love her too. Now she was coming back to the Island as mistress of the Bennett homestead, and Joanna was making the house ready to welcome her, with no tinge of resentment at all. This was Mateel's place, because it was Charles' home, just as the other house was Joanna's place because it was Nils' home.

There'd be lights in the Bennett homestead at night now. There'd be children spilling out of the back door, a dog or two, chickens in the barnyard, trap stuff piled up in the barn for the two Charleses to build their new gear.

The schoolhouse would be opened again, too. Nora Fennell was to board the teacher. She had volunteered for the job. "Maybe she'll take walks with me," she explained. "It'll be sort of fun this winter, too. I hope there's lots of courting going on."

"There's only Owen to go courting," said Joanna.

"Well, maybe some of the Brigport boys will give him some competition." Nora was excited, and Joanna hoped for Nora's sake that the teacher was as young and congenial, and as susceptible to courting, as Nora wanted her to be.

Charles had plans, too. He was going to put sheep on the Island. He'd already bought them, a hundred ewes and two rams, and he wanted the Bennett meadow fenced in so he could keep the sheep there until after lambing time. Then he would turn them out on Souwest Point, in the early spring. When Owen had come back from the mainland, with the *White Lady* loaded with fencing materials that Charles had sent in advance, she cried out at first.

"Oh, the strawberries!"

Owen gave her a darkly ironic glance. "You women and your goddam strawberries! They don't amount to Hannah Cook. There's plenty more places on the Island to pick 'em, anyway. Listen, wool is over a dollar a pound now, and it'll stay high. Charles splits with the rest of the family when he sells the wool. There'll be a sight more profit in sheep than in strawberries."

"Well," Joanna began doubtfully, and then grinned. "It'll be exciting in a way, won't it?"

Owen grunted. "Puttin' up that fence'll be excitin', too. Where's that long-legged gandygut?"

"If you mean Young Charles, he's down in the fish house." Owen went out, and Joanna began to tell Ellen about the days when Grandpa Bennett had raised sheep on the Island. There'd been the time when her father and Uncle Nate, as young boys, had camped out on Souwest Point with shotguns to find out whose dogs were chasing and killing sheep. It had seemed like the loftiest pinnacle of adventure to Joanna; she had begged for the story so much that she'd half-believed she'd been with them, crouched on a grassy slope above the sheep who filled the hollows like snow in the moonlight. Telling it, she saw the rebirth of her own passionate interest in Ellen's eyes.

"They felt pretty good, being down there alone with shotguns," she said. "Your grandfather used to tell me just how the stock of the shotgun felt, and how the barrels gleamed, and how the food tasted. I used to think nothing I'd ever eaten could taste as good as those cold biscuits with thick slices of veal and Red Astrakhan apples from that tree up in the orchard."

"I'll bet they were good," said Ellen rapturously.

"And they had gingerbread too—Grandma Bennett used to make a good solid kind that stuck to their ribs—and cold tea in a jug."

"Gosh," Ellen breathed. "Sometime I'd like to have some cold tea in a jug, just to know how it tastes."

"It sounds lots better than it tastes," said Joanna briskly. "Now let's get up there and black the kitchen stove like new for Mateel."

A sardine boat, skippered by a friend of Charles' from Pruitt's Harbor, brought the hundred Cheviots, and Charles moved his family in the *Four Brothers*. Another boat came along too, with Philip Bennett at the wheel; a thirty-four-foot lobster boat, the *Dovekie*. Philip would take the big seiner back to Pruitt's Harbor and continue to work with her, and a new crew, and Charles would go lobstering in the *Dovekie*. Her name belied her, for she had long, racy lines, and looked nothing at all like the plump, round little bird.

The dinner that Joanna and Ellen had ready for the family when they arrived was something monumental. The big kitchen at the homestead was full of light and air, with windows wherever you looked; the breath of August blew in, and the breath of lobster chowder, baked potatoes, baked stuffed lobster, with green peas from Joanna's garden, blew out, sweeter than all the perfumes of Araby to a crew who'd been on the water for three hours. Afterwards there was green-apple pie and good strong fishermen's coffee.

Walking home afterwards through the alder swamp with Jamie and Ellen, after helping with the dishes and delivering the schoolteacher to her boarding place, she felt tired and somewhat stranded. For weeks now, ever since Charles had written he was coming, she'd been on the crest of a wave of industry; there'd been hardly any lying awake at night because she was so tired when she went to bed. Now they were here, the house was cleaned, the sheep were in their meadow, everyone was established . . . and Joanna felt like a dory beached at flood tide and left high and dry when the water went out.

Now, all unbidden, as if it had been waiting for this very moment of inertia and reaction after the momentum of the last weeks, the night of the full moon and the blackberry blossoms came back to her. Worse was the memory of her bitter and futile weeping.

At the edge of the barnyard she stopped and looked at the house.

Jamie was running, scattering the duck family, Ellen was trying to coax the drake in a soothing, comforting voice, Dick stood on the back doorstep, waiting for someone to open the door so he could get a drink.

I don't want to go in, Joanna thought. *Not when Nils isn't there. I don't want to sleep alone any longer.*

26

SEPTEMBER WAS A LOVELY MONTH. Sometimes it was as pastel, as silken-hued and textured as mid-summer, sometimes there was a procession of warm bronze-and-sapphire days when the nights were powdered brilliantly with frosty stars; the northern lights spread their rosy fan above Brigport, the dawns were clear and chill. Joanna thought of the thick tropical stars that blazed over Nils and Mark and Stevie, the warm winds, the nightmare sense of fantastic beauty mixed with the perpetual threat of attack. Somehow Nils had conveyed that sense to her.

Here at home, while her brothers and her husband were at war, there was more money being made along the coast of Maine than had ever been known by the lobsterman. Usually the lobsters slacked off in the summer, but this year they'd kept up, and in September the hauls were phenomenally high. So were the prices. In a way, it was a little frightening. You felt like bracing yourself for the crash; this couldn't go on forever.

The strawberries had been long gone, the blueberries had ripened and been picked, and then the raspberries; in late August and early September the blackberries were heavy and rich on the trailing bushes, shiny as lacquer, bursting with purple juices. And while you picked them you saw cranberries turning waxy pink against the thick, glossy green carpet their vines made along the ground. In the orchard the

Yellow Transparents gleamed among the leaves, and when you stood under the twisted trees you could see golden fruit against the hot hard blue of the Maine autumn. The crickets chirped in the windless hush at noon, the asters bloomed along the paths in chalky-lavender drifts and the little blueberry bushes turned red as fire in the fields.

School started, and one afternoon Miss Gibson, the teacher, came to make a formal call on Joanna. She laughed about it. "I always call on my pupils' parents right off," she said, "as a teacher. After that I hope I'll be considered as a friend."

"You've been considered a friend ever since we found out you were willing to come out here," said Joanna. "You don't know what it means to have Ellen home with me."

"And Ellen's a darling. I love her already." It didn't sound like saccharine gush from Miss Gibson. She was young, and she'd come from Aroostook County. Her body was compact and strong under the yellow skirt and sweater, her movements were vigorous; her hair was vigorous too, hanging in a thick, shiny, brown page-boy bob. She looked at Joanna with unreserved friendliness in her bright blue eyes.

"I didn't know what Island people would be like," she admitted. "I took the job when your brother offered it to me, because everybody told me the Bennetts were fine people—and because I wanted an adventure." She grinned diffidently at that. "I had no idea what the Island would be like. I thought of little camps hanging onto bare rocks by their toenails. But this is so different—and everybody is so easy to like."

"I think everybody likes you, Miss Gibson," Joanna said.

"My name is Laurie, outside of school." She rubbed Dick's head, and admired the truck Jamie showed her. "He's about two, isn't he?"

"His birthday's next week."

"That's his father?" Laurie Gibson had discovered the photograph of Nils on the sideboard. "He's the image of him." The bright eager face sobered abruptly. "I wish it were all over! I wanted to join the Wacs or the Marines, but Mr. Maxwell—he's the principal of the Normal School—kept telling me that I was needed as a teacher—that people were neglecting the generation who would inherit the world after the war. So here I am. Still a teacher."

"I'm glad you didn't go into the service," Joanna said sincerely. "The children need somebody like you. The teacher's a very important person here."

Miss Gibson glowed. She had abundant, lovely color and a quality of becoming radiant in an instant. "I want to do my best, and I've got a lot of ideas. I'm qualified to teach First Aid, so I thought I'd do that, and have Home Nursing — most especially for Ellen and her cousin Donna, but anyone who wanted to could join that. And then I think children should have more music in the schools, so I'm going to have that, and teach them handicrafts —" She blushed suddenly and beautifully. "There I go again, getting enthusiastic."

The girl was a fresh, springlike, uncomplicated presence in the room. Joanna brought out apple pie and made coffee, wanting to keep her there for a while longer. She loved to hear her talk. For her, Bennett's Island was an adventure, she probably slept as deeply as Jamie at night and awoke as eager and hungry for the day's activities as Jamie did. She had what she wanted, she didn't know anything about the torment of dreams or of twisting restlessly at midnight, or tears that meant nothing because they could gain you nothing; perhaps she would never know what Joanna had known only recently, the swift awakening to the sound of weeping, and the realization that it was yourself who wept, without understanding why.

Owen came in while they were drinking coffee. It was too windy to haul, and he'd been working all day in the fish house, heading pots. Now he stood in the doorway, smiling, running a hand through his hair.

"Afternoon, ladies. You bein' hoggish with that pie?"

"Come and sit down," said Joanna. "Have you met Miss Gibson face to face yet?"

"No, I've been admirin' from afar." His black eyes were bold and bright on the girl's face, his white grin shameless. *Now, Owen,* Joanna cautioned him silently. *She's much too young for you. It'll be like killing a sitting duck.*

But Laurie wasn't flushing, or looking away uncertainly, as he meant her to do. Her eyes didn't move from his.

"How do you do?" she said pleasantly. "I know already which boat is yours. The *White Lady.* It's beautiful."

"*She's* beautiful," Owen corrected her.

"Oh, I'll learn. I know more about logging and raising potatoes than about boats." She smiled at him and went on eating pie.

"Go and wash if you want a mug-up," Joanna said to Owen. Her mouth twitched, and Owen lifted one eyebrow at her in a Mephistophelian threat before he went out into the kitchen.

The teacher stayed a while longer, playing with Jamie, talking with candid enjoyment to both Joanna and Owen. If she was conscious that Owen watched her, that his eyes held a gleaming devil, she was not at all disconcerted by it, and Joanna felt like chuckling. This would make rich material to write to Nils.

When the girl left, Owen went over to the windows, walking cat-like in his stocking feet, and watched her cut across the field toward the lane that led to the Fennells'. She walked briskly and well, her head up.

"Well, Cap'n Owen?" Joanna said softly. "She didn't react, did she? Too bad Charles didn't let you pick out the teacher."

"You're feelin' pretty perky, huh? Pretty chipper?" He glared down at her good-naturedly. "But don't start crowin' too soon, darlin' mine. I've met that kind before."

"She's probably engaged to some nice boy in the service," said Joanna. "She has his picture on the dresser, and she writes to him every night—"

"But she's down here on Bennett's Island, don't forget. And she's not sixty-five, she's about twenty-five." Owen was still staring across the field, though she had gone out of sight by now. His voice dropped, he looked as if he were contemplating something utterly delectable. "She looks like a nice ripe berry. All ready to pick. Damn' encitin', if you ask me."

After supper Ellen went out to the barnyard to give the orts to the ducks, and came in with her eyes glowing. "Bobby Merrill from Brigport's just gone up to Fennells. I know he's calling on Miss Gibson! I saw him going up the lane, and he's all slicked up with a white shirt on!"

Owen tilted back in his chair and blew smoke rings at the ceiling. "Now that's what I call an enterprising boy," said Joanna, without looking at Owen. "It's choppy out, too. And he came all the way over here to go courting. I think they'd make a nice pair."

"Me, too," said Ellen with heartfelt conviction. "Maybe if she had a boyfriend down here, she won't get homesick."

"That's what your uncle thinks," said Joanna. She got up from the table. "Why don't you two settle down and have a nice chat about Miss Gibson's welfare while I put Jamie to bed?"

She went upstairs, Jamie toiling ahead of her. *I feel so good,* she thought. *Maybe I haven't been laughing enough. I can write Nils a good letter tonight!* She bent swiftly, thankfully, and kissed the back of Jamie's neck.

Time slipped away; Jamie's birthday came and went, with a cake for which his grandmother sent the sugar from Pruitt's Harbor. Joanna had a party for him to which everybody came, and Jamie distinguished himself by hitting Charles' youngest on the head with his new dump-truck. There were gifts from everybody on the Island and his Sorensen and Bennett relatives on the mainland.

The weather held out. A hurricane was reported, and everyone got ready for it, but Maine escaped with nothing more than a gale which wasn't as bad as most of the gales which were simply reported as "strong winds."

October had a dreaminess which no other month could have. The horizons were hidden in a melting lilac haze, the distant islands were painted against a tender sky, the gulls dreamed in the somnolent hush of noon. It was an exceptionally beautiful fall; the last fall that Joanna remembered like this was in the year when she married Alec. She found herself thinking sometimes of that fall. She would be walking along the curve of Schoolhouse Cove, while Jamie threw stones into the water and she would see a thicket of wild roses tumbling over the old sea wall, their hips a brilliant, burning red; and instantly she would be surrounded with an atmosphere that she had not sensed for years. That first fall with Alec had been touched with indefinable magic. Never, before or since, had there been an Island autumn like that one; and now, fourteen, fifteen years later, the magic could wrap itself around her again, as gently and tenuously as fog, and it filled her with vague alarms. She would hurry Jamie up over the beach and along the road through the marsh, leaving that unnatural nostalgia behind. She would start a letter to Nils as soon as she reached the house, setting his picture before her to strengthen her heart's image of him. Then the other feeling would be gone as if it had never existed, as if even Ellen were no bond with that distant past; as if Ellen were Nils' child as well as Jamie was.

It would go then for a while, until some morning in the first instant of waking, she would hear the sweet, stubborn "yank-yank" of the nuthatches in the spruces, and the "dee-dee-dee" of the chickadees in the alders, and she would remember helplessly how she'd listened to the little birds when she awoke before Alec, and his head lay heavily against her.

But in the crib across the room slept Jamie, with his flaxen bang and his eyes as blue as larkspur, and he was the fruit of a love that had come late, but richly; and Nils' heavy clothes still hung in the closet, so she could see them when she opened the door, she would even lay her cheek against the warm stuff of a wool plaid shirt and pretend that he'd be in from hauling in a little while.

She was not always unhappy except for these moments. The Island was too lovely, and there were good moments in every day. Thea didn't disturb her now, except when Dennis came up to the house for something, or when she met him in the road and was obliged to stop and talk, out of courtesy. Then she'd remember Thea, uneasily, and at the same time feel like cursing her, because Thea had cast a blight over her acquaintance with Dennis. She had to put her mind forcibly on whatever they discussed, she had to make her eyes meet his gray ones openly, and she had to will back the color that wanted to creep up into her cheeks. Her inner confusion on these occasions infuriated her and she blamed it all on Thea. . . . Almost all.

Sometimes, in spite of the fine case she'd built up against Thea, she would know doubt that spread through her self-righteous anger as insidiously as smoke. Perhaps the confusion had its roots within herself; perhaps the frankness had gone from their relationship at the time when they sat on the stile at the cemetery and she had surprised that look on his face. Perhaps—but she shifted quickly away from the blackberry blossoms above Barque Cove in the moonlight. She'd simply been tired, and lonesome for Nils that night.

No, it was Thea who was responsible for the lack of ease she felt when she talked with Dennis now; and she, Joanna, was an idiot if she heeded the blatherings of an idiot.

In late October, Nils wrote in one of his letters: "I know it's cold there. It doesn't change here. I'd like to see a no'theaster blowing down between the islands, and have to wear mittens, and come down into a cold kitchen in the morning and build up the fire."

It was the nearest thing to homesickness he had ever expressed and Joanna, knowing him as she did, understood what other things he meant. He meant herself, and Jamie; he meant the house, the big spruces stirring blackly against the star-powdered sky, the frosty dawns when each twig and blade of grass shone silver in the first sunlight, the pure, sweet, icy water that came up from the mossy darkness of the well. Yes, she knew what Nils meant in that sparse paragraph. He was homesick. Even in peacetime, when he had sailed on a freighter before he married Joanna, his Scandinavian blood had rejected the warmth and lushness of those tropical islands.

But mostly this letter meant that he was homesick for Joanna. *I'm homesick for you too, Nils,* she said to him silently.

27

OWEN'S COURTSHIP OF THE TEACHER PROGRESSED at an incredibly slow pace. Joanna had long since stopped worrying about Laurie's susceptibility, and had come to admire the girl for her poise and common sense. There were two Brigport boys calling on her, when the weather permitted, and Owen had to take his turn. It was rather amazing that he kept on courting, since he was used to being the only one; he was fond of saying that where he set his pots, nobody else dared to follow. Now the Brigport boys were on his grounds, but he was taking it with remarkable equanimity.

He took Laurie for long walks on Saturdays and Sundays. Joanna saw them sometimes when she was picking cranberries. They were usually on the far side of Old Man's Cove, on a sunny slope, Laurie taking excellent potshots at buoys with Owen's .22 while he sprawled on the grass beside her. He was apparently at a standstill, since Miss Gibson seemed to be more in love with his rifle than with him. But still he followed her, and whenever he came home with the black Bennett look on him, and stalked up to bed without speaking, Joanna had an amusing postscript for her letter to Nils.

Owen didn't go down to Sigurd's much these days. Francis Seavey went down several nights a week to play cribbage with Sig. Owen snorted at this.

"I guess Leonie's satisfied with Franny, if she's still worryin' about her honor. He wouldn't know how to muckle on to her if she showed him how."

"I suppose you don't go down there any more because Leonie's likely to hit you with something," Joanna suggested.

"Oh, my God!" Owen looked at her in rank disgust. "I'm sick of that set-up, that's all. Guess I'll have me a housekeeper of my own. Build me a little camp on the back shore, and find me a woman who'll keep her mouth shut all day and be ready for bed when I am, and—"

"Spare me the details," said Joanna. "And what are you moaning about a housekeeper for, when you're courting the school-ma'am?"

"Laurie's a good girl," Owen stated emphatically, and put down his cup with unnecessary firmness. "Give me some more coffee. Laurie's a good girl, and it looks like she'll go back to her mother just as good as the day she came down here. Lord, Bennett's is slipping."

"*This* Bennett is, anyway." Joanna patted his head as she passed him. "Looks like you've met your match, chummy!"

She dodged his big brown hand and went out into the kitchen, laughing.

In the fall there was always torching, when the ocean was full of herring that fired the water as the stars fired the sky. One night when it was particularly mild, Joanna went up to the Fennells' to get Laurie. The men were going to torch in the harbor, and it was too good an opportunity to miss watching them.

Nora waved them out wistfully when they asked her to come. "Nope! I've got a little cold, and Dennis told me that if I kept healthy, and remembered to take my vitamins, I'd be okay—you know." She grinned at Joanna. "So long, Laurie."

"She's a happy thing," said Laurie when they were walking down the dark lane toward the harbor.

"Yes, she is . . . There's a hole here, be careful." Joanna flashed the light on a dip in the path.

"Gram is always telling me I should get married," Laurie chuckled. "She looks over all the boys as if she were *my* Gram instead of Matthew's. She inclines toward Owen, I guess. Says the others aren't dry behind the ears."

"Which one do you incline toward?" Joanna asked casually.

"I don't think I incline toward any of 'em, really," said Laurie frankly. "I haven't thought much about getting married. I haven't been a teacher long enough yet."

"And you're doing all right at that . . . Well, here we are." They had come to Nils' fish house. Joanna led the way around to the front of it; from the little wharf, with the water gurgling and swashing underneath, they could watch in comfort. The night was strangely mild, and free from wind, and before them the harbor was brilliant with the ruddy flare of the torches. There were two dories at work; Francis and Sigurd rowed one, with Owen in the bow with the dipnet, and Matthew and Young Charles rowed the other, with Charles in the bow.

A torch made of oily rags, and flaming in a wire basket, was projected from one gunnel on each dory. The men at the oars rowed fast and hard, as the man in the bow directed them. It was hard to tell which job was the more exacting. There was more to handling the dipnet than the lowering and lifting of it, heavy with the dripping, squirming, silver fish. The man who stood in the bow in his oilskins must spot the herring and give the word to the oarsmen; then, as the herring swarmed upwards to where the torch burned above the glassy, emerald green surface, the net would swoop down, sweep in the fish, and lift again, to tilt its cargo into the dory. After a while the men would be knee-deep in herring, the tiny scales would glitter in the light from the torch, and the faces of the men would be smeared with soot.

Joanna had loved the torching ever since she was a child, and once it had been her most passionate wish to be able to row hard enough to help out. She told Laurie about the old days when there would be five or six dories in and out of the harbor, instead of only two.

"They never depended on the lobster smack to bring their bait then," she said. "They got out and worked for it, like this."

"They must get awfully tired," said Laurie, watching Owen's dory gliding past the wharf. Owen stood up in the bow, the torchlight shining on his yellow oilskins.

"They do get tired, but it pays off. Some places swear by bream, but there's nothing like good corned herring to fetch in the lobsters."

In the flickering glow Laurie's eyes were as wide and entranced as a child's. "It may be hard work, but it's a beautiful sight. It's sort of — romantic." She laughed shyly, and Joanna said seriously, "I always thought it was romantic too."

Laurie leaned against a stack of traps and looked up. "The stars are lovely. And it's so warm, too. I had no idea it would be like this. Every time I get a letter from home they think I'm kidding about the weather."

"This is unusual for the Island. It's the first of November, do you realize that?" She knocked on one of the traps, and Laurie laughed.

"What are you worried about?"

"This is a weather-breeder, I'm afraid. You may see some real Island stuff in a few days — wind and surf. Everything's been too good."

"I'd like to see a good storm," Laurie said. "But I suppose it's hard on the traps and the boats."

"Yes, sometimes it is," Joanna answered absently. "Let's walk around to the wharf and watch them bail out the herring."

She was more afraid of a storm than she would let anyone know. The September hurricane had passed them by; there'd been hardly one big gale this year, the traps were intact, the lobster prices high. Tonight she was more apprehensive than she'd been all fall. It was much too warm, the stars were too close, too softly brilliant. Oh, everybody was looking for a blow, but no one seemed very worried — no one but herself. The men had grown soft this year, she thought grimly; soft with good weather, good living, good money. But the crash would have to come sometime, and then there'd be a decade of poor lobstering, beginning just about the time the war ended and the other lobstermen came home.

She threw off this ominous mood when they reached the old wharf. There, by lantern light, the men were bailing out the doryloads of herring into bushel baskets. Matthew, in one dory, and Sigurd in the other were doing the bailing. The other men stood on the wharf, operating the hoist and reaching out for the loaded baskets when they came up. A space was penned off in a low shed and the filled baskets were dumped in there. The growing pile of herring made a shining mass on the rude board floor. In the morning the men would divide them, and lightly salt them down, and each man would have his share of bait for the next few days.

Thea and Leonie were on the wharf, watching what was going on; Thea had been laughing shrilly at some exchange of ribald banter between Sigurd and Owen, as Joanna came around the corner of the boat shop. But she seemed to fall back out of the radius of the lantern glow when she saw Joanna and Laurie.

Dennis was there too, pulling on the hoist. He glanced back at Joanna and nodded. *He has a nice smile,* she thought involuntarily, and then asked Owen quickly how thick the herring had been.

"We're through for the night," he said. "There's not much doin'. Damn' things have gone out to sea I guess — must be a storm on the way." He grinned at Laurie, his teeth startling white in his sooty face.

"Want to get down here and bail herrin', Miss Lady?"

"Sure!" said Laurie, unabashed. He laughed, and went back to the hoist. The smell of fresh herring was clean and acrid. Leonie was holding a pan in which Sigurd had arranged a half-dozen plump, glittering fish; they'd be good for dinner tomorrow, fried crisply, or corned in the kettle. When the last basket came up, and Matthew and Sigurd began to clean up the dories with buckets of sea water, Joanna called to Owen.

"We're going along, Owen. Bring up some herring, will you? Some to fry, and some to have corned."

"Hey, wait a minute!" Owen roared after them. "You gonna have coffee, and cut into that spice cake you made?"

Everybody was moving homeward, toward soap and water and coffee. Scales sparkled on everything, the men walked in an aura that smelled of salt water and herring. Laurie was watching happily the shifting figures in the lantern light, as if they were characters in a strange and fascinating book, and Joanna looked back at Owen.

"I guess I can cut the cake if you want some."

"Laurie wants some too. Huh, Laurie? I'll take you home afterwards!"

"Well—" Laurie looked doubtful. "I've got papers to correct—"

"Fine!" said Owen triumphantly. "She's stayin'. Well, you women get up there and get the coffee made, and I'll be along. Dennis, too." He put his big hand on the other man's shoulder. "You want some coffee, don't you, Doc?"

"I guess Leonie's got some ready, Owen." Dennis was filling his pipe.

"Oh, to hell with that. You know you want to come up with us. Set out four cups, Jo."

Joanna hesitated. She was oddly happy, knowing that Owen would prevail; at the same time she could have slapped Owen for making an issue of this, for being so loud about it. For Thea hadn't gone yet. Joanna could sense her presence, she knew that when she turned around she would see the pale blur of Thea's hair and face over against the boatshop wall. She'd be lingering there, listening, even though Franny had been one of the first to go home.

Thea, hating Owen because he'd always ignored her or laughed at her, hating Joanna for being Joanna, despising Laurie and Dennis on principle, would love to make something out of this. No one else on the Island would care much, they would only notice after Thea had listened, conjectured, and then made her sly suppositions. The thought of it was an uncleanliness, to be "talked about" was to be soiled.

Beside her Laurie was saying happily, "That's what I like about this place! Everything's an excuse to have coffee!"

And Owen, closing the door of the low shed so the gulls couldn't walk in and have an early morning feast, was shouting at her. "Go on, woman! Don't stand there gawpin'!"

She went, without looking toward Thea at all. Laurie said, "I didn't really have papers, but it sounds so professional!" She laughed aloud. "With five pupils, I get everything done in jig time. It doesn't seem right to have things so easy, and to be having so much fun at the same time."

"Oh, you'll make up for it later on," said Joanna cheerfully, forcibly ejecting Thea from her mind. "Wait till you're in a big school, with forty pupils under your nose."

"Oh, I'll get along," said Laurie confidently.

Ellen was in bed. Joanna and Laurie set out cups and saucers, crackers, and strong, old-fashioned, rat-trap cheese. The spice cake was golden-brown under the Aladdin lamp. Laurie was as enthusiastic as if it were really a party, and it was impossible not to respond.

The men came in, minus oilskins and rubber boots, and washed up at the sink. Owen was in one of his exhilarated moods. He teased Laurie unmercifully, watching her with glinting black eyes, and Laurie laughed back at him, confident and poised. Dennis was quiet, sitting back out of the Aladdin's yellow glow, smoking his pipe and watching Joanna. She tried to joke with the others, she laughed at Laurie's quick answers, but she found herself forever glancing back at Dennis; and always he would be watching her. Owen and Laurie were too absorbed in each other to notice, and she was thankful for that. She wished she could be oblivious, but instead she felt as uncertain of herself, as quick to blush, as a sixteen-year-old.

She kept busy, bringing more coffee until no one could possibly drink any more. Every time she was obliged to call Dennis by name, she was sure her voice sounded peculiar. She was furious at her own self-consciousness. *I'll have to conquer it,* she decided stoutly, *or I'll never get rid of it. And its so unnecessary.* She turned toward Dennis brightly, decisively.

"Dennis, how do *you* think we should treat the war prisoners?" she demanded. "There was a man on the radio at supper time who says we're too soft — what do you think?"

Dennis smiled. "Do we have to bring the war into this pleasant little interval?"

"Why not? What right have we to forget it?" Then she turned hotly red. "I'm sorry, Dennis. I didn't really mean to say that."

"I'm sure you didn't." He put his pipe back into his mouth and nodded at Laurie and Owen. "This is the best thing I've heard in years. Who's ahead?"

"They're neck and neck," said Joanna, and Owen swung toward her.

"What's that about neckin'? Laurie, my fair one, you ready to go home yet?"

"I'm ready to go home," said Laurie with dignity. "Home, that is. On the double, with no time out."

Owen brought her coat. He exuded masculine superiority as he towered over her. "What is this power I have over women? She argues, but I know damn' well she doesn't mean it."

"It's the biggest love affair in history," Joanna said to Laurie. "Owen's in love with Owen. I don't know how you stand him."

Laurie laughed, and glanced up at Owen, her thick hair shining in the lamplight, her eyes as bright as his. "Oh, we get along. Good night, Jo—good night, Dennis."

Dennis stood up. "Good night, Laurie."

When they had gone, the silence was too strong. Joanna began to gather up the dishes, making unnecessary trips to stretch the task. "Let me help you," said Dennis politely, picking up the sugar bowl. She took it from him, shaking her head.

"No, sit down and relax," she said gaily. "You've been working hard all day."

"So have you."

"Look, it's practically done. I'll just rinse out the cups and dry them, while you smoke your pipe and get the late news."

She was being a little too brisk; she saw him glance at her, side-wise, one eyebrow lifted faintly. His mouth quirked a little. "I thought we were leaving the war out of this."

"Then just smoke your pipe." Her voice rose nervously, and stopped. For a moment her mind went helplessly blank, she found herself staring at him, her lips parted, her hands lifted in a little futile gesture.

"Joanna," Dennis said gently. He stood across the table from her, she saw his square-tipped fingers, with their clean, short-clipped nails, resting on the cloth. "Joanna, do I bother you, being here like this?"

She answered too readily. "No, of course not! How could you?"

"I don't ever want to be in your way, Joanna. Do you under-stand that?" His voice was low, but each word was edged distinctly, as they had been the night above Barque Cove. She looked from his hands to his face; it was grave, and kind, and there was a sort of shining intensity in his deepset gray eyes. "I'd leave the Island before I'd cause you any—annoyance whatever. Do you believe that?"

"Dennis—" She stopped, and then tried again. "Please—I wish you wouldn't talk like this. You ought to know me well enough to realize how much I like you." Color rushed into her cheeks, her eyes were wide and very dark. "Everybody likes you. And you're the last person on earth who could annoy *anybody.*"

There was nothing else to say. She turned away from the light and walked out into the dim kitchen. He came behind her, and stopped in the doorway. "You know, Joanna, I've had a strange feeling lately, whenever we've been talking, that things aren't the same between us as they were. I feel a sense of strain since — shall we say? — that night after the dance." He hesitated, as if he were waiting. Then he added quietly, "I hope I'm wrong."

She swung around then, goaded beyond poise, and faced him. "Of course you're wrong! How could there be any difference between us? And certainly that walk couldn't make for any sense of strain!" She shrugged as if in utter impatience. "How *could* it? It was perfectly harmless, wasn't it?"

"Yes." Dennis nodded. "Perfectly harmless."

She leaned back against the sink, her hands reaching behind her to hold the cool molding. Inwardly she was trembling but she forced her eyes to hold his, she lifted her chin in the old defiant gesture.

"Well," said Dennis at last. "I'm glad I spoke about this, Joanna, because I wanted to know."

"You'll take my word for it, won't you?"

"Certainly I'll take your word for it." He smiled at her, and the inner trembling increased until she was sure she couldn't hide it. He took his mackinaw and hat from the hook behind the door. "As you said, I've been working hard all day. I'll go along now, and get some sleep."

"That's what I need too," said Joanna. "In spite of all that coffee."

"Don't come to the door with me. Good night, Joanna. Sleep well." He went out. Slowly, and with infinite care, she unclamped her fingers from the edge of the sink. Her one aim at the moment was to get up into the protective dark shell of her room before Owen came in.

And yet, when she reached that room, she was not comforted; there could never be much comfort against the turmoil that beat inside her mind and body.

28

THE VERY NEXT MORNING the warmth was gone, and the clarity and brilliance of the air. The harbor was the color of pewter, and the smoke from the chimneys went down on the wind. Ellen put on mittens that morning when she went to school, and it was too raw to put Jamie outside. In the sitting room, out of the way, he sat in a cardboard carton and rowed with two laths, going to haul. Joanna could hear him talking brightly to the "lo'sters," coaxing them aboard. Owen went down to the shop to work. There was always work to do, no matter whether it was a fit hauling day or not.

Joanna studied the barometer, tapped it at intervals during the day. It was not very menacing. She stopped worrying about a storm. There was a big ironing to do, and while she ironed she remembered how the harbor had looked in the torch-light last night, and the thick shimmer of the stars overhead. She knew that her mind would move inevitably to the later part of the evening, and this time she didn't steer it firmly in the other direction. There was no harm in knowing that Dennis Garland's eyes had followed her; the time was past when a woman was dishonored by the admiration of a man who was not her husband. Dennis was fine, and good, he was never anything but courteous. And there was a small, secret warmth in the knowledge that he admired her.

I'm flattered, I suppose, she thought bluntly. *Any woman would be flattered to have Dennis Garland care for her. The woman who let him down was a fool, or worse.*

But was it because she was flattered that she felt confused by him, that she'd wanted him to go last night, and then had wanted him to stay? Was it because she was flattered that the now-familiar tension had begun as soon as they were alone, and she'd lashed out at him so senselessly?

The irons were suddenly heavy, the sound of Jamie's voice monotonous and irritating. The house was too small, too close. She was glad beyond reason when Owen and Ellen came home to dinner, yet she was relieved when they went out again, and she could get Jamie to bed for his nap.

It was not a good day. With all she had to do, there was nothing she wanted to do. It took all her self-control not to be short with Owen and the children. She lit the lamps in mid-afternoon to hasten the evening, and went to bed when Ellen did. She read until after midnight. Nils' evening letter she put aside altogether. Each attempt only reflected her own state of mind, and perhaps in the morning she could write a really good letter.

She should have been sleepy by the time she blew out her lamp, but she lay awake for a long time in the chill darkness, listening to the gusts of wind rattle the windows at the side of the house. It had gone around to the westward during the day, and whether it was blowing hard or not she couldn't really tell, for this was when Gunnar's windbreak served its purpose.

She had always loved to lie in bed and hear the wind rising outside, but tonight it was a lonely sound for her. Yet the loneliness she felt could not be assuaged by contact, it was far too remote for that. It made her vividly conscious of Nils' absence from her side; her skin seemed sensitive where the bed clothes touched it, her nightdress constricted her, her scalp itched. She slipped at last into a restless sleep.

It was dark at six o'clock in the morning now, and so she did not wake until the sun touched her face. It was after seven. Jamie still slept; no one else stirred in the house. She knew the weather before she got up; behind the spruces the huge, purple-shaded wind clouds sailed toward the east, and the sound of the wind came to her, a high, steady wail. It was a westerly, a dry, brilliant westerly. And a crazy westerly, because it could roar into the harbor and set the boats to pulling and plunging at their moorings like terrified horses. They'd had a long time to lunge and rear, for the wind had begun to rise at midnight, on the flood of the tide.

She went downstairs and inspected the oil bottle in the sitting-room stove. In the kitchen, she put kindling in the cookstove and started the fire. From the stove, with its satisfying roar and crackle of flames, she went to the sink, to dip cold water into the basin and wash her face. After she had dried her tingling skin, glad of the icy shock, she looked down at the harbor. The early sun sent the long shadows of her own house and Thea's across the field, and touched the dead grass with bright gilt. The air was heavy and trembling with the sound of surf, it even penetrated the walls of the house.

Across the open space between the Sorensen fish house and Grant's wharf Joanna could always get her first morning glimpse of the harbor and the eastern point, and now she saw the rising wall of rock, topped by its wind-twisted spruces; she saw the long dark ledge that reached out to the deeper waters of the outer harbor. Surf piled upon the ledge, dazzling white in the sunshine, and spray flew like smoke to the higher ramparts of rock. It was a beautiful shoreline with its slanting cliff, its crest of spruce, its surf thundering below; but it was a wicked shore when a helpless boat was drifting down upon it. She couldn't forget—ever—how the *Donna* and the *White Lady* had looked, that day in the spring when the ground line had chafed. It had been just such a day as this, cold and diamond-bright.

She looked at the eastern point now, and then looked again; for a moment she stared blankly, but only for a moment. Then she understood.

A boat lay defenselessly on her side against the dark, wet, rockweed. The boiling surf that sent spray flying on the wind did not touch her now; the waves that had flung her ashore had been pulled back by the retreating tide. And now the boat lay quietly, a spent thing, like a gull tossed away by the sea, its life taken by the very force it had loved.

It was the *Donna*. Joanna knew it before her eyes scanned the moorings. She could see Sigurd's boat riding wildly, but safely; Francis' boat, Matthew's, Charles', even Owen's, which shared the *Donna's* mooring. The emptiness where Nils' boat should have been was as shocking to her as a physical hurt. For so many years the *Donna* had lain safely at her mooring, she had ridden out one storm after another—until that day in the spring. It had been a close call then. But this storm had taken her.

For an instant longer Joanna looked, her throat thickening. Then she shut her eyes. The boat seemed unscathed lying there, its rounded,

sleek, white side gleaming in the morning sun. But no one needed
to go and look closely at the *Donna* to realize what had happened to
the other side, the side on which she lay.

Joanna's closed eyes stung. How long had the sea wrenched and
pulled at her until she had parted her mooring and drifted into the
surf? She had been such a proud and graceful thing, but now she
was wreckage. She had never been known to let her captain down,
whether he was Stephen Bennett or Nils Sorensen. But somehow,
someone had let the *Donna* down, and while the Island slept, this was
what had become of her grace and beauty and loyalty.

Joanna went upstairs, past the sleeping children, and into Owen's
room.

"Get up, Owen," she said. She blinked the tears back and stared
hard at his sleep-heavy dark face to keep them from returning. "Nils'
boat has gone ashore. She parted her mooring somehow. She's lying
on Eastern Harbor Point now."

"Jeest," said Owen on a long slow breath, and sat up. She went
downstairs again, fixed the fire automatically, and put on her coat.
She was past the windbreak when Owen caught up with her. He
didn't say anything as they walked together around the shore and
out on the Point. She knew what he was thinking. He was responsible for the care of the moorings, and he'd slipped up, he'd forgotten.
He'd been so intent on his pursuit of Laurie Gibson that he hadn't
checked up on the mooring since that storm in the spring. He'd
mentioned the need of a new pennant but evidently he'd let it go,
putting off the task until a gale had come to catch him with the job
undone.

She was not angry with him. He was suffering enough. It
wouldn't help anything, or bring the *Donna* back again, to resent his
neglect. She thought wryly, *He must be really smitten with Laurie.*

The side upon which the boat lay had been bashed in as if it
had been no more than an eggshell. The wind tore at Joanna with
its full strength out here on the Point, and fine, stinging spray blew
against her face, but she didn't notice. She looked impassively at the
wreck. She knew enough of boats to realize how much the *Donna* was
bruised and broken beyond immediate repair. The splintered plank-
ing, the twisted timbers, the great hole where there had once been
a graceful curve; she looked at it all, and reckoned the loss, but it

was as if another Joanna stood there on the shore with Owen. Some part of her that could not bear this blow had shut itself away.

She glanced at her brother. His face was hard, cut like red-brown stone. There was a quick glitter on his lashes, and she turned away, shoving her hands down hard into her pockets. For Owen it was still their father's boat, and since they had been children the *Donna* had ridden the same mooring, and had never once broken away. Whenever they saw her there, it was something of their father left to them. And now Owen stood on the wet stones in the biting November wind, and knew perhaps a heavier, more barren, solitude than he had ever known before.

Joanna saw it all, without pain. The pain would come later. She began to walk away from the boat, wanting to get home before she broke down. She heard Owen's boots on the stones and knew he was coming behind her.

They met Sigurd coming around the beach, his yellow hair blowing in the wind, his heavy shirt open over his chest. "*Allsmägtige Gud!* It's Nils' boat, ain't it?"

Yes, it was Nils' boat, and she would have to write and tell him what had happened. But there was something else. All the way to the house she moved under the shadow of it, like someone who had awakened to the vague knowledge of tragedy and is trying to remember what it is.

Owen stopped to speak to Sigurd, and she went on. In the house the teakettle was boiling noisily, and she pushed it back, and stood by the fire as if to warm herself. But she knew that no fire could reach the coldness she felt. . . . Other boats had gone ashore before this, and had been as badly broken up as the *Donna*. There had never been any good reason to believe that the *Donna*'s security was a sure thing; every boat took a chance lying there in the harbor. But yet she could not help saying to herself, *Why should Nils be the one to lose a boat?* Of all the boats in the harbor it had to be his that had broken away from her mooring.

She would not listen to any reasonable thought that came to her; that it was Owen's fault and no unfair gesture of fate. If he'd been on the alert and had seen to the pennant in time the *Donna* would be riding the waves this morning with the rest of the fleet. . . . To dwell on this would have quickened her with the wholesome invigoration of justified anger. But she couldn't think about Owen, only of Nils.

Nils would be heartsick when he got her letter and knew what had happened to the white boat he'd put on her mooring that noon-time when he'd said good-bye to the Island and all it held dear for him. She could almost see the way he would look, the quick tighten-ing of his face, the shuttering of his eyes, when the letter was in his hands and the written words were flat and cold and cruel with the message she had sent. No matter how she tried to sheathe the truth, nothing could really blunt its edge. The *Donna* lay ravaged and bro-ken on the rocks; there was no miracle that could restore her over-night to her mooring.

She went to the window and looked across the harbor toward the Point, and at the boat lying upon the coarse, jagged shore. Owen was coming toward the house, walking slowly, his head down as if he were tired. He stopped and waited, looking down past the Binna-cle. Someone was coming; out of apathy rather than curiosity, Joanna watched, and saw Dennis Garland joining Owen in the path. They talked for a few moments, turning to look across the harbor, and she knew that Owen was explaining the cause of the wreck. Then she saw Owen glance up toward the house; her apathy vanished before a tide of dread that threatened to roll over her completely, until she saw that Dennis was not coming home with Owen after all. Owen was walking up the path alone. The tide ebbed out, leaving her as spent as the sea had left the *Donna*.

She shut her eyes against a sudden terror from within. What was there about Dennis that should affect her so? She looked back over the days since she had first known him. But now she couldn't think clearly about their congenial talks, their shared jokes, the safe, *good* part of knowing him; she was thinking about the way she had come to feel when she saw him, when she heard his voice, when she met his eyes. There was nothing either safe or good about this, and she hated it, she loathed it, she had refused to face it until now. The tide of dread began to race back, it caught her and tumbled and buffeted her in the surf, it tried to pull her out into the inky-green depths and then tossed her back again into the breakers.

Was it true, then, that like the *Donna* she was slipping her mooring—the strong, secure mooring of Nils' love—and drifting toward Dennis? She shook her head wildly, trying to stop the pounding in her ears. *Think calmly,* she told herself. *Think straight.* There was no reason on earth that should draw her toward Dennis. He had charm, yes; but Nils had charm too. He had a strong personality, but so did Nils. She liked the cut of his face, the shape of his hands, his build; but this shouldn't constitute love, or even attraction. And his gray eyes could not stab her as deeply or as sweetly as Nils' blue ones could do. Dennis loved her; but she had been loved before, and had never looked back at the lover.

Then why this quickening whenever she saw Dennis on the road, or when he caught her glance? She could not deny it, although she wished with all her heart that she could. Dennis drew her in spite of herself; merely to hear his name stung her with a pain as elusive and bright as quicksilver.

It was time to take it all into account. She stared out at the *Donna,* whose wet white side gleamed against the dark rocks. Owen was coming up by the windbreak, and she looked past him as if he didn't exist. She must write and tell Nils that he'd lost his boat. But she mustn't tell him that he was in danger of losing something far more important.

She looked down and discovered that her fingers were clenched tightly on the edge of the sink, so tightly that the tips were white. She loosened them, one at a time.

She knew what she must do now. From this moment on, she would have absolutely nothing more to do with Dennis Garland. Whatever he might think or wonder, she must keep far away from him.

29

WHAT WAS LEFT OF THE *Donna* was hauled up on the grassground, where no waves could ever reach her. Owen was moody and downcast about it, and a pall hung over the house. Jamie was fractious, Ellen looked wan, and when the children were thus affected, Joanna took steps.

"Forget it, Owen," she said to him one evening, after the children had gone to bed. She spoke with a philosophical crispness which she didn't feel. "Forget it, will you? I'm thankful it wasn't a boat that's in use. We can rebuild her sometime, after the war, when we can get the material. And for the time being we might as well forget about it."

"Damn all women," Owen said savagely. "If I hadn't been chasin' after one, I'd seen what was happenin' to the moorin'."

"Well, you never let anything go before like that, and *I'd* hate to be condemned for *my* first mistake." Her knitting needles made a tiny, cheerful clicking, making a sweater for the Red Cross.

"By Christ, it's my last mistake then," he growled. "And if I want to look at a woman I'll go to Limerock—instead of this gormin' around takin' walks, and all the rest of the foolishness."

Joanna smiled, and went on knitting. As deeply absorbed in Laurie as he was, his threat was a hollow one. And henceforth he'd be better company around the house, and that was what Joanna wanted; it would be easier to get used to the loss of the *Donna* if Owen were not stamping in and out in a black fury of self-accusation.

She had written to Nils at once about the boat, and the answer came back by air-mail. They would repair the *Donna* somehow, he told her, no matter how badly she'd been smashed. He gave directions for the care of the engine.

Thanksgiving was coming, and then Christmas. The Island winter set in all at once, after the long and dreaming fall. Snow drifted down across the harbor, and outlined each dark spruce branch with white; the fields were as dead, as snow-bound in the lee, as if they had never known summer. In the early mornings after a snowfall, the white was penciled delicately with the tracks of chickadees and juncoes and crows. The brook froze, and the ducks moved into the barn, the alder swamp was a tangle of bare branches through which the sunlight fell freely on places that it could never reach when the leaves were green.

There were flashing, sunny days when the sea smoked with vapor; it was calm enough to go to haul, but the vapor at once burned and froze the flesh. There were mild days, when the clouds were soft and delicately tinted over Brigport, and the paths grew muddy. Then there were blizzards when the steady pounding of surf was drowned out by the high thin wail of the wind. The snow blew, and cut like fragments of ice, and left the Island bare in some places, deeply drifted in others. There were days to go haul in, and there were many more days that weren't fit, except to row out to the mooring and pound the ice off the bows and decks. In the fall the men shifted their traps to deep water, far from the Island. The lobsters went there in the winter time, to live in the protective mud. So when the gales came, the traps were fairly safe. They might drag, but there was less chance of their being splintered into matchwood against the rocks. During a blow the Islanders settled in snugly, with a minimum of worry. There were long hours of radio, hours warmed by aromatic fires of spruce wood that had been cut in warmer weather and had had time in which to season. There were card games, and the sewing afternoons, and the children coming and going from school; reading, knitting, quilt-piecing.

And this was the time when the Islanders ate summer from the jars that stood on the celler shelves; vegetables, strawberry jam that tasted of sunshine, raspberries and blackberries, the mackerel and herring that had been caught on still, mild, nights full of stars. Life on the mainland offered steam heat, movies, stores; but they'd all had their fill of mainland living, and for the most part they were content on the Island.

For the first time in many years there was a Christmas party in the clubhouse, with recitations and songs, and a little play by the children. Laurie Gibson had been keeping them busy all fall with the preparations. After the children's part was over, there was the Christmas tree, with a present for everybody; ice cream the Fennells made, cakes contributed by everyone who had any spare sugar. Then the dance came. It was just Bennett's Island people this time, and it was a happy evening, even though a steady undercurrent of sadness beat through the music for Nils and Mark and Stevie.

Joanna was glad when New Year's was past, it meant that it was the turn of the year, and anything could happen now. Germany could be beaten, Japan could surrender, and Nils would come home.

She hadn't gone far from the house during November and December, and Dennis Garland hadn't called. They'd danced together at the Christmas party and had been pleasant and polite to each other. *It's really easy to be like this,* Joanna thought, but sometimes she found herself wondering what she would do if she should glance out the harbor window and see Dennis coming. The very fancy caused a sickening constriction in her breathing, and so she did not think of it often. She thought instead about how it would be if she should see Nils coming up the path.

Nora came down one raw, slate-gray afternoon. In her dark-blue ski suit, with her visored red cap and woolly mittens, and her cheeks as red as the cap, she wore a sparkle about her, a gayety, that took Joanna back to the time when Nora had first come to the Island.

"You look happy," Joanna said appreciatively.

"I am! Guess why I'm out? Gram shooed me out. Said I wasn't to poke around the house all day with an old lady!"

"Well, take off your things then, and be comfortable. . . . What's come over Gram, anyway?"

"Oh, she's been that way ever since I fell down stairs that time. Now that she knows I'm perfectly willing and able to give Matthew an heir, she's been fine." She gave Joanna a sheepish glance. "Of course, I've been meeting her half-way."

"Good for you," said Joanna dryly. "Well, how about some coffee? I was just going to make some."

"Grand!" Nora dropped down on the floor beside Jamie. "Hi, old-timer! Let me see your new boats." Joanna left them and went into the kitchen to start the coffee. It was good to see Nora looking so well; perhaps it had been all for the best that she'd lost the baby, since the change in her—and in Gram—had dated from that time.

The world wasn't so badly off, after all. It gave her an optimistic lift, and she went back to the other room in anticipation of an afternoon of lively conversation. She found Nora still kneeling beside Jamie, while he demonstrated his new boats. But Nora's eyes were shadowed and remote.

"That's fine, Jamie," she said absently, and got to her feet. "Joanna, what I really wanted to tell you about—" There was trouble in her voice, and in the set of her mouth. "Well, I don't suppose you can do anything, or anybody can, but it's been on my mind. It has to do with Laurie."

"Laurie?" Joanna took out the inescapable knitting and Nora curled up opposite her in the other big rocker. "I thought she was more fun than a basket of pups. Don't tell me she's hard to live with."

"No, she isn't hard to live with. She's swell, really." Nora gazed out through the geraniums at the wintery field. "But she isn't so gay these days. I don't know whether she's run-down, or if it's something on her mind. Matthew noticed it too, especially after she came back to the Island after Christmas."

"Maybe she doesn't like winter on the Island after all," Joanna suggested.

"I don't know," Nora said somberly. "Sometimes in the morning her eyes look bad, as if she might have been crying."

"The children don't complain. But she might have had words with Owen—he doesn't go up there much lately." She tried to think back to the last time Owen had gone to see Laurie, and discovered with a faint shock that she couldn't remember. Had he really taken the *Donna*'s loss so seriously, then? She doubted it.

"Whatever it is," Nora was saying, "she covers it pretty well. It only comes out when she's off guard. You catch her staring into space."

"Poor Laurie," Joanna said absently. "Maybe she's worried about things at home."

The conversation turned to other things, and she did not think of Laurie again—consciously—until just before supper, after Nora had gone. She was alone except for Jamie and the dog. Ellen had gone to the homestead from school, to play with her cousins. Joanna lit the lamps, and started supper, and while she was cutting out biscuits, the idea came to her. It hit her with all the unpleasant impact of a door slamming on her fingers, and it sent a vibration of astonished dismay along her backbone that swung up her chin and left her staring at the cupboard doors with narrowed eyes and tightening mouth.

I may be wrong, she thought. *But I could be right. God knows I don't want to be right, but—* Out in the sun parlor the door banged. Dick bounded through the kitchen on his way to meet Owen, and she knew that sometime within the next fifteen minutes, she was going to break a cardinal rule and ask Owen a personal question—about Laurie.

He had nothing to say when he came in, but then he never did when he'd been working on gear all afternoon and came in hungry. She gave him a cup of coffee to hold him until supper time, finished cutting her biscuits, and put them in the oven. Then she went into the dining room and sat down opposite him at the table.

He was sprawled low in his chair, his head tilted back, his black eyes heavy-lidded and sleepy as he watched the smoke from his cigarette rise toward the ceiling. She tried to study his bold profile impersonally, as if he weren't her brother, as if she hadn't always possessed a fierce sense of pride where her brothers and their behavior was concerned.

He was a handsome devil, and he was old enough, and practised enough, to know just how to sweep a girl like Laurie off her feet. But how did you go about asking your brother how far he'd gone with a girl? There was a time, when they were in their rowdy, blatantly honest teens, when she could have asked him and been answered. Now, she didn't know.

She would have been willing to swear, before today, that Owen couldn't talk his way around Laurie. But today all that was changed. She knew what the Island could do to a girl who was not Island-bred and more or less immune. Laurie was warm-blooded, as sensitive as Joanna to fragrances and atmospheres; from the first she'd been highly infatuated with the Island. And as the year deepened from the rich bloom of early September into fall, she'd spent hour after hour with Owen on the warm slopes of the West Side. Joanna knew those dreamy days, when a lilac mist hung over the horizon, and the water rippled in little quicksilver curls around the rocks, and a silence like that of an enchanted land hung over the woods where no one ever went but children—or lovers.

She wished she knew if Owen, by some incredible freak of affairs, really loved the girl. But a man like Owen didn't have to be in love, he needed only to be tempted by the fact that the fruit was ripe.

"Owen," she said at last. He gave her a lazy glance through his lashes.

"Yeah."

"Nora says that Laurie isn't very happy. She's got something on her mind." This was blunter than she'd intended to be, but at least he was listening.

Owen dropped ashes in the cuff of his rubber boot and said deliberately, "What do you mean — unhappy?"

"Well —" Joanna shrugged. "Preoccupied. Moody. You know."

"No, I don't know." Owen was sitting up now. His black eyes were hard and direct and hostile. "What are you gettin' at?"

"Maybe she's in love. Girls get sick with it, I've heard. It strikes in, or something."

"If you're fishin' for information, I can't help ye any. Jeest, I haven't talked with the girl since way back last November sometime." He crushed out his cigarette in his saucer, and stood up, stretching till his fingers touched the ceiling. "You think she's got caught on a stump, or somethin'? Lost your good opinion of her, ain't ye?"

"I didn't say anything of the sort," Joanna protested, and Owen laughed.

"What in hell are you hennin' around for, then?" He pulled on his mackinaw and picked up his cap. "Well, I'll get a few more buoys strapped before supper, I guess."

He went out whistling, and she sat still, looking at his coffee cup. She had found out exactly nothing, and all she had was a soiled and uncomfortable feeling. She hadn't lost her good opinion of Laurie; but she knew what it was to be a girl like Laurie, and she knew her brothers. She had known Island boys all her life and had seen the effect of their particular brand of romantic hawk-wildness on the women who had come in contact with them. Islanders were *different;* and mainland girls were fascinated and drawn by that very difference. If anything had happened to Laurie, she needed a friend.

30

SOMETIMES SHE SAW LAURIE walking up the lane on her way home from school in the late afternoon. The firm, spring vitality wasn't there now. Ellen observed that Miss Gibson seemed tired these days, she wasn't so much fun as she'd been.

Then Young Charles and his sister Donna told Joanna that Bobby Merrill wasn't coming over from Brigport any more. The teacher didn't have any boyfriends now, they said. Everything added to Joanna's apprehension, and when she saw the girl at a distance— Laurie never dropped in, these days—she felt a helpless compassion for her.

But she lacked courage to ask Owen any more questions, after that one attempt. And so she had to make up the story herself, and she didn't like it. It spoiled everything that was in the least degree enjoyable about the life she was living now, when she must always remember that Laurie Gibson was miserable, that she was a long way from home and in alien surroundings. She found herself watching the spruces as Laurie must see them, tossing and swaying against winter-blown skies. She saw the rushing clouds, listened to the wind and the sea's rote, watched the surf forever piling in deadly white chaos on Eastern Harbor Point, and their familiar response in her was deadened, because of Laurie.

Owen never spoke of Laurie. Then he came in at the edge of dark one night, with fine crystals of snow powdering his black brows and hair, and said with savage abruptness, "Matthew Fennell's been holding forth all afternoon down in the shop."

"What about?" Joanna asked idly. Ellen was with her cousins again, the house was quiet.

"Laurie Gibson," said Owen. He shook his mackinaw with a fine disregard for the clean kitchen floor, and hung it up; then he sat down to pull off his boots. Joanna waited for him to go on, her impatience making knots in her stomach. But Owen wasn't to be hurried. He put his boots behind the stove and padded around in his stocking feet, whistling softly.

"Your moccasins are on the woodbox," she said at last. "What about Laurie?"

"Oh, her." Owen gave her a bright, mocking glance. "Nosey, ain't ye? What's your pucker?"

Joanna turned away from him in annoyance, and his voice followed her, softly and slyly. "Even if I didn't tell you, darlin' mine, you'd find out in a couple of months. So'd the whole Island. It's practically a sure thing."

"Owen . . . no."

"Yes. She hasn't said anything, but Matthew's sure of it, and he's all hawsed up. Says some beggar left her in the lurch."

She said hesitantly, "Who?"

"Matthew thinks it's Bobby Merrill."

Joanna hardly heard him. She was staring at him and seeing something else. "Poor Laurie," she said. "The poor kid. She must be terrified."

"Poor damn' fool, if you ask me. And Bobby'll be a bigger fool, if they haul him into it."

"Who'll haul him into it, if she's not saying anything?" Joanna demanded.

Owen dropped into a chair and took out his cigarettes. "Then she's about as numb as anyone could be and live. Wouldn't you think that little idiot would want to get married right off? The kid's got to have a name. But no, probably none of us Islanders are good enough for the likes of her. So she's lookin' down her nose at us."

He stared at the match flame for an instant before he lit his cigarette, and Joanna realized that he was really enraged; he was smoldering. Because young Bobby got there and he didn't?

"You don't know much about women, Owen," she said. "You think you do, but you know just about *nothing*. Laurie's a kid, and she's away from home. You and the others gave her a grand rush. Now she's fallen in love and gone over the edge. Can't you imagine how she must be feeling? Scared to death, and wondering if it's a false alarm, but if it's true, how's she ever going to face her people? She's probably carrying all the guilt in the world on her shoulders and thinking she's the lowest thing in creation. Laurie's a *good* girl, Owen."

Owen said, grinning, "Amen to that."

"It's not your fault that she stayed out of trouble as long as she did," Joanna flared at him.

"Oh take it easy! What I want to know is, what's she have to act this way for? So high-and-mighty?"

"Oh, you're so *stupid* about girls! Maybe Bobby Merrill, or whoever it is, hasn't asked her to marry him! Maybe she's heard of men who turn against a girl when they've got her into a mess, and think she's cheap, so she's afraid to approach him. And maybe she's so upset that she's wandering around in a sort of fog." She took a long breath. "I think if that ever happened to me I'd want to jump off the nearest wharf rather than admit it."

"Quite an oration," said Owen lazily. "Just goes to show what a mess a woman's mind can be. If she's thinkin' all those things at once, she's just about half there. A man's better off without her."

"I could brain you, Owen Bennett," she began hotly, and then Ellen came in.

Clear days in winter had a particular gloss and sparkle of their own, from the first apricot glow of sunrise until sunset, when the woods threw shadow as purple as grapes across the fields, and the harbor rocks turned red in their reflection of the west. It was this sort of gem-like day that followed the evening when Owen told Joanna about Matthew. There was a light fall of snow on the ground, and it glittered like diamond dust where the sun struck it, and reflected the skies' brightness even after the sun had gone down behind Pete Grant's house.

Joanna took Jamie out for a walk after his nap. Buttoned and zipped securely into his snowsuit, his round cheeks framed by his helmet, he marched ahead of her across the Island to Schoolhouse Cove and back again without stumbling. She watched him, thinking how much he had grown since the spring. Now he was a real little boy instead of a baby, his very walk was different, his sense of humor had enlarged, his expressions had changed. Her letters to Nils were making a record of Jamie's growing-up.

When they came to the harbor beach he wanted to climb in and out of the skiffs; but Dennis was on the lobster car, buying Sigurd's haul, and she wanted no conversation with him. She waved and smiled when the two men looked up toward the path, and led Jamie firmly away from the beach.

"We'll see what Owen's doing in the shop," she comforted him, when his lower lip came out, and he grudgingly conceded that it would be all right.

The fish house smelled of the drying-out traps that were stacked to the ceiling, and of the roaring fire in the pot-bellied stove. Owen stood at the bench strapping bottles for toggles. Above the bench the windows faced the south-west and the late sun shone in, hot and yellow. Perhaps it was the sun across his face that made him scowl so; his brows were drawn together, his jaw was set, and he knotted the pot warp with quick, vicious thrusts and pulls.

"We came to see you, Uncle Owen," said Joanna tranquilly, turning Jamie loose among the buoys.

"So I notice," Owen muttered. "Don't scatter those buoys around, Jamie. Leave them alone."

Jamie, unused to such restrictions when he visited the fish house, straightened up, his blue eyes rounding and his lower lip coming out again. This time it was trembling.

"Here, Jamie," Joanna gathered up some lath ends, gave him Nils' hammer and a handful of wire nails that had been bought for traps and then discarded as no good. "Temper, temper, Uncle Owen," she said lightly. "What's biting you?"

"What the hell? Does anythin' have to be bitin' me? What are you doin' down around here anyway?"

"Just out for a walk, Owen. There's no call for you to be ugly." She walked across the shop to the window in the end that faced up toward the house. "School will be out in a few minutes. As soon as I see Ellen coming along, I'll leave you in peace and quiet."

She stood there idly, watching Jamie hammering nails. The sound of the hammer, the snapping of the fire, the click of bottles, were serene and homey sounds she had heard all her life; there'd been times when she'd loved the atmosphere of a fish house far more than the tidiness of a house. When Nils came home, she'd come down often to talk with him while he worked, or just to watch, without speaking, like this. The thought of it was like drawing a long, refreshing breath of clean air, it spread through her like the balm of peace.

She glanced out at the village now and then. The snow sparkled, and every house and tree seemed to be gilded by the sunshine.

Ellen came by Sigurd's house, arm in arm with her cousin Donna. They wore bright parkas, gaudy socks and mittens, and their feet fairly skipped on the frozen ground. *I'd better go up and tell them what they can have for a mug-up,* she thought absently, watching them with pleasure as they turned up the path toward the house. But it was nice standing here, almost imagining that it was Nils working at the bench instead of Owen.

Then Laurie Gibson came by. Involuntarily Joanna moved back to where the traps shadowed her against any glance from the outside. Without knowing why, she said quietly, "Owen . . . look here."

He came over to where she stood, and they watched Laurie in the interval of time it took her to go by Sigurd's and then disappear behind the Binnacle. She wore a bright pleated skirt that should have swung saucily about her knees, if she had walked as vibrantly as she'd once walked; the hood of her parka was thrown back, and against the dark wall of Gunnar's windbreak her young profile showed set and white and lost.

When the Binnacle hid her, Joanna looked up at Owen. "Poor kid—" she began, and stopped. Owen was staring at the empty path where Laurie had just been, as if his black eyes were still seeing that gallantly straight small figure. There was a whiteness all around his mouth; he was oblivious of Joanna, he was lost in some wasteland of his own. She walked away from him then, without speaking, and beckoned to Jamie.

Her lips formed the enticing word, "Mug-up," before he could protest aloud, and she took him home.

The two girls, who were eighth-graders in the school, were preparing to do their homework on the dining-room table. She looked at them in surprise until they explained that Ellen was invited up to Donna's that evening to make popcorn balls, and they wanted to get their school work out of the way. She nodded, and smiled at the happy excitement in their faces and went to make cocoa for them and set out a bowl of molasses cookies. But all the time she was working she was conscious of a driving urgency, as if there was some violent reason for her hurrying.

When Owen came in, scarcely ten minutes after she'd left him in the shop, she knew the reason. She was putting Jamie in his high chair, and Owen came and stood in the doorway. Across the girls' heads, one fair and one dark, he looked at Joanna long and hard. Then, with a slight hunching of one shoulder he went out again, through the sun parlor and out the back door. Joanna followed him; that was what he'd meant her to do.

She found him standing on the doorstep. His back was toward her as she came out, his shoulders were broad under the red and black plaid; his legs were braced as though he stood at the wheel of the *White Lady* in a choppy sea, and he was looking up toward the Fennells'. With one hand he was breaking the brittle lilac twigs, the snapping sounds were loud in the still cold. Joanna watched that hand for a moment before she spoke to him. There was a repressed but passionate emotion in those brown fingers, they cast the broken bits of twig away from him with something like angry revulsion.

"Well?" she said quietly.

He didn't turn around. "Start talkin', Jo," he said harshly.

Her amazement made her catch her breath. She forgot the cold that stung through her dress. "About what?"

"Tell me what to say to her."

"Why do you have to say anything, Owen?" But it wasn't as if she didn't know. She moved slightly until she could see the line of his forehead and high, jutting cheekbone, the flat slanting stroke to his chin. A tide of dark color was flowing under the skin.

"I'm really sold on the kid, Jo." His voice came with difficulty, he was playing a role alien to him. "I guess I'm—in love with her all right. Joke's on me." He didn't look around at her, he held his head stiffly high. "I didn't catch on to the love stuff till after I got her where I wanted her." The red deepened even more. "If you don't think I know what kind of a son-of-a-bitchin' bastard I am, you're crazy."

There was no time to be shocked, no time to criticize. "Have you been to see her at all—since?" Joanna asked.

He cleared his throat. "I went around by the school the next day, when the kids were gone. She was markin' papers and when she saw me she turned white as chalk, and wouldn't look at me. I tried to tell her . . . but she asked me in that damned stuck-up voice if I'd please go. So I went."

Joanna saw him standing inside the schoolhouse door, immense against its child-scaled furnishings, watching Laurie, trying to say tender words with a mouth that was shaped for mockery and cynicism. "She was too upset then, Owen. You should have tried again."

"I did, but she was so goddam stubborn. . . . She was crazy enough about me before it happened, too."

"I'm willing to bet anything she's still crazy about you. Girls like Laurie don't do what she did unless they're in love. They're not like Thea."

He looked at her then, or rather turned on her, like a hurt animal goaded into fury. "What are you tellin' me that for? Don't you think I know it, for Christ's sake! Don't you think I want to make it right?"

"But don't tell her that," Joanna warned him. "Don't tell her you want to make it right. Tell her what you told me—that you love her, and you won't leave her alone till she promises to marry you." In her eagerness she took hold of his forearm and shook it. "Tell her what she wants to hear! Don't let her think she's lowered herself, but that she'd be honoring you if she married you—"

His rigid mouth relaxed enough to twist in a faint grin. "You want to do my proposin' for me?"

"No. I'm going in and start supper." She left him abruptly, knowing that she had said enough. The rest was up to him.

In the next few minutes she made herself very busy, trying to explain an obscure problem to the girls, taking Jamie out of his high chair again, now that he'd finished his cookie. She felt curiously lightheaded and taut, she knew the suspense of the next hour would be all but unendurable.

Going out into the sun parlor once, she glanced out the back door and saw that Owen had gone. When she'd first questioned him about Laurie, she'd hoped with all her sincerity and her pride that Owen wasn't responsible; for she had never once considered that he might love the girl. His almost inarticulate confession there on the doorstep had moved her deeply. Now her chief emotion was astonishment, and not dismay. And the astonishment was tinged with satisfaction. If Owen had really fallen in love with Laurie, she was truly glad. He was nearly forty, he should have a home of his own to anchor him, and Laurie would make him a good wife.

Nora came in while she was cutting strips of dried fish for soaking.

"You look good," Nora stated. "Happier than a lot of people I've seen lately. . . . The schoolmarm came home looking as if she'd been dragged through seven cities, and she wouldn't eat anything. She went out for a walk. Then your brother comes up, looking even worse. I told him she'd gone for a walk down Chip Cove way, and he hiked off without another word."

"That's what you call the troubles of young love," said Joanna with a warning tilt of her head toward the apparently oblivious children in the dining room. "What's in the dish you're hugging so fondly to your bosom?"

"Oh, Gram's been baking!" Nora grinned, and set the little dish down on the dresser, uncovering it. "It's some sort of custard, and she fixed this 'specially for Jamie."

It was a good world. Suddenly Joanna liked it very much. In it she could conquer anything, nothing could daunt her. Was it possible that she'd been apprehensive about *anything?* Oh, yes, it was possible; she had worried about Nils, Owen, Laurie, and about herself. But not now. Loving-kindness flowed around her in as tangible a stream as the heat from the stove.

31

NORA STAYED ONLY A LITTLE WHILE. Then Donna, having done her arithmetic with Ellen's assistance, gathered up her things. She was fourteen, a pretty, vivacious, black-haired girl who found life on Bennett's Island very dull after the comparative brillance of Pruitt's Harbor. But she was gay about her boredom. Ellen walked home with her through the frozen alder swamp. The day was still bright; wartime daylight saving had pushed back the early winter dusk.

On the back of the stove the teakettle hummed as busily and contentedly as a bee tumbling in and out of a honeysuckle vine. The sounds Jamie made as he played were contented too; he murmured to his boats and trains and trucks, weaving a long involved story about them. Joanna was to remember that small tranquil interval for the rest of her life.

It ended when she heard running feet on the long doorstep at the back, and Ellen's voice, high and piercing with terror. "Mother— mother—"

Joanna was at the door before the child could get it open. For a moment Ellen wrestled with the knob in wild desperation before she glanced up through the pane and saw her mother. Her eyes had darkened incredibly, or else her face had grown unbelievably white.

"Mother," she sobbed, as Joanna swung the door open. She caught at Joanna with the strength of pure panic. "Mother, it's Owen—he's coming across the meadow now, and he's all dripping blood—" Her voice rose, and she began to choke. Joanna took her by the shoulders. Resisting her own impulse to run out and see, she spoke with authority.

"All right, Ellen. Don't cry. You'll frighten Jamie."

The girl stared up at her, her thin shoulders moving convulsively under Joanna's fingers. She took a long gulping breath, and then nodded. "We heard the noise, up at Uncle Charles'. But we thought it was a ship having target practice down off Pirate Island. And I started home, and then I saw Owen coming from Goose Cove." The wild trembling began again. "He's all covered with blood, Mother, he *is!*"

Oh, Lord! said Joanna silently. She tightened her grip on Ellen's shoulders.

"We've got to help him, then. Can you run?"

"I ran all the way home—"

"Then go down and get Dennis."

Ellen ran through the sun parlor and out the front door like a wild creature escaping from a snare, her bright hood flapping.

"Mama," Jamie said from the doorway. He was mildly curious. "Where did Ellen go?"

"She'll be back in a minute." Joanna picked him up and put him in his high chair, into which he fitted so snugly there was no chance of his standing up. She forestalled his howl of righteous indignation with an unprecedented handful of cookies. "Ellen's coming right back. Dick's here. Stay with him, Dick. . . . Mother's got to get some wood for the fire, Jamie."

She snatched a jacket from the row of hooks as she passed and ran out, pulling on the jacket as she went. The frozen ground rang under her feet, the first onrush of cold air in her lungs was like fire. In the alder swamp there were the new tracks made by Donna and Ellen, and then by Ellen as she ran home. Joanna was the one who ran now, steadily, trying not to conjecture, trying not to wonder what she would find.

When she broke out past the belt of spruces into the meadow, she found Owen. He was a scant fifteen feet away from her, but he didn't see her; he came toward her at a staggering, lunging pace, that managed to be fast, but blind. The blood was there, and Ellen had been right. It dripped from the arm that he held rigidly against his side, it ran off the tips of his fingers, or where the tips should be, in a steady scarlet stream that splattered the snow between the grass-clumps. The other hand, pressed awkwardly against the front of his jacket, was red too. The jacket itself was ripped and shredded, one shoulder had been almost entirely torn loose.

Joanna moistened her lips, and conquered her nausea. *"Owen,"* she said, and stepped in his way. He stared at her from a face that seemed burned and blackened.

"Must have been a mine," he said thickly. "Floated ashore. I poked it. Goddam a fool!"

Joanna felt a maddening helplessness. It was surely wrong to let him walk another yard while he was bleeding like that; but the wonder was that he had walked all the way from Goose Cove.

"Out of my way, woman," he muttered. She stepped back dumbly; and then she heard Sigurd call from the alder swamp. He came in sight first, and then Dennis, with Franny behind him. She was grateful for them all, with a gratitude that made her eyes swim; but it was Dennis she saw with a prayerful relief that seemed to sink into her bones and melt them so that she wanted to sit down on the ground with her back against a tree and not move for an hour.

"Well, I'll be a son-of-a-bitch," Owen muttered in vague amazement as the men surrounded him. He began to waver. Sigurd caught him by the shoulder that was intact, holding him with his great strength. Franny stood by, holding the things that Dennis had brought, and Dennis began to make tourniquets. Joanna could not keep from watching him; first, his hands, as they bound and tied and twisted, working with strong and competent agility to stop the bleeding. Then his face. . . . Reaction was setting in; the scene blurred and writhed before her eyes. She thought dimly, *I don't have to worry now, Dennis is here. . . . Dennis always comes.*

"*Joanna!*" Dennis said, without stopping his work. His voice was like a slap across her fading consciousness. She shook her head hard, and everything became clear at once; Owen's face, set like dark iron, his eyes gazing into space as he tried to stand alone and not lean too much on Sigurd; Sigurd's face, red, sweating, as he bit at his lower lip; Franny, pale and intent, like a frightened white rabbit; and Dennis. He was in command. He was looking out for Owen, but his skilled eyes had time for her too, and they were warning her. They held her up as if they had been his hands.

"You'd better go up and get Charles," he said, nodding his head toward the homestead. "I don't need you here."

The meadow seemed miles wide, and the Bennett house seemed very small with distance, up on its rise. Its windows blazed with the sunset, the snow on the slope was tinged with rose and gold. Yes, it was a long way when her legs were trembling. But he had told her to get Charles.

She looked back once. Where they were, there was no sun, it had gone down behind the solid black wall of the tall old spruces; the snow was overlaid with purpling shadows, and against it the men stood in a tight, dark knot. She went on, and after what seemed a long while, she climbed up into the sunshine. The snow crystals glistened in tiny jets as she walked through the powdery stuff. Charles' windows winked and gleamed. From here she could look down at Schoolhouse Cove on her left, and Goose Cove on her right; and she wondered if she'd ever again be able to look at the long oval of Goose Cove, dark sapphire as the shadows thickened over it, without this instant drying of her throat and difficulty with her breath.

She stepped up on the wide granite doorstep under the front door, laid her hand on the knob, and went into the house.

*   *   *

When she and Charles came down through the meadow, ten minutes later, the men had gone. The snow where they had been was trampled and stained. Charles looked at it with his chin jutting out, his eyelids drooping. He said nothing at all. They went through the alder swamp to the house.

It was oddly reminiscent of the time Owen had collapsed at the oars. The other men stood around the kitchen nervously, giving Charles quick nervous grins, glancing sheepishly at Joanna as if they expected her to give way in customary feminine fashion. But the moment had passed when she might have given way. She spoke to them briskly, and went into the dining room, where Ellen, still woefully white, sat in the rocking chair holding Jamie; she was keeping him turned away from the sitting-room door, and was talking to him in a low voice.

Joanna brushed a lock of hair back from Ellen's forehead and tucked it carefully under the ribbon. "Good girl, Ellen," she murmured. "You're a real help." Jamie struggled to sit up, and held out his arms imploringly. She shook her head at him. "Stay with Ellen, Jamie. If you're a bad boy, you'll have to go upstairs in your crib."

She turned inquiringly toward Dennis as he came out from the sitting room, trying to read his face; but he had the same unemotional, preoccupied expression he had had when he worked over Nora.

"How bad is it?" Charles asked.

"I've stopped the bleeding for the time being, but we can't leave the tourniquets on too long. I don't know what I'll find when I get his jacket off. . . . Can you put leaves in this table, Joanna?"

She nodded, and began to clear things away. She felt as calm as Dennis looked. It was impossible to be afraid now. She realized her faith in Dennis might be childlike, but at the same time it was a wellspring of strength.

Behind her Charles and Dennis talked in low, unruffled voices. "I'll want all the first-aid material there is on the Island," Dennis was saying. "I've got some sulfa powder, but I'll need more dressings. We'll fix him up so we can get him ashore—I don't dare take a chance on sending him in as he is now."

"I'll take him in," said Charles. "In his own boat. She's the fastest in the harbor."

"Good. And before we start, call up for an ambulance to meet us, will you?" He went over to Ellen's chair and looked down at her. She smiled back at him, and the last of her wan pallor went. "Want a job, Ellen?"

"Sure," she said promptly.

"Take Jamie down and park him with Leonie for a while. Then, you can start collecting everybody's first-aid stuff, and all their hot-water bottles. We'll keep him as warm as we can on the trip."

There was a comforting stir of activity at once. Joanna stuffed Jamie briskly into his snowsuit, and for once he was too overwhelmed to protest. She led him to the door, and Ellen followed, zipping her parka. She said soberly, "Gee, Mother, I'm glad Dennis is here. It's just like when Nils is here, he knows what to do and he makes everybody stop being scared."

"Yes," Joanna answered. "He makes us all stop being scared." She shut the door behind them, and went back to Dennis, giving Sigurd and Franny a small reassuring smile as she went by.

"Well, Dennis?" she said quietly. "What do you want me to do?"

"You can hold the lamp—we'll need it now. I'll want Charles and Sigurd to stand by and steady Owen, if he needs steadying." For the smallest fragment of a moment, he smiled at her, and then moved away. "I think we can get started."

She had thought of strength, she had believed she *had* strength, and at the end of the half-hour during which she held the Aladdin lamp, she knew beyond a doubt that she was strong. She stood without moving, holding the heavy base of the lamp so that the incandescent mantle cast a maximum of light over the table and yet didn't dazzle Dennis' eyes. First her wrists ached, then her forearms, then her shoulders, and finally a red-hot knife was pressing into her backbone. At the end of the first ten minutes her legs were beginning to ache from their tense immobility. But the lamp remained motionless, from beginning to end, shedding its yellow brilliance over Sigurd's agonized, sweat-streaming face and Charles' stony one, over Owen's closed eyes and moving lips. Softly and steadily he was swearing. The light shone on Dennis' hands as they cut away the tattered sleeve and laid bare the mutilated flesh.

Leonie came in quietly with the first-aid materials and the hot-water bottles. She stood for awhile behind Franny in the kitchen doorway. Joanna was conscious of the light flashing on her glasses. Then she and Franny went away.

Dennis sprinkled the bloody hands thickly with sulfa powder and dressed them loosely, and did the same with Owen's arm. "How many fingers can I keep, Doc?" Owen asked, opening his eyes.

"I don't know," said Dennis frankly. "I can't do much more for you here, Owen. This is just to fix you up for the trip."

"What about my arm?" Owen persisted. He tried to lift his head and look down at his arm, but Charles pressed him back.

"I'm not promising you anything at the moment," said Dennis. Owen closed his eyes again. His face, scratched and cut slightly from flying fragments, looked sick and gray under the iodine.

"Goddam a fool," he muttered. "Pokin' at somethin' that looked like a dishpan full of electric light bulbs. . . . Sounds like one of your fool tricks, Siggy. . . . When are we leavin'?"

"As soon as we can get you on your feet," said Dennis.

"Sigurd," said Joanna quietly. "Take the lamp, will you?" He took it, and the relief in her cramped muscles was at first an agony.

32

FRANNY WENT DOWN TO THE STORE to call up for an ambulance which would meet the *White Lady* when they reached Limerock. Charles went to bring the boat in to the wharf while Dennis and Sigurd took charge of Owen. It would be a difficult chore to get him aboard the boat when he couldn't use his hands, and while Sigurd looked as if he'd like nothing better than a stiff drink and a chance to sit down, Dennis wouldn't let him go. They started down to the wharf with Owen, and Joanna hurried up and downstairs, her head wonderfully clear now, collecting clothes for Owen and for herself, gathering up blankets and extra cigarettes—Owen was chain-smoking in long, hard puffs.

By this time Mateel had sent Young Charles and Donna down

to find out what was happening; Joanna ran downstairs to find them waiting in the kitchen, their dark eyes wide and glowing with horrified excitement. She gave them each a hug.

"You're just the people I wanted to see!"

"How is he?" said Young Charles hoarsely.

"He's able to walk, kids. Now you've got to buck up and not worry, because I want you to stay here and keep house with Ellen tonight." She looked long and somberly at each one in turn. "Have fun, and cook up anything you want to, and stay up late if you feel like it—but don't chew about Owen. Ellen was the one who saw him first, and it was a terrible shock to her."

"Sure, we'll take care of her," Donna promised. "We'll have a keen time—huh, Charles?"

"Yep!" Charles was very much the young rooster left in full control of the barnyard. "You care if we dance, and stuff?"

Joanna laughed, thankfully. "You know how crazy Ellen is about waltzing. . . . Now help me carry these things down to the shore." She put on her reefer and tied down her hair under the bright wool kerchief Ellen had given her for Christmas.

"Jeest, this is hotter'n the hinges of hell," said Young Charles, wincing, as she filled his arms with a blanket-wrapped bundle.

"It's hot-water bottles. . . . You take these blankets, Donna, and I'll carry the bag."

She gave a last look around the house, remembered to turn down the Aladdin so it wouldn't stream up, put a thick piece of birch in the fire to keep it until the children came back; and then she was ready.

The sun had just gone down, and the sky in the west was a luminous apple-green, its clear pale color intensified by tiny, motionless clouds flushed with violet and coral. The air was pure and still and cold; it seemed to Joanna as if she had not had time for a deep breath in the past hour, and she took one now, as if it would be a long time before she could breathe so freely again. The worst was not yet over, perhaps it had not really begun.

There was no time to waste. In the echoing hush they could hear the *White Lady*'s engine idling at the old wharf. When they reached Sigurd's, she sent Young Charles and Donna ahead with the blankets, and took a moment to kiss Ellen and Jamie, to say that Owen would be all right and she'd be home in a day or so. Ellen accepted it calmly, and Joanna got out of the house before Jamie had a chance to pucker up.

It was while she was hurrying the last few steps between Sigurd's house and the wharf that she remembered Laurie, and involuntarily she looked back. If Laurie knew what had happened to Owen, surely she'd be here by now. But there was no other moving thing in the shadowless light cast over the village by the white eastern sky and the afterglow in the west. And there was no way to tell Laurie—not now.

She ran the rest of the way to the wharf.

The *White Lady* swung slowly away from the spilings, her engine responding as silkily as if Owen were at the wheel instead of Charles; her propellor stirred the shadowy smoothness of the water into bubbling foam, and sent small lacy wavelets up the beach. Sigurd, Franny, and Matthew Fennell stood on the wharf watching, and Young Charles—Donna had gone back to stay with Ellen. Joanna waved to them all, and saw them turn away as the *White Lady* headed out among the moorings with gathering speed. She didn't join Charles and Dennis at the wheel, but went down into the cabin. Owen was established snugly on a locker, hemmed in with blankets. He appeared half-asleep, as she studied him in the dimming light. His color was better, he seemed relaxed and fairly comfortable. That was a good sign, wasn't it?

It was warm in the cabin; they'd built a fire in the stove. She sat down quietly on the opposite locker. There was a change in the engine's tempo as they reached the harbor mouth and Charles opened the throttle. The *White Lady* would have a chance now to show what she could do.

Joanna drew up her knees and laid her head down on them, and made herself think of the *White Lady* instead of what was going to happen to Owen's hands. But it was impossible to think of the boat without remembering how Owen's hands had first drawn the plans for her, and then built her; and how, when he had lost her for a while, it was the work of his hands that had gained her for him again. Owen's hands, so quick at striking out, at teasing, at working, at loving—

Her eyes stung with tears; and in the same instant Owen said quietly, "Jo—"

She lifted her head, knowing he couldn't see her wet eyes in the shadows. "What is it? Do you want a cigarette?"

"No. Jo, I didn't get to where Laurie was. I saw that thing on the beach and like a fool I had to see what it was." His mouth was sardonic. "She won't want me now. But I—God, Jo, it's my kid, too, isn't it? If somethin' goes wrong, and I don't pull out O.K.—she's got to marry me, even if she don't want to."

"If she isn't in Limerock tomorrow, she's not the girl I think she is," said Joanna. "But you're going to pull out all right. Dennis said so."

"You think he's God Almighty on a stick, don't ye?" he teased her faintly. "Well, light me a cigarette, Brat, and tell me a dirty story to cheer me up."

"Why, Owen Bennett, you don't talk fit to eat! You know I don't know any dirty stories!" She bridled like Aunt Mary, and put a cigarette in his mouth. In the brief bright flare of the match he winked at her.

She was standing beside Charles at the wheel when they came into Limerock Harbor. Owen's discomfort had mounted steadily, and he had finally ordered her profanely out of the cabin, saying that he couldn't stand to look at her. "I'm gonna say words I wouldn't say even in front of you, Brat. So get the hell out of here, will ye?"

She went out of the dimly lit cabin into the cockpit. The dusk was pierced with stars, Orion swung in the sky as the *White Lady* swung on her course across the wide bay. Charles was a tall silhouette against the spangled sky, but Dennis spoke to her just outside the companionway.

"How is he holding up?"

She turned toward him eagerly in the dark. "Maybe you'd better go in to him. He's pretty uncomfortable."

"I wish I had something to give him. But I can't do a thing."

"Just the fact that you're here counts for a lot. Owen trusts you."

"Do *you* trust me?" Dennis said.

"Of course I do. I trust you so much that if you told me Owen wouldn't lose his arm, I'd believe you completely."

He sighed, and turned away from her to look out across the sea. To the westward the lights of Two-Bush and Whitehead bloomed against the dark. The faint wind blew against his face in a cold, steady stream, and the water rushed by the side of the boat, chuckling endlessly, gleaming with phosphorus.

Now Joanna was accustomed to the dim illumination of the stars; in this world through which the *White Lady* beat her rhythmic way, half was the black sea, the other half belonged to the stars. The lights along the horizon seemed to be the product of no human agency, but bigger, more brilliant stars. In the day, the bay was strewn with islands, but at night there was nothing but an apparently limitless sea, a half-globe of starry sky arching down to meet it, and the boat.

And in the cabin Owen swore softly and steadily; he was aware only of pain and fury, not of Orion swinging over the sea. What Charles thought, standing by the wheel, his cigarette tip a glowing coal, there was no knowing. The boat moved under him as the wind freshened, his legs shifted his weight easily and automatically, the wheel was responsive to his faintest touch. He would not be thinking about the boat, it wasn't necessary. But no one would ever know what he thought about Owen.

And just outside the cabin Dennis leaned on the washboards and watched the lighthouses without speaking, and Joanna still heard in her head her last words. *I'd believe you completely.* And she wondered in deepening dread why he didn't answer her.

"Joanna, I can't tell you that he won't lose his arm," he said at last. "But I've seen cases that looked worse, and healed perfectly. I didn't have the facilities to examine his arm, or his fingers." He straightened up, and she could see his face dimly. "I don't want you to stop trusting me, Joanna. But I can't tell you what you want to hear."

How do you know what I want to hear? The words broke through the surface of her mind as suddenly and violently as a porpoise breaking water. They left her shocked and uncomprehending. She drew back from Dennis, shamed, as he moved past her. "I'll go in and stay with him now," he said.

She stood for a long while in the shelter of the cabin. Then she went after to the wheel and began to talk with Charles about lobstering, the Island, the last letter from Nils.

When they were in sight of Limerock Harbor, the whole mainland seemed alight. It was the first time Joanna had come in past Owl's Head Light since the blackout had been lifted, and the city lights seemed strung along the shore like incandescent beads, each one sending its long bright streak of reflection across the harbor's sheltered waters. The *White Lady* ran across a surface that was like polished black glass until her bow shattered it into splinters of green-white light, sending the bubbling, unearthly radiance rushing aft along her sides to die out in a wake that reached back endlessly into the dark.

Just inside Owl's Head a small Coast Guard craft bore down on them and slowed up alongside to identify them. Charles was well-known; the skipper waved him on with an "O.K., Cap'n!"

In just a little while now they'd know. The ambulance would be at the wharf, and Owen would be taken away from them, and then someone would tell them — *what?* For the first time during the two-hour trip she began to feel cold. Her bones ached with it.

33

JOANNA SAT GAZING AT A PAINTING of a windjammer rounding the Horn and remembered the other times she had waited in this room at the Limerock hospital; when Ellen had her tonsils out, for instance, or when one of Mateel's babies had been born. She'd thought then it was a rather lovely room, she'd enjoyed the marine paintings, the deep chairs, the thick carpet, the lighting; she'd watched with admiration the nurse at the desk, who so obviously knew just what was going on all over the hospital at the moment. Now those other occasions were so alien to this one that they might never have existed; instead of comfort in the room, there was an atmosphere of hushed terror. Terror for what they would say about Owen, terror for Owen himself when he found out.

She saw her mother looking at her, and she tried to relax, muscle by muscle, nerve by nerve. She even smiled. Donna moved closer, her blue-gray eyes resolutely calm.

"After you've raised five boys, you're never really surprised at anything, Jo. You simply learn to hope for the best."

"The whole thing was so sudden, though," Joanna said, wondering, as she had always wondered, at her mother's inner serenity; it glowed through her worn, strong face like a candle behind a window. Perhaps this tranquillity was a defense. She'd had to learn it early in life, when she first married a Bennett, or be overwhelmed. "The way Ellen screamed at me, then finding Owen like that, and then the trip—" She caught herself quickly. "But it must have been even worse, the way Young Charles told you. I didn't tell him to call you up, Mother. I could shake him."

"I admit I expected that Owen would be in worse condition than he is. Young Charles didn't leave out any details, and I guess he added a few." She shook her head, smiling faintly. "Thank goodness for Helmi. I think she'd be calm if the sky fell. She called up the Coast Guard to locate Philip—the *Four Brothers* was up near Isle au Haut when they found him—and then she loaded me into the car and drove me up here."

Helmi, Mark's wife, sat across the room from them, a little apart from Philip and Charles, who were smoking furiously and talking shop with the concentration of escape. She was knitting, and the light fell across her bent, silvery-blonde head. As if she sensed that someone was looking at her, she glanced up and nodded. Her eyes were the same pale ice-green as her sweater, they were startling color set against her white Finnish skin. Her wide mouth was as composed and disciplined as it had always been, her long slim body in perfect repose. Joanna had known Helmi to be emotionally upset just once in the years since Mark had brought her home to his family. Since then she'd respected the girl's poise; she knew it to be made of fine steel, and not stolidity.

Tiredness seeped over Joanna, dulling the knife-edge of tension. She sank a little deeper into her chair and shut her eyes, but she saw Owen against her lids, the red fingers at which she had been afraid to look, the stained snow.

Her mother's voice came quietly, "I don't know how we can ever thank Mr. Garland."

"We'll never be able to, Mother." She shook off the heaviness that wanted to seal her eyes and looked over at Dennis. She had not looked at him directly since the moment on the boat when the darkness had half-hidden them from each other, and her brain had uttered strange and incomprehensible words. . . . *How do you know what I want to hear?*

The orderlies from the hospital had helped get Owen out of the cabin and into the ambulance, and Dennis had ridden up with him. Charles had to find an anchorage for the boat, and Joanna had gone to the hospital, alone, in a taxi, to find her mother and brother and Helmi there. Dennis had come to them after a while, from some other part of the hospital, and she had not looked at him frankly even then, but covertly, through her lashes, while he talked with the others. But she had taken in the details of his tiredness, the tinge of weary grayness in his skin, the lines around his mouth, the slow way he'd pulled off his trench coat and sat down, the grateful gesture with which he'd taken out his pipe.

Charles had cleared his throat. "I had an idea maybe you'd do the job. I don't guess there's any here better than you."

"Thanks." Dennis smiled briefly. "But I'm not fit, right now, and it's something that has to be done immediately. I talked with the surgeon, though. He's a good man. I've heard of him."

He'd settled back then with his pipe, and had not spoken since. Now when Joanna looked across at him he seemed unaware, his gray eyes were fixed on a point in space.

"He seems very tired," her mother murmured.

"I'm afraid he is," said Joanna. Other words seethed in her head. *You don't know all that he's done . . . what sort of man he is. . . . He's so much like Nils, in doing for people and knowing what to do. . . . One could get to lean on him — too much. . . . I'm afraid of it. . . . And when I see him looking so drawn, it hurts me. . . . I'm afraid of that hurt. . . .*

But you didn't say things like that. You shut them deeply inside of you, and you ignored their existence, because the very fact that they *had* existence was terrifying.

How long would it be before someone came and told them about Owen? After she found out, she'd get herself a room somewhere and sleep and sleep and *sleep.* She'd go home on the mail boat tomorrow, where familiar things set a rampart about her and she was not laid bare and vulnerable to her thoughts by foreign surroundings.

Beside her Donna sat straight-backed, her head erect, her dark blue coat and gloves immaculate, her good shoes without a speck on their polish; her hair, silver-gray where it had been fair, was no doubt satin-smooth under her hat, as glossy and ordered as the twist at the nape of her neck. She was reading a magazine, not just idly turning the pages. She had the calm, yet spirited, endurance of one who has had to weather a good many storms. She was hoping for the best, as she had said. And as far as Owen was concerned, nothing that happened to him could really surprise her, the only wonder was that something far worse hadn't occurred long before this.

Helmi went on with her knitting. Helmi had married Mark because she loved Stevie; it had probably been the most desperate gesture of her life. She'd accepted Mark because it meant she could be near Stevie, she hadn't looked ahead and realized the heartbreak of living with one man, who worshiped her, and seeing daily—on sisterly terms—another man whom she loved. Now both brothers were in the Pacific, Mark sure of her love, because she had never denied him his worship; Stevie unaware. And Owen, lying under the white glare of the operating-room lights, had fastened his hand once in the silver-gilt hair and kissed her until her lips were bruised. Mark had tried to kill him for that. The family thought afterward that Helmi hated Owen; but it was only Joanna who knew that Helmi didn't hate him, she had only wished with passion that it had been Stevie, who'd kissed her. Was she remembering those things now, as she calmly went on knitting?

A short, stocky, graying man in a tweed suit, hat in hand and a topcoat over his arm, came into the room and spoke to Dennis, who got up. The lights reflected, twinkling, on the man's glasses. His movements were crisp and concise; so was his voice.

Joanna straightened in her chair, Donna let her magazine close. Charles and Philip stopped talking. Dennis shook hands with the man, who glanced around at them all, nodded, and went briskly out.

"That's Dr. MacLeod," Dennis said. He smiled faintly. "He was in a hurry. Dinner engagement. . . . Owen's in bed now, he won't come around for an hour or so."

Donna stood up. "What did they have to do?" she asked steadily.

"They've taken three fingers off his right hand. The other hand they patched up. His right arm is badly lacerated, but they've done what they can. It'll require watching, but MacLeod's optimistic."

"Thank you," said Donna. Her eyes were radiant. "I'll wait until

I can see him. Joanna, come here." She laid her hand on her daughter's arm. "You and Mr. — Doctor Garland have been through a lot; now, Helmi's driving home, because she has to be at the library tonight, and there's a pot of beef stew on the back of the stove —" She turned back to Dennis. "I wish you two would go down there with Helmi," she said with gentle firmness. "You could eat a decent meal, and relax. Philip and I plan to stay uptown all night — there's no need for you to wait around when you're both so tired."

Joanna didn't look at Dennis. "Maybe Dennis has other plans —"

"I don't like to impose, Mrs. Bennett," Dennis said. "I can stay at the hotel here —"

"Fiddlesticks," said Donna, with a sparkle beginning in her eyes.

"When she says that, you'd better hark to her." Philip grinned. "My bed's ready and it's a good one, Doc. And I can guarantee the beef stew."

"Sure, go on and take it easy for a while," said Charles. "If anybody deserves it, it's you." His dark face was curiously softened. "He'd be dead if you hadn't been there. Don't you think we all know that?"

"Stow it, Cap'n Charles," said Dennis, and reached for his trench coat. "I'm outnumbered, Joanna. It remains for you to convince them that you can relax better by yourself."

"I'm afraid they'd all disown me, since they're so set on your having beef stew and a good night's sleep." She kissed her mother's cheek. "All right, Lady. Ready, Helmi?"

Outside, the night had a still cold and the first deep breath of it stabbed the throat. The snow sparkled under the street-lights. Joanna, going down the steps after Helmi, was unwillingly conscious of Dennis coming through the door behind her. Why couldn't she have what she wanted for once? Solitude — some sort of peace —

A taxi door banged, a girl ran across the sidewalk and up the steps. Joanna heard her short breathing, each breath caught with a sound like a sob, and she thought with impersonal pity, *Poor thing.* The glow from the door shone on a strained young face.

"Laurie!" Joanna said it aloud, and the girl cried out, "What is it?" She came to a stop, facing Joanna there on the steps. "Is that you, Joanna? Sigurd brought me over. Where's — is he? —"

"Come in," Joanna said simply, and took Laurie's hand. Dennis held the door open for them, and Joanna led the girl into the warm, clean-scented corridor and thence into the waiting room. Donna rose to meet them. Philip and Charles turned away from the window where they stood.

"Mother, this is Laurie," Joanna said. "Owen must know she's here, the minute he wakes up. It's important." She looked into Laurie's face; cheeks stung red with windburn and tears, blue eyes bright with more tears. "You've got about an hour to perk up in—Owen hates people to cry, especially over him." Then more gently . . . "Tell my mother who you are. You can tell her anything, and she's never surprised."

When they went through the door again, Dennis said, "That was well handled, Mrs. Sorensen."

"Thank you, Dr. Garland," she answered almost gaily, and they went down to where Helmi was waiting in her small car.

34

It was seventeen miles to Pruitt's Harbor. Seventeen miles of sitting in the front seat between Helmi and Dennis, because it would look idiotic to insist there wasn't room; seventeen miles of trying to make conversation stay alive, when her brain kept lapsing into futile wrath with her family, who were responsible for this.

In the five years that Joanna had lived with her mother at Pruitt's Harbor, she had gone over this road innumerable times, but tonight there seemed to be no end to it. The last stretch, of frozen dirt winding through dense spruces that made a serrated black barrier high against the stars, was maddeningly long, even though Helmi drove fast and with expert ease. At last they came out on the crest of a hill, and below them the little town of Pruitt's Harbor twinkled and gleamed, scattered down the hillside and into the hollow. It ended where the sea began. Joanna felt a quickening of interest; for an instant, before the road tipped over the brow and descended, she could see Matinicus Rock Light out there in the distant dark.

The house was half-way down the hill, nestled into a spruce growth, and fronted by two towering elms whose branches made a clear and intricate silhouette against the sky. Helmi turned the car into the drive and stopped it. For an instant the silence beat hard in Joanna's ears.

"I'll drop you people, and get over to the library," Helmi said.

"No supper?" Joanna demanded in sincere dismay.

"I haven't time. I'll eat when I'm through for the evening." She waited for them to get out. There was no arguing with Helmi.

The house was dark but when Joanna opened the door the warmth came out to meet them and the faint but savory scent of beef stew, and there was a gracious purring about their legs, a small blunt head pushing against their ankles.

"I hope you don't mind cats," Joanna said as she groped for the light switch. "That's Priscilla."

"I can tell that she's a very superior cat." His voice came pleasantly through the dark. "I can always tell by the purr. . . . Hello, Priscilla."

Joanna found the switch. The light went on in the narrow, old-fashioned hall with its landscape paper, the open doors that led invitingly into the square dining room on one side and the square sitting room on the other side, with the steep white-painted stairs curving upward. Suddenly it looked very good to Joanna, after her silent rebellion during the long drive. It was warm, it was familiar, and the gray cat with the white face, and the tail held straight up in ecstatic vibrations of welcome, seemed the very personification of hospitality. She was a small, old-fashioned cat, like the house.

It was easy now to smile at Dennis, to say with eagerness, "Hang your things up there on the rack, and I'll get supper on as quickly as I can."

Afterwards she knew she would have been miserable if she had been alone; for she had to talk. The accumulated tension of the last five hours had to work itself out, and to talk was the only way she knew. Over the lamplit supper table in the kitchen, she began to tell Dennis about earlier days, and it was amazingly easy to feel as if they were back at the first of their acquaintance, when he had been such an interested and encouraglng listener, and she had known no self-consciousness but a deep and candid satisfaction in knowing him. It was a relief to remember Owen as he had been once, instead of the way he looked when they loaded him into the ambulance. When Dennis laughed at the stories she told, she thought of more stories. Relaxation came; she began to feel happy and at ease. They went into the sitting room, and built up a fire in the fireplace. Then Dennis sank into Philip's chair with a deep sigh, and reached inevitably for his pipe.

"Your mother's a wonderful woman," he said. "Her idea was worth a million. . . . Well, talk on, Joanna. That clubhouse row sounds like something out of a western movie."

"Of course Owen wasn't half so much interested in saving my honor as he was in having a darned good tousle. So he moved right in on the boy who'd tried to kiss me, and then the other boys got into it, and Nils —"

"And where were you? Standing on the sidelines wringing your hands?"

"No, I was out in the raspberry bushes listening to the noise and feeling pretty excited. . . . I was a brat, I guess." She curled up more comfortably in the corner of the sofa.

It was dark in the room except for the leaping firelight. Dennis watched the flames.

"Nils was always sure to be where Owen was, I take it," he said.

"They were pals from the time they could walk. Nils was a sort of sea-anchor for Owen." Her voice slowed as her memories shifted, like the ashes under the logs. "Then they drifted apart for awhile, when Alec came. He was more exciting than Nils, and besides, he came from away." She laughed. "Jonesport. It was practically New York in those days, when there was none of this commuting across the bay."

"You've never mentioned Alec often," Dennis said. "What was he like? I try to imagine, when I look at Ellen, but I can't get any ideas."

"You'd never get any idea from Ellen, anyway. About Alec, I mean. She's her Grandmother Bennett all over again." The flames drew her; she spoke dreamily as she watched them, remembering Alec in this small detached interval between today and tomorrow. "Ellen's tall and slim like Alec, though. He always looked so thin, almost gaunt, even when he was well-fed. He played the fiddle, and his eyes used to twinkle even when he wasn't smiling. He'd inherited a house on the Island—where the Fennells live now—and that was why he'd come down there."

Her lashes drooped. Almost she could imagine the fire's warmth was the May sun on her face, and if she opened her eyes it would be to see gulls scaling against the blue, and Alec and Owen up there on the ridgepole of the Whitcomb place, shingling. They'd been mending the roof, fitting new window-frames, repairing the steps, for her, because in October of that year she would marry Alec. Owen had been cavorting so foolishly up there against the sky—

"It's odd," she said aloud, "how many chances Owen's taken, and never been hurt. When he and Alec were shingling the roof, he acted like an idiot, just showing off. . . . It's a wonder he didn't fall and break his neck." There, she was talking about Owen again. Her thoughts were an odd confusion of Owen, because of the last few hours, and of Alec, because Dennis had asked about him. When she tried to talk about one, the other always intruded.

"They were a pair," she said. "They dreamed up the idea of taking sixty pots out to set on Cash's. If they could stand it, they could make hundreds of dollars apiece in a few days. Owen needed a new boat—his old one had sunk in the harbor—and Alec wanted money to get married on." She glanced at Dennis, but he was watching the fire, his profile remote and peaceful. Yet she knew he was listening.

"Alec was a gambler, you see. That was something he and Owen had in common. But they got Nils to go with them—and take his boat. Father told Nils he was a fool to go, and take a chance on losing his boat if a gale came up while they were out there. But Nils went."

"Why?" said Dennis suddenly. "What did he want out of it?"

"I don't know. I think he couldn't refuse Owen, and maybe he thought he ought to go along with them because they were so irresponsible."

Now she could see the wild-rose dawn, born in unbelievable stillness after that long and horrible day of wind and lashing rain and surf; and she could hear Nils' boat beating her weary way home. . . . "They didn't lose the boat, but she was a heart-broken sight. They lost the traps, and they didn't make any money, and Alec was so seasick out there that he looked like a scarecrow." He had come up the beach, hollow-eyed, white, unshaven; he'd smiled, and opened his arms to her. And they'd got married without any money.

"There was always something happening around where Owen was," she reflected. "But he always came out untouched. Maybe he began to think he was charmed."

"But no one else was charmed," he suggested. "The others had bad luck, didn't they? Nils lost you to Alec—"

"And I lost Alec," she said steadily. She heard the words and was amazed that she could speak like this. "That's another time Owen was charmed. He was drunk, and he upset the peapod. They all went overboard . . . but it was Alec who was drowned."

Dennis said, "You stood it alone though, didn't you? You're not the one to ask for pity."

She was grateful for his cool impersonality. If he'd turned sympathetic, she would have hated him. "I was carrying Ellen then. Alec didn't even know about it—I'd meant to tell him when he came home that night. Instead, it was Stevie who came—to tell me that Alec was dead. You see how it was? I couldn't grieve, except deep inside, and I didn't dare do that, I thought it would hurt the baby."

"Owen told me about it," Dennis said. "I think he's carried the scar on his conscience all these years. . . . He told me that you never cried."

"I did—once or twice. But I knew if I really let go, I'd go out of my mind."

He tapped his pipe against the hearth, and began to fill it, his fingers leisurely. "Then, after a long time, you married Nils. And you've been really, richly happy with him, haven't you?"

"It was like coming home," she said simply. "I think Nils and I are part of each other, as—" she hesitated, the color rising in her face—"as I didn't believe two persons could be, even myself and Alec."

Now she knew she was talked out. She leaned back and let waves of quiet wash over her; if only she could sink beneath them, and not feel her nerves grow taut again! There was no reason for tautness, nothing but her imagination. What an impossible, conceited fool she'd been all these weeks!

But it was beginning; now that she was not speaking, she found herself watching Dennis, his hand lying on the arm of the chair, the other hand holding the pipe bowl. The long line of his jaw, the poise of his head, the fire making bronze highlights across his hair.

She stood up suddenly. "I'm going to make some fresh coffee and bring it in."

"All right." He glanced up at her, but didn't offer to help, and she was glad. She went out into the kitchen, and Priscilla, who had been asleep, came out to help her, purring extravagantly and winding around her ankles. Joanna looked at her watch and compared it with the kitchen clock. Helmi was taking her own good time driving home from the library in Port George. But perhaps she had some work to do after the library closed. Perhaps she'd come in any time now.

35

THE COFFEE TOOK an indecently short time to perk. She arranged a tray, with some filled cookies she found in the cake-box, and took it in. Dennis had replenished the fire, the mingled fragrances of birch logs and steaming coffee made a subtle and delicious blend. He'd cleared off a low end table and set it before the sofa.

She gave him a quick, brilliant smile. "Thank you!" Now she was uncertain again, and it maddened her, because all the while they had been talking she had felt so free and contented with him. "Both cream and sugar for you—"

"Yes, please." He sat down beside her on the sofa. Priscilla climbed into his lap and lay along his thigh, cupping her white forepaws over his knee; she looked at the fire with gem-like eyes.

Joanna felt curiously light-headed as she poured the coffee. Her desperation was slightly intoxicating, coming on the heels of the afternoon's shock and then the heady pleasure of relaxation. *This is the way it's always going to be,* she thought. *I'll never be rid of him, he's bought a place on the Island and he's going to stay there. Am I to be afraid the rest of my life? Shall I always have to run? Why can't I face it down, the way I've been willing to face down everything else? I've never been a coward. . . .* Her desperation increased, and so did her light-headedness. She felt as if she were swinging on the brink of an abyss, but oddly enough she was *not* afraid; only slightly breathless with daring, with the realization that if she took the right step she would know something that was inexpressibly important to know. And once she knew it, she would be safe. She would no longer be haunted, no longer afraid.

Dennis said, "The coffee is excellent."

"I'm glad," she answered. But what if the right step were the wrong one, what if she were not set free afterward. . . . What if there should be an abyss waiting for her? But if she ran away now, she'd never know, and within the next few minutes her freedom might lie, and she would be herself again, Joanna Bennett Sorensen, unclouded, unshadowed —

Her decision was made, and she would not revoke it. And now that it *was* made, she would not fight her consciousness of Dennis. It was as valid a substance as the fire's heat and glow, and she welcomed its growing force, for it brought the answer nearer.

Dennis set his cup down on the tray. "I think you're feeling better," he said gravely. "Back there in the hospital, you didn't look well. And when we first came into the house here, I was worried about you. But I think your nerves have loosened up this evening."

"I do feel better." She met his eyes in the half-light; she was through with avoiding his glance, with making up little tasks to keep a silence from coming between them. "It's because you're such a good listener, and you let me run on. I —" But it was growing hard to look at him so steadily, her face felt hot and she could sense a little pulse beating in the hollow of her throat. *But I won't look away first,* she promised herself with the old stubbornness.

"I can't ever thank you for everything," she went on. "Ever since you came to the Island you've been doing things for me — for us, and I — well, I know this sounds silly, but I don't know how I'll ever get along without you!"

There were pulses beating all over her now. The rhythm was deafening. *Get up and move around, you fool,* she thought, and in the next breath she knew she didn't want to move around. She didn't want to move away from Dennis now, she didn't even want to look away.

"I don't know," said Dennis soberly, "how I'll ever get along without *you.*" He put his arms around her shoulders and pulled her gently toward him. She let herself flow on the tide of instinct; as naturally as a flower her mouth lifted toward his, and he kissed her. It was a quiet gesture, no more than a brushing of his lips over hers, with perhaps a faint, pleasant pressure. The tide lifted her as if she had been a chip in the foam, and she leaned against his shoulder quiescently. For a long moment he looked down at her, his face gone impassive, her own lifted and waiting, no veil of pretense between them. Then she felt him sigh, his arm tightened around her swiftly, and his other arm caught her around the waist; for an instant she wondered at the warm hard compulsion of his hand against her back, and then the impression was gone under the impact of his second kiss. It was neither quiet nor faint; it shocked her with its passion, but it was a shock of ardor toward which her senses rose eagerly and hungrily. After the first moment she was surprised neither at herself or him, there was no room for surprise, or doubt, or guilt.

After a few moments he let her go, enough so that he could hold her back from him and stare at her face in the uncertain firelight. She looked back, smiling faintly, her mouth burning, her eyes heavy, a singing in her ears. The ruddy glow highlighted one side of his face, the way his hair grew at the temples, the line of the cheekbone; feeling as though she moved weightless through a dream, she lifted her hand and touched his cheek. He turned his head with a quick, famished gesture and pressed his lips into her palm, and shut his eyes.

Somewhere, as if it were quite outside of her immediate consciousness, there was an odd response to his gesture; the dreamlike sensation increased, and she knew a faint bewilderment, as though she had dreamed this dream before. His mouth against her palm, her fingers cupping his face. . . . Her head felt unclear. She slid her hand away from his mouth, around his neck, and found the back of his neck.

"Joanna," he muttered. "We mustn't —" but while he was saying it he was drawing her tightly against him, and her hand was imperative on the back of his head, pulling him down, until with a small, despairing, yet triumphant sound he buried his face against her throat, and she felt his mouth there at the warm beating hollow.

He always loved that little place, she thought, and the words left a track of cold across her senses. Bit by bit the warm flood was receding; his face lay against her throat, her hand curved over the back of his head, but her eyes stared past him at the flickering red light on the ceiling and they were no longer heavy and bemused with long-denied hunger, but wide with a trembling, fluid brightness. *He always loved that little place.* . . . She could not escape from the words, and because of them she was terrified, she felt the woe and confusion of a lost child, and she began to weep, without sound.

He must have felt the warm splash of a tear against his face, and then another, for he lifted his head, and said, "Joanna, what is it? My darling, tell me—"

She couldn't answer. For seeing him now, she *knew;* and she couldn't tell him. She cried harder with an anguished intensity that shook her whole body. He still held her, but not with passion, and his tenderness only increased her torment. "Joanna, please," he begged her. He was shaken, he was afraid for her, and she wanted to comfort him and to help him comfort her, but she could only put her face against his shoulder; there was no end to the tears.

"Joanna," he said against her hair. "Tell me. You can talk to me—you've always talked to me. I'm Dennis, remember?"

She lifted her head then. "No, you're not. You're Alec. You've always been Alec!" She stared at him from drenched eyes. "Don't you *see?* Oh, please understand!" She began to shake violently.

For a long moment he looked down at her; his face changed subtly, until it was no longer the lover's face, but the friend's. There was a shadow across it, like grief or exhaustion or illness, and she saw it with pity that was made remote by her own tragedy. Her breath still caught sobbingly, and she remembered Laurie on the hospital steps.

But that was in another life, another year. Now she didn't know where she was in Time.

"I think I'm beginning to understand," Dennis said at last.

"Am I insane?" she asked him, pleadingly. "What's happened to me?"

"Nothing very terrible," he said. His mouth had a quirk to it she had never seen before. One arm still loosely held around her shoulders, he leaned his head against the back of the sofa and shut his eyes.

"Something rather natural, Joanna. Tell me—" His voice was tired, but as calm as it had ever been. "When did you first begin to think that you might be in love with me?"

Now that the storm was passed, she felt weak but lucid. Their past relationship was crystal-clear in her mind. "I think it was the day when we met at the stile up by the cemetery. We were looking at the apple blossoms—"

"I remember looking at you that day with my heart in my eyes," he said with mild irony.

"I know," she murmured. "There was a change in me, too. I couldn't understand it."

"Did you and Alec sit on the stile, too?"

She began to tremble as the pattern cleared. "It was just that same sort of day, with the apple blossoms and the song sparrows, when he—when we found out we loved each other." The trembling increased, and the next words had to be forced out, because she had never said them, even to herself. "And when he was buried, the apple blossoms were drifting down. The earth was so ugly and raw, and the apple blossoms kept drifting against it, and a song sparrow kept singing all through the—the service. . . . I thought I was going insane."

"Did you ever tell anyone these things?"

She shook her head. "How could I?"

"Joanna." He had the familiar look now, kind and good. "How else do I make you think of Alec?"

"You're built somewhat like him, the same coloring. . . ." She felt exhausted but she made herself go on. Somewhere in her brain she knew this was perhaps the hardest thing Dennis had ever done; for each question he put to her, each answer she gave him, must have stabbed him deeply. "I guess I've always had little flashes of recognition, without knowing what they meant. The night we went for a walk in the moonlight, and found the blackberry blossoms; I know now why I was so upset. Alec loved them, he was always putting them in my hair. . . ."

She shook her head. "Dennis, I don't know what to say. How could I have been so confused? I only knew that I—" She blushed painfully, and groped for words. "For a long time I felt so—so *peculiar* about you that I didn't want to be near you, and yet I did; and

I was so afraid of what it might mean that I felt as if I—" She stopped helplessly, her eyes appealing to him to understand.

"You felt as if you were guilty of something horrible," he finished for her. "You've been torturing yourself, thinking you were disloyal to Nils. But you know now that you haven't done anything wrong, don't you? There's no flaw in your loyalty and integrity."

"How can you say that?" she whispered. "How *can* you? After tonight."

"Don't you understand yet?" He laughed at her gently. "First, stop thinking that you've fallen, like Lucifer. And listen; whatever I tell you, don't ever forget it. Promise?"

"I promise—"

"You never cried when Alec died, you never openly grieved. Don't you know that there was still something locked in you that should have been freed long ago? If you had cried then, as you should have, you wouldn't have cried tonight. You wouldn't even have found yourself in my arms."

The fire was dying down, and she could hardly see his face, but his voice was quiet and impersonal. "I've been two men to you, Joanna; I've never really been myself, as far as you're concerned. Because I could help you, because I happened to be around whenever you needed me and because I could lend you strength—I became Nils to you. In a small way I helped to fill the vacuum his going had left. And, because I bear some resemblance to him—and had the misfortune of falling in love with you, and showing it—I became Alec. That was a trick your subconscious played on you; it unlocked everything you thought you had stowed safely away, out of existence."

"You've made it very clear," she said slowly. "At least you've made *me* clear to myself. I still don't feel as if I'd behaved very well, though."

"Joanna, listen. I'm the one who hasn't behaved well." His voice roughened. "Tonight, I might have taken another man's woman— the way another man took mine while I was away in the Pacific. It's enough to have fallen in love with you. I shouldn't have kissed you as I did a while ago!"

"You've *helped* me tonight," Joanna said. "I know that now. I don't regret what has happened. It shows that you are strong, Dennis." And while she said it, she knew it was true. She had found the answer, after all. "I'm sorry if you're in love with me, because I want you to be happy as much as I ever wanted anyone—even Nils—to be happy. But I'm not sorry that you kissed me the way you did, or that I wanted you to kiss me."

Joanna stood now, her chin lifted, and met his eyes sincerely. "Thank you, Dennis. Thank you for everything." Her thanksgiving came from her heart, like a prayer. "And now let's go make some more coffee."

Dennis did not try to reply. He picked up the tray and followed her silently to the kitchen.

36

HELMI DROVE THEM up to Limerock in the morning. It was dark when they left Pruitt's Harbor, the stars still blazed with cold fire; but they saw the dawn before they reached Limerock, and it was the beginning of another blue-bright, glistening day. Joanna had slept heavily, without dreaming, until Helmi woke her to tell her breakfast was ready. She had met Dennis without embarrassment, and with a sense of well-being that seemed incredible after the multiple shocks and confusions of yesterday.

Riding up to town, sitting between him and Helmi, she treasured her peace of mind as a rare gift. If only Nils would be kept safe, now, and Owen would be all right, she could ask for nothing more, ever.

They let Dennis out on a corner of Main Street. He had errands of his own to do. As they drove away, leaving him on the curb, waiting for the lights to change, Helmi said casually, "I like him. Don't you?"

"Very much," said Joanna freely. "I hated to think of him when Aunt Mary sold the place to him. Now I hate to think of the Island without him." She watched her sister-in-law's cleanly cut profile, serenely concentrated as she maneuvered her small car through the tangle of trucks that comprised Limerock's early morning traffic. "I haven't had much chance to talk with you, Helmi. I wish you'd come out to the Island."

"When I have a vacation, I'll come. I get homesick for it, Joanna—believe it or not." She gave Joanna a brief wry smile. "There are times when I think of the loneliness at the Eastern End and get very homesick indeed."

"Do you think you'll ever live there again?" There were several meanings to the question; she hoped Helmi would catch them, and give her the right answer.

"If Mark wants to live there, we shall," said Helmi. "It's up to Mark."

"Not wholly," suggested Joanna. Helmi gave her another glance, unequivocal and green.

"I said *Mark*. I want him to come home, Joanna—and soon. Mark has—" She swung the car out of traffic at last into a narrow side street; the early sun threw the blue shadows of houses and bare trees across the snow. "Mark has become very—dear to me, Joanna." Her hands tightened on the wheel. "That's what you want to know, isn't it?"

"Yes," said Joanna. There was nothing more to say but it seemed as if the one laconic word wouldn't cover the warm spring of relief that she felt.

"I don't know why it happened like this. Maybe in some queer way I've come to know him better since he's been gone . . . through his letters, and through remembering things he's done and said. Now he is real, and Stevie isn't." She said the brother's name without a change of tone. "It used to be the other way around. Stevie used to be the only solid thing in my life, and now he grows fainter every day." She shrugged. "I used to hate the woman who was going to have Stevie some day. Now, I wonder about her, and I hope that she deserves him, whoever she is; but I'm content to be waiting for Mark."

"The world is full of women who are waiting for their men . . . and they're content about it," Joanna said. "I mean, they don't want anybody else—"

Helmi nodded. "It's a good thing to be able to see the way clear ahead, if only they come safely home." She stopped the car; they were in front of the big, old-fashioned rooming house where Bennett's Island people always stayed when they came to Limerock.

Donna had just come back from an early breakfast, and Charles and Philip, who'd slept aboard the *Four Brothers* in Limerock Harbor, were with her. Laurie came in after Joanna and Helmi arrived. She had a room down the hall. She had little to say, and she was pale, but luminously so; her pallor deepened for a moment to its lovely rose when both Charles and Philip offered her chairs, and when Donna called her *dear*. The family spoke freely of Owen, now that the peak of the strain had passed. He had been clear-headed in the evening, grim about his lost fingers but not as despondent as they'd feared. And Laurie had been there, as Joanna ordered; Owen seemed more engrossed by her than by his injuries. Now, in the morning, they all looked at her kindly and with a sort of reverence, because Owen cared for her more than for himself.

Charles was leaving for home at noon. He had his own pots to haul, and Owen's, and he was anxious to get at them. Joanna would go with him.

The *White Lady* was tied up beside the Public Landing when Joanna came down. She'd shopped for a few groceries, and for some birthday gifts for Ellen, who would be thirteen in another week; she'd gone around to the hospital to see Owen, who lay regally in bed with his arms in splints and bandages to the shoulders, and grinned at Joanna with a gallantry that made her forgive him for all the devilish, infuriating things she had once thought she could never forgive. It was amazing how you could know a man for all your life as well as she thought she knew Owen, and still be astonished as this.

Dennis and Charles sat on the *White Lady*'s engine box, smoking their pipes in the mild noon, when she came aboard. "Been waitin' an hour," said Charles, but not sourly. They took her packages from her and stowed them in the cabin. The engine tuned up sweetly; the big harbor was calm and blue, there was an air of enjoyable industry around its shores, the islands made a wavy pale violet line along the horizon. *And I'm going home,* thought Joanna, with the winged lifting of her heart the phrase had always given her. She was going home. Far beyond those near islands—Vinalhaven and North Haven sprawled along the sea—Brigport and Bennett's Island waited, unseen as yet, but waiting as they had always waited for their own to come back, whether across twenty-five miles of water or a whole continent.

Half-way, they met the *Aurora B.* coming in. Link Hall hung out of the pilot-house window to wave at them, grinning all around his cigar. They waved to him with eagerness and affection.

It was a pleasant, uneventful trip. Joanna spent most of it sitting on the engine box, watching the distant island slide by, watching the gulls, and the boats at work. The men talked by the wheel, but she felt no impulse to join them. She sat there, looking at the great bay, half-dreaming, half-planning. . . .

It was not quite three o'clock when the *White Lady* put into Brigport Harbor, to pick up the Bennett's Island mail. Dennis and Charles went ashore, to walk up the steep rocky hill to the store. Joanna stayed aboard the boat, too contented to move. An occasional boat came in from hauling and tied up at the lobster car out in the harbor; then the polished surface of the water was broken up into endless ripples of silver on blue, and the rock reflections were shattered into splashes of wavering rose and tawny color. Between the brief interruptions of an engine, or a man's voice calling from a wharf, or the sound of oarlocks, the silence was absolute. Of course it meant a storm, but how lovely it was, how wonderful the stillness, and the splendor of light. . . . She was almost sorry when she heard the footsteps sounding hollowly on the wharf, and Charles and Dennis came aboard again.

"Old Fowler's in a mellow mood," said Charles, tossing her mail into her lap. "Prob'ly figgered out a way to get out of payin' his income tax."

"Or he's had a fruitful week cheating widows and orphans," Dennis suggested. He cast off the lines, and Charles started the engine. As the *White Lady* backed and turned, he went into a lucid and profane discussion of the Fowler dynasty of Brigport. Joanna heard him only distantly. One of her letters was from Nils.

They were going down through the Gut now, among the moorings where the Brigport power boats and sloops rolled in the *Lady*'s wake, and where the high rocky walls on either side of the narrow passage magnified the engine's roar tenfold. But Joanna didn't look up. She read Nils' letter twice before it really penetrated her awareness, before she could grasp in its entirety the fact that Nils was on his way home. There were no details. *He was simply coming home.* By the time she received the letter, he would be on his way across the country. He'd written from San Francisco.

She had always imagined that if she ever received such a letter she would shout it out wildly; but now she stood by the cabin with the letter in her hand and she didn't want to shout, or to cry, or to laugh. She didn't know what she wanted to do; she only knew that in a little while her happiness would descend upon her and she would feel like shouting *then.* But now the knowledge belonged to her alone, and it was too soon to share it with others when it was hardly real to herself.

Little things would make it real; when she told Jamie and Ellen, for instance. And when Jamie did or said something, and she could think, *Nils will be seeing him soon.* And when she remembered she could tell Nils things instead of writing them. And when she went to bed at night, knowing that in a little while, when she put out her arm in her sleep, Nils would be there.

Her heart began to beat hard, suddenly. She stared over the *White Lady*'s bow at the Island coming out beyond Tenpound, its rocks rosy in the lowering sun, and knew that the letter was real at last; her happiness was beginning.

37

SHE TOLD CHARLES AND DENNIS when they reached the wharf, she told Ellen when she reached the house. And when the storm broke the next day, with wind and snow, never had a blizzard been more completely ignored. There was a holiday air in the house. Jamie talked constantly about Papa. Ellen moved around with a look of secret happiness. She said nothing, because it was her firm philosophy that if you talked about anything too much, it was likely not to happen.

Sigurd tramped up the path through the storm. He was boisterously happy. He'd sagged when Owen was hurt, and he was still horrified about the lost fingers, but at the same time he was so excited about his brother's return that he couldn't speak without shouting; his great voice reverberated through Joanna's small kitchen, and Jamie stared up at him in fascination. He went out to the barn and split wood for an hour, as if he were compelled to do *something* strenuous. He filled the woodbox to overflowing, piled more wood in the sun parlor and then went home, singing lustily in the teeth of the storm.

The storm gave way to a thaw. Then it appeared that the holiday air belonged to the whole Island. Nora called, and Mateel, and Leonie; and whenever Joanna went out, the men spoke to her about Nils.

Laurie came back to her teaching, with a wedding ring on her finger and a bloom of happiness about her that enchanted her pupils. The news that she and Owen were married diverted the attention from Nils for a day or so, and of course there were daily telephone bulletins about Owen that were good for several hours' conversation at least. But Nils was coming, he would be here any day now, and so everything swung back to him, sooner or later.

The thaw and its deceptive tinge of spring added to Joanna's intensity of waiting. Every morning she awoke at dawn, to the early morning crying of the gulls, who seemed to think it was March instead of the first of February, and wondered how she could bear this day if there were no word from him. At night she went to bed tired but happy in a light-headed, incredulous way. Young Charles bounded in daily; he had his heart set on a big time at the clubhouse by way of a welcome home. Finally, she vetoed it as tactfully as she could.

"Wait till he's home awhile," she told Young Charles. "Then we'll have a big supper and dance, the way we used to have back in the old days. Maybe Owen'll be here by then, too. But if you have something just for Nils, he'll be embarrassed."

"By gorry, I wouldn't be!" the boy said fervently. "I'd expect the brass band and flowers and speeches and the whole works!. . . Hey, you know what, Aunt Jo? I'll lay you any money the Huns and Japs are goin' to kick in right off. Why, they've got the papers all ready to sign, most likely. Else why is Nils comin' home now?"

"I don't know," said Joanna truthfully. "I don't know whether he's discharged or if it's a furlough. But I don't think he's won the war single-handed, even if he *is* pretty good!"

Young Charles responded to her smile, but shook his head. "My father says he'll be damned if he knows why they'd let a good man off, unless they don't need him any more."

"I'm not worrying," said Joanna. It was true, in more ways than one.

Thea had barely noticed Joanna ever since the discussion about Young Charles, back in the summer. And as far as Joanna was concerned Thea was nothing more than a shadow. For the past six months she had come and gone, shaken her rugs from the back doorstep, hung out her clothes, gone to the well, and yet, for Joanna, she might not have existed. The ugliness of that evening had long since faded, with all her other private ghosts. It was with a start of surprise that she saw Thea coming across the yard one morning, picking her way around the damp places while her freshly made curls bobbed like premature dandelions in the wind.

She met Thea at the door. "Good morning, Thea."

"Hi, Joanna." Thea smiled widely, not at all abashed. "I just wanted to tell you—it's swell about Nils comin' home."

Joanna was faintly touched. "Well, thanks, Thea. I guess everybody feels pretty happy about it."

Thea turned away, and then looked back. "I been wonderin'. . . Did he say why he's comin'? There was a feller over in Port George— he come home suddenly like that. His face was sure one nasty mess. His wife like to died when she saw him." She stepped blithely off the doorstep. "Well, I got a molasses cake in the oven. Franny likes molasses cake. I know he ain't much, but at least he's all in one piece."

She went back across the damp dead grass, the brassy curls quivering. Joanna watched her from the doorway. The wind that blew against her face seemed tinged with April and not with February, and the chickadees were happily busy in the bare alders; but she hardly felt the wind or heard the birds. The hobgoblins were surrounding her again, the early dreams of a bloody and shattered Nils. She shut her eyes against them, and they gripped her throat. Then she heard Thea's door slam, and at that loud and insolent sound, anger swept over her, as revivifying as a pail of cold water. She opened her eyes and her sane serenity came back to her. "Thea's a bitch," she said distinctly to Dick, and went back to her work.

Every boat-day was, in its own way, an ordeal. She didn't look for Nils, but for some word from him, and no word came. After that one brief note, there was nothing but silence, and the hope that beat in her like a hundred pulses; and the moments when expectation poured over her in an almost sickening wave. On boat-day mornings she awoke before daylight to these waves, and by the time the *Aurora* whistled at Brigport, Joanna would be inwardly trembling from weariness.

The week of good weather broke. It was winter again, with a knife in the wind that was all the more sharp after the warm spell. There was a day of spitting snow, of sullen, heavy clouds, and a penetrating cold that crept into the house and overruled the fires. Joanna awoke to the certainty that Nils wasn't coming, after all. Something had happened. There'd be a letter presently, explaining everything, and written in brief cool words to hide his bitter disappointment.

She didn't tell Ellen anything of what she thought, but Ellen was in a silent, downcast mood of her own by the time she left for school. Jamie was fractious, whining at nothing, throwing his toys, bullying Dick until Joanna had to spank him. He wouldn't take his nap, but she made him stay in his crib; it was a relief when he fell asleep in the late afternoon, worn out by the many frustrations that had upset him all day.

Joanna made coffee and drank it slowly, luxuriating in the sudden silence. Ellen had gone to Charles' house straight from school. No one had called all day; the cold spell was keeping them in as surely as the warm week had brought them all out like the chickadees. She sipped her coffee, with Dick's head warm and heavy on her foot, and wished that Owen would be coming up from the shore at any moment now.

She took her empty cup to the kitchen and put it in the sink. Through habit she glanced down toward the harbor. The village looked shuttered and locked, as sleepy and withdrawn into itself as Dick. There was no smoke from Nils' and Owen's fish house, and only a thin, tired thread of it, white against the pewter-gray sky, from Sigurd's shop. A few gulls huddled on the ridgepole of the Binnacle, but they seemed to have no relation at all to the shrill, joyous creatures that had looped and soared over the harbor for the past week.

There was a boat heading toward the mainland, past the southern end of Brigport. It was gray like the sea around it, but she saw the white wake foaming back toward the Island, the huge wings of water curving out from either side of her bow. A Coast Guard boat going in from the Rock, probably. There were men aboard the boat, and those men and herself might be the only human beings alive in the world of black spruces and cold white foam and gunmetal sea.

Except for the gulls, there was no other sign of life anywhere, and then a man came around the corner of the Binnacle. He walked slowly, and used a cane. His head was bent against the raw sweep of the wind, which cut across the Island from the east. She stood watching him in absent-minded interest, wondering if he were someone from Brigport. But it was only for a moment that she didn't know. He lifted his head to look up at the house behind the windbreak, and she saw the cap; he straightened his shoulders, and she saw the cut of his belted dark coat. *It was Nils.*

How she held herself so still for the next five minutes, she never knew; but something held her there, some stubborn refusal to meet him where Thea, or anyone else, might see. What was in her now was not for anyone but Nils. She stood like stone, her breath coming shallowly as though her lungs were cased too tightly. It was Nils, yet he moved so slowly that it seemed not to be Nils at all—not Nils, who had always walked with such a quick, light step. This man limped, and as the cane pressed against the damp ground, it pressed against Joanna's heart. The cane was familiar to him, it was a part of him, and Joanna felt a coldness settle around her, the chill pang of jealousy. All of the time that Nils had spent away from her, all of the life he had lived away from her, was like something stolen from her, and she had been cheated even of sharing his pain.

The thought of that pain, which he had hidden from her in his letters, only hardened the rigidity which she already knew. Then as he came abreast of the well, she saw his face clearly for the first time, she saw the searching look of him as he stared toward the house. He was so thin that there were hollows between his cheekbones and his chin, and his eyes were deepset and shadowy. He hesitated; then he moved forward again, as if he had to prepare himself for the effort, and she sensed his tiredness, and the awkwardness of his body, as if they were her own. She could wait no longer.

He came up past the end of the windbreak and between the bare white lilacs toward where she stood on the step. His eyes were hollowed, but so blue that they hurt her. She had forgotten how blue they were.

"Nils—" Her voice turned back on itself and almost didn't come. "Nils."

The cane clattered on the doorstep as he reached her and took her into his arms. At first his lips were cold, but soon they were warm against her temples, her cheeks, her mouth. They held each other desperately, like two people drowning; as if they couldn't hold each other close enough, ever. She forgot about the cane, now that she could feel him through his uniform, the hardness of his bones and the lean spare flesh over them; it was really Nils, that was really his warm breath mingled with hers, his flesh under her lips, his mouth searching blindly for hers.

38

THERE WAS SHRAPNEL in Nils' leg. They had gotten out most of it, he said, but not all. That was why he hadn't been discharged yet. Not that he'd ever be of any use to them again, he added dryly. His ship had gotten a direct hit during the invasion of some tiny but important island, and most of his crew had been killed. He told it quietly, without drama, after they had gone into the house. It had been some time ago; he had been writing from sick bay for several months now.

Joanna listened to him as calmly as he was speaking, while they sat over their coffee cups in the little interval of solitude granted them before Ellen came home and Jamie woke up. But inwardly she was anything but calm. All this had happened to him and she had known nothing of it; while she had been engrossed in her own whims and fancies, Nils had been a few inches from death.

He had been lying in sick bay, expecting to be told every time a doctor approached him, that he must lose his leg. And yet he had written her the sane, reassuring letters that had been her one link with the life they had known together.

He should not know how shameful a failure she had almost been. He needed her now, if he had never needed her before. How he needed her, she wasn't sure. But she would be ready when the sign came. In the meantime she must wait without words, and she knew already that it would be heartbreakingly hard not to tell him that she understood what his lameness meant to him, and why an impersonal blankness settled mask-like over his face when he glanced down at his leg. But she could not speak of it until he did; and when that would be, she didn't know. But if there was waiting to be done, she could do it.

Dick heard the back door and grumbled, but refused to move away from Nils; then Ellen came through the sun parlor, singing under her breath. Joanna and Nils looked at each other, their eyes smiling as their hands touched, and didn't speak. Into the silence Ellen came, all oblivious, her blue-gray eyes bemused with her daydreams. She stopped in the kitchen to take off her parka, turned from hanging it up, and saw Nils.

She looked at first as if she were seeing visions; as if her imagination had placed him there, as if the Aladdin lamp were casting spells. "Hello, Ellen," he said, and his voice dispelled her doubt. She ran to him in silent rapture, her eyes so wide, so shining, that Joanna's own eyes blurred.

By the time Ellen was in the chair with Nils, her arm around his neck, Jamie awoke with a roar, and so they were all together again.

Though nobody had seen Nils walking up from the wharf where the Coast Guard boat had left him, by evening everyone knew he was home. Laurie, down in the store to call up about Owen, heard the news from Philip, who'd met Nils on the street. By the time supper was over, they were beginning to come in, everyone on the Island who could possibly come.

No one offered to stay long, even Franny—he came without Thea—whose meager face was all but exalted when he saw Nils;

Sigurd hugged Nils ferociously, heard the cane fall to the floor, and stood off with his big face contorting oddly. He stayed only a few minutes longer. When he had gone Nils said with his faint smile, "Poor Sig . . . he takes it hard."

The Fennells came and went, and Laurie, in her new status as Mrs. Owen Bennett; Leonie ran in when she'd finished her dishes. Charles and Mateel, with Young Charles and Donna, came in for a little while. Most of them ignored the cane after the first glance. Joanna found herself looking for Dennis, and yet, by all processes of reason, it was foolish to expect him. He would not come, because he didn't know Nils, and he would consider it an intrusion for a stranger to come into the house.

When the others had all gone, Thea came. Ellen opened the door for her, following her into the dining room with an expression of mild bewilderment. She glanced at Joanna with an almost imperceptible shrug.

"Hello, Thea," Joanna said pleasantly. Nils, who had begun to read, put down his book and stood up.

"Well, Thea, how are you?"

"Just fine, Nils!" Thea, with her best dress showing a vivid, snug, electric blue under her open coat, long earrings swinging and flashing from under her curls, kissed him soundly while Joanna and Ellen looked on with amazement. Then she stood back to look at him. "My, if you don't look distinguished! I'm proud to claim you for my cousin, Nils. Not that I haven't been proud all along—I've tole *everybody* every chance I got!"

"Thanks," Nils murmured. He sat down again, stretching out his stiff leg, and Thea stared down at it. Her eyes had the glassy, bulging look they sometimes had when she was highly excited. "What happened to you?" she demanded avidly.

"Accident," said Nils. "How's your father and mother these days?"

"They're fine." She sat down. Joanna resumed her knitting. She didn't dare look at Nils' gravely polite face, she would want to giggle. Well, she'd save the giggle until after Thea had gone, and she and Nils could laugh together.

She glanced up once, during the course of Thea's spirited conversation, and Thea looked across at her with a full and insolent stare. Joanna's mouth trembled, wanting to smile. She rummaged busily through her knitting bag for her instruction book and studied it fervently.

"How do you think your wife looks?" asked Thea. "She's stood the war real good, hasn't she?"

"Joanna always looks the same," said Nils.

"I expect you worried some about her, but anybody could've told you there was no need to worry about that one."

"I didn't think there was." Nils opened a fresh package of cigarettes, shook one out and put it between his lips. Ellen held out a match, helpfully; he took it, with a little sidewise glance of thanks.

"You was smart not to worry, because she got along just fine. Had somebody to look out for her—didn't you, Jo?" She rocked back and forth, and spoke with gusto, as if the words tasted good and she was very happy. "She and Dennis Garland—but I s'pose she wrote you about all the good times they had while you was gone."

Nils' thumbnail moved and the match flared hissingly into life. He lit his cigarette carefully, and blew out the match. "I'm looking forward to meeting Dr. Garland," he said.

Thea stood up and wrapped her coat around her briskly. "Well, I'll be goin'. You prob'ly ain't interested in talkin' to *me.*" She laughed, and it was an odd, jangled sound. "Good night, all." Abruptly, she was gone, her high heels making a staccato rhythm through the sun parlor.

"My gosh," said Ellen expressively. Nils blew out a smoke ring, watched it with peaceful blue eyes, and said, "Thea's quite a character." He picked up his book again.

Outwardly the room was as it had been before Thea came in. But it had changed. It was as if the dank chill outdoors had come in to stay, for Joanna at least. She was not angry with Thea, but suddenly sick and weary with knowing that Thea had come for the sole purpose of making her ugly hint. Well, she had made it and gone, and now everything had changed. It *looked* the same. But Nils could be different behind that untroubled face. If he had not been away, if he had not come home lamed, she wouldn't have feared the difference, or even dreamed of it. But no man could go to war and come home the same; and where once he would have laughed at Thea's broad, transparent insinuations, who could say that he was laughing now?

The silence in the room frightened her. She said quickly, "Ellen — it's bedtime." Then, afterwards, she wished she hadn't said it, because the silence was only more intense after Ellen had gone upstairs.

Eventually it was bedtime for herself and Nils. She moved quickly and nervously about her chores, letting Dick out, filling the oilbottle, making a mug-up of lobster sandwiches. She waited for Nils to say something about the lobster, the aromatic smell of the spruce fir for which he had been homesick, the sound of the wind and the surf when the door was open for a moment. But he had little to say. She tried to read his face; certainly there was nothing there of which to be afraid, no shadow of suspicion or brooding. But Nils had never shown anything.

When they went up to bed, she remembered how she had reached for Nils when he wasn't there, and had wept at the emptiness. She remembered what she'd thought when the letter came — the lift of pure ecstasy she'd felt, knowing that the emptiness would be gone. Tonight there'd be no need to be lonely. But Thea had come in, and so — Moving numbly, she took Jamie up from his crib while Nils watched. Jamie was befogged with sleep. He grumbled at her ominously, and when she looked up at Nils he was smiling; but at Jamie, and not at her.

They lay side by side in the dark without moving or speaking. As the darkness became familiar, she saw the spruces blowing against the moving masses of cloud. Strange to hear Nils' breathing while she watched. She began to ache, wanting to turn to him and touch him, and yet held back. *Why doesn't he speak?* she asked herself miserably. Hadn't he longed for her at night as she'd longed for him? But suppose he too felt cheated and chilled because of what Thea had said?

In another moment she would reach out to him, she wouldn't be able to help herself; and if he lay as cold and remote as granite, what would she say to him then?

She gathered herself together, steeling herself, and in that same instant he turned over and put his arms around her. She moved close to him with inarticulate gladness, waiting for the familiar possessive tightening of his arms.

"I wanted to think about it first," he whispered against her cheek. "It's been so damned long — "

So that was it. And Thea didn't matter at all. Thea had never mattered. A sob rose in her, stifling all words. She put her arms around his neck and drew his head down until his face was against her throat. She felt his breath flow out against her skin in a long sigh. Their arms tightened around each other and they were held in a long embrace of passion tinged with desperation; it was like that first moment, on their own doorstep, except that it was more intense, hidden in the familiar safe darkness of their room.

39

BUT THERE WAS A STRANGE QUALITY to the days that followed.

On the first morning Joanna had awakened to the atmosphere of pure happiness which she had missed the night before, and she could hardly wait to begin the day. There would be one day after another for years and years that would be hers, to spend with Nils. The gift of time was unbearably precious, since she had learned what it was to be deprived of time. She was humble, too, as she had never been humble, with a new tolerance for Sigurd and his drinking, even for Thea, who was what she was because she must live within her own narrow limits. *I can't judge anyone,* she thought with cold logic, knowing how her own weakness had been so nearly perilous.

So the first day had begun. The sun came out and sparkled on the snow, the wind died down, and the men went out to haul. After Ellen had gone to school, and the morning was under way, Joanna and Nils went for a leisurely walk around the shore, Jamie and Dick in advance. Neither talked much. Nils watched Jamie, who'd been so much of a baby when he left, and Joanna watched Nils, content only to look at him and not to speak.

When they went by the beach, Dennis was on the lobster car,

bailing lobsters into crates. With his winter cap, his heavy plaid shirt and moleskin trousers, the rubber boots he wore now with considerable ease, he looked more like an Islander than the Islanders had ever believed possible.

Joanna made Nils stop. "There's Dennis—"

"He slings that bail-net around as if he'd done it all his life," said Nils.

"Come and meet him." Joanna was eager. "This is something I've been looking forward to." Then she hesitated, remembering Nils' cane. "Or I'll call to him."

"No, we'll go out on the wharf," said Nils quietly. "Come here, Jamie." He took the red-mittened hand firmly in his. Jamie made his usual violent wriggle of protest and Nils stood still. "Would you like to go home, Jamie?"

Jamie, suddenly awed, shook his head, his eyes growing round, and stopped wiggling. They walked out on the wharf at Nils' pace. Dennis looked up, narrowing his eyes against the sun's wintry brilliance, and then climbed the ladder to meet them.

"Nils, this is Dennis," Joanna said. "Dennis—" She looked from one to the other of them, her glance quick and bright with her pleasure in this moment, and thought with instant astonishment, *Why, Dennis is more like Nils than I thought.* It was not in appearance, for Dennis was tall and rangy, sandy-colored, with spare, rugged features, and Nils was more compact, wheaten-blond, with an unmistakably Nordic cast. But in the moment that their hands met, she had that knowledge, and it was a comforting one.

They stood talking for a few minutes, the sun warm upon them, the sky blue. When at last they separated, Dennis to go back to the car, and Joanna and Nils to walk slowly toward the house, she could hardly wait until they were out of earshot. "What did you think of him?" she demanded. "Do you like him?"

"Why is he burying himself here, thickening his hands with bailing lobsters," said Nils, "if he's a surgeon?"

He asked it mildly enough, but it was uncharacteristic of Nils, and she found to her chagrin that she wasn't sure how to answer. The explanation that she had accepted as logical seemed suddenly inadequate. She waved absently at Leonie, who stood by her kitchen window, and said, "Why, he—well, he's resting."

"He didn't look very tired," Nils observed. "But I know what you mean. This place probably looks like Eden to him."

"Yes, it does," Joanna agreed. "Can't you see why he likes it here? You should have seen him when he came." And then she remembered, unexpectedly, that Dennis had not been obliged to walk slowly, stiffly, over ground that he had once covered as lightly and swiftly as an Indian.

She slipped her arm through Nils'. "It looks like Eden to you, doesn't it, darling? Well, it *is* Eden, because you're in it." Her voice faltered. "It'll take me years to tell you just how much I've missed you—"

"You don't have to tell me, Joanna, any more than I have to tell you what I thought during all those nights when I couldn't sleep."

She should have felt at peace; but the strangeness began to seep back.

Nils was neither surly nor restless. He was quiet, as he had always been quiet. But sometimes when he came from out-of-doors, from a walk down to the store to call up about Owen, or from Sigurd's, his eyes had grown remote, and he would speak to her briefly, and go upstairs to their room. Joanna would stop her work to listen to that slow step and the tiny sound of the cane, and her throat would tighten. Later, no matter how bitterly hard she tried to leave him alone, she would have to go up, and she would find him lying asleep on their bed. Then the fancy came to her cruelly that his face was the thin worn face of a stranger who looked like Nils but was not Nils. The war had taken Nils and sent this man back to her.

She fought to discourage the fancy. Nils was tired, that was all. It was nothing but weariness on his part, and he was counting on her to understand, to make no demands on him yet. There was no other reason for him to be like this. *No other reason,* she told herself stubbornly.

He was tired at night, and usually went to bed before she did, and appeared to be asleep when she came up; but she couldn't pick that up as a sign or an omen, for it was natural for him to be tired when he spent so much time outdoors, and had to move so awkwardly. He played with Jamie, talked with Ellen, smiled at Joanna and discussed Island and family affairs with her. But even while she assured herself that she had all she wanted—Nils home and safe—she knew she was fighting to keep that assurance.

It wasn't fair, she thought wearily. Must she always be fighting something? And Nils was no Bennett, to be challenged openly; there was no way here to bring out boldly the thing that lay between them, to spit out the corroding doubts, the hidden fears, and see them vanish as soon as the light of understanding touched them. She could not say to him bluntly, "What have you been thinking since Thea said what she did the other night?" That wouldn't work with Nils. No, she must wait for common sense, and faith, and Nils' own incorruptible belief in her, to take over. What else was there to wait for?

This was never Nils, dwelling on the cruel idiocy of Thea's remark; but the familiar Nils that she knew had never been lame, had never faced the prospect of limping for the rest of his life, of moving about his boat with difficulty, of getting awkwardly in and out of dories under the carefully indifferent eyes of the other men who were whole. He was no longer a perfectly coordinated human being; he was defenseless against stares and pity. He had taught Joanna to dance when they were children, and now he couldn't dance with her. Even little Jamie, in a few days, had learned to be careful of Papa's leg.

Nils might face death with equanimity, but not lameness. And because he never spoke of it, never complained, it would go harder for him than Owen, who could swear freely about his missing fingers, and pity himself intensely and eloquently.

Joanna found herself brooding on Nils' lameness until her own leg seemed to ache intolerably. Now, when she looked at the *Donna,* lying on her side in the grass with her shattered timbers bared and ugly, she knew at last what the shipwreck had meant; it meant this thing that was happening to their marriage now. And it was so foolish, so maddeningly simple, and she was so helpless to do anything to save herself and him.

After that first night, when they lay side by side without touching, she listened to his even breathing and willed herself to lie still and not reach out to him. With a clarity that devastated her as soon as she attained it, she rehearsed his thought-processes. Dennis was whole; he was not. Dennis moved swiftly and lithely on two legs. . . . She tried to remember how Nils had looked when Dennis came up the ladder that day. But she couldn't remember because she had been watching Dennis, smiling, eager, happy. . . Perhaps Nils had been looking at her — she almost reached out to Nils then, she almost turned to him and cried out that he *must* listen.

But to protest, to try to explain, would only make more questions in his mind. So, lying rigidly still, she thought of other things. While Nils was gone, living in crowded, suffocating quarters where he'd been denied the long hours of solitude which he needed as men need water, Dennis and Joanna had become friends; there was no denying the atmosphere of intimacy and comprehension that lay between them. But after a while she had not mentioned Dennis in her letters again. And she couldn't explain. There was no way of explaining the long silence, and the true friend Dennis had been to them both.

Lying there one mild, windless night she talked to Nils without words, *He's your friend as much as he is mine. If I didn't write about him it was because I was in torment, as you are now. If your leg wasn't lame, you'd have laughed in Thea's face.*

But there was nothing to say aloud. But could his body reject her, even if his mind had set a barrier between them? Her arms gathering him in, her warm willing body, her passion — they were all here beside him in the dark. She moved almost before she knew it, turning to put her arm across him, to lay her face against his shoulder. He'd always loved the smell of her hair.

There was a long moment when she lay quietly against him, waiting for him to respond. If he barely brushed his cheek over her hair — She waited, without trembling, but it was torture to keep so still.

He stirred, finally. She sensed his desire; it was to escape, and she let him go, sickly, slackly. She gave up in the instant when she took her arm from across his body, and moved back so that her face touched his shoulder no longer. He got up in the darkness, she heard him gathering up his clothes, and then he went downstairs. When the door closed at the foot, there was no other sound but the muffled, heavy beating of her blood. She was too desolate to cry.

40

NILS DID NOT COME BACK TO BED that night. In the morning she got up as soon as the daylight began, and found him sleeping on the sitting-room couch. He got up when she brought Jamie downstairs, and they were no different with each other at breakfast from the way they had been since he came home. Joanna was doggedly pleasant, though her whole body ached with the effort. She must go through the motions of daily living. The rest of the Island was sure that she must be sublimely happy, and she would give that impression. But she must avoid Dennis; Dennis saw too much.

February gave way to March. There came a day that held a luminous softness that was like April. It was too windy for hauling; Charles would be home, and after breakfast Nils went up to the homestead to see him.

She watched him from the back door as he walked across the barnyard toward the alder swamp. In his plaid shirt and dark trousers he looked almost natural, except for the limp. He could go without the cane now, and he moved as if he had gathered strength from the Island in the short time he had been home. The odd tinge in his skin had disappeared. He walked with his head up, as if he were consciously breathing the wind that smelled of spruce, of warm damp earth, of salt, of rockweed at half-tide. *The Island hasn't let him down,* Joanna thought. She leaned her forehead against the doorframe for a moment and shut her eyes, letting her spirit's exhaustion flow over her in waves. It would be good to surrender to it entirely; but Jamie called from his pot-chair, and she went to him.

When Nils came back it was dinner-time. "Hello," she said brightly when he appeared in the kitchen doorway. "Hungry?"

"Can you give me a mug-up, Jo? I'm on my way to Sou-west Point."

She looked at him in honest surprise. "But you—" She glanced swiftly down at his leg and then at his face. He had a preoccupied expression, as if his mind were busy with plans that were shut away from her. "Can I ask why you're on the way to Sou-west Point?" she inquired lightly.

"I'm going to kill an eagle, if I have any luck." He went through the dining room and into the sitting room, where his rifle hung. His voice came back to her remotely. "Charles wants to put his sheep down there after lambing time. But there's an eagle to get rid of, first."

"I didn't know anything about an eagle," Joanna said slowly. She put a baked potato on his plate, ladled out creamed codfish, added a good spoonful of deep gold squash.

"Oh, Young Charles has seen it, Charles has, Sig—" He came out into the dining room, the rifle in his hands. "Owen's kept her in good condition for me. . . . You know, I think I'll really enjoy killing that eagle." He laid the rifle down gently, running his hand along the polished stock. "I've never been much of a hunter. But this is a little different."

She set his place for him at the table and poured his coffee. "Here you are, Nils." He was looking out past the geraniums at the field whose dead grass was bronze in the sunlight, his face quiet and far-away. She had to speak to him twice before he came.

"Thanks, Joanna." He glanced up at her as he sat down. "Aren't you going to eat with me?"

Her heart quickened slightly, and then slowed again. Nils would be polite under any circumstances; naturally he would be unfailingly courteous even if he had left her bed because he believed another man had possessed her. He slept on the sitting-room couch all the time, now. She shook her head. "I'm not hungry—I'll eat with Ellen."

She went back into the kitchen again, and made herself keep busy there until he was ready to go. He stopped behind her for a moment, and she held her breath, so conscious of his nearness that she felt sick with dismayed longing.

"Don't worry about me, Jo. I'll take my time, and besides, I'm not going alone."

This time she didn't watch him go away from the house.

The afternoon crept on hands and feet toward dusk. There was only one break in it. Leonie came up.

"You look bad," she said frankly. "Headache?"

"I'm getting a cold, I think." Joanna managed to smile gaily. "I may *look* bad, but I feel good, except for my nose prickling."

"Well, I'll only stay but a minute. I'm scared to death of catchin' cold." She left in ten minutes, during which short interval she touched comprehensively on Island affairs, leaving nothing out; Owen's state of health, the surprise of his marriage to Laurie, Charles' children and his wife, the Fennells and the inordinate stubbornness of Gram, who plainly intended to live forever. She stated bluntly that Sigurd was driving her crazy, and that she couldn't abide Thea.

"It's a relief to find one of that breed that's got some sense," she observed. "And that's your husband. Land o' love, you'd never know Sig was his brother nor Thea his cousin, now would you? And that *Franny*—if she'd feed him up and put a little meat on his bones, and look out for him a mite—" Leonie shook her head, her glasses flashing as emphatically as she moved, and prepared to leave. "When he comes down I try to get some good food into him, but I dunno as it's much use."

"Poor Franny," said Joanna.

"Ayuh . . . Well, I hope the men get their eagle. Lord, I s'pose you'd be worried sick about Nils hikin' off to Sou-west Point if he hadn't taken Dennis with him."

"I never worry about Nils," Joanna answered. She went to the door with Leonie, forcing the stiffened muscles of her face into a casual smile. "He always manages to take care of himself. Of course, I'm glad Dennis went along."

When she had shut the door behind Leonie she knew she was afraid. The men had been gone for nearly four hours. It would soon be starting to get dark; they should be on their way home. *They.* What if it were not *they,* but *he?* She fought like a drowning person to prevent herself from being dragged down by the powerful undertow of her dread. But there was no denying that the remoteness of Nils since he had come home was unlike the natural quiet thoughtfulness that had always been so much a part of him. And the way he had stood by the window while she had put his dinner on the table, his eyes distant and faraway, had there been dangerous planning behind that gaze?

Ellen had gone home with Donna after school but she should be back in a little while now. But it was almost dark enough to light the lamps when Ellen came in. "Hello, Chick," Joanna greeted her. "Mind standing watch for a while? I'm going out to meet Nils." As quickly as that she made up her mind. She could not stay in the house another moment and do nothing but wonder, and be afraid. She must get out, do something—

"Sure, I'll start supper, too." Ellen sang to herself as she hung up her parka. She was very happy these days.

If nothing's happened, she said to herself as she ran upstairs to change her clothes, *I'll have it out with Nils tonight, whether he wants to talk or not*. It was a life-giving thought, and it strengthened her as she moved with frantic haste, getting out of her skirt and into her slacks—the skirt would hamper her walking. She put on her old saddle shoes, and made herself think of each motion as she performed it. She didn't dare think ahead; if she did, her panic would constrict her chest so that she couldn't breathe. And she needed all her breath.

She ran downstairs again, trying to appear nonchalant, and put on her jacket. "Well, I'm off! Here's hoping I meet him by Barque Cove!" *And pray God he would not be alone.*

She went out the back way, and walked across the barnyard. Once out of sight of the house she began to run. She was on her way to Sou-west Point, but not by the familiar walk along the rocks of the west side. It was not the way she had first planned to go, but it was the way her feet were now taking her, because it was a much shorter, straighter way of reaching that lonely shore. It was an old wood road cut through the woods along the very crest of the Island; when Joanna was small, her father and uncle had agreed to sell some of the Island's pulp wood, and the choppers had cut the road from above Goose Cove to the farthest limits of the woods, beyond which Sou-west Point rose to its grassy, treeless heights. It had been a long time since Joanna had followed the wood road, but as a child she had known each bend and twist of it as intimately as she knew the Bennett homestead. With her strong flashlight, she would find—she hoped with all her being that she would find—she hoped with all her being that she would find *nothing*.

She had forgotten to put anything on her head, and as the alders along the path pulled stiffly at her hair, she struck out at them fiercely.

When she came to the meadow she stopped for a breath, consciously flexing her shoulders; she had carried herself so tensely that there was a pain in her chest. This wouldn't do. She must relax, walk easily and without strain.

The late afternoon was clouding up, dark masses of fog and mist were rushing in from the east and hastening the dusk. Across the meadow the old fence along the rim of Goose Cove stood silhouetted against the ragged sky. She walked toward it, trying to keep an even pace. Her shoes sank in water in places; at other spots the long dead grass tangled with fiendish persistence around her ankles.

The Bennett homestead looked massive and foursquare on its rise to the left of Goose Cove. As she looked up at it, a light appeared in the sitting room. Her brother and his family were settling in for the night, and if the east wind beat gustily against the seaward windows, and the rain came, it would only enhance the security they felt within the four walls. The house was for others; for her there were the woods, beginning at the right of the cove and marching thickly and blackly down the Island to Sou-west Cove. It was growing colder — or was the cold within herself?

At last she reached the broken-down rail fence and climbed over it. There was a noisy chug on the shore, and before long there would be the crash of white breakers in the dusk. She turned away from the beach and went up into the woods.

She found the beginning of the wood road before it was dark enough to use her flashlight. Then, with the strong beam to pick out the trail for her, she set off. It was impossible to walk. The darkness, the immense quiet that surrounded her as soon as she had left the shore, impelled her to move quickly. It was as if the very stillness fed her fears and she must run along the rutty, overgrown path, scrambling in frantic haste over trees that had blown down during the years when she had never come here.

She had to stop to rest, finally. She sat down on a log, switched off her light, and tried to calculate where she was, in relation to the shore. She must be at least half-way to the end of the woods, she thought in relief that was almost painful. . . . It was very quiet here, and black, after she'd put off the light. The blackness accentuated the silence. This was the very heart of the woods. Far off, along the rocky shores, the surf was white in the dusk, and there was the sound it made, and the rising wind; and there'd be the first glimmer of Matinicus Rock Light against the thick night.

But here there was nothing. In the spring or summer there would have been birds. Now there was no living thing to make a sound except herself. Her feet were wet, and because they were not moving, they began to feel cold, and the chill was creeping through her body. She switched on the light again and stood up.

After that, though she still hurried, time seemed to go backward, and there were always the woods around her with no sign of thinning out. She realized that the network of trails and paths she had known so well had grown over with ferns and blackberry bushes since there was no traffic here. Sometimes she felt a little confused; she found herself several times at an impasse, unable to break through a thickly laced wall of spruce that meant she had followed an opening which wasn't a path at all. Then she must find her way back to the wood road again. At least she could always recognize the wood road, because of the deep ruts where they'd brought the pulpwood out through the mud.

But the wood road had branched off too; she remembered now how many of those little side roads there were, reaching to the various cuttings. It had been fun to walk here once, to spend a whole afternoon wandering along the paths, with the sun falling in a pattern of misty gold through the trembling birch leaves, and the ground covered with young, tender green things, ferns and bunchberries and a hundred other little plants that grew wherever the sun could reach between the spruces. It had been lovely then, and the raspberries had grown huge and purple-red, quivering in the cuttings, their fragrance warm and rich in the still hot air. The trees had been alive with birds —

But this was March, the birds were gone, and on Bennett's Island there was not even a rabbit to give some life to the woods. Besides, it was confusing and difficult to try to keep to the right road when vision was confined to the small radius of the flashlight, and the landmarks had changed with the years.

But I'll come out to the shore some time, she argued with herself. Now she concentrated solely on that, she tried not to think of Nils and Dennis. She could think of them after she found them. *One thing at a time,* she cautioned herself.

Her feet were cold — they'd been wet ever since she'd crossed the meadow—and her legs were aching with weariness. She pushed on stubbornly, expecting that every twist of the path would bring her to the place where the trees thinned out suddenly, and through them she would see Matinicus Light. But with every turn, the flashlight's ray shone on impenetrable ranks of spruces that grew thicker and more hostile.

It was because she was in such a hurry. Five minutes could seem like an hour when you wanted so passionately to get somewhere— perhaps she'd been traveling for no time at all. . . . She came to a place where the road lay well-defined ahead of her for as long as the beam of light could reach, and her relief sent miraculous new life through her aching legs. She could make good time here; she began to run, stumbling at first.

But some instinct stopped her. For a long time she had been searching for a familiar sign, and hadn't found it. Now, without warning, almost without conscious thought, she recognized the ground under her feet, and stopped.

The light swung forward, and down; it touched the bare tips of little maples and birches growing far below her. From where she stood, the earth dropped away, a granite-faced cliff descended sharply into the ravine which the great glacier had scooped harshly out of the Island thousands of years ago. If she had kept on running, or if she had stumbled again, she would have gone over the edge.

She sat down abruptly on the ground. She lifted a shaky hand to her forehead and found that her face was wet. It was not the escape that sent weakness through her instead of new strength. It was the knowledge that she had gone far off the right path. And now it was really dark, and whatever had happened at Sou-west Point could have happened a dozen times, and she would have been helpless to stop it . . . if she'd really thought she *could* stop it. But who could stop Nils? She wanted to cry. But if she cried, the last of her energy would have melted away, and it was hard enough now to think of moving, of finding her way out of this place.

She knew the ravine. She knew that if she could find the path that led steeply into it, and then made her way across it, she would come eventually to the western shore. She'd still be a long way from Sou-west Point, and just as far from home. But she'd be on the shore, anyway. The woods were beginning to stifle her.

She stood up stiffly; perhaps if she waited long enough in the dark, she could get her bearings. The same instinct that had stopped her at the edge of the ravine would tell her where the path was. Her feet were so numb that she felt clumsy. As she stamped them, trying to bring some feeling into them, one foot hit against something which moved lightly away. A rock, she thought vaguely. She'd knocked it over the edge. . . . And at the same time she went down on her hands and knees, feeling wildly for the flashlight which she'd laid beside her when she sat down. Old spruce cones were in her groping hands, and that was all. The light was gone.

She almost cried then. In the woods, with no light, and so cold and tired — she wanted to cry aloud, to blubber like a lost child.

But in a moment her poise came back to her. After all, she had two hands, and it had been her lifelong belief that as long as you had fingers with which to cling, you couldn't fall too far. She'd go down into the ravine, and make her way across it to the shore if she had to creep. The soldiers had done it in the jungles, hadn't they?

In this interval of determined calm, she moved cautiously backward away from the edge of the cliff and felt her way from tree to tree, her hands before her, until the earth slanted under her feet, slippery with spruce needles. There, this was the easy way into the ravine, and if it took her an hour to get down there, it would be all right. At least she would not be lost any more.

Now she could look up and see the sky, where there would have been stars if the night had been clear. Instead, rain dashed against her face. She began to cross the floor of the hollow. At her first step her feet sank into icy water, and she remembered the swamp; the recent thaw had softened it thoroughly. The tip of a branch scratched her face and made her jump, she pushed it away fiercely and her mitten caught, and pulled off. There was no way of finding it. She kept on, her hands out before her, moving constantly to keep the alder branches from scratching her face again. But they still caught at her hair; and she still walked in water. It was too late now to turn around and go back to solid ground.

After a while she became aware that she was breathing in shallow gasps, her mouth opened. When she stepped on an alder root and her foot slipped, almost making her plunge forward, she cried out, and the sound was eerie through the echoing stillness. She had to stop for a moment then, to control the sick shaking that went all over her body. It was so cold, so black, so quiet; it was all the nightmares she'd ever had, rolled into one horrible eternity. She tried to think back to when she'd been walking across the meadow, seeing the rail fence against the darkening sky, but it was made faint by the haze of time and distance. This was the real thing; there had never been anything but this, the branches dragging at her, scourging her like living, evil things, the water welling icily around her ankles, soaking through her already-saturated shoes and socks and the cuffs of her slacks.

Panic exploded in her suddenly, melting her bones. A treacherous weakness made her reach out with trembling hands to seize the bare smooth trunk of an alder. She knew that she was afraid as she had never been afraid in her life on the Island. She had done a criminally foolish thing in coming here, in rushing like a madwoman through the woods. Had she really believed she could stop Nils from doing what he had set himself to do? And if she sprained her ankle, how was she to save herself? Who knew she was here? She'd let Ellen think she had gone by the west side. She could slip and fall, and hit her head, and if she drowned in six inches of swamp water, who was to know where to find her or what had become of her?

Nils, Ellen, Jamie — their faces swirled in her mind until she grew dizzy and thought she would fall. She could hear her terrified whimpering breath, and knew that in a moment she would have surrendered completely, without shame or dignity, to her dissolving fear.

But she couldn't do it, after all. "I can't stop here," she muttered. "I have to get out of here, there's nobody else to help me. I *have* to —"

Trembling, breathing hard, she forced herself to step forward, not knowing where her feet would go.

She stepped on another root; her ankle gave, she lunged forward, her hands clutching wildly at space, and found herself on her hands and knees in the water. She laughed at that. She could hear herself laughing, and kept on, because it broke the stillness and she could almost imagine that someone was laughing with her.

After that, she didn't think much about the malicious branches or her feet. She was so cold and wet all over that her feet didn't matter, and when something scratched her face she hardly felt it. She stumbled, fumbled, crawled when she fell, and then at last there was emptiness ahead of her; a whole sweet chill world of emptiness. There was hard grassy ground under her, and somewhere below her there were blessedly solid rocks, and the surf was piling against them with the rote she had believed she would never hear again.

She lay on the grassground, breathing in long shuddering inhalations, and shivering as a dog shivers, in spasms. She was confused as to where she was. She knew she had to find Nils; his name kept beating through her, it kept her from sinking into a warm and pleasant sleep that wanted to envelop her. She murmured aloud. "Nils . . . I'll be along as soon as I get warm. If I can just find a little place to get warm. . . ."

As soon as she was warm, she'd find Nils and stop him from doing some terrible thing. She saw him standing before her, smiling a little with his blue eyes, his hand gentle on the rifle's polished stock. He said, "I'm going to kill an eagle." And she had known then that she had to stop him, because Dennis was the eagle he meant to kill; Dennis, the man who had been a true friend to them both. And if only she could have gotten to them in time —

Her clothes clung to her wetly, and there was a taste of blood on her lips. She had bitten them when she'd fallen, one time. She flattened herself weakly and without hope against the frozen earth.

She didn't know whether she had been there for five minutes or an hour when it appeared as if she were besieged and then surrounded by light that pierced her eyelids when she lowered them against the brilliance. The sound of the surf had lulled her, and now it was breaking up into voices. Between the voices and the light she was startled into a sudden outbreak of strength. She tried to scramble to her feet, frantic and not knowing why.

"*Joanna!*" It was Nils' voice and she reached for it pleadingly. "Good God, where have you been?" he asked. He loomed between her and the light; he was wonderfully real, and stronger than rock or sea as she clung to him.

"Nils, I've wanted you — I've been looking for you!" she cried with one final, passionate outburst of energy. And then her brief vitality was running out like a fast-ebbing tide. As Nils' arms tightened, she sagged. Light, surf, voices, the whole world, circled her giddily; and the last thing of which she was sure was Nils.

41

"Nils, did you really kill an eagle?" she asked him.

She had opened her eyes to see him standing by the window that looked out toward the spruces. The room was full of sunshine, and his head seemed very bright; perhaps because she hadn't seen it for so long. His hands were in his pockets, and he wore a blue shirt that fitted him well across the shoulders. She lay for a few minutes admiring the back of his neck, knowing how it would feel under her fingers, before she spoke. And then her voice came out clearly in the quiet, sunny room.

"Nils, did you really kill an eagle?"

He turned around and came toward her, and he was smiling as if he were happy. "You've been worrying about that eagle for a long time." When he reached the side of the bed, he leaned over and kissed her forehead. She shut her eyes so that she could savor completely the way his lips felt against her skin.

He put his hands on either side of the pillow and looked at her very steadily, his face close to hers. "Dennis killed the eagle," he said. "I've been telling you that for three days. Now you're going to have something to eat. . . . I'll be right back." He went out of the room and she looked at the pattern of sunlight on the ceiling, and then at the small, delicate clouds blown over the spruces by the March wind. Everything looked new and bright and shiny, and she enjoyed seeing it all. But then she tried to remember when he'd told her about the eagle, and all she could remember was darkness. She shivered. He said she'd been talking about the eagle for three days; had they all been dark?

When she tried to divide the blackness into three days, her head swam with dizziness. There would be no way, ever, of breaking that long night into conventional patterns of time. There'd been the sound of surf in her ears for a long period, even after the men's voices and the lights had come. It seemed as if the surf had stayed with her until one instant, sharp as pain, when she was catapulted suddenly through space and found herself in her own room, with the lamp turned low. Then the roar of the waves had stopped so abruptly that her ears had rung with the silence.

She had lain there looking at the lamp for a little while, feeling as if she had no body. She listened to the stillness, she wondered vaguely about Jamie and Ellen, and then Dennis had spoken to her from the foot of the bed. She smiled, and tried to shake her head at him, to show him that she knew he wasn't really there. Then she had fallen asleep. It was real sleep, without dreams; and she had awakened from it just now, to Nils and sunshine, Jamie's voice downstairs, and the fact that she did have a body, after all, because it hurt whenever she tried to move.

She thought back to that long blackness, when the roar had hung perpetually in her ears. It hadn't been an unbroken darkness, because there were faces in it, swimming out of the swirls of dark mist, coming toward her, fading back, shifting. She'd called each one by name, Dennis, Alec, Nils. . . . That was why she hadn't believed it was really Dennis standing there at the foot of the bed, because all the time that she was seeing the faces against the dark, she had known that only one was real; Nils. Always, his was the strongest and clearest, it was to him that she spoke the most often. Now she smiled weakly. She'd been asking him about the eagle.

Bit by bit her mind cleared, groping its way backward toward the truth. She knew then, with a stubbornness unhindered by her body's weakness, that she must have *all* the truth. She could not live without knowing it.

She heard Nils' step on the stairs. It was almost even now, his lameness was growing less all the time. She waited, breathing lightly in her expectancy, and he came in with a tray.

"Special nourishment contributed by Gram and Nora Fennell," he announced. "And your new sister-in-law's been doing up the dishes and looking out for us more or less." He set the tray down on the stand beside the bed, while she stared hungrily not at the dishes but at him, his cleanliness, his quiet competency, his air of serene happiness. "I've had orders to feed you every time you open your mouth," he told her.

"I'm going to open my mouth, but I won't eat until you tell me something, Nils." There it was. She was surprised at herself for approaching him so bluntly. He sat down on the edge of the bed and put his hand on her forehead, pushing her hair back gently, and she laid her fingers over his. "Nils, please—,

"I'm listening, dear."

"Nils, I know this sounds silly, but it's probably because I've been sick that I'm asking such foolish questions." She smiled at him, hoping he'd think it was just an idiotic whim that she must know these things. "But why did you ask Dennis to go with you to Sou-west Point?"

"Because I like him. And he's quiet." He dipped a spoon into soup, and the aroma made water run in Joanna's mouth. She felt starved. But she had to talk first, for she would want to sleep afterwards, and she had to know before she slept.

"Is that important—being quiet?"

"It is to me. Garland didn't ask me questions, and he didn't look at my foot when he thought I wouldn't notice. He'd been through all hell down there in the Pacific, so what had happened to me didn't matter to him—except that he knew what it was like. . . . Aren't you hungry, Joanna?"

"In a minute. Nils . . . did it bother you, what Thea said that night?"

"What night? Did Thea ever say anything important in her life? Anything worth remembering?" His smile deepened, as if he were thinking of a very funny joke. "She said plenty *last* night, as I recall, but I don't remember anything else—" He looked at her questioningly, and stroked her cheek with his finger.

Some force stronger than herself impelled her to speak up, when she could have let it go. "She said some nasty things about Dennis and me. Remember? That first night you were home."

"Thea's humor. You don't take her seriously, do you, Joanna?" He poised a spoonful of soup invitingly. "Dennis is all right. I've thanked God many times because someone like him was here on the Island and you weren't alone when Owen kicked up." His eyes darkened and his face grew somber. "Any man who could do what he's done with Owen—stopped his drinking and set him on his feet—" He shook his head.

"There's something else, Nils," she said haltingly. "That night when you—got up, and then you began sleeping on the couch in the sitting room. . . . What about that?"

He put the spoon back in the dish, and took both her hands in his. She felt the warm, firm clasp of his fingers over hers, and it was as if he had taken her in his arms. His eyes held hers steadily.

"Joanna," he said in the quiet voice she knew so well, because its quietness was not remote, but very close to her. "I knew I was hurting you, but I couldn't help it. I knew that if I tried to tell you, you'd be sympathetic, but at the same time you couldn't really understand what was tying me up in knots. Nobody can *know*, unless he's been through it." His clasp on her hands tightened. "I got up and went out for a walk that night, Joanna. I could have told you, yes—but in another way, I couldn't make myself tell you. Joanna, that boat down there was a hell of a place for a fisherman to be! It was like tying down a gull. There was never a minute to myself, never a place to be alone—never a time when I wasn't under orders."

Her eyes filled with easy tears, she wanted to speak, but he shook his head. "I'm not complaining, Joanna. I'm glad I was in it. But if you could just see how I felt—and not be hurt—" Far within her a small, surprised, and rejoicing voice said, *This is when he needs you, Joanna. He's asking you for help.* "All the time I was overseas, Joanna, I never slept a whole night through. I almost forgot what quiet was, except when I dreamed of it. . . . When I had a chance to dream."

If she'd had any intelligence at all, she wouldn't have made a fool of herself, she wouldn't have caused all this bother and worry for him. If she'd only left him alone. . . . The tears rolled down her cheeks, and he took out his handkerchief and began to wipe them away. "Listen, dear, it's all over now. It's past. Don't think about it. Just try to see how it was to want to sleep at night when I'd forgotten how. After that first night, I was pretty discouraged. I'd lie here with my skin crawling, not wanting you to know I was awake." He leaned forward and kissed her mouth gently. "I wanted you—God, I wanted you, but there was that damn' crawling and twitching going on inside of me. When you reached out to me, I wanted to take you, I'd been thinking about you and these Island nights for a year. And now I had them . . . and I began to wonder if I was going insane. . . . I had to get up, Jo, and go out."

"Now," she whispered. "How is it now, Nils?"

"Maybe we owe something to that eagle, Joanna. I asked Garland to go with me — I had some idea of talking to him because I'd got to the state where I had to talk to somebody. But when we got down there, sitting around waiting, I didn't seem to want to talk about it. We covered about everything else, and that was good in its own way. And then, when we got home, you were gone." His arms slipped around her suddenly, lifted her to him and held her in a steel-muscled vise. "I can't tell you about that, Joanna. I don't think I'll ever tell you what I thought. But we found you, and brought you home — with pneumonia coming on — and —" He smiled faintly and kissed her again. "Well, I stopped thinking about myself, that's all. The crawling and the twitching's gone. Crazy as you were to run off like that, you helped me. . . . Are you going to eat now?"

"Yes, I'll eat now," she said. Her eyes were shimmering, she felt light-headed and radiant with joy. The trip hadn't been in vain after all; there'd been some sound and valid reason behind it, even if she had only known of the wrong one.

"I'll tell you the news while you eat," Nils said. He laid her back against her pillow and turned to the tray. "There's been a Navy officer to see Owen, and there's going to be a routine search of all the beaches to find drifted mines. . . . And Franny and Leonie eloped in Franny's boat yesterday."

She choked on her soup, in incredulous laughter, and he nodded his head. "That's right. He couldn't stand Thea, and Leonie couldn't stand Sigurd. She can mother Franny. . . . Do you want to know about Dennis?"

Her laughter died. But Nils said quickly, "He's all right. But he's leaving us, Joanna. He told me that down on Sou-west Point."

"I knew he'd go sometime," she said, feeling a repose, a hushed acceptance that was a fusion of grief for herself and the Island, and of rejoicing for Dennis, who was no longer running away. "He couldn't forget, after all, what he was."

Nils shook his head. "He said he'd tried to forget, but everything conspired against him. No matter what he did, or how hard he set himself against keeping any part of the other thing, there was always something he couldn't turn away from." Nils' simple words dropped peacefully into the quiet room. Far away, Jamie was calling to Dick, someone dropped a pan in the kitchen, but these sounds had no relation at all to the present. Nils went on. "This business with Owen was the final thing. Fixing Owen up and going with him, talking to the man who was going to operate—" Nils shrugged. "He knew, that day, that he'd be leaving here. He'll sell the Place, by the way—to Owen, if he wants it."

She should have felt wild delight at that, but she didn't, only this quiescence. "He wasn't really a coward, was he?" she said briefly. "I knew he wasn't." *And I wasn't a coward either,* she thought. *I thought I was, but I'm not. Silly, but not afraid.* "Will he be up before he goes?" she asked.

"Yes, he'll be up." Nils looked at her with the slight smile she loved; it held all the warmth and truth she would ever need for the rest of her life. "We've come round in a circle, Joanna. It's been just a year since he came and I went. Now we'll be back where we started."

"No, we won't, Nils," she answered him with clear and honest conviction. "I don't think we've come round in a circle, neither you nor Dennis nor I—nor Owen, for that matter. To me it's just as if—" She drew her black brows together, seeking for words within her tired but eager head. "As if we'd been on an ebbing tide. But now the tide has turned and we're with it, going back into the harbor that we'd never have left, if something hadn't cut our moorings. Isn't that true, Nils?"

He nodded; and their eyes, holding, grew lost in each other's gaze until she reached up; she cupped his head between her hands as if it were infinitely precious, and drew it down to hers.

About the Author

Elisabeth Ogilvie lives for the better part of each year on Gay's Island, Maine. There she enjoys long walks among the rocks and woods of the island, reveling in air and space and sky. The remainder of the year is spent across Pleasant Point Gut, at her nearby mainland home, where plumbing, a telephone, and other amenities await. Her interests include the Nature Conservancy, Foster Parents Plan, reading ("a necessity of life!"), and music of just about any kind.

Miss Ogilvie's latest book is a historical romance, the second of a planned trilogy. Despite some thirty-six books for children and adults produced over the past forty years, though, the author is still caught up in the spell woven by Bennett's Island and its inhabitants and is presently at work on a fifth installment (the fourth, An Answer in the Tide, was published in 1978) in the continuing story of Joanna Bennett.